FOOLS RUSH IN

Across the hall, Justine struggled with her reaction to Duncan's almost kiss. She had wanted it. She rolled over to untangle the sheet twisted around her body. Her unloved body. Behind closed eyelids she saw his lips moving toward hers, slowly. Teasing. Tantalizing her. She parted her lips for the taste of his hot velvet tongue and moaned in despair when it failed to penetrate her welcoming mouth. When her breast began to ache for his stroking fingers, she swung out of bed, took off her gown and showered. She didn't fool herself. Duncan wasn't the only source of her discontent, nor could she attribute it to celibacy, for she'd never been fulfilled. The certainty that she'd never been loved, that her failure at lovemaking with her husband wasn't her fault, had triggered in her a need to explore herself, to fly. Because Kenneth Montgomery hadn't loved her, his heart hadn't been in his lovemaking. She knew that now. And sleeping within fifteen feet of her every night was the epitome of temptation in the person of Duncan Banks, a good-looking, mesmerizing, and powerful hunk of a man who wanted her and whose lure beckoned her. Torment was right here on earth.

Excerpts From Reviews of BEYOND DESIRE

"By now readers have become obsessed with the incredibly skilled Gwynne Forster, whose relationship romances are constantly among the top novels available to readers. Her latest story, BEYOND DESIRE, takes the trite marriage of convenience theme and, against all odds, turns it into a brilliant tale of redemption and love. As usual her protagonists are caring, charming and compassionate. No one on the scene today mixes romance and social issues with more class and finesse than the Great Gwynne Forster."

—Harriet Klausner, *America On Line Reviewer Board; www.Amazon.com*

"Only a gifted writer such as Gwynne Forster can coordinate these elements while literally making words dance on the page. Her gift for weaving sensuous love scenes between the heroine and hero without even touching is nothing less than amazing. It is as if she reaches down in her soul and pulls out characters who are nothing less than incredible. This is such a heartwarming story of family love, challenges, heartbreak and joy. The heroine and hero exhibit such a commanding presence of character and dignity that impresses this reviewer no end." Five stars.

—*Affaire de Coeur Magazine*

"Well worth the read. Wonderful characters. Rich, complicated and very human. Marcus and Amanda come to life in Gwynne Forster's newest romance, ***BEYOND DESIRE***!"

"A story with a thread that might be all too common today, yet ***BEYOND DESIRE*** raises social and personal issues that will make you stop and think. Gwynne Forster is a terrific romance author who possesses the rare talent of combining contemporary issues in a satisfying romantic story." —*The Literary Times*

"This is an honest look at the lives of people who are facing circumstances beyond their control and seek help. The strong characterization makes this a must read. The tension is fierce as both sides hide their feelings from the other and, at times from themselves. Ms. Forster does an excellent job of keeping the pace just right and providing dimensional characters. Excellent and emotional reading." —*Rendezvous Magazine*

"Ms. Forster has once again showcased the phenomenal talent that has become her literary signature and professional trademark. She creates a hero who isn't too proud to love and a heroine who embodies the quintessential '90's woman, a true Proverbs 31 woman—ageless, timeless and without equal." 4½ stars. Top Pick. —*Romantic Times Magazine*

"Gwynne Forster has written a great piece of work here. This story was so believable that at times I found myself talking to the book—"Just tell her, Marcus, just tell her!" Sounds crazy, but it is true. That's how well done this novel is. Not only does the reader become so involved in the story, but there is also sound advice to walk away with. Never does she become preachy, but it is evident that Ms. Forster has done her homework on the way men and women truly interact with each other."

—*Interludes*

FOOLS RUSH IN

GWYNNE FORSTER

BET Publications, LLC
www.msbet.com
www.arabesquebooks.com

ARABESQUE BOOKS are published by

BET Publications, LLC
c/o BET BOOKS
One BET Plaza
1900 W Place NE
Washington, D.C. 20018-1211

First Printing: October, 1999
10 9 8 7 6 5 4 3 2 1

Printed in the United States of America

ACKNOWLEDGMENTS

To my husband, whose love and unfailing support sustain me and enrich my life, and to Karen Thomas, my editor, whose helpfulness, competence and upbeat approach make writing a pleasure and deadlines a less ominous thing.

CHAPTER ONE

Justine let the white vehicle take her weight as she stood alone at the edge of the crowd, staring at the gutted Falls Church, Virginia motel in which, hours earlier, her faithful and loving husband of four years had perished with his white mistress. Perspiration matted her hair even as she tightened her jacket against the early fall chill. Her dry, tearless eyes stung their sockets as she gazed at the burned-out ruin still ripe with the smell of singed carpet, incinerated furniture, odoriferous rubbish, and charred flesh. Shivers coursed through her at the sight of the smoke-darkened glass and fragmented windows. Blackened bricks that had once gleamed red in the sunlight mocked her with their message of gloom and death.

"They shore musta been busy," a female voice declared, "if they was the only ones in there that couldn't hear the fire alarm."

"You tell it, girl," another agreed.

The only love she had ever known. Why couldn't she cry? Echoes shouted at her from the black ruins that jeered contemptuously at her. "Love ya, Baby!" He said it that way every time he left her. "You be ready for me, Baby." She opened the crumpled note that he'd left tacked to the refrigerator and read it again. "Sorry I couldn't reach you at work, Baby, but the company's got an emergency of gargantuan proportions, and I'm on my way to Boston to straighten things out. May take a couple of days, but I'll call you. Explain it all when I get back. You be ready for me. Love ya, Baby. Your devoted husband, Kenneth." Boston! And here he was, dead in a Falls Church, Virginia motel.

She looked up and stared in horror as men approached her wheeling gurneys carrying one long, black plastic bag and one shorter bag, each tied securely. Dazed, she would have touched the remains of her husband if an ambulance worker hadn't jumped between her and the lifeless object. Her fist pummeled the man's chest until he held her hands to restrain her and folded her shaking form to his body until she gained control. She looked at the note, read it again, shredded it into bits, and let the wind have it. Then she turned from the horrifying scene where Kenneth Montgomery had perished with his lover, rested her hand on her belly—distended with their eight-months-along unborn child—and walked away. Thirty-five minutes later as she drove the Ford Taurus home, the first pains of a premature birth began. . . .

Justine's screams awakened her, and she sprang forward in bed, tugging the sheet to her as though to protect herself, and gazed rapidly around her bedroom. It wasn't a dream. If only it was. If only that morning had never been, and she could sleep through one night without reliving it exactly as it had occurred that awful day. For nearly twelve months, that scene had been her constant companion, filling her thoughts during the day and her dreams at night. She wiped the perspiration from her face with her left hand and shook her right fist.

"I won't let you do this to me. I won't let you destroy my faith in human beings. You with your goodness, your humanitarianism, and your love for the common man. You for whom I ruined my relationship with my father. You treacherous bastard. You robbed me of my child. You . . .

"*My child.* Why did I . . . ?" She rested her head on her raised knees and folded her arms around them. *What had she done?* She jumped from the bed, got dressed, rushed to the social service department of the hospital in which she'd given birth, and paced in front of the door for an hour and a half until the workers arrived at nine.

Maybe if she said it often enough, they'd do something. *"I want my child back. I was sick. You can't do this to me."* Her screams reverberated through the social service department of Alexandria, Virginia's Presidents Hospital. She tightened the woolen stole that she wore to ward off the September chill and leaned across the social worker's desk, oblivious to the tears that wet the corners of her mouth.

"I . . . I'll sue you. I'll . . ."

"You signed the papers, Justine. You couldn't stand the sight of that baby and it was our duty to protect her."

"But I was sick, and you knew it."

"You said you didn't want the baby. We know you sustained an unusually deep postpartum psychosis; many women do. Some of them have killed their babies when the psychosis was a deep one like yours. We thought you'd never come out of it. A week ago, I'd have sworn you never would. Your refusal to look at the child, and your insistence that we do whatever the law allowed, left us no choice, but to do as you said. Your therapist agreed."

She stormed out of the social service department and, nearly blinded by her tears, made her way to the maternity ward to find the doctor and nurse who had taken care of her when she developed an embolism following the birth.

"After about a week," the nurse told her, "you became withdrawn, refused food, wouldn't talk to anybody, and wouldn't take the baby. You refused to take the baby with you when we discharged you. We had a conference with you and your therapist, and when the therapist asked you what you wanted us to do, you said, 'Suit yourself.' I've never known postpartum psychosis to last as long or to be as deep as what you've been experiencing. Look at you now. You're a changed woman; I can see that. But it's too late. We can't help you."

Nurse Jane Wilkerson watched Justine's heavy steps as she left them. "What else could we all have done?" she asked the doctor who had joined her. "Every time she saw that child, she sank deeper into depression, screaming and crying like we were beating her. I never felt so sorry for anybody in my life."

"Yeah. I don't think many women could handle learning that her husband died in a tryst with a woman he'd had a steady affair with since before he met her, and especially not if she was eight months pregnant."

"Are you saying . . . ? You're joking."

"Wish I was. Alexandria's a small town, and the upper middle-class African American community here is minuscule. Marian Iverson had been Kenneth Montgomery's mistress for at least twelve years—since their college days, I'm told. Uninterrupted. Long before he met Justine. But he couldn't marry a white woman and run for congress in that all-black district he claimed to represent. African-American women don't seem able to hack that from us black guys; though, believe me, they take whoever they please."

"Well, I'll be. Can you beat that? I never would have thought it of him. And such a distinguished man, too."

"Yeah. But if his wife didn't know about it, he must have done his best to be good to her. Poor fellow just got caught."

Jane Wilkerson adjusted a blond curl beneath her crisp white cap and walked off, more certain than ever that being single and staying that way made good sense.

Justine walked aimlessly out of the building as a white Cougar pulled up, and the Washington, D.C. license plate on another white car flashed through her mind. Eleven months earlier, she'd just left her therapy session when a man walked out of the hospital carrying a newborn baby, and the woman beside him had seemed to drag her steps. They got into a white Mercedes, and the man held the tiny form wrapped in a little pink blanket as the woman drove them away. She hadn't associated them with her child, but the scene had made her curious about it, and she had run back inside and asked the social worker's secretary if they'd found an adoptive family for her baby.

"Yes," the woman had beamed, "they just left. Now you can relax and get on with your life."

Not one emotion had made its presence felt. She hadn't tried to understand her unusual behavior, her lack of concern that her child had a new mother. She and Kenneth had planned to have three children—one every two years—but he wasn't there and he'd lived a lie. Every time he'd held her and made passionate love to her, telling her that he loved her, that she was his world, he'd lied. He'd made a mockery of her love. She shivered, wondering if he had laughed with his mistress about his unresponsive wife, frantic to climax with him only to have it elude her every time. If only he were alive so she could despise him!

She shook off the unpleasant memories and gathered her wits. She'd get her child back, no matter what anybody said or did. They shouldn't have let her sign those papers, knowing she had an illness fairly common among women who had just given birth. She couldn't undo the past, but she was back to her old self now, and getting her child would be her number one priority. Her child would be hers again. She'd find her and nobody was going to stop her from getting her back. She remembered the license plate number now—dredging it up from the bowels of her subconscious mind. At the time, she'd thought that only someone rich and famous would have the number *GDB 1800*. She wrote it down and headed for Indiana Avenue and the municipal building in northwest Washington.

Hours passed while first one official and then another treated her to a dose of government bureaucracy, bouncing her from office to office. Anxious and frustrated, she called one of Kenneth's fraternity brothers in the mayor's office and, an hour later, had the information that she wanted. That car belonged to G. Duncan Banks, an investigative reporter for *The Maryland Journal*, a paper in Baltimore.

She searched in the Library Of Congress, the internet, and records of the Society of Professional Journalists, learning all she could about the man whom she believed called himself the father of her child. The information she treasured most concerned his character and his address. He lived in affluent Tacoma Park, at the edge of the Maryland/District line. Now, what could she do with that information? She couldn't drive up to his house and demand her child, because he had a legal right to the child, but he'd hear from her. And soon.

Duncan Banks stretched his long frame out on the floor beside Tonya's crib, his mind idling while his eleven-month old adopted daughter's chubby brown fingers examined his right thumb. She had wedged herself so deeply into his heart that he hated being away from her. He couldn't understand how Marie, his ex-wife, could have agreed to their adopting a child if she hadn't wanted one. He understood her disinclination to interrupt her career as a rising criminal lawyer in order to have a baby, but it hadn't occurred to him that she hadn't wanted to be a mother. And she'd quickly tired of it.

"I just can't spend the rest of my youth taking care of somebody else's kid," she had announced. "I'm sorry."

Every time he thought about that night when she'd asked out, pain seared his heart. "What about the indescribable, boundless love you feel for me? Your words. What about that?"

She'd looked him straight in the eye—insolent as usual when caught out. "Love doesn't conquer all, Duncan. You're old enough to know that."

"No, but money does. Doesn't it? Now that I've paid for your law degree and your career is humming and you can support yourself in the manner to which I have accustomed you, it's bye, bye birdie, eh?"

She had the grace to be flustered. "Don't be crude."

"And don't you be so high-handed."

She was right; love didn't conquer all. He wouldn't let himself think about how he'd loved her or that his heart threatened to explode in his chest. And when she lowered her lashes in that way she did when she wanted to control him with her body, make him forget whatever she'd done and make love to her, he'd clenched his fist.

Her lashes swept down over her large brown eyes—eyes that made a man stare at her beautiful brown face—and then came up slowly. "I'm not planning to ask for much of a settlement."

"Smart girl. Collect your clothes. If you ask for more, I'll take back that mink. Trust me." He looked away to hide from her the pain he knew his face reflected. He'd loved her—really loved her with every atom of his being. "If you're going, Marie, don't draw it out."

Three hours later, the door had closed on his dreams. But what the hell! The day before yesterday, he'd shot a perfect game of pool. From now on, nothing would surprise him.

For months, he had sensed a widening rift between them, a drifting away from each other, though he'd done everything he could think of to turn their relationship around. Nothing he did had touched her. He had thought that a baby would bring them closer. He wanted a family, and if she didn't want the burden of bearing their own he'd take what he could get. Many babies needed parents he'd told her and she had agreed to their adopting Tonya. He'd been satisfied so long as he had a child to love and to raise. But he couldn't take care of an eleven-month-old baby girl.

Duncan pulled his mind back to the present, got off the floor, and leaned over Tonya's crib. "I'll advertise for a wife," he told his laughing daughter. "If the woman's intelligent, loves children, and promises to spend the rest of her life being sweet to you, that's as much as I want; I've had it with love—biggest hoax ever foisted on a man." She raised her little arms to him, and he lifted her into his embrace.

"Daaaaddy," she sang, clapping her little hands together. He sat with her in the rocker beside her crib and rocked her while he sang Brahms Lullaby, her favorite song. When she fell asleep, he put her into the crib and rolled it into his office so that he could work and keep an eye on her.

He had no luck advertising among his friends. Dee Dee Sharp, the feature editor of *The Maryland Journal*, told him she could get him someone to keep the baby, that she only had to drop a hint and even society women might show up if they knew he was single. He shook his head and went on to Wayne Roundtree's office. Wayne owned the paper.

"Get a wife," Wayne advised. "Tell her you want a marriage of convenience. You'll take care of her and she'll take care of your child. No emotional involvement."

Duncan's look of incredulity brought a wicked grin from Wayne. "Who'd fall for that?" Duncan asked him. "She'd have to be ninety and have all the beauty of a wet field mouse."

Wayne leaned back in his high-back swivel chair. "Wake up, man. A lot of women would like a soft life, especially if they're childless, out of work, down on their luck, jilted maybe, and—"

"Naaah, man. I can't hack that."

"But you said you'd had it with women. This way, your emotions won't get you in trouble, and you might luck up on a great gal."

"Is that you talking? I didn't think you believed there was such a woman."

"No? Well, that shows how well informed you are. Think about it."

"Man, I haven't the slightest notion how to go about a crazy thing like that."

"Why not ask Dee Dee to stick a line in her column. Trust me, you'll spend the next six months interviewing twelve hours a day."

"Heaven forbid." He passed Dee Dee on the way out of the building and wished he could close her grinning mouth. "The boss told me you'd be by to see me. I've got just the idea."

* * *

"Do you DC ladies know that a prominent, recently divorced gentleman with the initials DB is in the market for a wife who'll be a good mother to his baby daughter? Send your love letter to P.O. Box 0001, Washington, D.C. 20017," Dee Dee wrote in her Thursday column. Duncan read it the next day and considered moving to Alaska. Letters arrived by the dozens and, though the procedure embarrassed him, he interviewed applicants, but didn't like any of them.

"Maybe getting a nanny is easier," his best friend, Wayne Roundtree suggested several weeks later. "Marriage can be such a permanent thing, man. Get a good nanny."

"To sleep in and take over my house? No thank you."

Wayne shrugged. "What have you got now? A cleaning woman who comes in every day at a time of her choice, leaves when she gets ready, won't answer the phone, and avoids anything that isn't six feet tall, male, and human."

Duncan couldn't help laughing. "Mattie's a real number, but I'm used to her and when I need her in a pinch to look after Tonya, she doesn't let me down. Besides, Tonya never stops laughing when she's around Mattie."

Wayne's left eyebrow went up. "Big deal. Neither do I. Tonya probably thinks Mattie's an oversized rag doll. Every time she looks at the woman, she's seeing a different color of hair."

Duncan's white teeth flashed against his dark face. "Took me a while to look at her and keep a straight face, but she's good as gold." He walked over to the big picture window with its tinted glass and ecru curtains and looked down on Charles Street. His hand fingered the change in his right pants pocket. Maybe a nanny was best. He didn't really want to be married. Not then. Not ever again. But Tonya needed a mother on whom she could depend, not a nanny who might leave at a minute's notice.

He whirled around and started out of Wayne's office.

"Man, I don't care who decorated your office, it would look a lot better without these fancy curtains."

"No argument here. My sister-in-law found me a decorator, and that's what she put there."

"You mean Adam's wife?"

"Who else? Adam's my only brother. He's a lucky man. Our families strew their path with one obstacle after another, but they persevered. She was made for him. You and I should be so lucky. Forget about that wife business, and hire a nanny."

"Yeah. You may be right, man." Duncan threw Wayne a high five and headed for the heart of West Baltimore, where he put in at least a weekly appearance at CafeAh-Nay—a local bar, restaurant, and billiards hangout on Liberty Street—to keep up his contacts. As an investigative reporter, he needed to maintain good relations with his sources.

Several days later, Mattie stopped Duncan when he walked into the house after work. "Mr. B, you know I think you're a good man, but you also know I don't do no full time housework and no babysitting I just been doing all this work 'round here to help you out. And I'm good and sick of all these women that's started calling here axing about you. It ain't my business, but having all these women chase you ain't a proper atmosphere for a baby girl. A sweet little tyke, she is, too. All the same, Mr. B, you know me and phones don't get along. I wish you'd get a nanny for Tonya. I'll help you out, but I ain't happy doing it."

He patted her shoulder "I've decided to do that, Mattie. Just bear with me."

He stared at her two front teeth, a perfect tribute to Bugs Bunny. "Mr. B, there ain't a woman nowhere what can resist you when you looks helpless like that. If I wasn't old enough to be your mother, and if I didn't have my Moe, I'd be in trouble. You make sure you get somebody me and Tonya can get along, with now."

"I'll do my best," he said and rushed past her to find a place where he could laugh in peace. She hadn't noticed that he had gaped at her orange hair, front teeth, red lips, and purple dress. She'd called it "looking helpless."

* * *

Justine listed her house with a real estate agent and began packing her things. She'd leave that torture chamber in which she'd lived with Kenneth, that brick and mortar vessel of pain and horror, if she had to give it away. She couldn't bear it any more than she could stand the pitying eyes of her neighbors and the thoughtlessness of the store clerks and delivery men who seemed to enjoy greeting her with, "So sorry to hear about Mr. Montgomery, Ms. Montgomery. It sure was a tragedy." As if they had decided among themselves how best to remind her that her husband would be alive if he hadn't been unfaithful to her.

She left the real estate office, bought a copy of *The Washington Post* at the corner drugstore, and went home, where she made a cup of coffee, went into the guest room, pulled off her shoes, and sat on the bed. She hadn't been in the master bedroom—the den of lies whose walls probably still echoed his false shouts of ecstasy in her arms—since the day he died, and she never wanted to see the inside of it again. The cleaning woman had removed her things and had packed his and taken them away. She flipped through the want-ads to check the job offers. She had to change her life, but resuming her profession as a clinical psychologist held no interest. She sat forward, more alert than in almost a year. Duncan Banks had advertised for a nanny and had given a postal address. She knew he'd gotten a divorce. Did she dare? She rushed to the phone, ignoring his request that the application be made in writing.

"Duncan Banks, speaking."

"Mr. Banks, this is Justine Taylor. I'd like to apply for the position you advertised in *The Washington Post.*"

The voice, soft and refined, set him back a bit. He expected a person applying for a job as babysitter to be somewhat raw around the edges.

"I prefer applications in writing, Miss Taylor."

"I know, but I figured I'd get a lead on the other applicants. I need a job, and I can provide good references. If I have to sleep in, I'd like to visit your home before we talk business."

That made sense. He gave her his address and realized that he hoped she'd suit him. "When can you come out?"

She didn't hesitate, and he liked that. Coyness in women had always put a sour taste in his mouth. "This evening, if you'd like. Say, a couple of hours from now?"

He glanced at his watch. "Perfect. I'll get Tonya ready for bed, but she'll still be awake when you get here."

Justine hung up, fell back across the bed, and kicked up her heels. She made no attempt to squelch the scream of joy that peeled from her throat. She had spoken with him, and she would see her child. She rolled over and said a prayer of thanks. She'd never wanted anything as badly as she wanted that job and the chance to nurture her own child, to know that her baby was well cared for and loved. Tonya. He'd named her daughter Tonya. She liked the name. Her heart thundered as it raced inside her chest like a runaway train. She didn't trust herself to drive in that state. After all this time. And all the pain. Maybe she was being given another chance. She didn't mislead herself into believing that what she was about to do was fair to herself, Tonya, or Duncan Banks, but what choice did she have? If she'd been a well woman, she wouldn't have given up her child for adoption. As a psychologist, she understood what she'd gone through and considered herself fortunate to have survived that awful trauma. She telephoned a deacon of her church who had a notarized letter of recommendation ready for her when she stopped by his house. She'd chosen him because he knew her only by her maiden name. The nursery school at which she'd volunteered since before her marriage and where she was known as Miss Taylor provided her second reference.

She styled her hair in a French twist, and in spite of the sweltering August heat, dressed carefully in a conservative beige silk suit and olive-green blouse, added brown accessories, debated the advisability of wearing lipstick, decided to apply it, and headed for her door. The phone rang and she almost didn't answer it fearing that Duncan Banks was calling to cancel their appointment

"Hello, Justine, this is Big Al. My sister is your real estate agent, and she tells me you're changing your life, selling your house, and leaving Alexandria for DC. Can't say I blame you, honey. How about doing that column I've been pestering you about?"

"Oh, Al. It's great to hear from you. Just because I wrote a gossip column for *The Hill Top* when we were at Howard U doesn't mean I can write a column for the lovelorn."

" 'Course you can, babe. You've got two degrees in psychology and plenty of horse sense. How about it?"

"How much of my time will that take?"

"Practically none. Three columns a week. For each one, you answer a minimum of three letters and write some family values stuff. You say the word, I'll put the notice in tomorrow, and bingo. End of the week you'll have dozens of letters. Just give me a P.O. box number." She thought for a second. She needed time to consider the risks. "I like the idea right now. Who knows, I may someday be syndicated. Tell you tomorrow."

"Two things. You'll be Aunt Mariah, and you will not tell anybody—I mean not one soul on earth—that you write that column. We gotta have secrecy. Otherwise, it'll be a total flop. Call me tomorrow before ten. See ya."

Justine walked on liquid legs to her car, got behind the wheel, and slumped against it. She had to go through with it. No matter what conditions she found or what she faced, she had to do it. She had to be with her child. She had read Duncan Banks's columns. Who hadn't? But she'd never seen him. Please God, don't let him be a slob, but the smiling, happy man she'd seen leaving the clinic that day carrying a newborn baby. Her shaking fingers stuck the key in the ignition, and she didn't know how she did it, but she managed to release the brake. "Mind over matter," she repeated aloud.

The drive along the Shirley Memorial Highway, over the Fourteenth Street Bridge, and on up Sixteenth Street didn't soothe her nerves. Horns honked, drivers darted in and out of lanes breaking traffic rules, but she managed to keep her wits until she turned into Primrose Street at the edge of Maryland and stopped. Her nerves rioted throughout her body. She sat in the car until she could control the trembling that shot through her, making her skin crawl and her teeth chatter. In minutes she would see her child. She took a handkerchief from the glove compartment and dabbed at her tears.

Calmer now, she walked up the long, winding bricked walk to the modern white stone building whose enormous glass windows were more off-putting than welcoming. Trembling fingers rang the bell, and the jitters commenced again. Duncan Banks opened the door, and she stared at him, wondering if she'd lost her mind. He was the man, all right. The same tall, dark man. And what a man. Not that she cared, she'd finished with men. But even in her baffled state, she had the sense to recognize male perfection. And danger. As if his stature and facial features weren't enough to sabotage a woman's will, he opened his mouth and released a deep, sonorous, velvet timbre.

"Hi. You must be Justine Taylor. Come on in. I'm Duncan Banks."

She found her voice and marveled at its even tenor. "Yes. I'm Justine. I'm glad to meet you, Mr. Banks."

His smile had the effect of termites hard at work on the foundation of a shingled building. "I'm glad you agreed to come today. I've got an assignment that'll take me away from home, and I have to be sure Tonya's taken care of. Tell me about yourself."

She told him as much as she wanted him to know, and she'd prepared herself for his misgivings. So when he commented that she seemed too polished to be working as a nanny, she countered that she was down on her luck and seeking to change her life.

He raised an eyebrow "What precisely do you mean?"

Don't forget that he's an investigative reporter, she reminded herself. "I plan to write, and this job will support me while I work at it. I know it may be years and years before I have any success," she added, to allay his qualms about impermanence, "but this way, I needn't worry about bills and a place to stay."

She must have said the right thing, because he nodded and a smile surfaced around his mouth. She pulled her gaze from it as quickly as she could and asked some questions so he'd know she was a careful, responsible person.

"Where would I sleep?"

"The guest room faces Tonya's room. You'd sleep there. It has a private bath and a small anteroom that you could use either for a dressing room or a little office. Did you bring your references?"

Electricity shot up her arm when his fingers brushed hers as he took the letters that she handed him. His gaze was that of a man who'd just had a surprise, one that he didn't necessarily welcome. Well, it was time she got some of her own back. She'd been reacting to him ever since he'd opened that door. Where did he sleep? she wondered, but didn't have the nerve to ask.

"Do you think I could see Tonya? Or is she asleep?"

His apparent pride in his daughter gave her a sinking feeling, even as it warmed her heart. He'd never give up that baby. Never. So she had better play her cards right.

"Come with me." He raised his long frame from the big wing chair that had no place in a modern setting and headed down the hall. She looked away from Duncan for fear that the guilt curdling her stomach would blaze across her face, and she had her hands full, so to speak, controlling the wild anticipation that danced within her at the promise of seeing her child.

His leisurely smile only heightened her anticipation of the wonder awaiting her. "She's wide awake, but she whispers to her bears so they don't growl at her. I don't know where in the devil she got that. Probably from Mattie."

Her joy bordered on hysteria, and she didn't think she could move another step, but she did. Icy marbles frolicked through her veins, and she had to bite her lips to control their quiver.

"Hi, Baby," his deep voice began when Tonya looked up at him, threw the bear aside, and smiled. "You have company. This is Justine." Tonya climbed to her feet with the bars on the crib for support and raised her little arms. Stunned disbelief spread over Duncan's face. "She's asking you to pick her up? Shy as she is with strangers? Can you beat that?''

If her life had depended upon it, Justine couldn't have said where she got the strength to reach down and pull her child into her arms. "Juju,'' Tonya said, pulling at Justine's dangling gold earrings. Justine gazed into eyes identical to her own and, in spite of her efforts to retain her sanity and maintain a professional demeanor, she hugged the child to her bosom and kissed her cheek, all the while praying for composure.

"Juju,'' Tonya repeated. Then, as if she'd had enough, she wiggled aside and raised her arms to Duncan. "Daddy. Daddy.''

He took the baby, held her with one arm and opened one of the references. Justine didn't have to be told that she'd get the job if he liked what he read.

He folded the second letter and stuffed it in his left trouser pocket. "If these check out, we're in business. Tonya seems to like you, and that's my main concern. When could you start?''

She hadn't gotten that far. "I need two or three days to get my stuff stored and settle my lease, but I'm fairly certain I could be here Saturday morning.''

He seemed to hesitate. "How do you expect to care for an active baby while you're writing?''

"I'll write while she's asleep. If an idea pops up at any other time, I may make a few notes so I'll remember it. Whenever I have to choose, Tonya will come first. I give you my word on that.''

His reddish-brown eyes seemed to penetrate her soul, and she knew she was looking at a man who relied on his own judgment, who didn't need the words of others for his peace of mind. "You're hired. Be here Saturday morning and do your best to make a hit with Mattie. "His grin nearly knocked her off balance.

"Who's Mattie?''

The grin broadened. "If I was sure, I'd tell you. Suffice it to say she comes in every day to do the cleaning and cooking. She'll surprise you, but take my word, she's harmless.''

He moved toward the bed to put Tonya back in it, but she didn't want to go there and reached for Justine.

"Juju."

Duncan laughed aloud "Oh, no, you don't. Think you've got an ally, do you? You're going to bed, and that's final." He glanced at Justine. "This little devil thinks she can wind me around her little finger."

"Can she?"

His sheepish expression grabbed at her feminine being. "Yeah. I guess so."

He kissed Tonya, but she yelled, "Juju."

Justine leaned over and kissed her cheek. She had to get out of there before she broke beneath the strain of it all.

"I'll show you your room. Of course, you'll have the freedom of the house. Your friends are welcome." He ran his right hand across the back of his neck and stopped walking. "My child means everything to me, Justine. I've decided to postpone that assignment a few days and stay home until she gets used to you, though I think she's already decided that she likes you."

He opened the door to a large bedroom that faced Tonya's and was decorated in mauve and violet blue. She would not have chosen those colors, but she found the effect appealing. A king-size bed bore a violet-blue silk spread and, except for a copy of Botticelli's "Spring" that hung beside a large mirror, mauve adorned everything else in the room.

"Like it?"

She caught the anxiety in his voice, and realized that he wanted her comfort and contentment "Yes. Very much." A smile claimed his incredible eyes, and she had to shake herself out of the trance into which they quickly dragged her. She had to get out of there.

"I'd better be going. Thanks for your confidence. I'll see you Saturday. Oh. Do I get a day off?"

"Yeah. I nearly forgot that. Sunday for sure, and we'll work out something else. Okay?"

"Fine." She wanted to avoid his extended hand, but

accepted it along with the feeling that she knew would come with it. "Good-bye, Mr. Banks."

"Duncan. Good-bye, Justine.

He'd said good-bye, but he didn't stop looking at her. A hammer began pounding her insides. Had he seen the resemblance? Had he noticed that Tonya had her eyes? Why was he staring at her? She forced a smile and reached for the doorknob, but his hand shot out to open the door, and landed on her own. He didn't move it, but looked down into her face with a strange and indefinable expression.

"Goodnight," he said at last, and opened the door.

She made her way to her car, got in, and sat there for a good half hour before she found the strength to drive away. Over and over she told herself that he hadn't seen the resemblance, but she didn't see how he or anybody else could be so unobservant.

Justine released the brake and started home, reliving the feel of her baby in her arms, pulling her earrings and pinching her nose. A screech of somebody's automobile brakes called her attention to the red light she'd shot through, and she eased up on the accelerator. Shocks scooted up her spine as she recalled the soft flesh of little fingers on the back of her neck, the child's joyous laughter, and Duncan Banks's indulgent words, "Some daughter you are. Ready to chase after the first stranger who comes along." She, a stranger to her own child. She attempted to pull out of the center lane, but a honking horn impeded her effort to get to the roadside and wipe the tears that blurred her vision.

When at last she reached the brown brick Tudor house in which she'd lived with Kenneth Montgomery, she parked in front of it, too drained to put the car in the garage. Sane enough not to sit in a car alone on a dark street at night, she dragged her weary body into the house she'd come to hate, changed her clothes, and washed her tear-stained face. The flashing light on her answering machine got her attention. Her real estate agent had a buyer for the house, a diplomat who didn't bargain, and two co-op apartments in Washington for her inspection.

Thank God, she could put Alexandria behind her. If she wasn't certain the buyer would object, she'd walk away from that house and leave everything in it except her clothes.

Duncan stuck his hands in the pockets of his trousers, fishing for change, and toyed absentmindedly with what he found there, something he did when he was thoroughly discombobulated. He tried to figure out his reaction to Justine Taylor, the strange feeling he got the minute he opened the door and looked at her. He'd swear he'd never seen her before, yet something in him said he knew her, had always known her. As if she'd somehow sprung out of him and had found her way back to where she belonged. It wasn't sexual, at least he didn't think so, though when he'd opened the door, she'd reacted to him as woman to man. But she had quickly controlled it. A refined woman. He'd give her that.

Tonya, too, had sensed something special about her. Granted, you couldn't miss her warmth and sincerity. And she was pretty easy on the eyes. For a second, he let himself imagine what she'd look like if she pulled her hair out of that old-lady's twist in the back of her head. He shrugged. A little too plump for his taste, but she had the height, around five-six, he guessed, to carry it. But why did he feel as if he knew her? He played with the change in his pocket and dismissed the thought. Some people had the kind of face that cropped up everywhere.

He started to Tonya's room to check on her and stopped. Dee Dee's notice had been in the paper more than a month, and Justine hadn't answered it. So she wasn't looking for a husband. Thank God for that. Accustomed to examining both sides of an issue or a fact, he considered the possibility that Justine hadn't answered the ad because she didn't read Maryland papers. Well, his daughter liked her, and that settled it as far as he was concerned. If Justine Taylor possessed any unsavory traits, Mattie would detect it at once, he could count on that. But he'd gotten good vibes from Justine—honesty, warmth, femininity, and self-confidence, traits he admired in a woman. And she clearly loved children. He phoned his sister.

"Banks speaking."

Duncan took a deep, impatient breath. If only he could knock some sense into his sister. "Leah, I've told you a few million times to stop calling yourself by our last name. It's too masculine."

"And I've told you not to call me Leah. I can't stand that name."

"Then change it, for Pete's sake. Oughta be easy, since nobody but the family knows what it is."

"Duncan, did you call me to fight with me? I'm sleepy."

"When will you have an evening free? I want to ask some people over. Seems like I owe everybody I know an invitation to dinner."

"I'm always free. Promise to invite some men who still have their own hair on their head. And I'd like to see their chests before I see their bay windows."

Duncan was used to his sister's cynicism, but he couldn't resist trying to change her. "Leah, your attitude needs refining. Learn to judge a man by the content of his character—to quote a famous one—instead of his girth and how much of his scalp you can see."

He imagined that she tossed her head and shrugged her left shoulder. She was the only person he knew who did that. "Thanks for nothing, brother dear. Most of us women like a guy we can get our arms around, if need be. Besides, Martin Luther King was talking about kids; I had in mind cool brown brothers over the age of thirty."

She never failed to amuse him—the best dose of anti-tension medicine to be had anywhere. Laughter flowed out of him. "Trust you to twist it your way. How about it?"

"Improve your list of men friends, and you can count me in. And no cigars. Why do newspaper men like those hideous things?"

"I don't smoke."

"Everybody needs at least one virtue. Good for you."

"All right. All right. You'll be glad to know that I just hired a nanny for Tonya."

"You mean you've given up the idea of marrying somebody to mother her? It's a dumb idea, anyway."

"No, I haven't, Miss know-it-all, but I haven't found anyone who suits me, and I needed somebody to look after Tonya. So I hired Justine Taylor."

"Well, this I've got to see. Is she good looking?"

Trust Leah to focus on a side issue. "Among other attributes. See ya." He hung up and called Wayne Roundtree in Baltimore.

"Say, man, I hope I'm not disturbing you," Duncan said when Wayne held the receiver a long time before speaking.

"Nah. I had to shake a couple of pests a few minutes ago, and I fully intended to hang up the minute I recognized either one of them. That's the life of a managing editor. What's up?"

Duncan trained his ear in the direction of Tonya's room. No, she wasn't crying, only talking. "I just hired a nanny. She won't be on the job 'til Saturday, and I want to spend a few days at home after she starts to be sure she and Tonya get on. So I'd like to postpone work on that municipal bribery case."

"Okay, but I hope it doesn't break in *The Sun* or *The Afro-American.* What does she look like?"

"Who?"

"You know who I mean. This nanny you hired."

Duncan leaned back in the big barrel chair, propped his left knee over his right one, and grinned. "Not worth a backward glance, man. And I'm going to introduce her to Listerine mouthwash the minute she walks back into this house."

His ears hummed with Wayne's roar of laughter. "No kidding. She must be a knockout. When can I come over for . . . well, for dinner?"

"Come to think of it, I'm planning a dinner party soon as my sister can get over here to help me. I owe everybody I know an invitation."

"Count me in. I have to meet this poor unfortunate nanny you hired. Let me know when you can get on that case."

"Will do. In a couple of days, I'll fax you my story on ward politics."

"Right on, man."

Duncan hung up and went into Tonya's room to turn out the lamp beside her bed and put on her night light. It worried him that she feared the darkness so much. Maybe having Justine—someone who'd be with her all the time—would give her a greater sense of security. Justine. Why had he felt so comfortable with her? He'd swear that she had in some way been a part of his life.

CHAPTER TWO

Justine took an old purse from a shelf in her closet and, for the first time in twelve months, looked at the picture taken of Tonya at birth. The little red spot at the top of her right ear was now brown, but it was there, the final proof that she had found her baby. She needed to talk with someone, anybody. But who? She couldn't expect another person not to divulge a secret as ripe for gossip and, at the same time, as potentially damaging as hers. She replaced the photo and lay down and, for the first time since Kenneth's death, she slept through the night, and no horrible memories invaded her dreams.

She rose early the next morning and began preparing for life as her child's nanny. Her first act was to phone Big Al, editor of *The Evening Post.* "You're on, Al," she squeaked out, less sure of her decision than when she'd made it. "As of now, I'm Aunt Mariah. I have to get a post office box. I'm moving to Tacoma Park, Al. You'll get it all by fax sometime tomorrow."

"Right. Soon as I get your P.O. address, I'll tell the world not to be troubled any longer," he crooned in his booming voice. "Aunt Mariah will solve all their problems. Just give 'em horse sense, babe. That'll do it every time."

The next three days were the busiest that she could remember, but knowing she was putting her life in order, folding the page that had been Mrs. Kenneth Montgomery, and beginning a life with her child—however impermanent it might prove to be—energized her and buoyed her spirit.

She got a post office box, closed the deal with the buyer of her house, and bought one of the co-op apartments that her agent reserved for her inspection. Then, she sent the fax to Al, and told her agent to find a tenant for her new apartment. That done, she invited the Salvation Army to come over to her house and take whatever it could sell, except for her blankets and Kenneth's expensive clothing, which she planned to divide among the homeless men along "East of the River."

She'd been determined to do it herself, and her stomach rolled from the stench of stale wine, the rags that served as the men's bedding, the unwashed bodies, and the refuse that some more privileged citizens had thoughtlessly strewn along the street. Their gratitude shamed her, but she persisted until she'd given out all of the blankets, gloves, sweaters, and other clothing. Still, a sense of guilt wouldn't let her leave the men without food. She counted them, went to the nearest McDonald's, and got eleven bags of coffee and hamburgers and gave one to each man.

"I would ask the good Lord to bless you," an older man said to her, "but it looks to me like he's already done it."

"You bet, " she answered, feeling good for the first time since she'd parked her car beside the rubble-strewn vacant lot two blocks away. She waved them good-bye and headed home.

Time crawled while her desire to see Tonya escalated. She examined the hands on her watch, thinking that it had stopped. Twice, a coffee cup slipped from her fingers and splattered the brown liquid on her legs and around where she stood. She turned off the radio, unable to tolerate music; even the soft strings of a Mozart quintet jarred her nerves.

Saturday morning arrived and she had to face another truth. The prospect of seeing Duncan Banks again excited her, though not as much as the thought of living with her child, but she gave herself a quick lecture and put Duncan out of her mind.

The response to her single ring of Duncan's doorbell gave her one of the biggest shocks of her life. Canary-yellow hair—or was it a wig?—topped the tiniest woman she had seen in years. Perhaps ever. And that small face wore enough make-up to camouflage a couple dozen fashion models. If that weren't enough, the two prominent upper front teeth that decorated the copper-colored woman's generous mouth—now curved into a smile—sent pictures of Bugs Bunny flashing through Justine's mind. What on earth?

"Quit staring and come on in," was the way in which Mattie Swindell introduced herself. Justine resisted asking why she patted her hair when the hair spray on it wouldn't allow it to move. "I just got it done yesterday," Mattie explained, oblivious to the fact that Justine hadn't uttered one word. "It'll look good like this for two or three days. Where's your things?"

"They'll be here later. I'm Justine Taylor." No wonder Duncan had said he wasn't sure who she was.

"I know who you are. Mr. B told me to expect you." Justine had almost gotten her breath when heavy footsteps on the stairs sent her pulse into a tailspin. If she didn't get a grip on herself, she'd fail before she started. She took a few deep breaths and looked toward the foot of the stairs. "Don't gasp, girl," she told herself, when her gaze took in his open-neck yellow T-shirt, white canvas Dockers, and toeless sandals. He stopped within two feet of her, his sleepy, reddish-brown eyes the focal points of the most breathtaking smile she'd ever seen.

"Welcome. What did you do to yourself? I've been expecting that nice prim lady who came here the other night." The fingers of his left hand toyed with the back of his neck. Then he shrugged his right shoulder. It was a series of gestures she'd seen him display several times when he'd interviewed her. A dimple transformed his right cheek, and she wouldn't have been surprised if she'd melted right there.

"I don't mind the change, but I hope Tonya recognizes you. She's asleep, and she should be after waking me up at five o'clock this morning."

She didn't tell him he'd done a number on her, switching from gentleman reporter to an advertisement for carnal joy. "My work clothes, " she said of her blue slacks and mauve-pink silk jersey shirt. "Unless you want me to wear uniforms." She let her grimace give him her view on that matter.

"Whatta you want with a uniform?" Mattie interjected. "I shore don't intend to put on one."

Once more, his gaze seemed to bore into her. "Uniform? Not for me, but do whatever makes you comfortable. We're all equals here. I see you've met Mattie," he said, changing the subject, and she could have sworn she saw a meddlesome twinkle in his eyes. "Just take good care of my child. That's all I want." He winked at her, and the drum started its roll in her chest.

As if he wasn't aware of his effect on women. Well, she would not give him the satisfaction of knowing that she was susceptible to his taunting virility. "Thanks. Maybe I'll wear jeans; they're more comfortable."

His raised eyebrow suggested that he didn't believe her, and he was right. She'd never pulled a pair of jeans over her ample hips, because she prided herself on having sense and taste, and she hated walking behind overly-endowed female bottoms that threatened to work their way out of stretch jeans. She'd just been testing the water. She'd wear cotton pants.

Hoping to distract him from any evidence she'd given of her background, she added, "I'm very casual."

His tongue poked the right side of his jaw. "If you say so." He turned to the other woman. "I've got to run down to the Library of Congress, but I should be back shortly after twelve, Mattie. A sandwich will do." He started for the door, checked himself, and walked back to Justine. "Seems I'm short on manners this morning. Mattie will get you settled. See ya."

Justine was thinking that she had to watch herself with Duncan Banks when she realized that Mattie was speaking to her. "When he says sandwich, I cook him a hot meal. What do you want for lunch?"

"A sandwich and a glass of milk or—"

"I ain't got no two percent milk in the house, and I don't expect you need whole milk. First thing you got to do is get down to a size ten. You must wear a sixteen. My sister is a nursemaid for this rich woman in the Watergate Apartments who wears a ten. I wear a size two. One of us has to make use of those designer clothes she throws away. Can you take tea?"

A full-throated therapeutic laugh flowed out of Justine, and she hugged the little woman as best she could, considering the differences in their size and height. "Mattie, I think I'm going to love you. I'd better tell you, though, that I do wear a fourteen . . . well, sometimes, and not after holidays. I get plenty of appreciative looks at my size sixteen, and I'm satisfied. How long have you worked here?"

"Me? I've worked for Mr. B on and off for the last six or seven years. Why you ask?"

"Just curious. You like him?"

"He's a real sweetheart . . . 'til you mess up, that is. And then he's got a real long memory. I mean long, honey."

Unaccountably, shivers raced down her back, and her fingers gripped the back of the chair near where she stood.

Mattie went on in a sing-song voice. "One thing you better be sure about and that is not to utter one word of what goes on in this house. That's his law. He's had me understand that a hundred times. He values his privacy and, being a reporter and writing things about people, he has to keep hisself to hisself."

"He needn't worry. I know how to be discreet." When Mattie stared up at her with both eyebrows raised, Justine amended her remark. "I know how to bridle my tongue."

"Discreet, huh? Well, hush my mouth."

Anxious to see Tonya, but afraid to reveal her longing to Mattie, Justine guarded her voice and spoke in casual tones. "You think Tonya is still asleep? She's awfully quiet."

"If she ain't, she oughta be. Mr. B said she was singing loud as you please five o'clock this morning and didn't stop 'til he gave her her breakfast. But soon as she got her oatmeal down, she started noddin'. Gimme your bag. Did Mr. B tell you your room is facing his? Soon as we get rid of your stuff, I'll show you around. This is one big house."

Just what she needed. She wouldn't be able to stick her head out of her room without taking the rollers out of her hair and getting fully dressed. Well, she'd asked for it. How was she to have known that Duncan Banks could spin the head of the most devoutly virginal woman? Best thing she could do would be not to care what he thought of the way she looked. She'd seen her own quarters and Tonya's room, but Mattie didn't open Duncan's door. Instead, she ushered her into the office that adjoined his bedroom. Soft beige tones and Royal Bokhara carpets in his office, in the hallway, and on the curved stairs. Mattie didn't pause at Tonya's room, and no sound came from it, so she didn't have an excuse to go in and fill her arms with her baby.

An arresting peaceful decor was all she could think of as they began Mattie's tour of the first floor. "Mr. B loves to sit in this big lounge chair with his hands behind his head and think. I declare that man can do more thinking than anybody I ever saw."

Mattie wasn't a slouch at thinking, Justine mused, taking in the tall cactus plants on either side of a huge picture window that were among the few things of nonutilitarian value in the living room. Everywhere, masculine taste. What was it about James Denmark's "Honky Tonk" that made Duncan Banks want it on his living room wall? She studied the painting of the itinerant guitar player, but got no clues. But it didn't tax her mind to understand his attraction to Ulysses Marshall's "Between Mother and Daughter." She turned quickly away; the painter had given them identical faces.

"These here pieces only been here 'bout a month. He took his time getting things for this living room," Mattie said, gesturing toward the comfortable beige leather sofas and chairs that rested on a cheerful Tabriz Persian carpet woven in beige, brown, and burnt orange colors. She noticed that the dining room was a place for eating, not for show. A walnut table, eight matching chairs, and a sideboard sat on a Royal Bokhara carpet. No curtains graced the windows.

"I'll see the kitchen when I get my sandwich," Justine told Mattie. One thing she had to ask, though, because she hadn't seen any evidence of a woman's touch was, "How long has Mr. Banks lived here?"

Mattie's method of clearing her throat was unique. And loud. "Well, 'bout four months, I'd say. Why?" And she let it be known that her yellow hair topped a fast mind. " 'Cause everything's new? Mr. B's been a bachelor since Tonya was four months old, and he been living here since Tonya was four months old. Anything else, ask Mr. B. We'd better go downstairs. That's where Mr. B spends most of his time, 'cept when he's in his office or off someplace."

She could find her way around Duncan's house on her own, and she hoped she had years in which to do it; what she wanted right then was to see Tonya. "Thanks for the tour, Mattie. I'd better see about Tonya."

But Mattie wouldn't be denied her opportunity to show Justine who ran Duncan's house. "Tonya's fine. Let's get this over with. I can't spend all my time giving out tours." Justine saw no junk or apparent storage areas in the basement. One large, wood-paneled room held an enormous television, a recliner, and what looked like the original Nordic Track machine. A refrigerator, bar, and pool table filled a far end of the room.

"This is gonna be Tonya's recreation room soon as Mr. B decides how he wants it fixed up," Mattie said, after opening the door to an empty little room with windows on three sides of it. "He can't figure out what color to put in there. Maybe you got some ideas." Indeed she did. Soft, pastel colors lifted the spirit, though she thought greens too cold for babies. But she didn't voice her opinion. She could too easily slide back into the skin of Dr. Justine Taylor Montgomery, clinical psychologist.

"I'll think about it."

"You reminds me of some kind of teacher, Justine. Ain't

no babysitter I ever saw talk like you. 'Course, it ain't my business. Mr. B's satisfied, and you seems nice enough."

Tonya's shrill cry served notice that she had awakened. "There's the bell, honey. When she starts crying, she means business. Thank goodness, she's all yours now."

Justine's throat constricted at the prophetic words. She had to force herself to walk up the two flights of stairs, when she wanted to run. When she crossed the threshold of that room, she would change her life for all time. At last she would mother her child, and from that moment onward, Tonya would be hers. She tiptoed into the nursery, looked at Tonya sitting up in bed, and smiled.

"Tonya, darling. Do you remember me? Justine."

Fear curled around her heart. Had that other night been a fluke? she wondered, as Tonya looked up at her with wide inquiring eyes.

She tried again, less confident now. "Darling, don't you remember Juju?"

"Juju?" Tonya pulled herself upright and lifted her arms to Justine. "Juju." A smile claimed her little face, and Justine leaned over to take Tonya into her embrace.

"Honey, you must be a magician."

Startled, Justine turned so quickly that she hit her head against the side of the bed bars, but Mattie shook her head in wonder and didn't notice.

"What kind of sandwich? Chicken? Low sodium, low fat cheese? Lean, low sodium ham?"

For a moment, she wondered whether Duncan's housekeeper was operating a health farm. Her glance lingered on Mattie until her eyes widened. It had to be the light. No, that hair really was fire-engine red. Good Lord, was the woman driving on four wheels?

"I decided this isn't my yellow day," Mattie explained after noticing Justine's prolonged stare. "I learned long ago that hair does things to a person's mood. Now take you. You ought to make yours a light blond or something. Anything but this dreadful neither black nor gray nor anything else these black women walk around with. Make it pretty so the men will notice you, honey."

Justine laughed. Mattie seemed to have a prescription

for everything. "Let Tonya and me get to know each other. We'll be down soon."

"Looks to me like she been knowing you all her life, the way she's acting. Content as a little bee buzzing roses. Never seen the beat of it. That child never did like strangers. 'Course, you do have a nice way about ya."

Justine breathed deeply as the door closed behind Mattie and prayed she wouldn't be caught out. She picked up the baby and walked over to the rocker, and Tonya's little arms curled around her birth mother's neck. When the baby kissed her cheek, as Justine had seen her do to Duncan, a bottomless well of emotion sprang up in her, and love such as she had never felt for another human being gushed out of her. She stumbled to the rocker and slumped into it, barely avoiding sitting on the floor.

Was this what she had missed as a child? Was this feeling that she would gladly give her life for the baby in her arms what mothers had projected to the confident and self-possessed schoolmates of her early youth? Not once had she felt such love. Not from Kenneth, nor her Godfather, and certainly not from her father or his sisters to whose care he had entrusted her. Tonya cooed and wiggled, demanding her freedom. She couldn't release her. Not yet. Softly, she began to sing, but tears choked her, and she closed her eyes and rocked.

A nearly unbearable sense of wholeness enveloped her. She'd come alive. The lifeless feeling that had engulfed her and crippled her emotions for a year lifted from her like a blanket of soot dissipating at the behest of a strong wind. Yes. Oh, yes. Her limbs no longer seemed deadweight, dangling from her torso like iron bars, dragging her down. But now, fear curled around her heart. Fear that Duncan would discover her deception and send her away.

Duncan answered his cell phone as he walked out of the Library of Congress and into the unlikely September heat. "Banks."

"Wayne."

"What's up, Wayne?"

"I'm not the only editor onto that case of municipal bribery, man. Can you get free to cover it? Can't you leave that new nanny with Tonya for a quick span? Man, if this thing breaks, and I don't have it, I'll lose readers."

"All right. Have somebody type me out a briefing. I'll get over there around three-thirty or four."

Duncan opened his front door to the aroma of frying chicken and buttermilk biscuits. If Mattie ever paid attention to his preferences for food, she'd be driven to it by a warning from St. Peter. He dashed up the stairs to change clothes.

"Patty cake, patty cake, loo, loo in the oven . . ."

"Baddy yake, baddy yake, ooh, ooh, wuwu," Tonya repeated after Justine.

His eyes widened at the sight of his daughter sitting astride Justine's lap, slapping hands with her and giggling, her little face glistening with joy. Pleased at that confirmation of his choice as the right one, he walked quickly to his room, closed the door and got into his daytime make-over: gray T-shirt, black cotton bomber jacket, crepe-bottom black loafers—in case he had to run—and dark gray Dockers. He wore that particular jacket because it had a place in which to hide his small, but powerful, recorder.

Duncan stopped in the kitchen for what he knew would be a tongue-lashing from Mattie. "Could you give me some biscuits and a couple of short thighs? I've gotta get over to Baltimore in a hurry. If you need me, call Roundtree at the paper."

"Now, Mr. B, these biscuits won't taste like a thing once they get cold. I puts my whole self into these biscuits, seeing that you're so crazy about them, and now you wants to go and eat 'em out of a paper bag whilst you're driving. And my chicken. Mr. B, if you try to eat my chicken and drive same time, you'll have an accident. Mark my word. Nobody can concentrate on my chicken and try to do something else same time." She patted her yellow hair and looked up at him. "Nobody, but my Moe, that is. 'Course, ain't many men equal to my Moe."

"I can believe that. Would you hurry, please? It'll all be hot when it reaches my stomach. Trust me."

She handed him the bag and patted his arm. "Y'all be careful now, Mr. B."

"Thanks." Mattie's southern notions and mannerism gave him old-shoe comfort. Dizzy as a drunken chicken, but he liked her. At the front door, he looked up to see Justine strolling down the stairs with Tonya in her arms.

"I'm glad you two are getting on. I'll be back sometime tonight. If you need me, call my cell phone number. It's on the side of the refrigerator, on Tonya's bed post, and on the side of my computer. See ya."

An hour and a half later, Duncan parked on Reisterstown Road just off Rodgers Avenue in West Baltimore, walked a couple of blocks, and knocked on the apartment door of an ex-girlfriend, the notes that Wayne's assistant had prepared tucked into his jacket pocket.

"Hi, Grace. Long time, no see."

"Believe me, that's not my fault. Come on in. You don't have to tell me this isn't a personal visit, though I'm more than willing to apply for the job of unrequited, unfulfilled wife just like the ten thousand other sistahs in this town."

He let a grin crawl over his features. "On target, as usual. Where do you think I'll find Buddy Kilgore?"

"Probably at the joint, but not before six or so. What are you doing 'til then?"

He wrote down "CafeAhNay" on a small pad, tucked it in his inside pocket, and prepared to make his excuses and leave. Not for anything he could think of would he get involved with Grace again. She'd been his girl in college, but she'd realized her dream of singing in jazz clubs and, somehow, had gotten into the dark side of life. That wasn't for him She'd put that behind her, but he saw her only as a friend.

"Grace, this is serious business, and you know I'm not for fooling around where my work is concerned. You and I are friends. Isn't that enough?"

Her shrug said he couldn't blame her for trying. "When

I make a mistake, I lay ostrich eggs. It's not enough, Duncan, but I have to accept it. We're friends."

He let go the breath he'd been holding. He needed her cooperation, because she had useful contacts that served him well from time to time. "Does Buddy have a manager for that cleaning service or does he look after it himself?"

"Duncan, honey, Buddy's got a cover for every one of his businesses; he owns 'em, but somebody else takes the heat."

Just as he'd thought. He leaned against the door and appraised her. She'd always been as transparent to him as pure water in a clean glass. "You going to tell him I asked about him?"

Her head jerked upward, and she glared at him, obviously affronted. "Of course not. That's all you think of me? That I'm a stool pigeon? Dunc, honey, you know I wouldn't do that."

"I didn't think so, Grace, but in this business, I can't take chances."

"No, I don't suppose you can. Lots of people are pushing up daisies for trusting the wrong guy."

"Tell me about it. I owe you one."

She flashed a smile, but it didn't ring true. Grace was suffering from a bad case of if, of what might have been. "Don't mention it," she said, grasping for her self-respect. "Just let me know what kind of payment you want to make and when you plan to pay."

Heaven forbid that Tonya should let herself slip into the clutches of degradation as Grace had. She'd pulled herself out of it, he'd give her credit for that much, because most people who flirted with the drug culture and got mired into it weren't so fortunate. Grace had been raised by a father who'd spoiled her, and she was one reason why he'd go to any respectable length to find a woman who'd be a good female role model for Tonya. A picture of her bouncing happily in Justine's arms as he left the house earlier flashed through his mind. She hadn't even cried when she saw him walk out of the door, and she usually kicked up such a storm that he'd taken to slipping out when she couldn't see him.

He wished he could figure out why the ease with which Tonya had accepted Justine didn't alleviate his concerns about the child's well being. Well, hell. He wasn't going to allow himself to be jealous of his daughter's seeming fondness for Justine.

He stopped by *The Maryland Journal* editorial office, got some blank press passes, and headed for Darby Elementary School. He looked around for a parking spot and glimpsed Buddy Kilgore leaving the school. He grabbed his camera out of the glove compartment and snapped the man's picture as his feet touched the bottom step, and stayed in the car until Kilgore turned into Dolphin Street and was out of sight. Sure that his hunch had been right, he barged into the principal's office unannounced just as the man began to cram papers into the shredder. He wished he'd brought his camera. With his recorder running in his jacket pocket, he walked over to the shredder, stopped it, retrieved the papers, and looked at the top page.

"What do you have to say?"

"Me? Nothing, Mr. Banks. I'm just getting my desk straightened out like I do every day before I leave."

Duncan released a half laugh. "So you know who I am? Who tipped you off? Kilgore?"

"I've seen you around, mostly over on Liberty Street in CafeAhNay. Nobody told me anything. Mr. Kilgore came by to ask me to vote for him for the City Council."

"No kidding. Hadn't heard he was running. And you'd think a reporter would know things like that."

"Whatever you're after, man, I don't know a thing about it; I'm just doing my job."

"Yeah? Well, next time, don't trash your invoices. Of course, if you're double billing or maybe giving your supplier a cut, I can see how that shredder over there comes in handy. Keep the faith, brother."

It didn't take genius to detect a lie that thin. He walked out of what the city fathers regarded as a bastion for the development of youthful minds, and shook his head in disgust at the debris and graffiti that decorated the building's exterior. How could a child formulate goals and pursue them in an environment that consisted of vacant buildings whose windows and doors stood shuttered with plywood? Every building in sight was an example of someone's failure, and every man-made thing that an eye could see stood in some stage of disrepair. He stopped at the sight of a two-story-high pile of rubbish that small children barely school age were using for a playground. No wonder childhood mortality was on the rise among the urban black poor. Broken glass, cracked sidewalks, and potholes were what most African Americans in West Baltimore got in return for their taxes. With an hour to kill, he headed for Micah's Restaurant to get some crisp fried lake trout and the best soul food in Baltimore.

At six o'clock, Kilgore was where Grace said he'd be. Duncan sat in a dark corner of CafeAhNay trying to adjust his nostrils to the mixture of dime-store perfume, beer, and sloe gin, a favorite of the locals. No matter how many times he sat there, he always left feeling soiled, not that he'd let on to the owner and habitués; his bread and butter depended on their considering him one of them. He whittled on his egg-sized carving of a Frederick Douglas bust—as the regulars were used to seeing him do when he sat there alone—and watched the school principal rush over to Kilgore. He'd seen enough, so he slipped out of the place, leaving the two men gesticulating as though nervous and excited, and went to find the manager of Kilgore's Cleaning Service. Two hours later, he had it on his recorder that Kilgore billed the system for twice the value of the merchandise, the principal signed the order to pay, and Kilgore gave the principal ten percent of the excess. One bill went to the school board and the other, a smaller one, Kilgore kept for the IRS. The scheme guaranteed that a lot of schools paid one dollar for a roll of toilet paper, fifteen dollars for a seven dollar box of Tide, and other exorbitant charges. He'd gotten the story, but he had a hunch that wasn't the end of it.

It had all gone too smoothly. He had the facts, but his sixth sense warned him that more would come. He wove his way through the dense, stop-and-go traffic on Highway

295 to Washington, and in the slow driving conditions, his mind flitted between thoughts of Kilgore and the immediate rapport between Tonya and Justine. Justine's odd femininity and warm personality could get to a man, but to a baby?

Justine put Tonya's car seat in her car and drove with the baby to the post office. She hadn't asked Duncan's permission to take the child out of the house, so she'd get back there as quickly as possible. The sight of a dozen letters to Aunt Mariah escalated her spirits, and she could barely wait to read them. She parked in Duncan's two-car garage seconds before he pulled into the other spot.

As she jumped out, he opened the back door and took Tonya from her car seat. "How's Daddy's girl?" But his gaze bore into Justine, unreadable and disquieting.

"I hope you don't mind that I took her with me; I had to run a quick errand."

"I don't mind." Did she imagine a reluctance in his voice? "Leave me a note, though, when you do that. I worry impatiently, Justine, and I don't like to waste my time like that." The smile that gleamed from his sleepy, reddish-brown eyes would have taken the sting out of his words and comforted her had it not sent hot darts zinging through her limbs.

But she refused him the satisfaction of knowing that, looked into his eyes as brazenly as he'd looked into hers, and assured him, "Of course, I'll abide by your rules."

He started walking toward the front door and stopped, when Tonya reached for her. "I can't believe what I'm seeing. When I'm around, Tonya sticks to me like glue. She's been with me a couple of seconds and wants to go back to you. I didn't hire a hypnotist, did I?"

"Children Tonya's age enjoy the comfort of a soft bosom, which you don't have." She wanted to eat the words even as they slipped out of her mouth, uttered in a desperate effort to divert his mind from its dangerous track.

Her normal composure nearly deserted her as his rapt

stare appraised her. Unwavering. She couldn't erase the words and didn't dare try to explain them, so she stepped past him and reached for the front door knob. His hand whipped out to grasp her elbow.

"I take it you weren't being provocative with that comment, but if you were, you might remember that children aren't the only ones who enjoy a warm, soft bosom." He released her arm, opened the door, and headed upstairs as Tonya looked over his right shoulder and sang out, "Juju. Bye, bye Juju."

Most men declared war when they wanted to fight, but this one gave no warning. She watched his long lithe body stride up the stairs as Tonya continued to wave good-bye to her over his shoulder. Several retorts surfaced to mind, but she couldn't afford flippancy. She would have to decide how to deal with Duncan Banks, and she wouldn't let his cool, self-assured manner tempt her into an ill-considered reaction to that taunt. After all, it was she who had everything to lose. Legally, he was Tonya's father, and he didn't have to make up stories or play games in order to be with her. But he'd better watch it; she had never played roll-over for anyone, and Duncan wouldn't be her first experience at it.

Duncan removed Tonya's jacket and cap and put the happy baby in her crib. He knew he should have let Justine do that, but he was close to furious at his reaction to her innocent comment. Yes, innocent. She'd been embarrassed at her words, for they had surprised her as much as him. He didn't need the reminder that he had a lovely, desirable woman sleeping across the hall from him, a woman who responded to him without his having to encourage her. He changed Tonya's diaper, as he had done for months past, without remembering that he was now paying a nanny to do it. He gazed down at her, lying there so peaceful and trusting while she fought her drooping eyelids and lost the battle.

What could he say to Justine after his own provocative and unnecessary remark? He stepped out of Tonya's room seconds before Justine closed her bedroom door. Whiffs of her gently seductive perfume assaulted his nostrils and quickened his blood, but her door, that cold, white barrier that separated them, stirred his common sense into action, and he shoved his hands in his pockets and loped down the stairs.

"You hungry, Mr. B?" Mattie called from the kitchen.

He wished Mattie would resist yelling at him when three rooms separated them. "A little, but I'll wait for Justine."

"Well, I gotta get home. Moe complains when I'm out late."

He looked at his watch. Seven o'clock. "Call me when Justine comes down." He headed for the basement. What he needed was a good workout. He discarded his jacket and shoes, did twenty push-ups, and threw a couple of dozen darts, each of which landed farther from the bull's eye than the one that preceded it.

"Mr. B, come on up. I got to get my dinner on."

He put on his shoes and jacket, washed his face and hands, ran up the stairs, and stopped short. Justine floated from the second floor, almost unrecognizable in a red silk jumpsuit, oversized gold hoops at her ears, and her make-up-free face framed with jet black hair that swung well below her shoulders.

When he could close his mouth, he asked her, "Going out tonight?"

Her raised eyebrow reminded him of the silent reprimands he used to get from his elementary school teachers. "I freshen up for dinner, even when I'm eating at home alone."

Oh, no. He might have eaten dinner by the light of a kerosene oil lamp a few times as a small child, but she was still the nanny, for Pete's sake, and she wasn't pulling status on him. "And get all done up like that? Well, it doesn't hurt my eyes one bit. Come on, let's eat."

Duncan reached for the cornbread, but Mattie sang out, "Dear Lord, we thank . . .," and he let his expelled breath tell her what he thought of her reprimand. From the corner of his eye, he could see the satisfied smile that claimed Justine's face as she enjoyed Mattie's audacious behavior. In his younger days, the devil would have gotten into him, and he'd have given himself the pleasure of seeing her eyelids pop open when he planted his mouth on hers. Better not entertain such thoughts. Besides, Justine would get her dose; nobody's business was sacred to Mattie.

"Mattie, what's the matter with this cornbread?" he asked when she'd finished her long supplication. She took a bite of bread and chewed it as though relishing rich ice cream.

"Come on, Mattie, What did you do to this stuff?"

"Nothing. Tastes good as it always did, and it's a lot more healthy. I just left out the melted butter and eggs to give Justine a chance to drop a few pounds. I'm surprised she could get into that thing she's wearing."

He pretended not to hear Justine's gasp. Now that Mattie was on her case, he wanted to see how she would deal with it. "Why do you want Justine to lose weight? As far as I can see, she's got what she needs, and nothing's out of place. Next thing I know you'll have Tonya on a weight-losing diet. Could you please put some butter on the table?" He ignored her loud grumbles as she went to the kitchen. "Don't pay any attention to her, Justine. You look good to me. Sometimes, I'm surprised Mattie doesn't have us eating dinner in the morning and breakfast at night—"

"According to my books," Mattie interrupted, "that'd be a lot healthier than eating all this heavy stuff and going straight to bed. Here's your calories, Mr. B." As though suddenly conscious of Justine's silence, she went on, "Hope I didn't upset you none, Justine, but you have to watch—"

"Mattie, I've already told you that I'm satisfied with the way I look. We'll stay friends if you stop talking about it."

"All right. All right, but you mark my word, men like little women."

He recognized in himself the desire to protect Justine from embarrassment, and he knew himself well enough to know it spelled trouble. "This man likes women of substance, regardless of size, and I hope this is the last time I hear this subject in my house, Mattie."

As usual, Mattie looked toward heaven before uttering what she considered a profundity. "Well hush my mouth. Like I ain't said one thing."

He spread his hands and let a helpless shrug tell Justine that doing battle with Mattie was a waste of time.

"How about a couple of games of pinochle?"

The shock of his suggestion had to show on her face. She hadn't thought that he would involve them socially, and she wasn't certain that she liked the idea. "I haven't played since college, so I'd probably bore you. Besides, I need to get Tonya ready for bed." She'd had enough of his charisma as well as his bluntness for one evening, and she'd as soon get to work answering Aunt Mariah's mail.

"Tonya's asleep. If you take her out, try to have her back before five o'clock so she can be in bed at seven. When she wakes up, I'll get her something to eat. It'll take you a while to learn her routine. How about a game? Give us a chance to get acquainted."

"Well, all right."

She didn't remember having played cards or done anything else to the tune of Billie Holiday's "Fine and Mellow." Her aunts would have had a hissy fit if they'd caught her listening to "that low class trash." The earthy and mellow voice and the suggestive rhythm made her wonder as to his motive. The track lighting threw round balls of soft light against the beige-colored ceiling and walls, and the floor-to-ceiling mirror that she faced reflected the intimacy of their surroundings at the far corner of the basement. An eight foot maroon-colored leather sofa graced the side of one wall and a large, framed Gordon Parks photo of an urban park in which children enjoyed greenery, flowers, and early spring sunshine hung above it. A gold patterned Persian carpet covered the parquet floor beneath their feet. The only things missing were lighted candles and sparkling champagne. She diverted her gaze from her seductive surroundings to see him studying her face.

"You don't feel like playing cards?"

"Not really. I suppose I need to take stock of things. I'm home, but it doesn't feel like it." She couldn't tell him that mothering her child for those few hours and having to deny their true relationship frustrated and saddened her, even as the joy of being with her baby had been almost intolerable.

He pushed away from the card table, got up, and changed the CD. Mozart's Concerto for Flute and Harp did nothing to lessen the scene's allure. He braced his shoulders, hips, and the sole of his left shoe against the wall, and stuck his hands in the pockets of his trousers. Her pulse quickened, and she had to lower her gaze, but he seemed oblivious to the picture of male perfection that he presented. If he knew the woman facing him doubted that she'd ever been loved and longed to know it at least once in her life, would he turn off the heat, or would he . . .

He trained his reddish-brown eyes on her. "This won't work if you're not content, and I don't want Tonya to get used to you only to have you leave. I know you haven't ever worked as a nanny, and I hope you'll someday trust me enough to tell me what this move is about. But if you intend to go, please do it now. Tonya needs a woman's love and nurturing, and I can see that you'll fill that role, because she seems taken with you, but I don't want her hurt. I . . . If I have to have a . . . someone living in my home, actually becoming a part of my family, I . . . well, I'd as soon it was you. I think we'll get along."

"I'm not going anywhere, Duncan, but living in someone else's home takes getting used to." She switched topics, because the atmosphere was ripe for personal questions. "You have a beautiful home; all you need is a swimming pool."

"There's one out back, but I'm keeping it covered 'til Tonya is older. I can't risk the danger."

This man loved her child. It came home to her with hurricane force that knowing what Tonya meant to him was enough to suck her into his orbit. Yet, she had to live independently of this new world of which she was now a part.

"I've enjoyed our talk, Duncan, but I'd better do a little writing before I turn in."

"Don't forget, journalists are professional writers. I'll be glad to read your stuff and give you some feedback."

"Thanks," she threw over her shoulder, petrified. She couldn't show him her writing, which was actually a newspaper column, because she'd taken an oath not to divulge Aunt Mariah's identity. And if he knew she worked for a paper, he could easily trace her to Justine Taylor Montgomery, daughter of the Virginia State Assemblyman and widow of Kenneth Montgomery, double-dealer and adulterer.

She stopped in Tonya's room, and her heart pounded as though to burst with the joy that suffused her as she looked down at the sleeping child. She thought of the horrifying feeling that had engulfed her when she'd come to herself, realized what her therapist, the social worker and nurses had allowed her to do and fought the threatening tears. They said she'd rejected the baby and gave that as their excuse, when they knew she was ill. She resisted the urge to lift Tonya to her breast and know again the happiness of holding her. She secured the baby's blanket, turned and looked into the shining eyes of Duncan Banks standing in the doorway. She had to pass him, and she didn't like the tension that danced between them like an unharnessed electric current, wild and dangerous. She suspected that he could get to her if she wasn't careful, and she wasn't going to tempt fate with a wrong move, because she didn't plan to let anything destroy her chance to be with her child.

Stiffening her back, she approached the door. "Excuse me, please."

When he didn't move, she had to stop. "Uh, would you please excuse me, Duncan?"

He glided in with the litheness of a wild animal on the prowl and gave her the door, but not without teasing, brushing close enough to let his heat envelope her like hot quicksand, signaling the certain coming of disaster. She opened her bedroom door and closed it, never glancing his way. Duncan Banks was honorable, she was sure of that, but he'd just let her know that he was a man—with limits. She couldn't imagine what she would have done if he'd decided to let her squeeze past him in that doorway. She hadn't felt lonely while in the grip of that terrible postpartum psychosis; she hadn't felt anything, and as a psychologist, she understood that she was only now experiencing the loneliness that she should have felt following Kenneth's death. Her need to reach out to someone, to have someone care, meant that her health had been restored. But she'd deal with it. One way to exorcise feelings for one man was to develop an attachment to another one. She rubbed her arms. Maybe Duncan wasn't her type; maybe she was only lonely. Her loud laughter confirmed for her the hopelessness of it.

CHAPTER THREE

Duncan fed Tonya and rocked her to sleep. Now what? His notes on Buddy Kilgore's scam operation didn't entice him. He couldn't recall a time when his work had failed to excite him, when the lure of his next winning headline didn't light him up like gasoline dumped on an open fire. He wandered back down to the basement and put on a stack of his old Ray Charles records, but after a few minutes, he switched off the record player, ambled over to the window, and looked out at the night.

What the devil had come over him? He'd flirted with her. In a way, he'd even challenged Justine. Thank God, she hadn't taken him up on it. He didn't know her, and even if he did, he wasn't letting another woman embroil him in an emotional web as Marie had managed with such wily finesse—withholding affection and sex to get what she wanted and pulling out the stops in wild, frenzied lovemaking if he capitulated. It had taken him months to develop an immunity to her brazen bargaining. Love. She hadn't known the meaning of it. He recognized something special and different in Justine, but he'd take an oath of celibacy before he'd get involved with his daughter's nanny. Besides, he liked his women willowy, svelte. Or had.

After his debacle of a marriage to tall, slim Marie, he'd be the first to admit the folly of picking women by their size.

Clouds covered the moon momentarily and raced onward. Somewhere a dog barked, not because of the moon's enticement, it seemed, but in furor, and he wondered at the intruder's fate. Disgusted with himself for his mental meandering and the images he conjured up to avoid thinking of Justine, he knocked his left fist into his right palm and let out a deep breath. His mind wouldn't be shackled, however, and he gave in to his thoughts. Something about her had gotten to him the minute he saw her. Her eyes seemed to . . . He couldn't name it. His hands moved ruthlessly over his tight curls. Had he known her before? And where?

Still restless, he closed the blinds and started slowly up the stairs. Was a failed love-marriage any reason for entering into one that was strictly a business deal? He had loved Marie, but soon after their marriage, he'd begun to wonder if she'd traded her freedom for financial security. She'd sworn that she loved him, but he'd never felt deep down that he was her world, her priority.

"I've never been anywhere or done anything," she'd announced, "but you've been everywhere and you've got your life the way you want it. I didn't want a baby, but you insisted on us adopting one, and I gave in. You love that baby more than you love me."

"If you're looking for excuses," he'd said, "that one will serve as well as any."

She'd merely shrugged and looked at herself in the mirror while she perfected her make-up.

"What's your bottom line?" he'd asked her, dreading the answer.

He had marveled at the smoothness with which her reply slipped through her lips. "I'm checking out. You've got your life. I have to make mine, and I can't do that tied to another woman's child. I'm sorry, Duncan, but this scene's not for me, and I'm tired of pretending. I wish you the best."

The finality of those words had slammed into him with the loud finality of a hangman's trapdoor. He glanced toward Justine's bedroom door, and a rueful smile claimed his face. That woman would show him what he was made of, sure as his name was Duncan Banks.

Justine read the last of the Aunt Mariah letters and decided to answer the least serious one first. "If you love this man and you're sure he loves you," she wrote to a senior citizen, "you don't need my advice. You want me to agree with your decision. If it feels right, go for it."

To the twenty-seven-year-old woman who complained that her father allowed her twenty-five percent of her earnings, saved the remainder, and kept her bankbook, she advised, "Grow up. Take your bankbook and your clothes and move into your own apartment, preferably in another city."

Wife abuse required more careful consideration. She wrote to a Washington, D. C. woman, "Eleven years of beatings and your husband's numerous other acts of mistreatment always followed by his bent-knee apologies should tell you that he will not change. You have no children and no excuse for putting up with his pathological cruelty. Leave him, get a job, and take care of yourself."

The sound of Duncan's footsteps as he loped up the stairs sent shivers from her armpits to her fingertips. His door closed and she let herself breathe. It had to work; this was the only way in which she could be with her child.

The next morning, she got Tonya settled and began to organize her day around the child's eating and sleeping schedules. She couldn't have been happier that Duncan wasn't around to disconcert her. She made a list of things she'd need—a child's record player, records, blackboard, little musical instruments, crayons, drawing paper, and books for Tonya—and shoved the note under Duncan's door. Then she called her editor.

"Big Al speaking. What can I do for you, Justine?"

She told him she preferred each column to have a general theme and answers to five letters. "I'll mail my first one this afternoon."

"Right on. Think you could come in for a conference Wednesday morning? We wanna talk syndication. If I can swing it, you'll make some money."

Money was not her first priority, but it wouldn't pay to say so. "Mind if I bring my little charge?"

"Sure, baby. Long as she's quiet. Eleven o'clock."

"Sweetheart, the sight of you still gives a guy palpitations," Al greeted Justine that Wednesday morning. "A nanny, huh? Well, honey, things are about to change. You won't be doing that for long. Warren Stokes says he can syndicate you easy as that" He snapped his long, thick fingers.

Justine gaped at him. "Warren Stokes? Is he the Warren Stokes we knew at Howard U?"

"That I am. Hello, Justine. Still beautiful, I see. And what a beautiful little girl you have there!"

That couldn't be regret she heard in his voice. "I'm her nanny."

His raised eyebrows and pursed lips didn't surprise her. He'd have been less astonished to see her get out of a chauffeured Town Car. "Nanny, eh? I suppose you'll explain that."

Their conference ended with Justine's agreement to syndicate after six months if the public's reception of her column warranted it.

"Have lunch with me, Justine."

She shifted Tonya to her hip. "That may not be wise, Warren. Best not to revisit the past."

His gentle grasp of her left arm was her clue that the old Warren hadn't changed. He still had the tenacity of an irritated bull. "I never married, because you have my heart. Always did and always will. We shouldn't have let a stupid misunderstanding separate us. Is there anyone in your life right now? A husband?"

She shook her head. "If we pursue this syndication deal,

I suppose we'll run into each other. It's been nice seeing you again."

It didn't surprise her that he wouldn't be put off. "I'll call you. You won't get away from me this time."

Something began to roll like rough ocean waves in the pit of her stomach. Warren never let anything get between him and what he wanted. She liked him, but she hadn't suffered when, in a fit of jealousy, he'd broken their friendship because she'd regarded him only as a friend. She didn't want a romantic entanglement with him or anyone else, and especially not now when she was trying to put order into her life.

She looked him in the eye. "Those were college days, and we were children. Let the past lie."

Tonya called "bye bye" to him as Justine walked away. The years could have whittled down Warren Stokes's ego, but she doubted it. As students, they'd talked of their future and shared their dreams. She had admired his dogged pursuit of his goal, loved his hip-swaggering way of dancing, and enjoyed arguing against his conservative views, but she hadn't wanted him as a man. This older Warren wasn't the man to be a woman's pal, and she didn't want a lover. She didn't intend to give Duncan an excuse to fire her. If necessary, she'd don a nun's habit.

Justine opened the front door and raced down the hall to answer the telephone. Mattie would let it ring indefinitely. No one had told her to identify Duncan's home, so she picked up the phone and said, "Hello." She couldn't find her voice when the caller, a woman, wanted to know whether GDB was still looking for a wife. She seemed to panic at Justine's dumbfounded silence, and an explanation of the notice in Dee Dee's column spilled from her mouth. So he'd advertised for a wife. She couldn't believe he'd need to resort to that. Unless . . . She promised the woman that she'd deliver the message.

Perplexed, she asked Mattie to watch Tonya for a few minutes while she went to the nearest drug store. She bought a copy of *The Maryland Journal* and scanned it until she found Dee Dee's column. Stunned, she threw the paper into a refuse bin and drove home. Why would he do such a thing?

"I'm so sorry. The position has been filled," she told the next caller.

The woman's disappointed, "Oh no. Oh no" didn't give her a sense of guilt. If Duncan married, Tonya wouldn't need a nanny, and she intended to be the woman who took care of her child. Besides, what kind of an environment would an arranged marriage be for a baby?

She put Tonya to bed, ate a sandwich, and settled down to work. To the next four women callers who wanted to marry GDB, she responded, "The position has been filled," reasoning that she hadn't lied, since she hadn't said which position was no longer open.

Several weeks later, leaving the house, Duncan collided with Justine as she raced out of her bedroom to answer the hall telephone. He couldn't have said when the phone stopped ringing, and he'd have sworn that she couldn't either.

"Sorry."

"I . . . I . . . Please, I didn't see you. I hope I didn't . . ."

"No. No. I'm . . . I'm fine, but you must weigh a ton."

Still holding her, he managed to say, "Well, no. Only about a hundred and ninety-five. I hope I didn't hurt you."

He told himself to take his hand off her, but his arms remained around her shoulders, and her soft, ample breast nestled against his chest. A stricken look spread over her face, and he realized that he had tightened his hold on her in an unmistakable caress.

"Duncan . . . Please . . . I . . ."

If her wide eyes hadn't silently pleaded with him, he didn't know how far he'd have gone. He doubted that he would have released her of his own will. It had been so long since he'd known the loving arms of a warm sweet woman wrapped tightly around him. So long since he'd floated out of himself in the hot haven of a woman's welcoming body. He wasn't fooled by her business-like manners, walking past him day after day with barely a smile on her face, always so damned civilized and courteous. If she'd behave a little more naturally with him, he'd believe he held no attraction for her. But she worked too hard at it, always making a point of not being interested.

"Duncan . . ."

He realized he'd been staring into her eyes, looking for he didn't know what. "You all right now?" He asked in an attempt to diffuse the situation.

She nodded and rushed back into her room. Only then did he realize that she'd been dressed in a silk Japanese kimono. No wonder she'd gotten away from him as fast as possible.

He got back into his room, closed the door, and leaned against it. That had been close. Too close. If he didn't want to start anything with Justine—and he didn't—he'd better let her go and get someone else to take care of Tonya. He slapped his left fist into the palm of his right hand until the sting of it stopped him. Shaking his head as though to admonish himself, he conceded that he couldn't do that either. It wouldn't be right. After a month, he didn't have a single complaint against her, and he doubted Tonya would have been as happy in Marie's care as she was with Justine. If he wanted his child to have a woman's love and caring, he didn't think he'd find a better source than Justine. Her presence raised his home environment to a higher level, gave it a true feeling of home. He straightened up and walked over to the window, examining his feelings. After over half an hour of musing over his life, he told himself that he, and not Justine, was the problem. He had to figure out what he wanted between them and behave with her accordingly. Armed with this determination, he crossed the hall and risked knocking on her door.

"Yes?"

"Did Mattie tell you I'm having a dinner party tomorrow night? If I had seen you, I would have told you myself. Just a few close friends."

"She said some people were coming over. Do you want me to help?"

He realized then that he didn't think of her as a servant, and maybe he ought to. Seeing her in that light might have a taming influence on his libido. "No, indeed. That's Mattie's job. You're invited as my guest. See you this evening."

For once, she didn't look him in the eye the way she did when she wanted to get a point over. Instead, she gazed so intently at something over his left shoulder that he had to control the impulse to turn around and see what had her attention. "Uh . . . Thanks for the invitation. How casual are your dinner parties?"

The question took him back a bit. What kind of dinner parties did she go to? "Well, I put on a jacket and tie. You mean what should you wear?" At the risk of annoying her, he grinned broadly. "That red jumpsuit would be just the ticket." He'd wanted to see her in it again.

Her eyes widened, and she shifted her gaze to his face. "Really?"

"You bet. And don't forget those big silver earrings."

She stared at him as though in wonderment. "Why're you so surprised? Believe me, you made quite a picture in that get-up."

"Thanks."

For once she didn't have a come-back, and he wondered what she thought of the way she looked. As far as he was concerned, she had what she needed and plenty of it in just the right places. "See you this evening. Oh, yes. Those things you ordered for Tonya . . . I'll pick them up Saturday." He braced his left hip against the doorjamb. "You grooming her for a show in the National Gallery of Art or for the Metropolitan Opera House? Hell, Justine, she's only a year old."

Her shoulders squared, and her back stiffened. She'd gone from kitten to lioness in a second, and he prepared himself for their first argument. But her gentle voice belied her battle-ready demeanor. "Duncan, she's a thirteen-month-old who sings all the time and draws on everything. If she doesn't have crayons, she uses her little fingers." She laid her head to one side, and he knew he could expect a challenge. "Do you know how Picasso and Leontyne Price got started?"

He didn't, and he expressed his capitulation in joyous laughter. "Remind me not to confront you unless I'm ready to do battle."

Justine hummed a few bars of "Mighty Like A Rose," one of her mother's few legacies. Whenever she hurt, her mother would kiss and rock her and sing a few bars of that song. She didn't remember the words, because she was five when her mother died, but the tune lived in her memory, a cherished possession.

Overjoyed as she was to be with her child, happiness eluded her. The flame between Duncan and her would someday erupt into an inferno, and when it did, the Piper would come to collect his due. She picked up a copy of *The Evening Post,* glanced at her column, and threw the paper aside. What would she do if Duncan's self-control deserted him and she found herself locked to him in the consuming passion of which she'd begun to dream? He'd send her away, because he didn't want an involvement with her any more than she wanted it with him. But oh, how good it had been to feel his hands on her and her breast against his rock-hard chest. She had wanted to scream at him, *Just take me and love me and show me what I've missed.* Shocked at her thoughts, she walked out on her balcony and gazed at the forest of oaks that proudly displayed their orange, red, purple, and yellow autumn leaves. She sucked in her breath in awe at the beauty her eyes beheld. Her mood of minutes earlier dissipated and a smile crossed her face. Maybe this was where Mattie got ideas for her hair. The thought enlivened her spirits.

Was she his partner? An extra woman for the unattached man? Would he have a date? She considered staying in her room rather than be seen as an extra at the dinner table. Her older aunt invited couples only to dinner, and the widowed one did the same, except for the "friend" who'd been a "friend" for as long as she could remember. Justine had long ago decided that her aunt's friend was her lover and had been years before Uncle Benedick had passed on. She wondered if she should check the dining room; Mattie could be sloppy. She stamped her foot in frustration at her awkward position in Duncan's house.

She hung a long rope of silver beads around her neck, setting off the deep red silk jumpsuit and silver hoops. She had always regarded that jump suit as casual wear, something in which she lounged in her room. But if he wanted her to wear it, she would. She didn't like high heels, but wore them anyway as she tripped down the stairs and nearly stumbled when she reached the bottom. Duncan stood nearby, tall and handsome in a dark business suit, talking heatedly with a tall woman whose flawless skin had the color of fresh pecans. She raised her head and started past them.

His arm lightly on her shoulder brought her to a quick halt "Justine, this is my sister, Leah."

Leah's knowing look told Justine that Duncan's sister had noticed her relief that she was his sister and not his date. "Hello, Justine. I've been anxious to meet you. Duncan talks about you a lot."

He looked down at his feet and then toward the living room. "Leah lets anything that comes to her mind drop out of her mouth."

Leah shrugged a shoulder. "I'm blunt. And nobody calls me Leah. I hate the name. Call me Banks if you want me to answer."

Justine extended her hand. "I'm happy to meet you, Banks. Duncan hasn't mentioned having a sister."

Banks let a rueful smile linger on her face. "I embarrass him, Justine. He'd love to have a dainty, ultra feminine little sister who's brainless."

Both of Justine's eyebrows shot up. "Are you sure? He's been acting like an egalitarian with me."

"I've known him longer. He thinks I need a total makeover."

The grin that settled around Duncan's mouth assured

Justine that she shouldn't take the conversation seriously. Duncan and his sister adored each other.

"I'd be satisfied if she'd quit walking around like a chimney belching bituminous smoke."

"Grant me my one vice, Duncan. I don't interfere with yours." She turned to Justine. "You'd think he'd introduce me to his boss. I've been trying for six months to meet that man on square ground when I have the advantage, and my own beloved brother has access to him every day, and won't get us together. I was just telling him what I thought of him when—"

So that had been their argument! "If he won't do it, ask somebody else."

"I asked my girlfriend, Melissa Grant Roundtree, to introduce us, but the opportunity just won't come."

"Excuse me while I answer the door," Duncan said, looking down at Justine's face. "Be right back."

Chills snaked down her back. What would she do if he walked back to them with a woman on his arm?

"Wipe the worry off your face, Justine. Duncan doesn't have a woman. He's sworn off them for life."

"Wh . . . What?"

"Sorry, but I saw right away that you like him. Just be careful. He's a great guy, but he goes by the title of man, if you know what I mean. And I don't expect he's going to expose himself to what he just got out of any time soon."

"Leah. I mean, Banks, what are you talking about? I'm Tonya's nanny."

"Come on back in the kitchen. Duncan won't let me smoke anywhere else in the house, and Mattie doesn't mind." They walked down the long brown and beige tiled hallway to the modern brick-floored kitchen. Banks kissed Mattie on the cheek and lit a cigarette. "I know you're her nanny," Banks said softly so that Mattie couldn't hear, "and we don't want to get into that yet. If you're a nanny, Wayne Roundtree's in love with me, and as far as I know, he's never met me. Did you answer the ad for nanny or the one for wife?"

I need my wits with this woman, Justine cautioned herself. "Nanny. Is he looking for a wife?"

Banks blew a few smoke rings. "Yeah. For a strictly business deal. Now who's crazy? Him or me?"

"There you are," Duncan's voice boomed. "Wayne, I want you to meet my sister, Leah—the one who's blowing smoke. And this is Justine Taylor." Banks quickly rubbed the cigarette against the sole of her left shoe and put it out.

"I'm glad to meet you, Wayne," Justine said, showing as little interest as possible in the man who was Duncan's boss and the object of Banks's affection.

Wayne grinned and winked at Duncan. "Not worth a backward glance, eh?" He took her extended hand. "A pleasure to meet you, Justine."

She looked from Wayne to Banks, hoping to see a spark of desire in his face and praying that Banks would say the right words.

"Hello, Wayne. It's a relief to see somebody from home down here among these jaded Washingtonians."

Wayne appeared suitably impressed, and his low drawl seemed to captivate Banks, who gazed unsteadily at him. "Well, hello. Duncan didn't tell me he had a sister. Where've you been?"

"Mostly in Frederick. I told Melissa I wanted to meet you, but the three of us are never in the same place."

"Melissa? My sister-in-law? Wait 'til I see her. All she had to do was tell me she had a nice brown, long-stemmed beauty she wanted me to meet. Duncan, what's the matter with these women?"

"Search me. Justine, you want to come with me and meet some of my buddies?"

At least he had the grace to leave them alone and give Banks a chance. Wayne seemed interested enough, but maybe his joviality was nothing more than courtesy. Duncan's fingers at her elbow were meant to reassure her, and she didn't attach any significance to the special attention. If only he wouldn't watch her like an eagle about to dive for trout while he introduced her to his friends. She'd been properly brought up by aunts with strict codes of behavior, and she knew how to act with people. What did he expect? She opened her mouth to tell him he needn't fear embarrassment, when it dawned on her that his interest was in another direction: she wasn't behaving as a servant would, but as Dr. Justine Taylor Montgomery. Too late to repair that damage; she'd have to watch it.

"You don't drink?" he asked after she declined all that he offered.

"I'll drink wine with my dinner, but Tonya could wake up any minute, and I don't want to be tipsy if she needs me."

He searched her face as though gauging some inscrutable object or investigating the unknown. "What do you usually drink?"

"A glass of white wine."

"Mr. B," Mattie yelled. "It's on."

He continued to gaze into her eyes. "Dinner's ready. Will you sit at my right?"

"But Duncan, that's . . . I work for you. Surely, you don't want to give the impression that I'm more than—"

His fingers tightened on her arm. "As long as I'm in my house, I can give any impression I like—provided I don't offend you. I wouldn't want to do that. Come with me."

None of his friends appeared to find it unseemly that Duncan escorted his daughter's nanny to dinner and gave her a place of honor at the table. She turned to find Duncan's gaze on her.

Unsure as to how she should deal with his attentiveness, she tried to divert his attention by focusing the conversation on Banks and Wayne. "They seem to have hit it off. If you knew she wanted to meet him, why didn't you arrange it before now?"

He placed his fork on his plate and leaned back in his chair. "Justine, my sister is as mercurial as a person gets. If Wayne makes one false move with her, she'll tell him to drop dead. He's my boss, and he's also like a brother to me, and I'd as soon not have to tie up with him because of Leah."

"But she's enchanted with him and has been for a while."

"Enchanted or not; if he doesn't toe the line, she'll give

him the boot, and he won't get a second chance, sure as my name is Duncan Banks."

She didn't like the sound of it. "Does that run in the family?"

"Hardly. I don't expect perfection from people."

She let herself breathe more deeply. "What do you expect?"

He leaned toward her and whispered, "Honesty. Weakness, I can understand, but not dishonesty. And whatever you give me, give it with your whole soul, every bit of yourself. I refuse to be anybody else's guilt or, for that matter, their charitable duty."

His stricken look told her he'd said more than he had intended, that he hadn't wanted to reveal so much of himself. She shuddered to think that, of their own volition, her fingers had found his beneath the table and grasped them as though in a gesture of comfort. When she tried to remove her hand, he tightened his grip.

"Look at me, Justine."

She cast her glance downward and closed her eyes, refusing him, but she was about to learn that he would always stand his ground.

"Justine, if you don't look at me, I'll make you do it right here in front of everybody. If you don't want my mouth on yours right here, open your eyes."

She had to open them. Not merely because of his threat, but because she needed to see his face. "Don't complicate this, Duncan. Please leave things as they are. I want to work here, but I can't if you start something with me. I—"

"Why do you want to work here? And another thing, I can't start anything with you unless I have your eager cooperation. You're as safe with me as you would be in the Vatican. And you know it."

His question, potent with danger, flowed out of him so readily that she knew it hadn't just occurred to him, that it nagged at him waiting for a chance to be asked. She dodged it and commented on his assurance of her safety.

"Thank you, Duncan, but I have never doubted that you are honorable. It blazes across your countenance like a big red sun just before it sinks beyond the horizon."

She glanced first at their entwined fingers and then toward the other end of the table where Banks sat with Wayne Roundtree in rapt attention beside her. "Duncan, please give me back my hand."

His answer was a wide grin, roguish but determined, and she shifted her gaze to find Duncan's sister watching them intently. She couldn't help wondering why Banks wouldn't use the opportunity to gain Wayne's attention. Instead, the woman's eyes seemed to pierce her, to scrutinize her insides, and she'd have thought it an act of rudeness if Banks hadn't suddenly smiled and then turned to Wayne.

When they finished the five course meal and moved to the living room, Justine expected Duncan to circulate among his friends, but he stayed close to her.

His long-lashed reddish-brown eyes seemed to measure her features, as he gazed down at her. "Enjoy the meal?"

She nodded and forced a half-smile. All right, he was honorable, but her nerves still rioted at the thought that he slept across the hall from her and that their bedroom doors didn't have locks. "Yes. It was wonderful. I had no idea that Mattie could turn out a gourmet meal. I had expected some first class soul food."

Looking at him, relaxed against the marble fireplace, she didn't think she'd ever seen a man so comfortable with himself. "Oh, she can cook that, too," he said, "as well as French or Italian, and always top fare. There's more to Mattie than those ridiculous wigs. Aperitif?"

"N . . . No thank you. I'd better run up and check on Tonya."

With a finger on her arm, he detained her. "I told you. You're off tonight. I'll check on her. If you want to get away from me, just say so."

She looked up quickly, startled. "Why would I want to do that?"

"You're asking me?" Ice laced his speech. "Look, Justine, I don't know why I'm pestering you. If you'll excuse me . . ."

To her amazement, he half-bowed and left her. What had brought that on? Surely, he wasn't so thin-skinned.

"What got into him?" Banks asked, her words and delicate spicy perfume announcing her presence.

Justine looked up at Banks, about five-feet-nine, slim, and beautiful. Almost enough like Duncan to be his twin. "You tell me. You've known him longer than I have."

Banks's tongue poked the lower side of her jaw, a gesture Justine had often seen Duncan make. "He's bothered about something, and maybe he ought to be."

Justine had to reach for self-control to avoid reacting to Banks's cryptic remark. Still, she couldn't refrain from glaring at Banks. "What do you mean?"

Unperturbed, Banks shrugged with the elaboration of royalty conferring an honor. "Why is an intelligent, well-educated, smart woman like you working as a babysitter? You're finishing school from your head to your toes, girlfriend, and I bet you never made a bed in your life."

Taken aback by the woman's shrewdness and blunt remark, Justine pretended to be unruffled. "Not everybody can judge a book by its cover. Congratulations."

"Save the sarcasm, Justine. What are you after?"

A sigh eased through her lips before she could stifle it. She lifted her chin in defiance, but thought better of the words about to spill out and decided to bridle her tongue. No point in making an enemy of Duncan's sister. "I'm trying to make a living while I develop some writing skills. That all right with you?"

Banks sat on the edge of a leather arm chair, leaned forward, and cupped her knees with her hands. "I'll buy that. For now. If I were you, though, I'd watch it with Duncan. For all that he-man front, he's as tender as Tonya, and I'll tell you one more thing. Girl, if you ever trip his trigger, you're in for a full-scale war."

"Thanks. But why are you telling me this?"

Banks's raised left eyebrow was meant to question Justine's intelligence. "You kidding? Deny it all you please, girlfriend, but you want Duncan just about as much as I want Wayne Roundtree. From what I've seen, I suspect you'd be good for him. Of course, what I've seen also tells me there's plenty more to you than meets the eye." At Justine's barely contained annoyance, she went on, "Don't mind me. I say what I think. That way you know where you stand with me. Can't say that for my brother, though. He's about as open with his thoughts as a deaf mute; by the time you figure it out, your name is Mudd." Wayne joined them and saved Justine a rejoinder.

"Are you headed back to Frederick tonight, Leah?"

Justine could barely refrain from grinning when Banks pulled air through her teeth and rolled her eyes toward the ceiling. "Wayne, we aren't going to get anywhere if you insist on calling me Leah. My name is Banks."

"Get real, Leah. I can't call you Banks; that's what I call your brother."

"Then call him Duncan," she huffed. "He loves his name. I can't stand mine."

"It's a lovely name, and I like it. Brings to my mind a graceful swan, long-necked and elegant, as you are," Wayne said, and Justine thought of telling Banks that Wayne Roundtree wouldn't be browbeaten. "I repeat, going to Frederick?"

"I have to," she mumbled, in a manner that suggested she wasn't pleased with him. "I'm working tomorrow." She bunched her shoulders. "Duncan would love it if you drove me. Save him the long trip tonight."

Wayne raised up to his full height of six feet, three inches and bestowed a cool smile on Banks. "Leah, I don't give two hoots what Duncan would love, and I'm not trying to save him a trip anywhere. I want to know what you would like. Do I drive you?"

"That would be nice," she said in a barely audible voice.

Justine left them to settle the matter and slipped upstairs to look in on Tonya. All evening, she'd longed to sit beside the child's bed and watch her sleep, to be there for her when she woke up and see her smile of recognition. Torn between the desire to nurture Duncan's interest into a living, permanent emotion and the need to preserve her status as Tonya's nanny, she'd needed reassurance of Tonya's affection—the one thing that could fill her life forever. Her heart pounded in joyous rhythm as she gazed down at the sleeping child.

"She's asleep."

The sound of his deep, velvety voice sent tremors of excitement ricocheting through her body. "I know. I just thought I'd check." She cut a wide swath around him, avoiding his eyes as she did so, rushed to her room, and closed the door. She'd never been afraid of relationships, had always delighted in exploring them, game for new experiences. And then Kenneth deceived her. She squeezed her fists tight, fighting to shut out the gnawing sounds of the past, to live in the present, grab whatever happiness came her way and hang onto it.

The stench of the burning rubble, the gutted remains of the Sutton Motel in Falls Church, Virginia and the sight of the black plastic bags tied to gurneys that passed within inches of her came back to her, bridging time, and she was there again. She hadn't known that she cried out until her door sprang open and Duncan Banks had her in his arms.

"What is it? Why are you shaking so? Justine, honey, tell me what's the matter." She had to pull herself together, to reclaim her dignity. She couldn't let him see her shattered this way. He held her closer in an unmistakable caress, and she wanted to luxuriate in the warmth of his embrace, but her relationship with her child was at stake. She rested her head on his shoulder for a second, lolling in what might have been, and then moved away.

"I'm sorry if I alarmed you, Duncan, but I'm all right now."

He wasn't easily pacified. "You don't get off that simply, Justine, and if you had heard the terror in your voice, you wouldn't blame me for insisting. What happened to you?"

She didn't question his right to an explanation, but she couldn't tell all. "You're right. It was the sudden memory of a terrible tragedy, so fresh and so real. I . . . I suppose I forgot where I was."

"And you're not going to tell me about it, are you?"

Still shaken, she had to control her voice, lest it tremble. "Some day, perhaps, if our relationship warrants it. For now, you'll have to trust me, Duncan. I promise I haven't committed any crimes, and I have no unpaid debts. You don't have to worry about my character."

His grim expression belied his words. "I don't question your good character, Justine. To mimic you, you wear it wrapped around you like a bold spring breeze. If you're all right, I'll leave you. But if you need me . . ." He let it hang.

She couldn't face the merrymakers downstairs, so she'd get Banks's phone number and apologize for not saying good night. She got ready for bed and faced a welcomed fact. That scream was at last a physical reaction to the pain of that morning in Falls Church, Virginia. She still hadn't cried.

Duncan walked down the stairs with heavy, burdened steps. He'd waste a lot of time if he tried guessing what could have been so horrible that its memory wrung such a terror-stricken scream from Justine. He ought to be grateful that it happened, because he needed a reminder that he didn't know Justine Taylor. Yet, it was no use denying his strong attraction to her. When he'd held her in his arms upstairs there, he'd felt her pain, and he knew the danger that presaged. A man was headed for trouble when his gut reaction to a woman was to protect her, and he'd wanted to shield Justine from whatever demons haunted and hurt her. He paused on the bottom step, unwilling to break his thoughts and join his friends. Maybe he'd take his annual hunting trip early. Justine was as capable of taking care of Tonya as he was. When he got back home, she'd be out of his system.

He pulled air through his teeth in disgust at himself. He had to straighten out his head. If she had so much as raised her face and looked at him or put her hands near his shoulders, he'd have taken her mouth, the consequences be damned. And that didn't make a shred of sense. He glanced up at Wayne Roundtree and his baby sister heading for the front door.

"You don't want me to drive you home, Leah?"

"Wayne's gonna drop me off on his way to Beaver Ridge."

He didn't suppose it was funny; nothing amused him

right then. But he couldn't help enjoying Wayne's apparent discomfort—until the man reprimanded Banks, "I'm not *dropping* you off; I'm taking you home. You said you'd like that, and that's what I'm doing."

She was about to learn that Roundtrees didn't let people jerk them around, and the lesson might do her some good. Still . . . Duncan ignored Wayne's scowl. "If you want me to take you, Leah, it's no sweat." He didn't laugh when Wayne glared at him, though maintaining a straight face took some mental discipline.

"What do you want?" Wayne asked her, his voice tinged with vexation and his stance just short of predatory.

Banks's sheepish grin settled it for Duncan even before she said, "He can take me home." Wayne Roundtree had her number, but it didn't surprise him when she took care not to get too far out of character and added, "You trust him, don't you, Duncan?"

A belly laugh rolled out of him. Trust his sister to squeeze the humor out of a situation. "Make him stick to the speed limit, Sis. Wayne drives like a bat out of hell."

"I'll open that door," Wayne said when Banks reached the car.

She shifted her weight to her left foot and let fly with, "Something wrong with my hands?"

She resisted squirming when he stopped inches from her, looked down into her face and said, "No. The problem lies elsewhere. And that's something you and I are going to get straight before I move this car."

Tough, was he? "Hmmm. Maybe I'd better tell Duncan he has to take me home after all."

His hand on her elbow said he meant business. Fine with her. "Leah, I don't care for this constant stream of sarcasm and cynicism. I'm with you because I want to be, and I assume the same goes for you. But if you'd rather be somewhere else, say the word and we won't start this. What'll it be?"

She wished she could see his eyes a little better and figure out what he thought, and she'd give anything to know how to talk to him. She opened her mouth to tell him he couldn't always have his likes, remembered how long and how badly she'd wanted to be with him, and said instead, "Are you always so cut and dried?"

"Not usually, but your constant challenges bring out a side of me that I'm not familiar with. Think you can mellow a little?"

"I . . . I thought I was."

He helped her into the sleek, maroon-colored Town Car, seated himself, and started the engine. "Do you want us to spend time together?"

Playing it safe, was he? She bristled. "Wayne, I'm not an authority on boy-girl behavior these days, but I think if you want us to see each other, you have to ask."

He glanced her way briefly before accelerating onto the Capital Beltway. "Okay. Okay. Will you spend time with me? I'd like to get to know you."

He was asking her out. Everything inside of her started swimming, and she grasped her forehead as though to quell an attack of vertigo. Only air came out of her mouth when she parted her lips to speak.

"Well? You turning me down? I thought you said you'd wanted to meet me. If I've bombed this fast with you, I'm in trouble."

She grabbed her middle when he zipped into Route 270 and nearly panicked when words still wouldn't come. In desperation, she placed a tentative hand on his knee and risked a gentle pat. The man had tied her into knots; she'd never been speechless in her life.

He glanced down at her hand resting on his knee. "What does that mean?"

"I . . . I think you're nice, Wayne, and we can go out sometime."

He rested his hand on hers. "On a steady basis?"

Just because the man was wonderful wasn't a reason to chuck her common sense. "Well, let's see if that's what we want. Okay?"

"Works for me."

They reached Frederick well before driving at the legal speed limit would have allowed. When Wayne parked in front of the white brick house at 75 North Teal, she breathed in sweet relief. "Thanks for the ride home. See you soon."

He took her hand and walked toward the front door. "I assume you don't live out here on Teal Street. Let me have your keys." He unlocked the door with his free hand and walked with her into the darkened foyer. "I'm glad we met. Goodnight, Leah."

She jerked her hand from his. "I told you not to call me—" His mouth warm and firm settled on hers and scrambled her brain, and she grabbed the lapels of his jacket to steady herself. She'd never felt anything like it. Shivers coursed through her body until she trembled in his arms.

He broke the kiss and gazed down at her as though in wonder. "Is there a guy in your life? Serious, I mean?"

She blinked her eyes. "Why'd you do that? You caught me off guard."

She luxuriated in his grin, its warmth toasting her like midday sunshine on a deserted beach. "If I'd asked you, I'd never have gotten that kiss, and especially not one that honest. And I'm calling you Leah. Period. Get that?"

He was out of the door before she could tell him he'd be talking to the wind, because she'd refuse to answer him. She lit a cigarette with shaking fingers and made up for lost time.

Duncan told the last of his guests good night, extinguished the lights, and headed upstairs. The light shinning beneath Justine's door caused him some concern, and he left his bedroom door ajar so he could hear her if she called out to him. He stripped and slid into bed. Justine was across the hall from him, crying for all he knew, since she hadn't come back downstairs, and he was helpless to do anything about it, because she hadn't trusted him. Then there was Wayne Roundtree and his kid sister. Kid? She was twenty-seven. He hoped the man had sense enough to realize that she was a tenderfoot, that she hid her innocence behind her sharp tongue. He flipped over on his belly. He'd hate to flatten his boss, but he'd do it in a New York minute and wouldn't think twice about it.

Across the hall, Justine struggled with her reaction to Duncan's almost kiss. She had wanted it. She rolled over to untangle the sheet twisted around her body. Her unloved body. Behind closed eyelids she saw his lips moving toward hers, slowly. Teasing. Tantalizing her. She parted her lips for the taste of his hot velvet tongue and moaned in despair when it failed to penetrate her welcoming mouth. When her breasts began to ache for his stroking fingers, she swung out of bed, took off her gown and showered. She didn't fool herself. Duncan wasn't the only source of her discontent, nor could she attribute it to celibacy, for she'd never been fulfilled. The certainty that she'd never been loved, that her failure at lovemaking with her husband wasn't her fault, had triggered in her a need to explore herself, to fly. Because Kenneth Montgomery hadn't loved her, his heart hadn't been in his lovemaking. She knew that now. And sleeping within fifteen feet of her every night was the epitome of temptation in the person of Duncan Banks, a good-looking, mesmerizing, and powerful hunk of a man who wanted her and whose lure beckoned her. Torment was right here on earth.

CHAPTER FOUR

"Phone for you, Justine. I'd appreciate it if you'd answer the phones; I can't stand those things. I like to see who I'm talking to."

"All right, Mattie. In a second." Justine put Tonya in her crib and rustled across the hall to her room.

"Hello."

"Hello, Justine. I told you I'd call. Big Al gave me your number."

She looked to the ceiling. Just what she needed, a pursuit by the biggest ego ever to strut on Howard University's campus. "Hello, Warren. I didn't tell Al to give out my telephone number. What can I do for you?"

"Well, thanks for the nice warm greeting. How about going to the automobile show with me tomorrow night?"

She had forgotten his passion for cars. "Sorry, Warren, but I'm working tomorrow night."

"If you weren't, would you go?"

No wonder he had amassed a fortune by the time he was thirty; he had the tenacity of an ant after sugar and didn't know the meaning of the word, no. Never had. She walked as far as the cord would reach, then back to her desk. She didn't need Warren in her life right then. He'd pick until he knew everything and wouldn't be averse to using against her whatever he uncovered.

"I don't think so, Warren. Would you excuse me now? I have to see about Tonya."

"All right, lady, but I'm not giving up. You remember that. I get what I go after, and a lot of people will attest to that fact."

She didn't want him plundering around in her life. "Waste your time somewhere else, Warren. We've got a business arrangement through Al. That's all. Look, I have to go. Good-bye."

Bulldogged as ever, he drawled, "That's my girl. Same Justine. If you committed a murder, I bet you'd do it in the best lady-like manner. Bye for now."

She hung up and regrouped. An involvement with any man, not only Warren, would complicate her life. Besides, she couldn't afford to have Duncan question her suitability as a nanny for Tonya, and he might if she had men visiting her. Still, if she concentrated on another man, maybe she'd spend less time thinking about Duncan Banks.

She got back to the nursery in time to see Tonya's shoe drop out of the crib. The baby smiled at her, banged her other shoe against the bars and sang out, "Juju."

Justine stopped herself just as the words, "Mummy's coming," perched at the tip of her tongue. She slapped her right hand over her mouth, horrified. Lord forbid that she should ever make that mistake. Weakened by the significance of what she'd almost done, she slumped into the rocker beside the crib, closed her eyes and leaned back. Instead of getting easier as the days passed, the pain became sharper and the charade more difficult. But she couldn't envisage turning back. Not now. She could never leave her child.

She lay Tonya in bed for a nap, put on a cassette of Mozart chamber music, collected several letters to Aunt Mariah, sat beside the child's bed and perused them.

"Dear Aunt Mariah, My boyfriend is seeing another girl. He didn't say so, but I know he is, because he hasn't called me in two months. Should I drop him? Tearful."

Justine controlled the urge to laugh, because Tearful

had a serious problem. You couldn't drop what you didn't have. She wrote:

"Dear Tearful, Be a good sport and let him out of it gracefully. A gentle note saying it's been nice knowing him, and all the best would sound just the right chord, though he doesn't deserve that. If he's cheating, forget him. Yours, Aunt Mariah."

A ringing phone sent her scrambling into the hallway to answer it before Mattie gave vent to her ire.

"Yes?"

"Hello, Justine, Big Al here. I got a couple of great letters about your column. I told ya people would love it, didn't I? Keep it up. You're doing good. Just give 'em plenty of horse sense and that family stuff But you . . . er . . . sat down pretty hard on . . . let's see, some woman wrote you that her husband—Linden, I believe—was fooling around. You told her to leave him. Justine, baby, that is not family stuff. The only advice you ever give to a woman who's man is unfaithful is to kick him out. You gotta do better than that, babe."

So that was why he'd called. Might as well set him straight. "Thanks, but that's what they deserve. By the way, why did you give Warren my phone number here?"

"You didn't want him to have it? He said you gave it to him, and he lost it. Wait'll I chew him out."

The man hadn't changed since school days. Dear as he was, she'd have to reprimand him. "Next time, please ask me first."

"Okay, but you could do worse than Warren. He's smart. A real go-getter. I know. I know," he said, as though he anticipated her censure. "He can stick to you like glue, but you can handle that. He's a good guy. Not a lot of 'em are your equal, you know."

"Speak for yourself, Al."

"Okay. Okay." She could imagine his hand palm out before him. "I won't do it again. Say, I could have your mail sent to you by messenger."

She knew that gesture was meant to appease her, but instead, it alarmed her. She didn't want him to have Duncan's address. Thinking rapidly, she said, "Then the messenger would know where Aunt Mariah lives."

She thought she heard air seep through his lips. "Fast thinking. You're on the ball, honey. We'll leave it as it is."

She hung up, slipped back into the role of Aunt Mariah and finished the column, but she couldn't make herself advise Rose Akers to stay with her abusive man. "Leave him," she wrote. At the other extreme, Annie K. couldn't make up her mind to marry a prince of a guy. Justine wrote, "Annie, dear, a woman who doesn't know champagne from grape juice doesn't deserve champagne. Yours, Aunt Mariah."

"Is she still asleep?"

Startled, her head jerked up. She hadn't heard him climb the stairs. Please Lord, don't let him ask to see what she'd been writing. She presented him with what she hoped was a smile. "Yes. She's asleep."

"How can she sleep with the radio on?" he continued as he entered the room and stepped with a jazzy rhythm directly to her. She didn't believe he did it intentionally, because there was nothing personal in his facial expression, only concern for his child. But intentional or not, his dancing gait set her on fire. Darn him. She looked away.

"It isn't the radio, it's a cassette. She sleeps most soundly when this music is playing, and if she's awake and I put on Mozart's "Concerto for Flute and Harp," she's very quiet and smiles a lot. I think she enjoys it."

She wished he wouldn't stare at her. Those sleepy-lidded reddish-brown eyes seemed to suck her right into his body. "I'd have thought she was too young to have preferences in music, but you've already made me ditch some of my ideas about bringing up children."

He stepped closer and pinned her with a hypnotic stare. "I'm glad you're here, Justine. You've warmed up this place, changed our lives for the better."

What had happened to his light manner of moments earlier? Vanished. His expression had dissolved into a somber cloud, and he stood so close that his knee touched the fabric of her slacks.

"I hope you'll be with us a long, long time, Justine."

His tone had gotten deeper, had softened. She had to observe him carefully in order to get what was behind his message, and as she looked into his face, his solemn words and the urgency of his manner sent warm arrows of excitement darting through her, and she closed her eyes to cover her feelings. But only for a second. The sensation of his warm fingers on her shoulders disconcerted her, and she looked into his eyes. He seemed to pull her into himself, to meld with her, to draw her into him as though he were quicksand. She drew back, away from him, but she couldn't loosen his hold on her, an indefinable something that seemed to tie them together. His hand moved to her face, caressed her cheek, and lingered there while he stared into her eyes. Abruptly, he turned and left the room.

Her left hand found its way to the spot where his had been and covered the warmth he'd left there. She heard his bedroom door close and gave silent thanks. She didn't know how she would have resisted pulling him into her arms, if his touch had lingered for a second longer. As she folded the letters and put away her writing pad, the thought occurred to her that, for her deception, she might get the trial of her life.

Tonya would sleep for another half-hour, so she slipped quietly down the stairs and out on the back deck. The mid-Autumn sun filtered through the red, gold, and purple leaves that signaled the changing season, and she stretched out on the chaise and drank in the loveliness that surrounded her. Peace. If only she could feel it inside. It was all around her, yet it didn't touch her. She loved the autumn with its calm winds and crisp, moonlit nights, and she adored the environment in which Duncan lived. Trees of many hues for as far as she could see, and neither a house nor any other man-made object to spoil the view. It would be so easy to pretend that life was perfect, to fool herself.

"Beautiful, isn't it?"

She nearly sprang from the chair. Didn't he ever make a sound? "I didn't know I had company."

"I come out here often when I'm home on afternoons like this one. A half-hour or so, and I'm rejuvenated."

She didn't risk more than a glance at him, for when his voice was lower than normal and the cadence of his speech unusually rhythmic, his eyes tended to have a dreamy, sexy look that took the starch out of her. "Ready to slay dragons?" she asked.

He shrugged as though her jab was of no import. "I never thought of it that way. The respite helps me put my work and other things in perspective. Are you contented here?"

So he was back to that dangerous topic. "Yes, I'm satisfied. Did you . . . think I might not be?"

He sat on the edge of a chair facing her, and she swung her legs off the chaise lounge and sat upright.

"It was only a question, Justine. I like stability in my life, and Tonya needs that. You're giving her more than I'd hoped for, and I'm grateful."

He'd made a perfectly reasonable statement, but it nettled her that anyone should thank her for caring for her own child, and she bristled. "Why shouldn't I take care of my . . ." She caught herself and dropped her head in her hands. Her palms dampened and chills settled over her body before she raised her head and looked in the distance.

"You're paying me, Duncan; I don't ask for gratitude."

He leaned forward, his long elegant fingers clasped loosely before him. "If I thought you meant that, I'd change my opinion of you. You care deeply for Tonya, and . . ." He stood. "I shouldn't have disturbed your peace."

Remorseful for the callous words she had uttered because she wanted to keep a psychological distance between them, she stood and reached out to detain him. "I do care deeply, Duncan, and I understand that it's important to you that your child's nanny love her. If that wasn't so, I wouldn't be comfortable here." She wished she could see past that blank expression that he'd draped over his face.

He grimaced. "And that's all you understand? I gave you credit for more than that." He studied her for what seemed a long time, and she forced herself not to flinch while his gaze first roamed her face and then settled on her eyes in a rapt stare.

Maybe that was his customary way at looking at people, but she wished he'd stop it.

"Want to go for a short walk in the woods? They're safe."

She did. She loved the woods, but she didn't dare go anyplace with him where they'd be alone. Not right then. "I'd love to," she told him, "but Tonya will wake up in a couple of minutes."

Lights danced in his eyes, and she realized he was laughing at her. Then he sobered. "You're a wise woman."

"I wish I thought it," she murmured.

"I heard that. One of these days, you're going to level with me, and I bet I get the shock of my life."

Her lip dropped, and she heaved when her breath caught in her lungs, but her composure returned as quickly as it had deserted her. "You've got one heck of an imagination. No wonder you're such a good reporter."

He jammed his hands on his hips in a belligerent stance and gaped at her. "*Imagination?* I'll have you understand, lady, that I don't make up stories; *I report facts.*"

She didn't know why she laughed, but she suspected from his stunned expression that no one should have had the nerve to say that to him. Shrugging, she did nothing to stop the grin that settled on her face. "Sorry. I have to see about Tonya."

She didn't ask, and this time he didn't get out of the way, but stood his ground and let her soft mounds brush his left shoulder as she squeezed between him and the door jamb sending a rippling sensation over her nerve ends.

His words followed her. "One of these days, you'll walk through these woods with me."

She would, too. And then what? His shoulder burned from the touch of her soft breast. Shaking his head in frustration, he stuck his hands in his pockets and headed for the trail that would take him on a winding trek through his beloved woods. In the months since he'd bought the house, he'd come to love and appreciate his solitary walks, and he had never shared his peaceful sanctuary with anyone. But for a moment back there, he'd had an urge to stroll that path with Justine. As usual, she'd had the foresight to refuse and ward off what they both would certainly have regretted. But he knew himself well enough to know that she had only postponed the inevitable and, clever as she was, she had to know it, too. Neither of them wanted an emotional involvement, yet it apparently wasn't the two of them, but fate, that dictated their course.

He stopped and leaned against a white-barked elm. What did he want from Justine other than the love and care that she gave his daughter? He couldn't recall being so indecisive about anything. He'd see her teaching, playing, and laughing with Tonya and watch the excited joy and happiness on his child's face and know deep down that if anybody or anything separated them, they'd both suffer. Another worrisome thing was the feeling he continued to get that he knew Justine from somewhere: at times he felt as though he'd always known her. He couldn't get a handle on it. It was as though an unexplained phenomenon dictated the course of their relationship, laughed at his vow to remain uninvolved with any woman, and elevated his testosterone level every time he saw her or thought about her.

Annoyed at the course of his thoughts, he started back to the house. What the devil? Killing time in the woods in the middle of the afternoon. He had to get that woman out of his system. He'd . . . He answered his cell phone.

"Banks."

"Hi, Duncan. I'm attending a workshop at the Library of Congress tomorrow. Mind if I bunk at your place tonight?" his sister asked.

He told her to get there in time for dinner, hung up, and sprinted the rest of the way to the house. With Leah around, he'd get no work done that night. As he strode through the kitchen, he alerted Mattie that there'd be a fourth for dinner.

"Justine," he called and tapped on her bedroom door.

"Over here with Tonya."

"Leah's spending the night. Just thought I'd tell you." He pushed open Tonya's door. "What are you—?"

"Three," Justine sang, and Tonya held up three fingers.

"Two." He stared as the child showed Justine two fingers, and got a round of hugs and kisses as a reward. He walked in, knelt before them, and rested on his haunches. Tonya reached for him, and he took her into his arms.

"She loves you, Justine. I don't want her little heart broken."

Justine had an urge to scream, why would she break her own child's heart? But she had to settle for wiser words: "I'd be the last person to do that knowingly, Duncan. I love her, too."

"I know you do."

Duncan gave the baby back to Justine, gazed down at the two of them already immersed in each other, went to his room, and got to work. She loved Tonya. He knew that, but why did hearing her say it give him such an empty, woebegone feeling? He couldn't put his finger on it, but something was not according to Hoyle.

Justine put on a pair of green silk wide-bottom pants and matching long-sleeve shirt, tied a mauve silk sash around her waist and strolled down the stairs to meet Leah Banks.

"Who's older, you or me?" Banks asked Justine after enveloping her in a warm hug.

"Justine's got two years on you," Duncan said.

Banks glided over to Duncan's favorite chair, took a seat, and swung her crossed leg. "Good. Then maybe you can give me some advice."

Justine's heart skipped a beat. Did Banks know about her column? If she did, they'd all soon find out, because she'd be her usual blunt self and say so. "What kind of advice?"

"Wayne. The night he drove me home from here, he kissed me like he was scared he'd forget how and said he wanted to see me regularly. We went to dinner a couple of times, but he doesn't call me. I can't figure him out."

"Try zipping up your lip when you get the urge to be clever," Duncan said in a tone that suggested exasperation.

"I'm serious, Duncan. I've fallen hard for the guy."

Justine couldn't help sympathizing with her. She was trying to tell them that she hadn't had much experience with men and didn't know what to do with Wayne. A babe in the woods. "Make him feel wonderful," Justine told her. "Don't lie to him, but let him know that you love being with him, that you'd rather have his company than anybody else's. When he does something kind or gracious, when he pleases you, let him know you appreciate it. You like to be treasured and admired, don't you? So does he."

Justine felt Duncan's hard stare on her before her glance took in his raised eyebrow and the impression of his tongue poking his lower right cheek. He made a ceremony of clearing his throat. "Well. Well."

Justine ignored him. "Just be honest about your feelings, Banks." She tried to act as though she didn't notice Duncan's look of surprise. "He needs to know you admire him just as much as you need to know he admires you," she went on.

As though unwilling to let an opportunity get past him, Duncan looked Justine in the eye and drawled, "I haven't noticed you knocking yourself out to make *me* feel great."

If he'd intended to surprise her, he had to know from her quick frown that he'd succeeded. "I didn't know you needed that nor that I was the one to do it."

Banks yawned deliberately and with all the drama of a great actress in a choice role. "Will you two stop fencing with each other? We're supposed to be dealing with *my* problem."

Duncan walked to the bar, glanced at his sister, and shrugged with an air of disdain. "*Your* problem? I'm not sure I want Wayne Roundtree kissing my sister. Would you ladies like some wine or something stronger?"

Banks took a spritzer, and Justine asked for a Lazy Mary.

"What's that?" Banks and Duncan asked simultaneously.

"A Bloody Mary without the vodka." From the expression on their faces, you'd have thought she'd dropped in from Mars.

"What am I going to do about Wayne?" Banks asked, bringing them back to the issue of most importance.

"Get rid of that crust you wear and be yourself," Duncan snapped. "What's so great about him anyway? There are plenty of other guys."

"I'm not interested in plenty of other guys; it's Wayne I can't stop thinking about."

"Maybe Duncan is right," Justine said. "I think Wayne likes strong, independent women, but he wants them soft. Feminine."

She knew she'd said the wrong words, though she didn't know which ones sent Banks's back up and changed her expression from suppliant to incredulous. "I'm not about to be responsible for any man's ego," she protested. "I'm going back there and talk with Mattie."

"What you're responsible for is your own femininity," Justine said.

Banks tossed her head and shrugged her left shoulder. "Looks like I'm gonna strike out then. Justine, you sound just like Aunt Mariah. Sometimes I could throttle that woman. She's so understanding. The correct answer to half the letters she publishes is a simple, 'Woman, don't be stupid.' "

Justine didn't want to look at Duncan, because she knew that, with Banks out of the room, he couldn't wait to pounce. And pounce, he did. "Well. Well. That little conversation was most revealing. You'd tell your man how great he was. And you'd be soft and feminine, too, wouldn't you?"

She got up and started for the door. "I'm not in a mood to tangle with you, Duncan. You've been floating those balloons past me ever since this afternoon. Please try to remember that I'm Tonya's nanny."

His half-laugh held a tinge of bitterness. "You don't think I could forget it, do you? By the way, that's a lovely get-up. Soft and feminine."

What next? she asked herself, as he propped his foot on the bottom rung of a Shaker chair that had belonged to his grandfather, and which occupied a place of honor beside the living room door, and gazed steadily at her. His face lost all expression.

"You waltzed in here and shook up our world. You brought us exactly what we needed and plenty of it. Don't you know what happens when you throw a pebble into a pond?"

"Are you asking me to leave?"

"God forbid." He stepped to the chair in which she sat and held out his hand to her. "Come on. Let's . . . Let's check out that kitchen."

When she stood, air and a few inches were all that separated them. His gaze nearly unraveled her as he focused first on her eyes and then on her mouth. Her quick intake of breath brought his ten fingers to her forearms, and a trembling of her lips telegraphed to him her anticipation of his kiss and her fear of the consequences.

"Oh, hell!" He spun around, bolted from the living room, and his steps could be heard taking him toward the kitchen.

After dinner, Justine went upstairs to check on Tonya, and Banks followed Duncan down to the basement. He paused on the bottom step and looked back at his sister. "You know, it's been months since a woman answered that notice that runs every week in Dee Dee's column. Strange. Well, what the heck! Maybe women don't think the offer is such a bargain."

Banks walked on past him. "It's only a bargain for a desperate woman. Most of us human creatures need to be loved. Anybody male or female who claims otherwise is either lying or peculiar. You included."

She reached for a cigarette, remembered where she was, and put it back. "If you ask me, and if you don't, the answer to your problem is right upstairs. You're not going to find a woman who'll be a better mother to Tonya than Justine. And you know it. That's why you're fighting so hard not to let your guard down with her. But you might as well forget it, brother. Justine beats any woman I ever saw you with, and she's got your number, too. Want to play some cut throat?"

He ran his hands over a piece of ebony wood that he wanted to carve when he got time. Whenever he saw Tonya's face blossom into a spontaneous grin, he wanted to engrave the image to keep it for all time. He studied his sister. Even as a small child, she'd had nearly infallible judgment about people. Perhaps if she and Justine were left alone, she could understand the puzzling relationship between Justine and Tonya. And maybe she'd remember whether Justine had previously been a part of their lives. He didn't want to cross examine Justine or to appear to distrust her, because he did trust her. It was a good time to check on the boys "East of the River."

"Not tonight, Sis. I've got a couple of errands to run. Why don't you keep Justine company? And try not to say everything that pops into your head."

"I don't do that, Duncan, which is why I haven't said you and Justine circle each other like a couple of Roman gladiators." She grinned as if savoring a sweet and wicked thing. "I'd love to be a fly on the wall when you two admit your little stand-off is useless."

He appraised her with brotherly indulgence. "You're hopeless. Justine has the guest room, so you sleep in the front bedroom." He hugged her. "See you in the morning."

He ran upstairs, got into the "street" clothes that he wore when roaming the slums for a story, covered up with a top coat, and slipped downstairs and into the garage. He removed the coat after he got in the car, zipped up his shabby black leather jacket, pulled on a woolen cap and headed for "East of the River." His beeper rang, and he picked-up his cell phone and called back.

"Say, Pops, this is Mitch. Hope I'm not botherin' you? man, but I thought you'd wanna know some guys about to get a rumble started."

"Yeah? Where?"

"L Street."

"Thanks. I'll be there."

"Watch it though, Pops. They're going with equalizers. It's Ghana and Kenya, man, so you better stay cool..

"Gotcha, Mitch."

He hung up. Mitch and Rags always used code names for the area's toughest gangs in the event that they might be overheard. Equalizers meant the boys would have guns and knives. In a gang rumble, especially that kind, he didn't stand a chance of making a difference; best he could do was report the news.

"Come on in," Justine told Banks, in response to her light tap on the door. "Where's Duncan?"

"He had a couple of errands to run, so I guess it's you and me."

Though she hadn't thought she would be, Justine was glad for Banks's company. The phone had rung twice in the past fifteen minutes, and each time she answered, only silence greeted her ears. If the caller knew that Duncan had left the house . . . She pushed back the thought.

"Tonya's asleep, but you may peep in on her if you like. She's growing so fast." Why was she nervous?

Banks leaned against the door and propped her right hand on her hip. "I'll see her in the morning. How's your writing?"

"How much writing can I do?"

Banks walked into the room and ran her fingers over the silk kimono that lay across a chair. "Good question. I see you've got a rich woman's taste. Say, why don't you ask my brother to bring you over to Frederick for a weekend so we can get to know each other. You can also have a mini vacation, because our mother will be delighted to look after her only grandchild."

Justine hoped her startled expression didn't register with Banks. It was another reminder that Tonya didn't belong to her. She pasted a grin on her face. "I'd like that little vacation, but why do you . . ."

Banks cut her off "We might as well start off right, Justine. I believe in facing facts. You are not going out of Duncan's life anytime soon." She let her gaze sweep Justine's bedroom, and Justine knew she was about to change the subject. "I never could figure out why Duncan put these washed-out colors in here. Dusty rose would have looked a lot better with this blue."

"You're probably right, Banks, but I've gotten used to it, and I find it restful."

Banks laid her head to one side in a frank appraisal of the woman facing her. "Yeah. Have you found anything wrong with him yet?"

"What?"

Justine gazed at the twinkles, so much like Duncan's, that danced in Banks's reddish-brown eyes. "Just checking. I think I'll turn in. I have to get up early, and that's against my principles. See ya in the morning."

Justine told her good night and gazed at her back as she left. She'd wanted the company, but she had a sense of relief that Banks had decided to go to bed. The woman missed nothing and had no qualms about commenting on what she saw. Justine switched on WMAL-TV for the local news round-up in time to see policemen herd a group of young boys into squad cars after a gang fight in Capitol View, while camera men documented the scene for the morning headlines and TV news stories. Several bystanders had been injured, and the police had their hands full dispersing the crowd. Her first thought was of Duncan. She didn't know where he had gone, but she suspected that his reporter's nose was on the trail of a story. Maybe that one. Wherever he was, she prayed he'd be careful. Anxious, she paced the floor, glancing at her watch every few minutes and listening for the sound of the Buick entering the garage. Well after midnight, she undressed and went to bed, but unable to sleep, got up and sat beside the window. She couldn't make herself move until she heard the motor as the car slowed down and turned into the driveway. Quickly, she got into bed, turned off the light on her night table and closed her eyes. In four years of marriage, she'd never stayed up until almost daybreak worrying about Kenneth's safety. She thought about that over and over, her belly knotting with tear at the implications.

* * *

"Do you know about that gang war in Capitol View last night?" Justine asked Duncan at breakfast that morning.

"I caught it on the news just before I came down." He chewed his bacon, absentmindedly she thought, and leaned back in his chair. "If so many boys didn't hang out on the street because they hate where they live, gangs wouldn't seem so attractive to them. The city doesn't have the resources to cope with it."

He wasn't telling all, but he was entitled to his secrets, and she wouldn't press him. After the night she'd spent worrying about him, she was too happy to see him sitting there all in one piece.

She accepted the coffee that he poured for her. "You care deeply, don't you?"

As though she'd spoken the obvious, he shrugged. "I could be one of those kids, Justine. When I was seven, our landlord put my family and everything we had out on the street on one of the coldest days I ever knew, because my dad couldn't pay four hundred dollars in back rent. The experience gave my father the heart attack that took him from us. But our mother used the insurance money to move us to Frederick, Maryland, where she bought an interest in *The Watering Hole* and made a down payment on our home. I've never forgotten that day, and I'll do whatever I can to help children caught in that kind of trap."

So he *had* been in Capitol View. She wanted to ask him how he'd anticipated the trouble, but instead said, "At least you had your mother."

He rested his cup with what seemed like special care and spoke softly, "You didn't?"

She had to tread carefully. 'I was five when she died."

"What about your father?"

She'd known he'd get to that. "He did the best he could, I guess, letting my two aunts take care of me. But they were long on discipline and short on affection. Both of them seemed to think the most important thing was making a lady out of me. Never mind how lonely I got."

"They didn't have children?"

She shook her head. "Neither of them. The younger one was married, and the older one was widowed, though she had a 'friend.' A circumspect one, mind you."

"And your father?"

That was the question she'd hoped he wouldn't ask. "She sucked in her breath and girded herself in preparation for grilling, reporter style. "I . . . I displeased him some years ago, and he's scratched me off his list of the living." When his brows furrowed in a deep frown, she terminated the discussion with, "So that's my story. Wonder why Banks is sleeping so late."

His reaction to what he'd heard was not as she had expected. Instead of an impersonal cross-examination, he responded with the gentleness that she'd seen in him so many times. "Leah doesn't get up until she has to." He said it quickly as though anxious to get back to the subject of Justine. "No wonder you're so giving, so full of . . . of . . . of warmth and . . . and affection."

Needing to protect herself, she lowered her gaze, lest the tender compassion mirrored in his eyes unsettle her. She hadn't made a mistake when she'd moved into his home, trusting him with her life. The affection for him that surged within her must have shown in her facial expression, for his mood seemed to lighten and, with his right hand, he reached across the table, pulled her left little finger, and continued to hold it while they sipped their coffee in contented silence. The sweet moments ended when Banks struggled into the dining room.

"Anything important happen since I last saw you two?" she asked.

Justine could see in his smile how much he adored his sister. "Morning, Leah. What do you want to eat?" She'd eat whatever he was willing to prepare, she told him, aware that Mattie stopped cooking at eight-thirty.

"He's a genuine peach, Justine," Banks said after Duncan went to the kitchen. "I'm single, because I could never find a guy like him."

Justine could believe that. "What about Wayne?"

Banks reached for the coffee Justine handed her.

"Notice I said *could never.* I didn't say *can't ever.* There's a difference."

Justine couldn't help laughing aloud. "All right. All right. Wayne belongs in the present tense."

"And if he wants to stay there," Duncan drawled, putting Leah's plate in front of her, "he'll toe the line."

"What?" Banks yelled.

"You heard me. If you don't make him do it, I will."

Intrigued, Justine asked Duncan, "Who makes *you* toe the line?"

"You do, and you will," he said, without a shred of humor."

Banks swallowed the last of Duncan's blueberry pancakes and looked toward the ceiling. "Oh. Oh. Here we go. The gladiators are at it again. Justine, if I didn't know better, I'd think a bomb dropped right in front of you. Pull up your bottom lip, girlfriend. Say, I gotta get out of here."

Justine watched Banks streak toward the stairs at a speed of which she wouldn't have thought her capable. Everything about Duncan's sister was laid back. She said as much to him.

"When it comes to her responsibilities, she doesn't fool around. Nobody is more reliable than my sister," he said, with obvious pride.

"I'm going to pop in on Tonya for a couple of minutes," Banks yelled down to them. "Could you call me a taxi?"

"I'll drive you down as soon as I get these dishes in the dishwasher and look in on Tonya for a few minutes. I don't like to leave home without spending a little time with her."

They left, and as soon as she got the baby comfortable, Justine called her father. Her conversation with Duncan had reopened those old wounds, the longing she'd always had for the only parent she knew. She had hurt him when she married Kenneth, his opponent for the Assembly seat. The two men had waged a bitter campaign, falsely accusing each other of unsavory deeds that in no way impinged upon their ability as legislators, and they had been equally guilty of the mud-slinging. She had begged Kenneth not to enter the race, but he had despised her father's politics—as she did—and made every effort he could to silence him.

She had loved Kenneth, but she might not have married him if her father hadn't forbade it—if he hadn't demanded that she choose between them.

"May I please speak with Mr. Arnold Taylor?" she asked the crisp, officious voice.

"Who's calling, please?"

Justine took a deep breath. "Justine Taylor. His daughter."

"One moment, please."

Justine held the phone away from her and stared at it as though it held a mystery. The women knew she was Arnold Taylor's daughter, but refused to acknowledge that fact to her, no matter how often she called.

"I'm sorry, Madam. The Assemblyman is busy. Would you care to leave a message?"

She shut off the word, no, as it slipped toward the end of her tongue. She would send the message that she'd buried in her heart while she waited for him to agree to hear it. "Yes. Tell him . . . Please tell him I love him."

She wouldn't let the woman's sputters and her disconcerted, "Wh . . . Wha . . . What?" deter her. She'd made up her mind that, if she couldn't tell him in person, she'd find another way.

"I said, please tell my father that I love him."

"Well . . . uh, yes. Of course. Good-bye," came the voice, less crisp now and far from officious.

"I'm not going to let it get to me," Justine told herself—aloud for emphasis. She did the one thing that was certain to buoy her spirits. She got a cassette of Mozart music and went across the hall to be with her child.

A car shot past on Piney Branch Road just as Duncan turned into it, barely missing a collision. He should have stopped at that intersection, but his mind had been on the events of the previous night. He couldn't protect every slum kid in the District of Columbia, but he had promised himself that he'd be there for Rags and Mitch whenever they needed him. He'd known from the distress in Mitch's voice that Rags would be involved in that rumble. The two boys, half-brothers, had spent more of their lives on the street than in a normal home. Thank God, he'd gotten there in time. Five minutes later and Rags would have been in the heat of it, or worse, a casualty. He had tried without success to convince the boy that carrying grudges and harboring hatred didn't hurt anybody but him.

Banks shifted beside him. He supposed his narrow escape from a collision had upset her, so it surprised him when she calmly asked, "Why do you persist in getting a wife you don't know and don't love? You struck out with Marie, and you'd known her for a couple of years before you married her. Duncan, you don't make sense."

Duncan moved into the right lane and prepared to exit Piney Branch Road onto Georgia Avenue. He did not want to rehash that topic with his sister, but she'd latched onto it with all the tenacity of a teenage boy on the trail of his first sex interest.

"Leah, I'd as soon not discuss Marie. I need a wife, and this is the best way to go about it, because I've sworn undying love for the last time."

"Humph." She sucked her teeth. "I wish you could hear yourself. Suppose the woman you do marry isn't good to Tonya? Uh . . . Tell me. What do you think of Justine, anyway?" He came to a halt at the red light. "Duncan, for goodness sake. You can't say a word about the way Wayne drives"

"Sorry. I thought I could make that light."

"Yeah. Just like you think you'll get married to somebody you don't know and could come to hate. Nobody you marry will get your mind off Justine."

He wished she'd get off that sermon. "Leah, for heaven's sake. Ever since Wayne got into your system, you've taken to some fanciful thinking."

She laughed aloud, surprising him, because he'd thought she might be annoyed. "He's there, all right. And he can stop running."

Duncan slowed down at Independence Avenue and turned left into the famous thoroughfare. I'll drop you at First and Independence. Okay?"

"Sure. Duncan, why won't you tell me the reason why Wayne is . . . well . . . kinda cool. He likes me."

Duncan pulled up to the curb and stopped. "I told you, and Justine told you. Be softer with him. Wayne's tough, but if he likes you, Leah, you can easily turn him off with your razor tongue. He's a good guy, but he's not going to stand for any nonsense. Just relax with him and be yourself." He expelled a long breath. "Look I am not going to help a man get my kid sister into the sack. So don't ask me about him again."

He couldn't believe it when she threw both arms around his neck and laughed. "You mean that's how to seduce him? Oh, Duncan, you're wonderful."

When he could get his breath, he took her face in his hands and stared into her eyes. "That's how you'll get seduced. So be careful."

"Not on your life," she sang, grabbed her briefcase, kissed him on the cheek, and got out of the car.

He watched her until she was out of sight. Wayne. The lucky dog. Did Justine think of him that way? He swore at himself, started the engine, and headed for Baltimore.

He bumped into Wayne when he got off the elevator in the Roundtree building, raised his hand for a greeting, strode past his boss without having said a word, went into his office, and closed the door.

Seconds later, Wayne pushed it open. "Which hornet's nest did you bump into?"

"What? Oh, sorry, man. How'd the pictures of the rumble in D.C. last night come out? The boys were all underage, so I couldn't get their names"

"Just as well," Wayne said. "If they see their names in the paper, they'll have something to strut about. How many paragraphs did you give it?"

"Three, and that's more than it deserves. I'm sick of glorifying these gangs. I didn't mention the gang names, either. Several bystanders were injured, but that was because some adults were yelling and shoving in order to get a good look at kids trying to kill each other."

Wayne punched air with his left fist. "With grown-ups

acting like that, what can you expect of kids? We'll trash the photos. What's eating you, man?"

"Nothing that won't pass. I suppose the Lord knew what he was doing when he made women, and I'm glad he did, but I wish to hell I could understand them."

"Justine?"

Duncan reached into his desk drawer, took out a wooden ball that he often whittled on, and rubbed it as though it were a pacifier. He didn't want to talk with Wayne or anybody else about his feelings right then He threw the ball up, caught it, and put it in his pocket. What the hell! Wayne was part of the problem.

"Justine and Leah."

Wayne took a seat in the office's only vacant chair. "Now, we're getting down to business. What about Leah?"

Duncan slapped his left fist into his right palm and stared into Wayne's hazel eyes. "Are you interested in Leah?"

Wayne took his time answering. "Leah? Yeah. I'm interested. Very much so. Anything else bothering you?"

Duncan rubbed the ball of wood in his right jacket pocket and let a smile float over his face. "Leah was six months old when our father died; I helped raise her. You're the brother I never had, Wayne, and I'd defend you with my life."

"But you'd mow me down over Leah. Right?"

"Just about right, man. I know she lets her wit get out of hand, but—"

Wayne held up both hands, palms out. "Don't tell me. I want to learn about Leah from her. Now that you've gotten into *my* business, when are you going to tell Dee Dee to stop running that notice?"

"But it was your idea."

"All right. So I'm not perfect. When you get back home, man, take a good look at Justine. From what I saw, I'd say she's choice. First rate."

Duncan stared at him. "You're interested in Leah. Right?"

Wayne enjoyed his big laugh almost too much for Duncan's comfort. "Man, you've got a problem. I want Leah to straighten out her act, but Justine's already got it together, and you're waltzing around her like you think she comes by the dozen. Man, good women are rare."

"You think you have to tell me? I've had a little more experience with this than you have."

Wayne showed white teeth in a wide grin. "Then I suppose you've given a lot of thought to your cockamamie notion of becoming a celibate—"

"What? Who gave you that idea?"

Wayne's face was the picture of innocence. "Well, if you get married, man, you're married, and you can't fool around even if it *is* a marriage of convenience. Vows are vows."

Duncan laid back his head against his chair and let the mirth pour out of him, laughing until his breath hung in his throat. When he could, he said, "Do you know, I never thought of that? Good Lord!"

"Dead issue?"

"Deader than an Egyptian mummy. At least the celibate part."

Duncan got home that evening around seven o'clock, and Mattie met him at the door.

"They ain't here, Mr. B. They been gone since noon, and they ain't got back here yet."

Her voice escalated with each word she uttered. He told himself not to let Mattie upset him.

CHAPTER FIVE

He had exhausted the possibilities, the places where logic told him they might be. Try the hospitals? He couldn't deal with that thought right then. He lowered his head into his hands and tried to think. Maybe if he changed the scenery, if he went for a walk, he'd think of something.

Mattie met him on the stairs. "Mr. B., Mr. B. Did you find out anything, Mr. B?"

For once, the purple bird's nest on her head that passed for hair didn't amuse him. Looking up at him, wringing her hands, and not bothering to hold back the tears that flowed down her cheeks, she was the epitome of misery. He lifted her and held her.

"Don't cry, Mattie. We don't know that anything's happened to them." He set her down and patted her shoulder.

"I . . . I'd feel a whole lot better if they was home here."

As if she needed to articulate that sentiment. Mattie was a riot even when she was sad and serious, but she'd said what he felt.

"And I'd feel a whole lot better if you did some of your famous praying right now. I'm going out back. I've got my cell phone, so transfer any calls that come in."

Her hands went to her practically nonexistent hips. "You

insult my religion. What you think I been doing, Mr. B? I already been praying. Ain't you worried none? This ain't a bit like Justine. She don't do things like this, Mr. B. Every single thing she do, she do it on time. Right by the clock. I tell you, it ain't good."

He put on the best face he could manage, because he didn't need to have Mattie break down and add to his problems. "I'm not exactly in a dancing mood, Mattie, but I have to keep a clear head. Now, you go back downstairs and try to make yourself busy. No news is good news."

She opened her mouth, then dropped her top lip over her upper front teeth—an act that changed her personality—and shook her finger at Duncan. "You ain't been doing nothing wrong that you're about to get paid for, has you?"

He shoved his hands in his pockets, loped down the stairs, and called over his shoulder, "I'm not the one keeping records, so I can't answer that. Call me if the phone in my office rings."

If Mattie knew how upset he was, she'd probably convene a prayer meeting. He stood on the back lawn with his left foot propped against a big piece of driftwood that he'd collected on the beach in Ocean City after a deep-sea fishing trip. He didn't know what he'd do if anything happened to them. Either one of them. She was in trouble, or she'd call him. Nothing would convince him that she'd keep Tonya out so late, without dinner, disturbing the child's sleeping schedule. He walked over to a rose trellis, pushed aside one of the stems that languished there—bare but for their thorns—and sat on the stone bench beneath it. The rising wind brought the smell of dying autumn leaves and the threat of a storm, and his belly knotted as tension coiled within him. Heaven forbid that they should be out in an electric storm. He unhooked his cell phone from his belt and called Wayne.

"I was just leaving," Wayne told him. "What's up?"

Duncan explained about Justine and Tonya's mysterious absence. He didn't expect Wayne to know where they were, but he might have some thoughts as to where to look.

"This is unlike Justine, Wayne, and I'm sure something's wrong."

"Did you call the police?"

"Not yet. I didn't want to do that 'til I had to. It's my last resort. In twenty minutes, every cameraman and his granddaddy would be parked in front of my house. You know that."

"Yeah. Look, buddy. I was about to go to Frederick, but I think I'll come over there. You might need me."

"I might. Why don't you stay there for another half hour. If you don't hear from me in that time, go to Frederick, and I'll call you at home."

After a long silence, during which Wayne appeared to consider Duncan's suggestion, he said, "All right. Hang in there."

He bunched his shoulders as shivers raced through him, not from the evening chill or the rapidly rising wind, but from the gnawing anxiety that he could no longer keep at bay. Scattered drops of rain dampened his bare head. Where could they be? He didn't want them out in that weather. Why didn't he get a call back from at least one of the fifteen inquiries he'd made? He walked forty feet to the edge of the empty pool and retraced his steps, looked up at the dark clouds, and admitted that he didn't want to lose Justine any more than he could bear the loss of Tonya. Maybe if he got into his car and combed the streets . . . He couldn't remember when he'd last prayed, but he found the words as he grappled with the pain that seared his heart.

"Mr. B., Mr. B."

He didn't wait to hear more, but jumped onto the deck, dashed into the house, and sprinted down the long hallway to the front door where Mattie stood tugging at the door knob. He slipped the lock and yanked open the door. His gaze landed upon the six-foot, five inches tall policeman who stood there, and his heart stopped.

"Duncan Banks?"

He'd never know how he managed it, but he heard himself say, "I'm Duncan Banks."

Simultaneously, he heard the words, "Daaaady. Daaaady," and shoved aside the massive form in front of him.

"Justine. Oh, sweetheart. Tonya."

She was there with his child, and he had her in his arms, feeling her warm life-filled body. He hugged and hugged them both until his arms ached.

"Uh . . . I take it these are your folks and it's all right for me to leave," the officer said.

Still holding them close, Duncan tried to remember why the man stood there.

"I escorted Ms. Taylor and your baby girl home," the officer explained.

"Oh, yes. Thank you, Officer. Forgive me, but I've been out of my mind for the last three hours, and—"

"No problem, Sir. I can imagine what you must have been going through."

"I doubt that, Officer. I can't thank you enough."

The policeman tipped his hat, turned and left. Duncan caught himself as he was about to lift Justine and carry them both into the house. He let out a tension releasing guffaw just as a torrent of windswept rain pushed him into the house. He slammed the door, looked down at the two people in his arms, hugged them close to his chest, and nearly wept at the feel of Tonya's little fingers on his face.

"I know it was awful for you not knowing where we were, Duncan, but I had no way of getting in touch with you. I'm sorry."

He wanted to erase the plea from her tired eyes. Didn't she know that he hadn't cared about anything but their safety? "We won't talk about it now. It's enough that you're both here and that you're all right. Are you hungry?"

Her attempt at a smile pulled at his heart. "I'm starved. The police gave Tonya some chocolate milk, but that's all they had. I expect she's hungry anyway."

"Maybe Mr. B don't need to know, but since I aged another fifty-two years, where y'all been? Your dinner's cold, and I practically used up a years' worth of prayers. I tell you, Justine, I just about died worryin' 'bout you and Tonya."

Duncan took the baby when Justine shifted the child to her left side. She thanked him with her eyes, and he could see her fatigue. "I'm sorry, Mattie. The drugstore clerk called, but there was no answer, and I didn't have Duncan's cell number. I couldn't call later, because I didn't have one penny, and the police didn't believe my story. You don't have to fix anything for me; I can do it."

"You got touched in the head since you left here, I see. You go get yourself together and look after Tonya; I'll have you something ready in twenty minutes. It shore is good to see ya." She looked toward the ceiling. "Yessir, it shore is."

Duncan carried Tonya in the curve of his left arm and, with his right arm around Justine's waist, walked up the stairs with them. "I'll give her a bath and feed her." He laid Tonya on her bed. "Justine, I want you to rest a little before we eat."

He knew he stared at her as though he'd never seen her before, but his heart said he must always have known her, for she'd so easily become important to him. "Go on. I'll look after her. You've got to be exhausted."

She moved away, then leaned to him, kissed his cheek, and rushed out of the room. His left hand drifted to the spot where her lips had been, and a wild fire of desire blazed through him. He started after her and stopped himself as his glance captured Tonya's restless turning and twisting on her bed.

He bent over and kissed his child. "But for you, Sweetie, I'd probably have done something I'd regret for a long time."

As soon as he'd bathed and dressed Tonya, she returned to her cheerful, smiling self. He answered the door expecting to see Justine, but Mattie handed him a bowl of Cream of Wheat and a bottle of milk.

"Thanks, Mattie. You're a peach."

She gave him a good look at her two upper front teeth. "That's what my Moe tells me all the time, Mr. B. Don't you men know no other ways to praise a woman?"

He concentrated on feeding Tonya and forced himself not to laugh. "I don't know about Moe, but I've got a bag full of 'em. Sure you want to hear a few?" He stuck his tongue in the lower part of his right cheek.

Mattie beamed at him. "You hush your mouth, Mr. B. I tell you, you shore is something."

He grinned as the door closed. She must have been a man's woman through and through when she was about twenty-five. More than twice that age, she still enjoyed her femininity. "Way to go, Moe," he said, sat Tonya on his knee, and rocked her to sleep while he sang "I Still Suits Me," one of the Paul Robeson songs that she loved.

Justine stepped out of the shower, dried off, and looked at herself in the mirror. Good Lord! The steam had kinked her hair and made it unmanageable just when she wanted to look decent. She could be signing her death warrant, but she'd never known the feeling she got when Duncan rushed to them and took her in his arms. It wasn't for Tonya alone. His hands had given her a lover's caress, and when he'd squeezed her to him, he hadn't communicated gratitude for their safety, but deep caring. She couldn't give what he would some day ask, but she needed to be needed, and she longed for the tenderness that he'd showed her he could give. Dear Lord, if only for a little while, for a few minutes, she could know his strength and passion without suffering consequences that could doom her forever.

She twisted her hair into a knot at her nape, slipped into her favorite ecru lace underwear and wondered what to put on top of it. She opened the closet door without turning on the light and, as she faced the darkness, the burning remains of the Sutton Motel in Falls Church, Virginia, flashed through her mind. She could almost smell the incinerating rubbish and hear the crackle of the roaring flames. She squeezed her fists tight and fought to shake off the gnawing sounds and sights of the past. She wanted to live in the present, grab whatever happiness came her way, and hold on to it.

"Don't fool yourself, girl. There's no happiness here for you." Her hand rested on an orange and black patterned caftan that had known years of wear. It made no difference what she wore, she knew, because she had cast the die against herself when she answered Duncan's ad. She slipped the caftan over her head, stuck her feet into a pair of low heeled black slippers and left the room.

Duncan rose when she entered the dining room. "It's pretty late, so I called a cab for Mattie and sent her home. She's got a pot roast, turnip greens, and candied yams." He took their plates, went into the kitchen, and filled them. "I'd like some good wine. How about this Chateau Neuf du Pap?"

She preferred white wine, but in the sweet aura that he wrapped around them, she would accept whatever he offered, and she'd do it because he obviously wanted to please her.

"Your dress is beautiful. Why haven't you worn something like this before? I like it. You . . . You're . . . well, lovely."

Maybe the evening's drama had left him in shock. Her hair was a mess, she didn't have on a speck of make-up, wore no jewelry, and looked maybe the worst he'd ever seen her. And he thought she looked lovely? She told herself not to believe it. Maybe it was because the caftan camouflaged her size.

"Thanks." It sounded lame, but she couldn't manage more.

"Don't you believe me?" He poured their wine and stopped. "We're going to start saying grace at the table. Mattie says I'll raise Tonya to be an infidel."

She bowed her head while he said grace. How had her child been so fortunate as to be given this man for a father? She raised her head and treated him to a luminous smile, lest a flood of tears break through her controlled facade.

He raised his wine in a silent toast to her. "You don't know how relieved I am that you're both here and all right. It's been decades since anything got to me like that did."

She'd known that not knowing their whereabouts at that time of night would upset him, but she hadn't imagined his reaction once he knew they were safe—not one cross word nor a reprimand.

"I knew you had to be miserable, Duncan, and I wouldn't have put you through that for anything if I could have avoided it."

"I know that, Justine."

"Aren't you going to ask me what happened?"

He sipped his wine, his fiery eyes bewitching her over the top of the glass. "You've had a bad time, too. I figure you'll tell me as soon as you can."

She blinked her eyes, hoping to break the spell. "After we left the doctor's office, I stopped at a drugstore to pick up a newspaper, went to pay for it, and realized I'd left my pocketbook on the floor in the front seat of the car. I had Tonya with me, because I never leave her anywhere, least of all in a car. I ran to the car and saw my pocketbook there, but the doors were locked and I couldn't get in. I didn't have a cent in my pocket, and the drugstore clerk didn't believe my story. He did make one call here, but there was no answer. I guess Mattie was in one of her moods and ignored the phones. Anyway, when I asked him to call the police for me, he refused. He asked for identification, but all I had was in the car.

"When a tow-truck came to tow my car out of the no-parking zone, I told the driver my plight, and he called the police on his cell phone. The policeman came and opened the car, handed me my pocketbook and asked to see my driver's license and car registration. Unfortunately for me, both were in the house here in my credit card case. He put Tonya and me in the squad car and took us to the station. By now, it's five o'clock, and I'm getting nervous. I asked them to call here, but nobody answered, because Mattie hates phones. The car went to the pound, I didn't have a cent, and your office phone went unanswered.

"Tonya began to cry, because she was wet and hungry, but she'd already made friends with the men, and one of the officers got a box of chocolate milk from the refrigerator, found a straw, and held her while she drank it. She went to sleep happy as a robin in a freshly dug spring garden. They wanted a social worker to interview me but, thank God, their regular one was out sick. The shift changed before they figured out what to do with us, and when the new chief arrived, I blurted out that they were holding Duncan Banks's child and that they could expect to see their names in the morning paper.

"Why hadn't I told the other officers? he wanted to know. I figured that wasn't the time for me to articulate my disgust. The one who brought us to the door said he'd drive us to your house and check my story. If I was lying, I could expect a nice long vacation in the clinker."

Duncan narrowed his eyes and tightened his jaw, his face clouded with anger. "What is that captain's name, the one who kept you there until the shift changed?"

His thunderous expression would have unsettled her had she been the object of his rage. She told him the man's name, reached over, and laid her hand on his. "We're all right now. If you want to scold him, please do, but don't make trouble for him on my behalf. At least they gave Tonya some milk."

"If those jackasses ever do something like this again, call James Randolph, my lawyer. If I could get my hands on—"

Shivers raced through her. If she got high-profile publicity, he'd soon know the story of her life. Just mention the names of either her husband or her father and the tabloids and supermarket trash sheets would descend like the vultures that they were.

She hastened to diffuse his anger. "Duncan, we came out of it all right, and don't forget I was wrong on two counts—driving without a license and without car registration—and I wasn't charged."

"That's because they were so busy being stupid that they forgot it. I'll get your car tomorrow morning." He stood and pushed back his chair. "They treat good citizens the same as they do criminals. No difference." He stopped his fist just before it hit the wall. "If I could get my hands on one of them, I'd—"

"Honey, let it ride. Call him up if you want to, but then drop it, please."

His body stiffened, and his reddish-brown eyes became orbs of sizzling heat. And like a big tiger stalking its prey, he moved toward her. "What did you call me?"

If she'd been standing, she'd have fled to her room, but he was there lifting her out of the chair as though she weighed sixty-five pounds instead of a hundred and sixty-five, holding her shoulders and staring into her eyes with his heat swirling around her and the man in him bellowing for release.

She'd never stuttered, but every syllable stuck in her throat. "I . . . I . . . s . . . said—"

"I didn't ask you what you said. What did you *call* me?"

If only she could know the man in him for one minute. Of their own volition, the words flew off the wings of her breath. *"Honey.* Oh Duncan. Duncan, Dun—"

His hot breath sent sensations hurtling through her, and his right hand pressed her buttocks and pinned her cradle of love to his hard frame. Then the earth stopped when he held her head with his left hand and took her mouth. Her blood raced wildly from her fingers to the tips of her toes, as his lips moved over hers. Seeking. Branding her. She sucked his bottom lip into her mouth, and his hot moist tongue rimmed her lips. The little sense that she had right then told her that she should push him away, but she needed the steel-like arms that held her as she'd longed to be held. Somewhere in the archives of her mind, she knew she had to resist him. She had to. But she was powerless to do so while tremors raced through her and his heat coiled around her making perspiration plaster tendrils of hair to her forehead. She braced with one hand, but the other caressed his head.

"It's too late, Justine. It's always been too late. Open your mouth for me, Justine. Sweetheart, I need to love you."

His fingers found her nipples, teased them while they flowered beneath his talented touch, and her woman's heat furled up to them until, besotted with him, she pulled his tongue into her mouth and nearly died of pleasure as he anointed every centimeter of it. More. She had to have more of him. Her tongue battled with his until he gave her what she wanted and let her feast on it. When her aroused body demanded everything that he could give her, he tightened his grip on her buttocks and let her feel his powerful erection. She moved into him, greedy for more, anxious for what had always been denied her.

His hoarse voice reached her as though from another planet. "Wait a minute here, Justine. Are you ready for this? Do you know what you're doing, baby?" He jerked away from her when her hand went to his belt buckle. "I want to make love with you, honey. I want it more than anything on the face of this earth. Are you sure?"

She reeled away from him as though in a drunken stupor. *"What?"*

"I said do you know what you're about to do?"

It could have been the tremors in his voice, or what looked like love in his eyes, or was it desire?—having been subjected to Kenneth's masterful charade, she wasn't sure she knew the difference—she didn't know. But she'd never been so certain that a man cared more for her well being than for his own. She stepped away from him.

"If you hadn't stopped us, I know I wouldn't have. Maybe it's everything that happened today; maybe it's you and what you are. I don't know the answer, Duncan. But I'm certain I've never before known what I felt just then, so don't think unkindly of me for letting it get out of hand."

He pulled her to him, and his hand stroked her back, soothing her. "It didn't get out of hand, Justine. We needed each other, and we had postponed that so long that I'm surprised I could back away from it. We'll have to talk about this, but not right now. You go on upstairs. I'll straighten up here."

"Why should you take responsibility for . . . for my behavior, I—"

His stiffened body sent her a message that his words confirmed. "You'd better get out of here, Justine. I don't want you one bit less now than I did five minutes ago. Leave while it's possible. Good night."

She knew he meant it, and she knew the price if she stayed. "Good night."

Justine closed her bedroom door and slumped against

it. Thank God, he'd called a halt to it. He didn't know the half of it. She'd never come close to losing herself with Kenneth, and she'd never known any other man. She rubbed her arms, stumbled to her bed, and fell across it. He'd lifted her as though she were a feather. Lifted her and held her to his body. Kenneth hadn't even taken her across the threshold of their apartment door on their wedding day. He'd jokingly said that life was full of choices; if he got a hernia lifting her, he wouldn't be able to make love, and he was sure she'd choose the latter. She gave in to the giddiness that swept over her, threw her arms open wide and let laughter pour out of her, as she gloried in her femininity.

Duncan finished straightening up the kitchen and dining room and looked around for something else to do. Nothing. Before he'd managed to settle down from his anxiety over Justine and Tonya's whereabouts, she'd revved his engine with a taste of the woman she was. He shook his head. Women were not strangers to him; he'd known enough of them well enough not to be surprised, but Justine Taylor had come around his blind side and pole-axed him. This perfect, well-mannered lady turned out to be the most sexually aggressive woman he'd ever touched. He rubbed the back of his neck, turned out the lights, and started up the stairs. And she was not only the sweetest woman he'd kissed, but the most honest about her feelings. *And sleeping across the hall from him in an unlocked room!* He laughed and started up the stairs. "Man, you've got your work cut out for you. Don't even glance that way," he told himself. He noticed the light that shone beneath her door. "Oh, no, you don't," he mumbled, retraced his steps, and headed for the basement. Two hours later, still pitching darts, he hadn't once hit the bull's eye.

The next morning, Justine opened the door of her closet and her gaze fell on the black and orange caftan, her idea of an old thing and Duncan's notion of a lovely dress. She resisted putting it on, but unable to forego an opportunity to make him notice her, she settled for a red-printed, Portuguese-style broomstick skirt and a white peasant blouse. She wasn't crazy about the effect, but it was at least feminine and, right then, pants didn't suit her mood. She bathed and dressed Tonya, whose morning greetings had already become the most cherished moments of the day.

"Well, now, I don't care what Mr. B says, that outfit is proof you don't need these pancakes," Mattie declared when Justine entered the dining room with Tonya in her arms.

"I thought we'd had the last of that song, Mattie. I am not interested in being like those tubercular models on the covers of fashion magazines, and since I'm satisfied with myself, don't let it bother you."

If Mattie was defeated, she didn't show it. "Magazines? I don't pay no attention to the women in those magazines. My sister—you know, the one who works for that rich lady in the Watergate Apartments—gave me one called *American Woman.* It didn't have one black face in it 'til you got to the last page and looked at Dionne Warwick advertising her psychic friends. And that in the year of our Lord about two-thousand. I bet if you pick up *Emerge* or *Today's Black Woman,* the women won't all look like they dying of consumption."

Justine shifted Tonya to her left hip and held up her right hand palm out. "Duncan said he didn't want to hear that again in this house."

"And he ain't hearing it, either."

"Who said so?" He bounded into the room, stopped within inches of her, and heat burned her face as he scrutinized it. "Hi, baby." Justine's eyes rounded, and she thought she'd swallow her breath.

"How's my favorite daughter?" he asked Tonya, though his eyes devoured Justine. "Aren't you saying 'good morning,' Justine?"

She spoke slowly, making certain of a steady voice. "Since you walked in and found me here, you should speak to me first."

His smile sent her pulse racing. "And you think I didn't?" he asked and took Tonya from her.

She decided to ignore his brazen comment. "Mattie, I want four pancakes oozing with syrup and real butter, please. None of that imitation stuff you keep back there."

Mattie put her left hand on her hip and waved a spoon with her other hand. "Oh, I forgot to tell you, Justine, I got a sister who sews. She don't even need no pattern. Just bring her eight or ten yards of cloth, and she'll make you a dress in no time. 'Course, for me, she only needs a yard-and-a-half."

Justine stared at Duncan, who gaped at Mattie. "I thought I told you, Mattie—"

Mattie put on an air of contrition. "My sister's a poor woman, Mr. B; she needs all the work she can get."

Justine thought it wise of Mattie to make a swift exit toward the kitchen. Ordinarily, the twinkling of his eyes and that shadow of a dimple in his right cheek mesmerized her when he lost himself in laughter, but what she felt right then was a desire to punch him.

"Walk Daddy to the door," he said to Tonya, who bounced up and down on his thigh. "Daddy's in a hurry this morning, but I promise to take you for a stroll this afternoon." Justine watched Tonya bubble with smiles as though she understood and anticipated the pleasure of their time together. She could hardly bear the mixture of pain and joy that swirled within her as Tonya looped her arms around her father's neck and left the print of oatmeal on his cheek after a long kiss. It amazed her that he neither complained nor wiped his face.

"Come on," he repeated. "Walk me to the door. It's time you used your two little feet."

"I'll take her," Justine offered.

"I guess you will," Mattie said, draining her coffee cup. "Otherwise, she'll have to crawl back here after she walks him to the door. I declare, men is so fanciful. Just 'cause Tonya's last name is Banks don't mean she super baby."

Tiny needles pricked at her insides, but she marveled that, only weeks earlier, pain would have seared her heart if anyone had mentioned Tonya's last name in that way.

Had she begun to accept the impossible, or were her feelings for Duncan going to betray her?

Duncan kissed Tonya, accepted her wet response, winked at Justine, and stepped out into the crisp, early November air. He paused on the steps for a second and counted his blessings. At last, he could go to work knowing that his child was safe, and that she would not lack for love, affection, and the best of care.

Dave Jenkin's taxi drove past as he started toward the garage and, on an impulse, he whistled for it, deciding to take the train to Baltimore rather than drive. The forty-six minutes head-time should be more than enough in which to make it to the station, especially with Dave driving. That and the thirty-minute train ride would give him an hour-an-a-half in which to edit his report. He finished it as the Morning Congressional rolled into Baltimore's Pennsylvania Station, hopped a cab, and was soon at the Roundtree building on Charles Street.

"Here's the story on chemical waste dumping," he told Wayne. "Got anything for me?"

Wayne scanned the story for a few minutes. "Man, this'll light up City Hall. Good going, Duncan."

"Thanks, but it couldn't have been more boring. I like to write about people."

"Glad to hear it. I'm thinking of a contrast in the life-styles of African American youth. I don't care what age group. How about it?"

Duncan didn't try to hold back the grin that spread over his face. "Bread and butter. I'll get right on it."

"By the way, how's your sister?" Wayne asked him.

"My sis . . . Leah? I don't know. You live in the same town as her. Why?"

"Whenever I call, I get a busy signal."

"What time do you call?"

"Between the hours of five and eleven. Continuously." The last word had the sound of a vile oath.

Duncan threw back his head and let himself enjoy a belly laugh. "Women! Call her at work. She's punishing you for giving her a cold shoulder." He gave Wayne his sister's office phone number.

"Wicked devil. And all that talk about wanting to meet me."

"She probably regrets having told you that. You guys get your act together."

Wayne lifted his left eyebrow. "Yeah. Wait'll I get my hands on that woman. Just wait."

Duncan made a ceremony of clearing his throat. "Don't forget who you're talking to, man."

"Not to worry, buddy, I'm a nineties man; she's more precious than a good rain after a long hot drought."

Duncan stared at him. "Are you being poetic?"

Wayne set his gaze on his desk. "Naah, man. She gets to me. See ya."

Duncan didn't succeed in avoiding Dee Dee, who kept her office door open to feed her curiosity. "How's it going, Duncan? You get engaged, yet?"

He flashed her the best grin he could muster and paused for as long as it took to say, "I'm a lost cause, Dee. See ya later." Dee Dee was his thrice-married colleague in whom he had no interest. She was a good gal, and he didn't want to hurt her, but he'd give a lot if he could figure out a way to tell her he wasn't attracted to her Creole beauty and that he wished she'd stop hitting on him.

When he stepped out into the dreary November afternoon, the excitement of beginning a new investigation sent his blood racing. He pulled his black knit cap out of his pocket and put it on, tightened the red and purple woolen scarf that Mattie had given him for Christmas—knitted by her sister's own hands, she'd said—and headed for CafeAhNay. He couldn't afford to look like a prosperous journalist if he wanted the CafeAhNay regulars and employees to consider him one of them. So whenever he went there on cold days, he wore his black cap, black leather jacket, long woolen scarf, jeans, and sneakers. And once there, he took his usual seat in a corner near the door and started whittling.

From the corner of his eye, he watched Lottie sashay from the bar to his table. "Hi ya doin' today? You havin' anything or just whittlin'?"

"Hi. I'll take a root beer and some fries."

"French or chitterlins?"

He grimaced. "Lottie, I don't eat the inside of anything."

"Okay. I always ask."

"Anything going on?"

When she looked from side to side before answering, he knew she had something. "Chuckie got a free ride last night."

He kept his gaze on his whittling. "What for?"

She lowered her voice. "Got caught in a sting selling stuff to kids over on Dolphin Street 'round Templeton. He had it coming. People been complaining about that mess for years. I hope this is the end of it."

He noticed two strangers staring their way, smiled, and raised his voice, "Sorry to hear it, babe. If I can do anything to help out, just punch my bell."

To her credit, she kept a blank expression on her face and didn't look around, only nodded. He drank the root beer, ate a few of the French fries, paid his bill, and left to find his contacts at Wilma's Blue Moon on Dolphin Street. The taxi shot along Dolphin well above the speed limit and, more than once, he had to ask the driver to slow down, lest he hit one of the children playing in the streets. He hated that section of the city. Every third house was boarded up, and broken windows told sad stories of some that were occupied. He stared at the endless pieces of broken furniture that littered the streets and wondered how the city could justify not collecting the garbage for people who paid taxes. When the taxi stopped to let him out, he released a breath of relief, but quickly covered his nose and mouth to defend his nostrils against the assaulting fumes of week-old refuse. He walked a block and a half to Wilma's, because he didn't know that taxi driver and didn't trust his health to fortune. For all he knew, the man was on the take from one of his enemies. As usual, he left Wilma with hot names, addresses and some crucial details. He flicked off his recorder and looked at his watch. Just time enough to make the Metroliner to Washington.

* * *

He walked into his bedroom and found Justine's note on his pillow. "I noticed that you do a lot of sculpting." He wondered how and where she'd noticed it and kept reading. "Would you please make some learning tools for Tonya. I'm not satisfied with what I can find for children her age. Thanks, Justine."

He read it again, looked at some sketches she'd provided, propped his hip against the wall, and urged his subconscious into action. That note was telling him something that wasn't written there, an important message, and he couldn't get a handle on it. His mind told him she couldn't be as simple a person as she'd represented herself to be. He couldn't believe that she was a part of a research experiment aimed at seeing what you could do with children if you started training them early; she loved Tonya too much to use her. Yet, fragments of information and inconsistencies, including that sophisticated note from a nanny, fueled his misgivings. He'd seen nothing about her that he couldn't admire, but he hoped his feelings hadn't begun to befuddle his brain.

His adrenaline kicked up when he knocked on her bedroom door, anxious for the sight of her. The surprise mirrored on her face was worth a laugh. Other than Mattie or himself, who else would be knocking on her bedroom door?

"Hi. Mind explaining this? he asked in reference to her note.

His misgivings must have shown on his face, because she reacted as one taking up arms, before telling him that she would use the sculpted figures to help Tonya learn counting and reading. He looked first at the note, then at Justine, whirled around, and went to Tonya's room.

Shock reverberated through him when Tonya saw him, laughed, and bounced up and down. "Tree, Daddy, tree," she said, holding up three fingers. "Tree."

He walked over to her, picked her up, hugged her, and carried her back to Justine's room. "You're right again.

But I don't want an exceptional child, Justine. I want her to be happy."

She took Tonya from him, and he couldn't imagine why she avoided his gaze. "You're exceptional. Has that caused you any problems?"

She had a quiet way of telling him off, and he'd do something about that if she wasn't usually right. "I hope we're not going to disagree about how Tonya should be raised, Justine. I have to depend on you for most of that, since I'm not with her as much as you are. So far, there hasn't been a problem, but I've always heard that parents are most likely to fight about money and how to raise their children. Let's not . . ."

Now, what the devil had he said to make her face lose its color? "Look, I'm not criticizing you, Justine. You're doing a wonderful job, far better than I could do or that I even dreamed you would do. Let's . . . let's leave things as they are."

But she wasn't pacified. Her face actually sagged as though its skin had lost elasticity, and her eyes blinked rapidly. "Justine, for heaven's sake."

She turned her back to him, and he walked around to face her, hoping he wouldn't see tears in her eyes. Water gushed from them, though she didn't utter a sound.

"My God! What did I say? What have I done to you? Justine!"

He tried to take Tonya from her, but she held onto the child, and he enclosed them both in his arms, close to his chest. He could feel her tremors and her struggle not to sob, and when she relaxed, he took the child from her, put her in her crib and hurried back to Justine, before she could close her door. His arms enfolded her and held her to him in a lover's caress, and he wiped her tears with his handkerchief.

"For whatever I said or did, I'm sorry," he whispered. "I'd as soon hurt myself as you."

"I don't . . . don't think we should be here like this, Duncan."

Her several quick, short breaths confirmed for him her struggle not to succumb to her tears. He tightened his hold on her and raised her chin. "You may be right, but I need to hold you. Can't you put your arms around me?"

"Duncan, we'll be sorry for this. I know it. I don't want you to mean so mu—"

He turned her to face him, and maybe he'd have heeded her words if her eyes hadn't held a desperate appeal when she looked up at him. Something in the vicinity of his heart grabbed at him and squeezed until he had to have her healing softness, that tenderness, sweetness that she showered on his daughter. That woman's loving that he'd never known.

"Can't you . . . hold me?"

He could see her fight it, and he could see her losing her battle as her arms crept toward his shoulders. Impatient for her caress, he brought her closer until he could feel the tips of her breasts through his shirt, shocking him as that evidence of her desire fueled his heat.

"Justine!

"Duncan, I . . . Oh, Lord!"

Her lips moved beneath his, eager, warm, and giving, and the pressure of her hand at the back of his head begged for more. Her fingers moved at his nape, and she opened her mouth for a test of his manliness. He couldn't deny her. He didn't want to and, with all the restraint he could muster, let her have what she wanted. Fire raged in him. Didn't she know anything about moderation? He jerked away from her, but too late to ward off a full arousal. He stepped away and sat on the edge of her chaise lounge.

"You can tell me we shouldn't be here like this and, a minute later, kiss me as though you could eat me alive? What am I supposed to believe?"

It didn't surprise him that she glared, but when she balled up her fists, he figured she'd show him something of herself that he hadn't seen. Her calm demeanor fooled him. "And what were you busy doing, Mister? All that proved was that I'm human."

"Human?" She'd probably get madder, but he couldn't help laughing. "Human, huh? You mean to tell me you think that's normal?" She continued to glare at him, so he got up and walked over to her. "Man proposes and

God disposes, Justine, so unless you and I have had a change of plans, we'd better give each other plenty of space."

"I didn't start that."

He took her right hand, turned it over, and looked at it. Soft, beautiful fingers. "I didn't start it either, Justine. And that's our problem. We're not engineering this thing. See you later."

She closed the door behind him, slumped against it, and let it take her weight. One day, she'd have to face the consequences of her hasty decision to move into Duncan Banks's home as a nanny to her own child. She ought to get out without damaging herself further, but she'd rather die than leave Tonya. And Duncan. He sent her will to the winds with his gentleness and the way he made her feel when he had her in his arms kissing her. How did he expect her to stop when, in all of her adult life, she had longed to feel with a man what she felt every time he touched her?

Icy tremors shook her body and she cringed remembering his innocent comment about parents fighting over the best way to raise their children. *Parents!* She had hurt all the way to the bowels of her being. If he had impaled her with a knife and turned it, she doubted the pain would have been as great. For that was precisely the situation: a mother and a father disagreeing about raising their child. She heard the front door close, looked out, and saw Duncan jogging down Primrose Street. She imagined that he was as unsettled as she. For however long Tonya needed a nanny—Lord, she didn't want to think that far ahead—she wanted that responsibility. After that, well . . . she did know that if she didn't eliminate the currents that zigzagged between Duncan and herself, or at least diffuse them, she'd have to leave, and soon. Nothing of merit could develop between them, because you couldn't build anything worthwhile on deception. Nothing.

The telephone ring interrupted her musings. "Hello."

She listened to the eager female voice and shivered as the reality of its message brought forcibly to her the hopelessness of her situation. "I'm sorry to disappoint you,

Madam, but the position was filled some time ago," she said.

Another woman wanting to marry Duncan Banks and take care of Justine Taylor Montgomery's daughter. She'd lost count of them. A white lie was as unforgivable as any other, but what choice did she have?

Desperate for a resolution, she called her godfather and explained the bind into which she'd gotten herself. "I don't know what to do Uncle Hugh. If I tell him the truth, he'll fire me, and I won't be able to see Tonya."

She could imagine that he chomped on his cigar while he thought about it. "That's just half of your problem, Justine, because it looks to me like you two ought to be together. From what you said, though, he's a man who won't hold still for double-dealing. Don't encourage any involvement, and cut him off if he heads that way. If you don't, you'll end up doing a lot of crying. What does your father say?"

"He still won't take my calls."

"Yeah. I'll bet. He's got self-righteousness down to an art. I expect he'll need you before you need him."

She periodically forgot that Hugh had never liked her father and had thought that her mother married beneath her. "I don't seem able to handle it that way, Uncle Hugh."

"Yeah, I know. You're just like your mother. Sweet and loving. You couldn't walk on her though, no more that anybody can do that to you. Be careful, child. I think you're dealing with your life. A man like that one won't forgive easily."

He hadn't told her anything she didn't know, but at least she had been able to talk about it with someone. Unable to work, she examined one of her emergency columns. Of the three letters, one was from a woman who longed for marriage, but whose youth was behind her. Another writer wanted to know if she should confess her infidelity to her husband, and the third wanted help with her troublesome teenage daughter. She considered it one of her better columns.

Thinking it a good time to stroll in the back garden while Tonya slept, she started out of her room and met

Duncan on the stairs. One look told her that his run had done little to cool his passion. She smiled and swept past him. The tension between them had to be diffused and, if Warren Stokes called her again, she wouldn't turn him away so readily. She stepped out onto the deck, looked up at the darkening sky, and remembered the night she'd brought Tonya home late to her desperately anxious father, the night she'd first felt his arms strong and sweet around her. She went back to her room and telephoned Warren.

CHAPTER SIX

Duncan rushed out of his office to answer the door bell and nearly knocked Justine off her feet. "Going out?" he asked, as he helped her recover her equilibrium. "Seems like we've collided in this spot once before. I don't mind bumping into you, but you always get the worst of it."

Why did she seem put out? "I know I'm heavy, but you've got a few pounds on me and a lot of muscle."

He didn't move when she attempted to pass him. "Want to get by? Just ask nicely. No red-blooded man could say no to such a lovely woman."

She still didn't smile. "You're too generous. See you later."

He didn't know why the devil got into him when it occurred to him that she might have a date. Feeling irritated, he plastered a grin on his face and touched her elbow. "I'll see you out."

"Thanks, but that won't be necessary."

He went with his grin again. "I know, but I was raised to be a gentleman."

Giving her no way out of it, he walked down the stairs with her, certain now that the caller was a man. To his amazement, he yanked the door open, and something akin to furor furled within him when he saw the man standing there. A stud, if he'd ever seen one. He told himself to cool off; it wasn't his business.

"Looking for somebody?" It was not a gracious greeting, but then, he didn't feel gracious.

"Is Miss Taylor here?"

In his heightened ire, he'd almost forgotten that Justine stood behind him. He moved aside, but he didn't look at her, because he'd rather not see the fire he knew would be aimed at him. "Yes. She's right here. Come in."

He couldn't help cringing when Justine brushed around him and held out her hand to the man. "Hello, Warren. I'm glad to see you. I'll be ready as soon as I get my coat. Warren, this is Duncan."

He took Warren's extended hand for the most limp handshake he'd ever participated in. "Hi. Come on in. Like a drink while she's getting ready?"

He grinned when Warren looked him up and down; he knew when a man sized him up as competition, and he also knew when he made the fellow uncomfortable. Feeling like getting some of his own, he took Warren's elbow and ushered him into the living room. "I've got a thirty-year-old Chivas Regal here somewhere, or would you like something else?"

Just as he'd expected, Warren seated himself and got comfortable. "Chivas would be fine. Don't I know you from somewhere?"

"Probably. Ice? Soda? How do you like it?"

From the corner of his eye, he saw Warren sit forward and look around the room, obviously appraising the quality of what he saw. "Why do you say probably? Do you know me?"

Duncan told himself to let up. He had assured Justine that she could entertain her friends as if she were in her own home, and he had no right to embarrass her. But he couldn't help it if the thought of her going out with that guy irritated him. He got his drink—club soda with a slice of lemon—and sat opposite the man. "I don't believe we've met," he said and raised his glass in a silent toast.

"You're familiar."

Duncan sipped his club soda and told himself he shouldn't be concerned about Warren, because no woman of Justine's intelligence could tolerate him for long. "One of those faces, I guess. You live around here?" He wished Justine would hurry.

Warren shook his head. "Bethesda."

Duncan hated making small talk, and especially with a man who wasn't any better at it than he was. He would offer the man another drink, but he didn't know the guy's capacity and he didn't want Justine out with a drunk. He stood when she walked in.

"You look beautiful, as always," he told her and took the coat that she attempted to hand to Warren. He wasn't going to laugh because it wasn't funny, but he enjoyed getting the better of Warren, though he knew there'd be hell to pay when she got back home. He noticed that she didn't thank him for the compliment.

"Nice meeting you," Warren said and extended his hand for another limp handshake.

"Have a good evening," Duncan replied. He was not going to lie and say he was glad he'd met Warren whatever-his-last-name-was, because it churned his gut to see Justine walk out of there with him.

"Nice fellow, Duncan," Warren said, opening the front passenger door of his powder-blue Cadillac.

Justine got in, adjusted the butter-soft leather seat, and fastened her seat belt. "You think so?"

She hoped that didn't sound like a sneer, but what she thought of Duncan right then was anything but complimentary. Just wait until she got back there.

Warren turned on the ignition and let the motor idle. "Seems first class, and he's got a nice place there. How can he afford you?"

"I've never asked him about his financial affairs. Why are we standing here?"

He patted the dashboard as though it were a lover, turned to her, and let her see the pride that glowed on his face. "I take good care of this baby. You blew my mind when you called; it was the last thing I expected you to do, and I'm curious. What changed your mind?"

Honesty is the best policy when you can manage it, she told herself. "You want to start up something with us, and I'm curious as to why you think it's possible or even a good idea. We weren't sweethearts in school."

He moved the Cadillac away from the curb, looked to his left and in his rearview mirror before heading down Primrose, and she remembered how cautious he'd seemed when they knew each other in college.

"I thought we were sweethearts, and I guess that was my problem. We went every place together, and as far as I was concerned, you were my girl."

"Come on, Warren, you never kissed me, and you certainly didn't ask me to go steady."

"I didn't think I had to. No, I was afraid you'd say no, and it made me mad as the devil if I saw you with anybody else."

"Tell me about it! Your temper broke up our friendship. I hope you've tamed it."

"After you walked off and left me on the dance floor, I was the butt of every joke in the men's dorm, though you can bet nobody said anything to my face."

He'd been a brother then, and after nearly a decade, she couldn't even muster a sisterly feeling for him. Still, maybe if she got to know him, her feelings would change. "Sorry about that, but you got hostile, and I never could tolerate frostiness from a man. Makes me uneasy."

"Can we start from here, then? I never got you out of my system, Justine, and Lord knows I've tried."

She couldn't encourage him too much knowing how she felt about Duncan, but maybe being with him occasionally might help her put her relationship with Duncan in perspective. "You deserve more than I have to give, Warren. My feelings haven't changed, and I don't know that they will. Friendship is all I have."

He paid the gas attendant and rolled up the window. "Déjà vu all over again, just like old Yogi said. Duncan is a lucky man."

"What do you mean?"

"You think I didn't notice how possessive that guy is about you? He'd probably have taken me on if I wasn't as big as he is."

For the first time that evening she could laugh. "Warren, if Duncan had wanted to take you on, as you put it, he wouldn't have cared how big you were."

He parked in front of Ludella's Restaurant on Georgia Avenue.

"The best soul food in the District," he boasted. "The Willard's fine when I want pressed duck breast."

She suffered through his tales of Rufus Meade's football genius and made herself attentive while he dropped other famous names. She noticed that he let his gaze sweep the room every minute or so. For a man claiming to want a woman, he had a peculiar way of showing it.

She declined his suggestion that they visit one of the Georgetown nightclubs with the excuse that, "It's almost midnight, and I'm not one for staying up late. It's been lovely."

She noticed that he could barely contain his displeasure.

They spoke very little on the drive back, each silently acknowledging that the evening had been more of a trial than a pleasure. Needles attacked her feet as they started up the walk to Duncan's front door. Maybe he'd left a light on in the living room. Surely he wouldn't sit there and wait for them. But to her chagrin, that was what he had done. Even as Warren reached for the doorbell, the door swung open, and a wide grin on Duncan's face greeted them.

"You two have a good time?" he asked, though he looked at Warren. "Thanks for bringing her back safely, man. This town can be rough at night."

Realizing that he didn't plan to give them a second of privacy, anger exploded in her head and, throwing caution aside, she reached for a startled Warren and planted a kiss on his mouth. "Good night, Warren. I had a wonderful time."

She disregarded his quizzical expression and brushed past Duncan. The front door closed and she quickened her steps.

"You had a good time, sure enough? " he asked.

She whirled around and marched back to him. "If I were you, Duncan Banks, I wouldn't say one word to me right now. Not one word."

He stuck his hands in his pants pockets and shrugged. "Why? What's the matter? What did I do?"

She took a few steps closer to him. "For one, you can wipe that look of innocence off your face. I'm twenty-nine years old, and what I do on my nights off is none of your business."

"You mean your business is my business the other five nights of the week?"

She took another step toward him. "I'm warning you. If you ever behave again the way you did tonight, I'll embarrass you. You've got Warren thinking there's something between us."

His eyebrows shot up so fast she almost believed she'd committed a sin. "You mean there isn't?"

"I'm going to bed. You try something like this again and, I promise you, I won't be so reasonable."

"Do I get an affidavit to that effect?"

She controlled her right foot just before she stamped it. "You . . . you . . . You think I don't know what you were doing?" She headed toward the stairs, stopped, and turned around. "I could . . . Duncan, I could throttle you."

"As long as you don't plant one of those cold, flat kisses on me like you did Warren, I won't complain."

She glared at him. "I like peace, Duncan, but there's a limit to what I'm willing to pay for it. Good night."

She didn't want to believe that Duncan was jealous of her, but what else would have caused him to act as he had? She wasn't entirely innocent, because she had gone for broke and dressed to the nines, and she had to admit that she didn't much care what Warren thought of the way she looked . . . .

Duncan watched her rush up the stairs—away from him. He knew he'd overdone it, and he owed her an apology. A couple of them. But it went against his grain to do it, because he'd lie if he said he was sorry. He climbed the stairs and knocked on her door.

"I don't want to be disturbed, Duncan."

"I need to talk to you."

He waited for what seemed like long minutes until she cracked the door and peeped out. "What is it?"

"I know I owe you an apology, but I don't feel like apologizing. I shouldn't have interfered with your date, and I won't do it again. Just warn me next time. Okay?"

"Why should I warn you?"

He stared at the red silk kimono hanging off the side of her shoulder and the smooth, beige-colored flesh that it exposed. Damn! Annoyance flared in him. Not at her, but at life's nastiness. "Don't ask the obvious, Justine," he said, taking it out on her. "Not unless you want some bare facts, and right now, I'm in the mood to give them to you. Just warn me next time."

He didn't wait for her response, but headed for the basement, where he kicked off his shoes and stretched out on the sofa. This night wouldn't be the first on which he'd gone without sleep. And probably not the last.

Duncan could hardly bear the diet of coolness to which Justine treated him during the week that followed. Pleasant. She was that, but not much more. All right. Let her stew. Around seven that Sunday evening, she appeared in the living room elegantly dressed in a blue suit and told him, "I should be back by midnight. Have a good evening."

He went to the closet for her coat and controlled his amusement when she attempted to take it from him and put it on. "Anybody picking you up?" He said it as casually as he could, because he didn't want to give her an excuse to be angry with him.

"Is there?" he persisted when she didn't answer. "Want me to call you a cab, or are you driving?"

He could see that her impatience was feigned. "Thank you, Duncan, but I'm fine."

He didn't release the coat. "How are you getting there and back? A sensible person doesn't cut off his nose because he has a cold, Justine. I'm only concerned with your safety."

"Oh, all right. I'm driving."

He relaxed. Maybe he'd scared old Warren off. "If you're going to a movie, I suppose I shouldn't detain you."

If his life had depended on it, he wouldn't have been able to say why he leaned down and placed a gentle kiss on her lips. Her right hand flew to her left breast, she sucked in her breath and her grayish-brown eyes seemed twice their size. He had to diffuse the tension and quickly, because he couldn't let her think he would take advantage of her, so he headed for the front door.

"I'll let you out. Be sure you have enough gas, and take care."

Her face still had that stunned expression when she turned to walk down the steps. He sat down at his desk and tried to work, but he couldn't do any hard thinking, so he pitched his pencil across the room, slammed his file cabinet shut, peeped in on Tonya, and called it a night. A few hours later, he lay on his back staring at the ceiling. A quarter to twelve, and she still wasn't there. He had a good mind to . . . He flipped over on his belly and gathered the pillow under his chin. *"Man, you're losing it. If she went to meet a man, you are not interested. You don't care,"* he said, and repeated it over and over like a mantra.

Twenty minutes later, he heard her footsteps on the stairs. He should go to sleep, but he couldn't, so he slipped on a robe, opened his door and stepped out in the hall. "You okay?"

Her startled look told him that he'd surprised her, that she'd trusted him not to meet her at the door, and he was glad he hadn't let her down. "I just wanted to know that you're all right," he said.

She smiled at him, warm sunshine breaking through a dark cloud. "Thanks. I'm just fine. It is a bit eerie driving up here at night, though. There're no lights along the park portion of West Beach."

"I'm glad I didn't know you took that route. If West Beach had red lights, I wouldn't even pause at one of them this time of night. Well, I just wanted to see that you're okay. I hope you had a good time."

"I went to see Jack Nicholson. That guarantees you a good time."

An unfamiliar glow suffused him. "I'm glad you enjoyed it. Good night."

He sat on the edge of his bed and tried to figure out why she'd been so friendly. So warm. One of these days, he was going to conduct a survey on the subject of women, and ask them why they acted the way they did. He wasn't stupid, and if he couldn't figure them out, he doubted a lot of other men could. He threw off the robe, got in bed, and went to sleep.

Justine resisted checking on Tonya for fear she'd encounter Duncan again that night. Much as she adored Jack Nicholson, she hadn't been able to concentrate on that movie, because Duncan had shattered her defenses with his kiss as she left the house. She'd been distant all week, hoping to set some rules for their relationship, but with that one gesture, he'd torpedoed the little progress that she'd made. The hole that she'd dug for herself got deeper every day. She shouldn't stay, and she couldn't leave. If that knowledge wasn't sufficient to set her nerves on end, she got a genuine shock the next morning. She took Tonya to the breakfast room, put her in her highchair, fed her, and went to the kitchen for her own breakfast.

"I tell you, Justine, that child loves you so much she starting to look like you. Mr. B don't know how lucky he was finding a good woman like you to take care of his child. Only the Lord knows how a mother could give away a beautiful child like this one. She gonna be sorry, too. You mark my word. What you want for breakfast?"

Justine couldn't move. She opened her mouth, but couldn't make a sound. Frantic, she rushed out of the kitchen and stopped when Tonya, laughing and shaking a rubber bird, sang, "Juju. Juju." She whirled around and bumped into Mattie.

"What you wanna eat, Justine? I got to get my housework

done. You don't have to watch that child every minute. I didn't even hear her cry. You want pancakes?"

Grateful that Mattie hadn't detected the effect of her words and that Duncan hadn't been there to hear them, she answered in a voice strange to her ears, "Juice and toast will do, Mattie."

The woman stared at her. "You ain't sick, is you?"

"The suit I had on last night was tight, and no comment on that, please."

"You ain't heard me say a word."

She had to get out of there, away from the stress of living a lie that threatened to encircle her like a coiling python. Maybe she'd take Tonya for a walk or a drive down to the paper. Mattie returned with orange juice, several toasted muffins, butter, and jelly. Justine wanted to push it all away, but Mattie stood at the table waiting to be treated to the sight of Justine devouring the food.

Justine drank the juice, nibbled on a raisin muffin, took Tonya, and left the dinning room. She struggled with the coming damnation that Mattie's innocent comment foretold, as she contemplated that time when Duncan would recognize the resemblance and know at last why he thought her familiar. Indeed, Mattie's shrewd eyes might soon conclude the truth. Well, she'd deal with that when she had to.

She dressed for the outdoors and looked around for something warm to put on Tonya. The idea that came to mind startled her. Did she dare? She went to her closet, opened the box of treasures that she stored there and took out the hand-made yellow sweater, one of two precious things she had from her mother. The other was a small bronze medallion blessed by Pope Paul VI. She gazed at the hand crocheted sweater with a large pom pom on each sleeve and smaller ones down the front. A garment for a two-year-old girl. Her eyes smiled down at the child who giggled and clapped her hands.

"Juju sing?"

She didn't feel like singing. She had never worn the sweater, because her mother had gotten ill right after she made it, and her father had packed it with the things she'd taken to her aunt's home. It rightfully belonged to Tonya, but a lump formed in her throat as she put Tonya's arms in the sleeves. A perfect fit. She pulled the child into her arms and spilled tears on her head, but she heard Mattie climbing the stairs, and her moment of weakness was a short one.

"Tonya sing. Juju sing?" Tonya said again.

She knew the child wanted to slap hands and play patty cake, but she hadn't the spirit for it, pretended she didn't understand, and sang "Here We Go 'Round the Mulberry Bush." Tonya yelled and jumped up and down in protest, but Justine was not moved. She finished dressing her and took her to the back garden for a walk. The telephone rang as she closed the back door, but she didn't pause.

"Justine, some man was asking if you lived here," Mattie yelled from an upstairs window. "He don't sound like nobody you'd be knowing, real rough like, so I told 'em he had the wrong number."

"I don't know what he'd want with me," Justine said.

"Me neither, but this ain't the first time he done that. I got a good ear, and I know he's called here before. Wonder if he's the one what calls, don't say nothing, and hangs up? I tell you whoever invented phones ought to be horsewhipped."

He'd called before all right, and he hadn't spoken a word. If only she knew who he was and why he called, she could protect herself. She had planned to put Tonya in the stroller and walk around the neighborhood, because the child enjoyed seeing the squirrels and chipmunks that roamed the area collecting their winter food, but who knew the whereabouts of that man? So much for her wish to spend some time out of doors, away from the claustrophobic atmosphere of her deception. She went back inside, put Tonya in her crib, and got to work on some letters that she'd procrastinated about answering.

"Dear Aunt Mariah, what do you do when your man catches you in a lie? It's not the first, and I don't think he'll forgive me this time. Help. Troubled."

Justine had thought for a long time about that letter. If

she knew the answer, she'd be less worried about Duncan's reaction to her own deception.

"Sometimes we have to pay the piper," she wrote. "You may have to take your medicine, and try to get on with your life. If that happens, don't let yourself become a pathological liar. Get some help. I wish you the best. Aunt Mariah."

But for the ringing phone, she might have gotten into a blue funk. "Hello." She nearly panicked as only silence greeted her ears. When it rang again, she asked Mattie to answer it.

"It's for you, Justine," Mattie called out.

"Big Al here. Loved your last column. Justine, I wish you'd sign those papers for syndication. You've already got a good local following, but in a few months you'd be the biggest name in the business. Feel like a personal appearance tour? I can get you ten thousand a shot if you syndicate, plus a six figure book deal within a year. So how about it?"

"Al, you promised me six months, and I want to stick with that. I'll let you know in April."

"All right, but you're blowing good hard cold cash, babe. We're speaking real money. But if you don't wonna be rich . . ." He let it hang.

Quadruple your income by syndicating. Go on a personal appearance tour at ten thousand dollars per one hour speech. Write a book for a six figure advance plus royalties. Get rich. And lose her child for the second time. Never! Yet she knew she could expect pressure from Al, for he, too, stood to gain plenty by syndicating her column.

Her private phone rang. "Hello."

"Hello, Justine, this is Warren. How about dinner Sunday night?"

She didn't want to go out with Warren, because he'd take that as evidence of an interest in him. "Hi, Warren. I don't want to encourage you, so let's just be friends."

His silence telegraphed his disappointment. "All right, if you insist, but I'd like to have dinner with my friend."

"Warren, I don't think so."

"Couldn't you at least give me that much . . . for old times sake?"

Maybe if she saw more of him, she could grow to care for him. "Oh. All right. Seven o'clock. Which restaurant? I'll meet you there."

Another long silence spoke eloquently of his reaction to her suggestion. "I won't ask you why, because I don't think I want to know. The Willard at seven."

She breathed deeply in relief, though Warren's ready acquiescence perplexed her. Duncan had said he wouldn't interfere with her dates again, but she didn't believe him, so she wouldn't let Warren call for her at the house.

She wrote a note telling Duncan that Tonya loved the stairs and asking him to install a gate upstairs so that she wouldn't tumble down them. And she thought it time to work on his plans for her playroom in the basement. She added that it wouldn't hurt to have a piano in the house.

If he'd gotten uptight about the learning tools, she recalled as she placed the note on his desk, he'd care even less for the suggestion that they needed a piano.

Thinking that he'd enjoy having Tonya meet him at the front door when he got home, she walked there with Tonya and stood her on her feet when the Buick turned into the garage.

"Well, who's daddy's baby?" he asked, picked Tonya up and kissed her while his eyes adored Justine.

If there had been any place to go, she would have gone there. He stared into her eyes until his reddish-brown orbs seem to blaze with fire, clearly oblivious to having his nose and ears pulled and his face rubbed and patted with baby fingers. If she'd been foolish, she'd have thought she was his world, but she wasn't, and she couldn't trick herself into believing that all was well when she knew her life could be capsized at any moment.

"There are times," he said, so softly that as close to him as she was, she could barely discern his words. "There are times, when I think I've known you before. Somewhere. Known you all my life." He shook his head as though in wonder. "I don't question my sanity, Justine, and I've always been sure of my hunches. But this feeling I have that I know you ties me in knots sometimes. Have I ever known you before you came here to apply for this job?''

She wanted to grab her knees to make sure he didn't hear them knock, but she stiffened her back and let him have the brilliance of a practiced smile. ''Duncan, that is not flattering. If I had ever met you, trust me, I would have remembered it.''

Obviously taken aback by her response, he nodded in a slow, deliberate movement. ''It's the darndest thing, but maybe that's it. Maybe you're in my subconscious somewhere.'' His demeanor brightened.

Was it possible to be jealous of a baby? Her own child? She watched the adoration that lit his face while he gazed at Tonya. Here was love. An almost overpowering desire to have that love, to belong to the two of them, gripped her, and she did the only thing she could. She kissed Tonya on the cheek and rushed toward the stairs.

''Come back here, woman.''

She whirled around, nearly missing the step. ''Are you talking to me?'' Her tone wasn't what a boss could expect of the hired help, but he hadn't spoken like an employer either.

He started toward her with Tonya laughing happily in his arms, taking the stairs slowly and deliberately. ''You bet I'm talking to you. You kissed Tonya, but you wanted to kiss me.''

''Why you . . . How dare you?'' He kept walking up the steps until he reached her. ''I dare because you won't deny it.'' His eyes stroked her. ''Oh, yes. You meant it for me, and I felt it.''

She had to put up some fences before the situation got out of hand, and she was going to call Warren and tell him to come to the house for her on Sunday. ''Don't fool yourself, Duncan,'' she said. ''And don't forget that I'm the hired help.'' She left him standing there holding their daughter in his arms.

Duncan admonished himself that he'd better behave more prudently with Justine. He was as certain as he was of his name that if he hadn't been holding Tonya, he'd have gone after her, and when he left her, their lives would have been changed forever. She wasn't responsible for the need that churned in him with increasing vigor and urgency, but he wished she'd learn not to post her feelings like a flashing neon sign. Trouble was, she had an aura of innocence that he suspected was anchored in reality.

"Juju sing, Daddy."

"Yeah. And that's not all," he said, taking her into his office.

He sat at his desk with Tonya on his knee, as she'd become too adventuresome to turn loose in the room, and his gaze dropped on Justine's handwriting. He read the note three times, because he didn't believe what he saw. The woman wanted to make a Mozart out of his child? He had hoped he wouldn't have to do it, but she was going too far, and he'd have to put a stop to it. He'd tell her as much at dinner that evening.

"You're going to your room and get a nap," he told Tonya. "Daddy has to work."

"Daddy work?" she asked. Her face crumbled into a frown. "Sing, Daddy."

He sang a few bars of "I Still Suits Me" as he walked her to her room. "Say, where'd we get this sweater?" He knew that only Justine would have given it to her; Mattie's taste didn't reach that level.

"I'd planned to order gates for the stairway upstairs and the one down here that leads to the basement," he told Justine at dinner. "I haven't decided how I want that playroom. It seems to me we ought to know more about what interests her, but I'll take ideas."

He didn't like the frown on her face and braced himself for her argument. "You teach children what to value; you don't wait 'til they're not interested in anything but cock fights to wish they appreciated and enjoyed the ballet. You take them to the ballet and keep them away from cock fights."

"Shore do," Mattie chimed in. "If you don't give her no turnips, she ain't likely to get a craving for turnips."

Duncan looked from one to the other. Justine's stare almost dared him to disagree, and he sensed that she'd fight him on this issue. "You seem certain of your ground, Justine, but even if you're right, I'm her father, and what I say goes."

She stopped eating, pushed back her chair, and folded her arms, and after one of the most pregnant pauses he'd ever witnessed, she looked him in the eye. "And what do you say?"

"She's not ready for the playroom and certainly not for a baby grand."

He had to hand it to her. Her face seemed to crumple, but only for half a second before her shoulders went back and her chin out. "I'm not so foolish as to start Tonya on the piano. Nor did I ask for a grand. Tonya likes piano music, and I wanted a piano so that she could see and hear me playing it and learn where the music comes from. But if we're back in prehistoric times with the dinosaurs, forgive me my twentieth century stupidity."

His left eyebrow shot up. "You know how to play hardball, don't you? You play the piano?"

The eyes that glared at him conveyed passion, but not the kind that usually sent blood rushing to his loins. She hardly bothered to suppress her annoyance with him. "Obviously, I do. If you'll excuse me . . ."

"Say, wait a minute. I shouldn't have brought up this matter here. Please finish your dinner."

"Thanks, but I really have finished."

"Now y'all ain't going to treat my dinner like this. My best roast veal, and you hardly touch it. I tell you, me and my Moe don't talk about nothing at the table but what we eatin'. That way, we don't get mad, 'cause I cooks good food. I declare—"

"It's okay, Mattie. We can eat it again tomorrow night," Duncan said, hastening to appease her. "Wait a minute, please, Justine."

She stopped but didn't turn to face him. "Yes. What is it?"

"I'm sorry, and Mattie's right. The dinner table is no place to discuss anything contentious."

She walked on. "You're right. Good night."

He caught up with her as she headed for the stairs. "I said I was sorry, Justine."

"Thanks. That and thirty-three cents will buy me a postage stamp. Duncan, if I'm allowed to, I'd like to go to my room."

He took his hand off her arm and watched her rush up the stairs. Something had happened, and he didn't think it was what they'd disagreed about. By then, she had to know that he was open to compromise. Frustrated, he stuck his hands in his trouser pockets and walked back to the kitchen.

"That veal was excellent, Mattie."

"I know that, Mr. B." She waved the scrub brush instead of her finger. "I been 'round a lot of people in my fifty-two years, and when I see a man and woman start arguing and fighting, I know that's 'cause they'd rather be doing somethin' else. 'Course, I ain't telling you nothing you don't know." She wiped her hands on her apron. "Y'all kept me here late tonight."

He looked at his watch. Seven forty-five. "Right. I'll run you home as soon as I let Justine know I'm going out."

"Mr. B," she called after him, "you ain't gonna find nobody else to take care of Tonya and love her like Justine does. She treat that child like she was her own."

"I know, and don't think I don't appreciate it."

He took the stairs two at a time, stepped into the hall, and paused at Justine's door. "I'm going to run Mattie home right now," he said when she opened it, "and I've got a couple of errands to ran. If you need me, call my cell phone."

"All right."

If only he knew what had caused her to fold up. "Justine, I know something happened at the table that upset you, and I know it wasn't our argument. Maybe it was the tone of my voice. Whatever. I want you to know that I appreciate the care and love you give Tonya more than I know how to tell you. Like that sweater. When did you buy it and where?"

Her obvious reluctance to answer baffled him. At last, she said, "It was mine. My mother knitted it for me, but she got sick and never put it on me. It's one of the few things I have from her, and I wanted Tonya to have it."

He hesitated to say the obvious and wondered at his

reluctance. Surely, she should have saved it for her own daughter. All he said was, "She looks so pretty in it, and it's probably the only handmade sweater she'll have. Thanks."

"It was my pleasure. Good night."

What could he do but leave? Yet it pained him to walk away from her not knowing what hurt her and unable to erase her forlorn expression. "Take care. See you in the morning."

He put his "street" clothes in a small bag, put on a pair of Nikes, and loped down the stairs. "Let's go, Mattie." He threw this bag in the back seat of the car and put Mattie beside him. As soon as he dropped her off, he'd park somewhere and change his clothes. Neither Rags nor Mitch had called him in the past few days, and he had to check on them.

"I'm her father, and what I say goes."

Those words had been ice around her heart, chilling her until she'd barely been able to breathe. In that moment, she could have hated him, though she knew he had a right to say it, for he was the only parent to Tonya that the law recognized. She had wanted to scream, *But she came out of my body with pains that almost broke me into pieces!* Yet, she couldn't say a word. They'd robbed her of that right. If she had known how much it would hurt, would she still have taken the job? She walked across the hall, went into Tonya's room, and looked down at the sleeping child. Her hand reached out to touch the hair of the beautiful, happy daughter that she might never have known, but whose life she'd been given a second chance to help shape. It wasn't an occasion for self-pity, but for gratitude. She'd just have to toughen her skin, swallow the pain, and enjoy what she could of the life she'd laid out for herself. Would she do it again? She left the room, counting the blessing that she had. Would she? In a New York minute! And she had to watch herself. Both Mattie and Duncan often inched so close to the truth that one more misstep on her part might open their eyes to her true identity.

CHAPTER SEVEN

That following Sunday evening, Justine dressed in a green velveteen jumpsuit, knocked with nervous fingers, and peeped into Duncan's office. "I'm going out to dinner. See you when I get back."

His quick frown and the sharp backward movement of his head confirmed that she'd shocked him. She closed his door, rushed downstairs, and got her coat from the closet just as the doorbell rang.

She'd startled two men in less than five minutes, she realized, for Warren's bottom lip dropped when she opened the front door, took his hand, and ushered him out, closing the door behind them.

"What's the hurry? I was hoping for some of your boss's thirty-year-old scotch."

Irritation swept over her. Wouldn't Duncan have loved that! "Are you serious?" she asked.

"Well, no. Where is he tonight?"

She didn't plan to spend the evening talking about Duncan. "Upstairs."

In the car, Warren fastened their seat belts and leaned over to kiss her, but she held him off with both hands.

"I see. So that kiss you pasted on my mouth the other

night was for your boss's benefit," he said, in words that sounded as if they came through clenched teeth.

He revved the engine, and the Cadillac jerked away from the curb, accentuating the atmosphere of hostility.

She had regretted that impulsive kiss many times, but she refused to let him make an issue of it. "Warren, a simple kiss is customary after a pleasant evening."

He turned onto Georgia Avenue without waiting for the green light. "Yeah. Sure."

At the Willard Hotel, he left his blue Cadillac with a parking attendant and led her to their reserved table. "You say there's nothing between you and . . . what's-his-name? Dunbar?"

So that's the kind of evening it would be. "There isn't, and his name is Duncan."

"Right. Glad to hear it." He leaned back and assumed the demeanor of a man assessing a deadly opponent. "What happened between graduation and now, Justine? I heard you were involved with some big shot. Did you marry him, or what?"

Thank God her shaking hands were in her lap where he couldn't see them. "Dull as I am, I never dreamed I'd be the subject of gossip. I'm still wondering why you didn't marry Wanda."

He pushed back his shirt cuff and examined his Rolex. "All right, if you don't want to talk about it. There's such a thing as public records, you know." He beckoned their waiter. "I take it Dunbar doesn't know much about you. If he does and still hired you as his child's nanny, he must think a whole lot of himself—considering who you are. My guess is he doesn't know you're Arnold Taylor's daughter."

Her damp, cold palms gripped the sides of her chair. "Why is this interesting, Warren? I thought I'd be having dinner with a friend, not a private investigator. I'd appreciate your changing the subject."

His grin was just short of feral. "And if I don't?"

"I can get a taxi home."

He leaned back and smiled. "Home? Did you say home?"

She stood to leave and his expression hardened. "No

woman has ever walked out on me except you, Mrs. Montgomery, and you won't do it again."

His words set her teeth to chattering as fear hurtled through her, and she groped for her chair and sat down.

"I see I got a rise out of you," he said, his voice a match for the iciness of his gaze.

"What do you want, Warren?"

He didn't mince his words. "You. I want you, and I'll take you any way I can get you. And when I unearth the rest of your secrets, you won't be so hard to get."

So he'd resort to blackmail, would he? Anger crowded out her fear. "You want to make it big in syndication, broker for Big Al and other newspapers, right? Well, try something dirty with me, Warren, and you can forget your grandiose plans. You can also expect front page coverage in at least two major newspapers. Did you ever hear of Hugh Pickford?"

He sat forward. "Who hasn't? Why?"

She stood. "Uncle Hugh is my godfather, and he carries a lot of influential people around in his pocket. Good night."

He stood and faced her, shaking with rage, though his calm voice belied it. "So Dunbar or whoever he is doesn't know anything about you." He placed both knuckles on the table and leaned forward. "The hell with Pickford. You do things my way, or your boss will hear from me."

In spite of her rioting nerves, she tossed her head and glared at him, "Don't forget any of this, Warren, because you will have to repeat it before a judge."

Outside, she hailed a taxi and headed for Primrose Street and home. Yes, home. How had she let herself forget the size of Warren's ego, his bulldog tenacity in getting what he wanted, and the lengths to which he'd go for revenge? Revenge for her having walked out on him ten years earlier. She heard Duncan in the kitchen, but went directly to her room, changed her clothes, and called her godfather.

"Give me Stoke's phone number," Hugh said after she told him what had transpired between Warren and her. "Unless he's foolhardy for sure, you won't have to worry about him again."

"You . . . You're not going to do anything—"

"Illegal?" he asked, interrupting her. "Of course not, but neither am I going to let him intimidate you. Sleep well."

But she didn't. Warren had intimated that he meant to have her, and she'd seen his ruthless streak, so she had to take him seriously.

Duncan's knock was not unexpected. She put on a kimono and opened the door.

"I don't usually go out on your day off," he said, "but this is an emergency, and I'd appreciate it if you'd check on Tonya while I'm gone."

She nodded. "Of course. Please leave her door open so I can hear if she calls."

"Thanks. Good night." His wink didn't have its usual punch.

Justine didn't want to answer the telephone, because her anonymous caller usually made his evening calls soon after Duncan left the house. When the ringing persisted, she stormed out of her room to the hall phone.

"Hello!"

"Hey, Justine. This is Banks. I was beginning to think you guys had taken Tonya and gone off somewhere."

Relief spread over her. "Banks. How are you? You just missed him."

"Missed who? Duncan? I'm calling you. I'll be over Saturday, and I thought we could have lunch or something. You need to get out of the house. Mattie can keep Tonya for a couple of hours."

"I know she can, and I'd love to have lunch with you, but I'm supposed to work on Saturdays. Besides, Mattie hates babysitting."

"You leave Mattie to me. She'll do anything I ask her to do. You need the company of some females your own age."

Justine couldn't help smiling when it occurred to her that Banks probably had "Wayne" trouble and wanted to talk about it. "I'm older than you."

"No problem. You can bring along your cane. Is it a date?"

"I'll have to ask Duncan."

Waves of laughter reached her through the phone. "That's right, girlfriend. Dot all your i's and cross all your t's, then lower your lashes and give him your best smile. I'll meet you at the Willard. Twelve-thirty."

Justine heard herself agreeing, and realized that she would enjoy an elegant lunch with a friend. "I'm looking forward to it," she told Banks. "Anything new with you and Wayne?"

"Depends on what you'd call new. I'll tell you all about it. See you then."

Justine said good-bye and hung up. Did she want to be friends with Duncan's sister? She liked the woman's intelligence and quick wit, but she was wary of Banks's uncanny perceptiveness. She doubted Banks ever missed much, and figured that she could even be on the trail of something with this luncheon date. Had she noticed the resemblance between Tonya and herself? She went back into her room but left the door ajar so as to hear Tonya if she called. Restless, she stepped out on her balcony, but the chill of the air sent her back inside. She realized that she was pacing the floor, something she hadn't done since her days as Mrs. Kenneth Montgomery, threw her hands up, and told herself not to be paranoid about Warren or about Tonya's resemblance to her. People don't spend all their time thinking about you, she admonished herself.

At that very moment, however, she filled Duncan's thoughts. He sat in the corner of a pool room just off Benning, greeting the regulars in the language of the street. He didn't doubt that if the men and women who habituated "the street," living on the edge and skirting the law, were aware that he was Duncan Banks, the well known journalist, at best he'd lose access to his most important sources of information, but the greater likelihood was that he'd lose his life. He let them think him a worn-out has-been, dressed the part, and they considered him one of them.

"Say, man, how's your old lady? Out of the bone factory

yet?" he asked Buck, a longtime informant. Told that the man's wife needed additional surgery and might be confined to the hospital for weeks, he stuck his hand in his pocket, balled up a fifty dollar bill, and slipped it to Buck.

"Gramercy, Pops," was the man's thanks. In Capital View, he was known as Pops, a guy who wrote for supermarket tabloids or some other periodical of low repute. "Any time you need the word," Buck told him, "you know where I am."

Duncan knew that if he sat in that comer for an hour any night, he'd see Buck and all the other regulars. He wasn't there seeking information, though he was always glad to get it. He was reminding himself that he worked at night as well as day, and that he had to stop finding excuses to stay home evenings because Justine was there. He'd hired her so he'd be free to work when and where he chose, but home was a different place since she'd been in it, and he pulled himself away from it with increasing difficulty.

"When did ya blow in?" he asked an interstate bus driver, who paused on his way to the pool table.

"Couple of hours ago. Say, Pops, you're in the wrong place. Bunch of flat feet pulling a sting 'round on Fifteenth Street. A lot of A-bombs going down the drain tonight."

Duncan was on his feet. "Owe ya one, man." Such contacts were reasons why he was one of the areas most respected reporters. He'd just been told that the police were carrying out a sting that would yield a mother lode of crack.

"Watch it, man," someone said as he rushed across the street. "These cops see ya running, they figure you stole something and let you have a couple of bullets."

"Thanks, buddy." He slowed down.

When he reached the crowd, he pulled off his woolen cap, put it in his pocket and hung his press pass around his neck. "How's it going?" he asked an officer.

"Same old thing. A bunch of idiot kids trying to kill each other."

He wanted a story, not tired philosophy. "You deserve credit for breaking it up. What's your name and precinct?"

Duncan asked him. Half an hour later, he had the first story in his series about American juveniles. Eleven black, white, and Hispanic boys under nineteen years of age were arrested for selling drugs. He shook his head. Was there no end to it?

After learning that Mitch and Rags were all right, he walked to his car. On the way home, he stopped at a convenience store for early editions of the papers and his glance caught a box of Godiva chocolates wrapped in gold foil and tied with a green silk ribbon. Justine loved green and looked good in it.

"One of those, please," he said to the clerk. "Do you have a little card to go with it?"

She found one and dropped it in the plastic bag along with the chocolates. He didn't let himself think about the impulsive purchase until he looked at Justine's room door, saw no light, and had to deal with his disappointment. He sat at his desk and wrote, *"Justine, I would never knowingly contribute to your discomfort or your unhappiness. Yours, Duncan."* He read it over several times, but didn't see there what he felt, what he wanted to say. He shredded it and dropped the pieces into his waste basket.

The next morning, Justine brought Tonya downstairs in her arms against the child's protests. Tonya wanted to walk down, but Justine didn't want to spend the thirty minutes necessary to accomplish it. She put her in the high chair, sat down, and prepared to serve herself a cup of coffee.

"What on earth? Mattie, where's Duncan?"

She picked up the box of chocolates, turned it over, around, and sideways. No card. Mattie, where did this come from? Where's Duncan?"

Mattie pranced into the dining room bearing a platter of eggs, sausages, and grits and a plate of biscuits. "You axin' me? His royalty didn't eat one mouthful of my breakfast. Said he had to go. Guess he don't want to be here when you see this candy he put here. I tell you, there ain't no figurin' out men. Who else you gonna think give it to you? Me?'' She patted her red and purple wig and looked at Tonya. "I forgot your cream of wheat.''

Justine looked at the box. No card. Nothing. Mattie returned with Tonya's breakfast, and Justine was glad to concentrate on feeding her. "Do you know what time Duncan left?'' she asked Mattie.

"I was too mad to look at the clock. My Moe woulda just give me the candy and sit down and eat his breakfast. I tell you, sometimes I think education makes people scared of theyselves.''

Best not to comment on that. She fed Tonya, drank another cup of coffee, and prepared to leave the table. "You ain't eatin' either? I tell you, you and Mr. B better get this thing straightened out, whatever it is, 'cause I don't cook for people what don't eat. Never seen the beat of it. First he bounces in here and says he gotta leave without his breakfast, then you show up and drink coffee. I'm supposed to be dumb?''

Justine stared at Mattie as she flounced toward the kitchen, lifted Tonya from the high chair, and escaped upstairs. She'd had as much of Mattie's outrage as she could tolerate. She placed the box on her dressing table, wrote a thank-you note, and went to his office to leave it on his desk. When her gaze found the small envelope that he'd left there, she pulled the waste basket from beneath the desk, looked at the tiny bits of paper, and knew that he had written a note to her, thought better of it, and destroyed the message. She didn't know why, but seeing the shredded paper warmed her heart. He'd written something and decided not to give it to her. If she had needed confirmation that he hadn't wanted to hurt her, here it was.

When she heard Duncan's car turn into the garage that afternoon, she rushed to the front door, waited for him, and opened it when he reached for the knob. "Well. Hi. What's up?''

Obviously, she had surprised him. She couldn't remember what she'd planned to say, and he stood there waiting for her to speak. She had a sudden overwhelming desire to kiss him, explanation be hanged.

"I . . . uh . . . You mind if I kiss you?" Where had those words come from? Her open palm flew to her mouth.

"Hell no, I don't mind. Come here to me."

He gave her neither time nor room to avoid his fire. His fingers grasped her arms, and jolts of electricity whistled through her veins. She moved toward him. Waiting. Wanting. He took his time and slowly lowered his mouth to hers. Her hands grabbed his shoulders and wound their way to his nape, while his hot mouth scattered her senses. She parted her lips in a plea for more, but instead of giving her what she longed for, he gripped her arms, closed his eyes, and brought her to him in a steely embrace. "One of these days, we'll go the limit, Justine, and I don't think either one of us is ready for the consequences."

He settled her against the wall as though she were a precious figurine and braced his hands on either side of her. "And one of these days, I won't be able to stop."

Giddy with lust for the aphrodisiac in front of her and all around her, she asked him, "And one of these days, will you decide you don't want to stop?"

He stepped back, his eyes stripping her bare. "Don't be reckless, Justine. I am well aware that you'd panic if I went after you. You're scared to death of involvement with me. And you ought to be, because it wouldn't be something either of us would be able to walk away from without scars."

"I know that, Duncan, and that's why I fear it."

"But don't ever be afraid of *me*, Justine. You live in my home and you're in my employ, so I'll protect you even from myself You may depend on that. But if you come to me, Justine, be prepared to stay a while."

He may have intended to warn her, but he'd only excited her. She stared at him, mesmerized. He had the most beguiling habits, as when his eyes suddenly blazed with humor and a grin spread over his face. "Why'd you want to kiss me?"

She stuck her hands on her hips and removed them just as quickly. "I think it had something to do with those chocolates. But I suspect any excuse would have served. They're delicious."

"Chocolates? What chocolates?"

She poked him in the chest with her right index finger. "The ones that you were too chicken to stick a note on, but I didn't care. I've never received anything that I appreciated as much."

She could see that as hard as he tried not to smile, her comment had pleased him, and a glow claimed his face. "Well, I'll be. It was my pleasure."

Several days later, she received more evidence of Duncan's kindness. "I'm here to put these guards at the tops of the stairs," a strange man told Justine when she answered the door several days later. If that weren't enough, a piano arrived. Duncan hadn't said anything more about the things she'd asked him to provide for Tonya, so she gazed in awe when a large truck parked in front of the house later that afternoon. The driver walked over to where she stood with Tonya on the front lawn and handed her some papers for her signature.

"I got a Steinway Grand for Miss Justine Taylor. You Miss Taylor?"

She steadied her fingers as she reached for the paper. "Yes . . . Yes, I'm Justine Taylor."

"Surprised you, did he?" the man asked, his amusement more suggestive than merry.

Not that she cared what he thought. "Indeed he did." She signed the papers and rushed into the house. Where would she put it?

"He said it goes in the basement where the long sofa is," the man informed her. "You just take it easy, we'll see to it."

She had to find a place to sit down. Two surprises in one day. And a Steinway Grand, at that. For the next three days, she waited in vain for work to begin on Tonya's recreation room. He had vetoed that suggestion, and seeing that he meant it reminded her once again that she was her daughter's caretaker. Nothing more. For the piano, which she discovered he'd registered in her name, she wrote him a warm note.

After reading it, he'd joked, "Changing your thank you style, I see."

"Do you think I can take a few hours off tomorrow afternoon?" she asked Duncan that Friday night at dinner. "Banks invited me to lunch at the Willard."

He stopped eating and stared at her, wide eyed. "Banks? My sister, Leah? I didn't know she'd be in town tomorrow. When did this happen?"

"She called me Sunday night. Will you be home?"

"He don't need to be here," Mattie interjected. "Miss Leah axed me to keep Tonya, and you know, Mr. B, I'd do anything for that sister of yours. You go right on, Justine. I'll be here."

Twinkling stars in his reddish-brown eyes danced merrily for Justine. "I'm not invited? Mattie's keeping Tonya, so I could go along."

She'd learned that he was pretty good at leg-pulling. Well, she wasn't too bad at it herself. "Sure. Glad to have you," she said and dared to add, "provided you take me along on your next midnight prowl."

His head jerked up and she delighted in seeing his Adams apple bobble up and down, while he wrestled with his answer. He hadn't thought she knew. "Just let me know when," she teased. "Should I wear my Dracula's cape, Nikes and hood, or my red mini-skirt?"

When his brow furrowed in a deep frown, and his eyes narrowed in a level, almost accusing look, she knew she'd come close to meddling in something that he chose not to share. Making light of it, she joked, "I have facets you haven't seen, so let me know what it'll be."

His eyes drilled her. "Mini-skirt, and make it a short one."

She held his gaze. Doggoned if she'd let him back her into a corner. If you don't play the fiddle, get out of the front row, was the message behind that cryptic remark. Well, she could give as good as she got.

"If you don't play basketball, stay off the court," she advised him.

"Right!" he jeered, "and always be sure the credentials you present match your talents."

The spoon slipped from her fingers, and her breath caught in her throat. She had forgotten her role again, and this time, he'd let her know that he was aware of it. He'd practically said, *you're anything but a nanny.*

Having to recover while he kept his gaze glued on her took some doing, but she squared her shoulders and stared right back at him. "May I have those few hours off?"

The dark clouds in his eyes forecast a coming storm, but his words belied it and would have given her an unwarranted sense of security, if she had allowed them to dupe her. "Of course. You ask for so little."

She thanked him, and when she would have excused herself and left the table, he leaned back in his chair and smiled, not in the way that could send goose pimples skittering about her skin as when it came naturally, but his cool, practiced smile. The smile that said he wasn't pleased. "I haven't heard you play the piano. Why is that?"

"As soon as the piano tuner comes over to tune it, that's probably what you'll hear most around here."

"Has Tonya heard you play?"

"I played for her the day it arrived, and I had to carry her kicking and screaming away from it. You should have seen her. She erupted in fury at me."

"Well, I'll be. So you were right about that, too."

She dared to say, "I was. And I'm right about that—"

His hand went out, palm forward. "Don't say it. You know my view on that, and it stands."

All right. She'd back off for now, but he hadn't heard the last of it.

She found herself eagerly looking forward to her luncheon with Banks and, in a fit of honesty, admitted that what she anticipated was the return to the life she'd known before Kenneth's betrayal and death—Seeing friends at lunch and dinner in elegant restaurants and dressing as a modern career woman. She dressed in a red wool gabardine suit and black accessories and walked into Tonya's room, where she found Duncan sitting in the rocker with the child in his lap. She bent down to kiss the child and he put his mouth in the path of her lips.

"Kiss Juju, Daddy."

She wanted to wipe the grin off his face. He buzzed the child's cheek and let his gaze caress Justine. "Have a good time, and stay out of trouble."

"If I don't get into any right here, I'm perfectly safe," she threw over her shoulder as she rushed out.

He was musing over her words when her personal phone rang. He put Tonya in her crib and dashed across the hall to Justine's room. "Hello."

"Is Ms. Taylor there?"

"She just left," he told the man. "Who's calling?"

"Warren Stokes."

The parasite. "Oh, yes, Warren. How's it going, buddy?"

"Fine. What time will Justine be back?"

He ran his hand over his hair, looked at the mouth piece, and told himself not to react. "I didn't ask Ms. Taylor when she'd be back, so I don't know."

"Where'd she go, do you know?"

Duncan told himself that Warren wanted to needle him and that he shouldn't give him the satisfaction of knowing he'd succeeded. He counted to ten. "My daughter is here with me, which means Ms. Taylor is on her own time doing whatever she likes wherever she pleases. Anything else?"

"I don't suppose I can rely on you to give her a message."

Duncan bristled. "I'll tell her anything you like, because it won't matter a damn to her. What do you say? You're wasting my time."

"You're pretty sure of yourself, aren't you? I'll call again when I think she's home."

"Suit yourself, buddy."

Duncan walked back to Tonya's room when he realized that she'd been calling him. He slapped his left fist into his right palm, thought of what he'd done, and laughed. It wasn't much of a consolation, but it relieved his desire to give old Warren a good sock to the jaw.

* * *

Justine parked in the garage of the Willard Hotel and took the elevator to the lobby. She looked around for Banks, didn't see her, and headed for the dining room.

"Miss Banks is waiting for you," the maitre d' told her.

She followed him to a table in the far corner of the room, which shone brilliantly with hundreds of tiny chandeliers, and knew a sense of wonder as Banks, tall, slender, and so much like Duncan, stood and rushed to meet her.

"You're practically a double for your brother," she told Banks. "It almost gives me the willies."

Banks tugged at her arm. "Our mother was supposed to have twins, but she decided two infants would be too much trouble and postponed me. I'm not as good looking as he is."

Justine couldn't resist hugging her. "God smiled on you, girl, so don't complain."

Each ordered a full course lunch, and Justine wanted to know how Banks stayed so slim. Told that smokers were less likely to eat between meals, Justine resisted telling her that they were also more likely to have some undesirable experiences.

"How's Wayne?" she asked, breaking the ice.

"He's just . . . I don't know how to put it. Special, I guess."

"Do you see him?"

"He took me down to Baltimore to see the Great Blacks In Wax Museum and showed me around the newspaper plant. Then he took me to lunch. It was on a Saturday, and he drove me all around Baltimore. Even showed me his pied-à-terre. That's where he stays when he spends the night in Baltimore."

Justine raised an eyebrow. "What about his etchings? Did you see any of those?"

Laughter rolled out of Banks. "I never cared for those things, so it's good that he didn't plan to show me any. He's a super guy, Justine, but he moves so slow. Darnit."

"I'm always worried when they move too fast. What attracts you to him?"

She almost envied Banks her dreamy-eyed demeanor as she talked about Wayne. "Honest, everything. But I think it's because he's so masculine. You should have seen him sitting on the sofa in his office with his hands locked behind his head and his long legs spread out in front of him. I practically incinerated."

"But there has to be more than that, Banks."

"There is, but I just like a man who sits with his legs wide apart." She whistled softly.

Justine finished chewing her shrimp and drank some water. She had thought Banks inexperienced and now wondered whether she might be naive. "Why? What does that say about a man?"

She needn't have worried. "I could be wrong but, to me, it says he knows who he is and what he's got going for him. Duncan sits like that. Haven't you noticed?"

Justine hoped that her face had an air of innocence. "Uh . . . Yes, I suppose I have."

Banks's eyes widened and a frown creased her face. "Look, girlfriend, I'm no expert on the man-woman business, but I bet there isn't anything about Duncan that you haven't noticed. Which side of his face has a dimple?"

Justine hesitated.

Banks laid her head to one side and shrugged. "Okay, don't tell me, but you know."

Justine blew out the breath she'd been holding. "The right one."

Banks nodded. "Yeah. And I bet you could answer every question I might ask you about Duncan."

"What's your point?" Justine asked her, though she might as well have been questioning the complexity of the universe.

Banks's expression sobered. "I like you a lot, Justine, so I warn you never to ask me a question unless you want my answer. I think you're crazy about Duncan, and I don't think he's immune to you, either. That's why I asked you to lunch today. He's been badly hurt, and you could be what he needs, but you have secrets. I don't want to know what they are. I just want to tell you that I'm in your corner, and that if you're loyal and honest, you've got a real prize."

The pain. Always the insidious pain of living a lie. A life that went against every principle that she held dear. And what choice did she have? She could promise loyalty and even a measure of honesty, but far less than he'd demand. And in the end, she'd have nothing. Banks's fingers touched her hand in a gesture of comfort.

"He's a wonderful person, different from any man I've known. If for no other reason, I'll always cherish this time in his home."

Banks's softly modulated tones reached her as though from a long distance. "Can you and I be friends, Justine? Real friends, I mean. Girlfriends?"

It wouldn't make sense, because you shared your innermost secrets with your girlfriends, and she couldn't promise that. "I want us to be good friends, Banks, but I'm in the peculiar position of working as a servant in your brother's home."

Banks threw up both hands. "Come off it! I'm not ready to pronounce on that yet, so let's not include that in our conversation Okay?"

She wasn't so daring as to question her. "All right. Friends."

Banks seemed unaccountably pleased, causing Justine to wonder if she'd acted wisely in agreeing to a closer friendship with Duncan's sister. "I'm not going to be paranoid about this," she told herself "Are you going to stay with u . . . at Duncan's house tonight?" she asked her.

"Nope. I'm not staying with you and Duncan tonight; I promised our mother I'd go with her to shop for antiques tomorrow afternoon, and if I stay over here, I'd have to get up too early. It's your day off, so why don't you come stay with me? Mama wants to meet you.

So she'd heard the slip. "Banks, I'm off this afternoon, but Duncan may want to go out tonight, and—"

She closed one eye and raised the other eyebrow as Duncan sometimes did when he wanted to show impatience. "We're friends, remember? Duncan will let you do anything you want to that's within reason. But I see I have to make appointments with you. Ready to go?"

After hugs that Justine realized were truly genuine, they

parted in the garage and went to their cars. She told herself that she was anxious to get home because she missed Tonya but, in truth, she felt like her old self—enthusiastic, bubbling with the wonders of the world around her—and needed to share that self with Duncan. She didn't know when her senses had been so alive, so open to life. She parked in Duncan's garage, and stood in front of the house letting the late autumn chill invigorate her. The breeze brought evidence of somebody's outdoor barbecue, as the scent of grilling beef provoked her olfactory glands and the quietly dying sun cast long shadows all around her.

"I hope you enjoyed the afternoon."

She should have known he was near, that he was part of the peace that had settled over her. She couldn't change the way she felt, but she intended to find the strength to avoid involvement and keep her sanity.

"We get on surprisingly well. I enjoyed being with her."

"Was she crying or jubilant about Wayne?"

He'd said it lightly, but she detected a concern. "Neither. She's enchanted with him, and he's gentle with her, but she's impatient, because he moves slowly. I told her I'm always wary of the ones who go too fast."

"Any woman should be. A man ought to give himself time to know what he wants before he makes a move on a woman."

She turned and faced him squarely. "Do you know what you want?"

He frowned, but a smile finally moved over his face. "Always. Knowing what I want has never been a problem for me; the trouble comes in deciding whether I should have it." The glow faded from his eyes, and he looked away into the distance. "You're the most frustrating dilemma I ever faced."

The minute his mood changed, his aura began to swirl around her, reminding her of his male strength and the treasures to be found in his arms. She took a step away from him.

"You say a man ought to know what he wants? I say a woman has to be certain she can handle the consequences of what she wants. You can do something in a moment and spend the rest of your life trying to heal the heartache."

Leaves now brown swirled at their feet, as the wind increased in velocity and the air snapped and sizzled around them. A squirrel raced across the lawn and over Duncan's shoes, the sun cast its last long shadow and slept for the night; far away a dog howled; over on Blair Road, an ambulance screamed for the right-of-way. They neither saw nor heard any of it. Her senses whirled dizzily.

Fists balled up. Legs wide apart. Heat in his eyes. She knew he wasn't going to swallow his truth and braced herself. "If I ever love you, Justine, if I ever hold you and love you . . . Woman, don't talk to me about consequences, because when we're on fire, they won't matter. If I ever love you, Justine, I'll damn well take the consequences."

The implications of his words all but sucked her into him, destroying her will and eating at her sanity. She wanted to leave, for the peace she'd had moments earlier lay scattered around her. Yet, he spoke the truth, and she couldn't deny that she wanted what that truth implied.

Still, she refused to bow to the torment he'd stirred in her. "Our consequences wouldn't be the same, Duncan, and I'm not rash enough to say I'd willingly accept them, because the Lord knows I wouldn't. I want things to stay as they are, and I intend to work overtime making sure of that."

His eyes narrowed, and he nodded as though comprehending something of importance. "Nothing will happen that you don't initiate, Justine. I told you once, you're as safe here as you would be in the Vatican. But like I also said, if you come to me, I will not send you away."

"I know, and I appreciate the assurance, but I have to tell you, Mr. Banks, your self-control is anything but flattering."

His gaze burned her. "You think you want to be around if I let it fly? Open my bedroom door any night your curiosity gets out of hand. Be glad to accommodate you." He slung his arm around her shoulder as he would his sister. "Come on. It's getting cold out here."

* * *

He walked into the house with her, but continued alone to the back garden, bunched his shoulders, and headed for the woods. She knew he wanted her, so he hadn't told her anything. But she'd told him plenty, and if he were unscrupulous, he'd research her life. After all, if anybody knew how to do that, he did. As an investigative journalist, he could get just about any information he wanted. He didn't let himself think hard about the inconsistencies that didn't add up, about his near certainty that he knew her from somewhere, and about her upper-middle-class polish and educated mind. He ought to, but for reasons he couldn't fathom, he couldn't make himself go behind her back for the answers. She did what he'd hired her for, and Tonya loved her. That was what mattered.

He kicked a patch of moss that clung to the roots of a pine, still green. Why hadn't he told her that Warren called? He walked on, enjoying the squirrels and chipmunks that carried acorns to their lairs for the winter's food supply. Ensuring their future. Warren. The man was no slouch, even if he did have a weakness for the connoisseur's whiskey. He didn't seem Justine's type, and he'd bet his last dollar that she didn't want him, but there was no accounting for taste, nor for a person's reasons for getting involved. The wind plowed into him with increasing force, and he turned back toward the house. He didn't want the guy near Justine, but he had no right to interfere.

He went inside, ran up the stairs, and knocked on her door, and his heart took off in a thundering race when she cracked it open and gazed up at him, her vulnerability spread across her face.

"Want to go to the movies tomorrow night?"

He'd known she'd be surprised. "What? Uh . . . I don't think so."

Her demeanor didn't match her words, so he threw in a teaser. "Jack Nicholson. I looked for something with Densel Washington, but nothing's around. How about it?"

"You know that Jack is my favorite."

His stroked the back of his neck with his left hand. He

hated to lie. "He is? Well, I'll be. Want to go? We can eat out first, and Mattie can have the evening off."

"What about Tonya?"

"I'll get a sitter, the one I always used before you came. She's very reliable. What do you say?"

She nodded. "All right. What time?"

"We can leave here anytime after five. See you later." He didn't want to give her a chance to change her mind, so he jogged downstairs to the basement and shot a few games of pool.

Justine couldn't decide whether to dress casually or go for broke. On an impulse, she dialed his cell number.

"Hello."

Strange that he didn't identify himself. "Hi, Duncan, this is Justine. Where are we going for dinner? I need to know what to wear."

"I like the Willard Room, but you had lunch there yesterday. So it's Rive Gauche, unless you'd prefer somewhere else. I already made reservations, though."

She sucked in her breath So he liked the most elegant places in town. She could handle that. "I see you like to go first class. Suits me."

She almost wished she hadn't said it. Maybe a nanny wasn't supposed to know about Rive Gauche. "I like first class," he told her, "but in my estimation the hamburgers at White Castle beat a lot of fifty-dollar veal cutlets. And you don't have to wear a tux in order to eat them."

"You've wearing a tux, for Pete's sake?"

"Not unless you want me to."

She'd love to see him in a tuxedo, but not at the movies. "Heavens no. I'll dress to your business suit. Okay?"

"Gal after my precious heart."

Five o'clock arrived at last, and she inspected herself in the mirror: blue, silk dinner suit; hair down around her shoulders; in her ears the big silver hoops that Duncan loved; and Dior perfume. She liked the effect.

He walked out of Tonya's room just as she started down the stairs. "What's a man to do when a woman is beautiful as well as elegant and clobbers him with a whiff of paradise? Have you declared war?''

''Thanks. I think.''

They walked down the stairs together and, by the time they reached the bottom step, his long fingers twined around hers. ''Let's have a good time,'' he said. ''We won't talk about anything that isn't pleasant. How's that?''

''Your wish is my command.''

He narrowed his eyes in a suggestive look and poked his right cheek with the tip of his tongue. ''Not if you know what I know. You'd be surprised what I wish for.''

Thank God for dark skin, she thought, as hers burned as though afire. ''I wouldn't dare ask.''

He parked around the corner from the Waverly theater in Georgetown at five-thirty, took her hand, and raced to the theater. As they sat down, the curtain rose for the beginning of the five-thirty-five show. He rested her head on his shoulder and gave her several pieces of chocolate.

''I'm already too heavy,'' she grumbled.

''Not for me,'' he whispered. ''To me, you're perfect. Every single, starved-to-death inch of you.''

She couldn't believe he'd said that. ''If I ate any more, I'd probably burst.'' His arm around her shoulder and his hand gently clutching her arm made her feel precious. Desired. It may never happen again, she told herself, using that as an excuse to snuggle closer to him. She closed her eyes, dream-like, and let her thoughts of him run wild.

''I thought that would wake you up,'' Duncan teased, when she sat forward at the sound of Jack Nicholson's voice.

''I wasn't asleep.''

He hugged her closer. ''I know. You were daydreaming.''

''Shhhh,'' came a voice behind them.

He held her hand as they left the theater. ''The restaurant's only a few blocks away. Feel like walking?''

She would have agreed if it had been a mile away. He had reserved a table near a window that faced an elegant courtyard where trees dressed with thousands of tiny white lights twinkled like earthly stars and cast a sensuous glow. Numerous crystal globes lent their radiance to the elegant room, and a sleepy, devil-may-care invitation shone from his eyes. They ordered, and while they waited for the meal, he reached across the table, took her fingers in his hand, and examined them. Was he looking for the print of a wedding band? The thought brought her out of her dream world, but not soon enough.

"You're an enigma," he said, turning her hand palm down in his. "I get so many conflicting signals from you that I wonder sometimes if I'm losing it."

Suddenly alert, she corrected her posture and sat forward. "I'm not aware that I'm doing that, so I hope you won't hold it against me."

"I guess you aren't." He snapped his fingers. "I just remembered my promise that we wouldn't talk about anything unpleasant, and if we get off into what is or isn't going on between you and me, we'll kill the evening."

The waiter brought their food, and he savored the quenelles that lay in a puddle of lobster sauce. "I love this dish, and it's one of the few things I can't get Mattie to try."

She made a note of that and told herself she'd stay home one Sunday night and surprise him. "My leek soup is good, too." She wanted to ask if they could go to one of the nearby clubs and listen to jazz, but decided she'd better let him take the lead."

As if he'd read her mind, he asked, "Want to hear some jazz? Not many of the greats around any longer, but Milt Hinton's over at Café Lautrec a few blocks away. What do you say?"

She realized that he'd planned an evening for them and let her delight in his thoughtfulness reflect on her face.

He looked around as though searching the room. "What is it? What brought on that smile?"

Watch it, girl, she warned herself. He's like a hawk. "I guess I'm . . . happy." There. He'd at least asked a question that she could answer truthfully.

"Aren't you usually happy?"

She reached across the table and took his hand. "Duncan, let's enjoy this evening together. No personal questions. All right?"

His gaze bore into her, burning her. Then as quickly, he smiled, befuddling her senses. "As the lady wishes." The smile vanished, and she knew she'd added one more thing to his lists of doubts and uncertainties. Too bad; she wouldn't let it spoil her evening.

She had thought that he planned for them to sit at a table and listen to the music, but he confided that he hadn't danced in over a year, that he loved to dance. "I feel like dancing. What about you?"

She did, she realized. Kenneth hadn't taken her dancing in well over a year before his death. She pushed thoughts of him out of her mind, raised her arms to Duncan, and gave in to the rhythm. When she danced a respectable distance from his body, he pulled her as close as the air between them would allow.

"You want people to think I've got a contagious disease?" he asked, sparkles flashing in his eyes and the dimple in his right cheek displaying its ability to mesmerize her. "Or are you telling some other guy in here that you're available?"

She stepped on his toe. "Hmmm. Is that the way it's done? If I was dissatisfied with my date, I'd ask him to take me home." She looked around, giving the impression that she was checking the supply of men in the room. "Nothing here worth the gamble, so I might as well enjoy myself with you," she teased.

His white teeth sparkled against his smooth brown skin, and when he winked his left eye at her, she didn't have to be told that he planned some mischief. His body moved into hers and swirled around as the alto saxophone moaned and cried, harnessing the blues for posterity. His steps caught the slow, suggestive rhythm and, with his hand at her waist, he brought her body in line. Teasing. Tempting. Filling her whole being with the heat of desire and her head with wanton thoughts.

"Quit fighting it, Justine. Let yourself go. Give into it. Let's show these so-called dancers how it's done."

Suddenly, the deep voice that could send shivers of delight across her nerve ends changed into a high tenor from her past. "Stop fighting me. It's your fault that you can't come. Let yourself go, dammit. I'm doing my part, for heaven's sake. I said stop fighting me." She grabbed his shoulders, let her head loll on his chest, and fought without success to control the tremor that shot through her.

"Justine! Sweetheart, what's wrong?"

She steadied herself, and his strong arms folded her to him and held her there on the crowded dance floor. "You all right now?"

"I . . . Yes, I'm all right?"

"Come. I'll take you home. If you were all right, that wouldn't have happened."

She had to gather her wits. Would she forever be Kenneth Montgomery's victim? Even from the grave, he could destroy her contentment, disrupt her life, undermine her sense of self. Never again. He had bedeviled her for the last time. She squared her shoulders. "I'm fine now, Duncan, and I don't want to go home. I don't know when I've had such a wonderful evening, and I'm not ready for it to end."

He eyed her carefully, as would a surgeon scrutinizing an x-ray. "Are you absolutely certain?"

"I'm sorry if I distressed you. It passed, and I'm fine now."

"Was it the way you felt? A dizzy spell?"

She owed him an explanation, so she said as much as she could. "No. Just an ugly memory."

He shook his head, and his facial expression was that of a saddened man. "I see. And it's cropped up before since we've known each other, hasn't it?"

"Yes. Please, don't ask more."

As though to protect her, he folded her in his arms and drew her close. "All right. We'll leave it. For now."

And she didn't doubt that, when he got ready, he'd demand some answers.

He had no choice but to take her word for it, so he led her back to the table and waited for a slower number. "It surprised me to learn that you like jazz," he said, hoping for a topic that would help salvage the evening. "At home, you listen to classical music, especially brother Mozart. How's that?"

He must have chosen the right words, because he could almost see the tension flow out of her body. "All my jazz is on long playing records, and I'm not going to buy the same thing on CDs. I don't have a record player, and finding one these days is like collecting hens' teeth. I wish I could play my records."

"Who's your favorite?"

Her smile lit up the dark room and made everything around them beautiful, but if he told her that, she'd probably turn around to see who he was talking about. "I love so many of the classical jazz musicians." Sadness momentarily streaked across her visage. Then, as if brightened by a memory, the sun shone once more from her face. "I could dance all night to Fats Waller's "Ain't Misbehavin' " and Jimmy Lunceford's "Uptown Blues." Problem is, all the great ones are gone."

He didn't want to change the subject, but he didn't want her reminiscing, either. Something in her past had nearly wrecked her, and he'd better forestall any reference to it or risk a recurrence of that throwback she'd had moments earlier. "Think you can risk a dance with me?"

Ah, things were back to normal. Her glare let him know that the Justine who never ducked a challenge was once more with him. "What is there about you that would make dancing with you risky?" She pushed back her chair as she said it.

He grinned, and then he laughed; his gaiety was as much a catharsis as jubilance. "If you didn't find out earlier, I'll be glad to show you."

On the floor, she moved with him, accepting every challenge and laughing at him. She stepped back so he could see her toss her head, wink, rotate her hips, and beckon him toward her with her right index finger, and he thanked God for the crowded room.

He pulled her to him and growled, "Keep that up and what you'll get will be more than a surprise. It's almost midnight, Cinderella. I'm taking you home." The smile left her face. "Wait a minute," he said. "I know what that's all about, and I'm not having it."

She shrugged. "But it was a perfect analogy. I'm Cinderella tonight, and tomorrow, I'll be Tonya's nanny again."

He helped her into her coat, paid the bill, and ushered her out into Eighteenth Street's brisk chill. They barely spoke on the drive home. He drove into the garage, walked around to her side of the car, and opened the door while she was trying to release the seat belt. When he took her hand to help her out, she stumbled into him, but he knew that her clumsiness was due to nerves.

"Like a drink?" he asked her, when they entered the foyer.

"Uh . . . No. No thanks. I'm turning in. Thanks for the evening. It was wonderful."

"We . . . Why don't you sit with me for a few minutes. I think I'll have a cognac. Let me help you with your coat."

Between her exquisite perfume that shouted her womanhood and the tension radiating from her body, he figured he stood little chance of telling her good night without incident. She turned toward him with a smile that she'd obviously plastered on her face and that told him he had read her correctly. Her nerves were as tangled as his own.

"Thanks. Good night," she whispered and started around him.

He wouldn't have touched her, if her soft breast hadn't caressed his arm, reminding him of what he needed and didn't have. He couldn't say how she got into his arms, but she was in them, squeezing him to her and moaning while his tongue circled her lips begging to get in. She opened to him. Took him. Welcomed him. *Stop it, man,* he warned himself, but she fought for his tongue until he capitulated and let her feast. Knowing what would come next, he sought to set her away from him, but she clung. Loving him. Cherishing him. His breath came fast and hard and, in spite of his efforts at control, he rose against her. Stunned by his wild response, he lifted her to fit him, and she held him, kissing and caressing him.

"Justine, for God's sake, I'm human," he whispered, unable to find his full voice.

When she didn't seem to hear him, he lowered her to her feet, hugged her close, and spoke near her ear. "Honey, you either get up those stairs right this second, or I break my promise to you."

"Duncan, I need you."

"And I need you. But if I do this, I will not like myself tomorrow and maybe not you either; you have to help me."

"I could love you. Oh, Duncan, I could love you."

"Tell me about it," he said under his breath. He watched her as she fled up the stairs with the speed of a five-year-old, then went to the bar in his living room and almost repeated what he'd done the day Marie walked out. He was on the third cognac, when he remembered Tonya, capped the bottle, and headed for his room. Some night! He needed to have a good long talk with himself, and he had a lot of questions for Justine.

He led the babysitter to the waiting taxi, went back in the house, looked up the stairs, and began what he figured would be the longest and most difficult climb of his life.

CHAPTER EIGHT

After the night she'd had, she wondered whether she'd suffer more if she left and tried to forget about Tonya. Memories of Kenneth's harshness—things she'd never taken exception to until she knew Duncan—had tortured her until daybreak. And her certainty that she would find in Duncan all she'd missed and all she could ever want had tormented her until she'd come close to walking across the hall and knocking on his bedroom door.

A look at her watch told her that it was early for a call to her godfather, seven-thirty, but she had to talk with someone.

"I've fallen in love with him, Uncle Hugh. I still haven't told him anything about myself, and I know he doesn't want to be involved, but we can't seem to . . . to keep our hands off each other."

She could imagine that last remark had brought him fully awake, for he was, if anything, a moralist. "Now just wait here, Justine. I told you not to take him up on it if he made a move on you. That's the worst thing you could—"

"Nothing like that has happened, Uncle Hugh, but I'm grown, and I know it's not far off. If I compromise myself, I can forget about Tonya."

"You didn't even tell him about that column?"

"My contract forbids my telling anyone. I had to tell you, because I'll go crazy keeping all this to myself."

"You know I wouldn't breathe it in my prayers, girl. How's Tonya? Do you get along?"

"She adores me. And that's another problem; she looks more like me every day. The housekeeper already mentioned it, and Duncan is bound to notice it soon. How many people do you see with these grayish-brown eyes?"

His long whistle irritated her ear. "I'll do all I can, but that won't be much. You just hope the guy falls so hard for you that he'll forgive you just about anything."

She paced as far as the cord would reach, then retraced her steps. "That's one more problem, Uncle Hugh. He loved his wife, and she stabbed him, so to speak, and turned the knife. He's not going that way again."

"Don't be too sure. Nature likes to take these things out of our hands."

If only time proved him right. *If.* That word had been her constant companion since she was five years old. She thanked him and hung up.

Duncan sat at his desk that morning, trying without success to outline his story on America's youth, his concentration shot. "Stop kidding yourself, man, and get out of here," he said, his patience with himself dwindling. He called Wayne.

"I need a couple of days to myself. I want to work out my plans for that series on juveniles and check out a few other things, so I'll be at my place in Curtis Bay on the Chesapeake. You have the number."

"Doing any fishing?"

"Depends on the weather. I'm taking along my gear."

"Get it straightened out, man. And give Justine my regards."

He thought he heard a snicker, and he wasn't in the mood for Wayne's antics. "What does that mean?"

"Don't get your back up. Just wishing you the best."

He hung up and began packing his books, notes, laptop

computer, tackle, and a few clothes. "I'll be away for a few days," he told Justine at breakfast, "but I'll call you. Remember if you ever have any problems, phone my attorney." He handed her the lawyer's card. "But if you need me, I'll have my cell phone with me. Just call."

At breakfast, they toyed with their food, and he wanted to close his eyes to avoid seeing the pain in hers. Her night hadn't been any better than his, but he could at least change the scene. He had to be honest with her, so he reached across the table and touched her hand. "Justine, I need to get away and do some thinking and, while I'm gone, you do the same. Tonya loves both of us, but if we don't get this thing straightened out, all three of us will lose something important. I'll see you next week."

Calm and self-possessed, as though she hadn't a care and giving the lie to the misery written on her face, she smiled and asked him, "Are you going far?"

"I have a place in Curtis Bay, Maryland, about forty-five miles from here. I thought I'd go there for a while."

"Have a good time," she whispered, and he had to steel himself against the urge to hold her. But he couldn't make it better, so he winked at her, sped upstairs to kiss Tonya goodbye, and headed for Curtis Bay.

Hours later, shielded from the rough ocean weather by his old leather jacket, he strolled along the narrow beach of the Chesapeake where the crabbers' buckets bobbled in the water, sand swirled around him, and the wind bruised his face. He wondered why he'd bothered. He'd thought he left her on Primrose Street, but she was on that beach with him. He walked around the cove, rubbing his numb fingers, picked up a few pieces of driftwood, and trekked back to the lodge. He made a fire in the fireplace, put some hot clogs on the end of a stick, and cooked his dinner. He'd gotten his life in order, or so he'd thought, but lately a feeling of being uprooted and displaced wouldn't leave him. Justine. Always Justine. If he believed in reincarnation, he's swear he'd known her in another life. Why did she seem so familiar?

He told himself he'd get down to work if he knew how

Tonya was, so he called home. "Let me speak with Justine," he told Mattie when she answered.

"They's in the basement with that piano, Mr. B. I tell you, that child loves that piano."

"Have you heard Justine play yet?"

"Now that is something for the ears. She plays in the mornings, but Tonya kicked up such a fuss after you left that she took her down there and played for her. I'll call her."

What was wrong with him? His heart seemed to have stopped pumping. Her voice came to him warm and sweet. "Hello, Duncan. Where are you?"

"At the lodge. How's it going there?"

When she hesitated, he knew she questioned his reason for calling. But he had to talk with her and, if it meant making small talk, he'd do it.

"Be sure to call me if you need me," he said after a few inconsequential words, and hung up. He paced the room for a few minutes. "She'll just have to go," he told himself, then laughed at the thought, opened his computer, and began to outline his research.

In the days that followed, he couldn't shake his feeling of rootlessness, of being adrift. He called home daily, usually twice, but his talks with Justine only whetted his appetite for more of her. Four days before his scheduled return, he called three times, hung up, said the hell with it and headed for home. Half way there, he passed a radio and electronics store and stopped.

"We do have one record player," the clerk told him, "but it's expensive. They're hard to find."

He fished in his pocket for his gold credit card. "If it plays LP's, wrap it up."

He didn't think he'd ever forget the expression on her face when she opened the package, and he marveled that such a small thing could bring so much joy. A sweetness radiated from her, and when she looked at him, her face glowed as though reflecting a light from the heavens. She walked as on wings while the house rocked with Jimmy Lunceford's "Uptown Blues." Even Tonya slapped her little hands to the beat. He'd never been more convinced that little gestures sometimes produced the most profound joy.

The morning after Duncan left for Curtis Bay, Justine received a menacing call. "You think you're so clever," the man said, "but you'll learn who to mess around with."

"Who's this?" she asked, trying to keep him on the line until she could press the record button.

"You think I'm stupid enough to tell you? You should've worried about that when you meddled in my business." He hung up.

The following night, he called again. "I have caller ID," she told him, "and you're in trouble."

His dark, menacing laugh sent chills through every molecule of her body. "So what. You think I'm stupid enough to call you from my house?"

"Who do you want here?" she asked, hoping to get a clue to his reason for calling.

"Figure it out." He hung up.

As far as she knew, she didn't have one enemy, so she wasn't going to be frightened. The idea began to recur that she'd better tell Duncan, but if she did, he'd have a barrage of questions to which she had no answers.

Deciding not to go to the post office for her mail, she called the postal clerk and asked him to hold it until she could get there, and learned that she had an armful of letters.

She looked through some unanswered ones and quickly wrote several columns for use in case of an emergency. One woman wrote that her teenaged daughter had run away. The letter amounted to pages of invective against the girl whom the mother called an ingrate for having fled after all she had done for her. The words brought back to Justine the days when she had wanted to run away, to find someone, anyone, who would show her genuine affection. She wrote a harsh letter, read it over, and tore it up.

"What your daughter needs is love, unselfish love," she wrote from her heart, words she wished someone had spoken to her aunts. "Love that asks nothing in return. No one on this earth would run away from that. And it wouldn't hurt to begin by telling her that you haven't been a wise mother. All the best, Aunt Mariah."

She answered four other letters, completed the column and peeped into Tonya's room. While the child slept, she could begin cataloging her collection of miniature busts. Forty-seven beautifully sculpted tiny busts of old black men, each one unique. She had procrastinated about doing it ever since she'd come to Duncan's home, because of the memories it was sure to trigger. She opened the box, found a soft cloth, and began dusting and oiling the wood, and didn't hear Duncan when he climbed the stairs, saw that her door was ajar, and paused there.

"Hello, Justine."

"Duncan! Where did you come from?"

He dashed into the room to catch the bust that teetered on the edge of her desk. "Hi. I cut short my stay at the lodge. How's Tonya?"

"You cut . . . She's asleep. She's . . . fine. Duncan, you frightened me almost out of my mind. I didn't hear a sound. Big as you are, you ought to make noise when you walk." She grabbed her chest. "You scared me."

His eyes devoured her, thrilled her with unuttered suggestions. "Sorry. Next time I'll blow a horn. Maybe then I'll get a decent welcome."

His gaze settled on the little busts, and she remembered them and began wrapping each one to put them away, but they'd already caught his attention.

"What are these?" He turned one over and around, examining it. "This is one exquisite piece of carving. Looks like something by Wesley Arne."

She nodded.

The eyes that perused her face asked for answers. But how was she to tell him that her aunts and her father had each given them to her whenever they'd done something to displease her, without giving him the whole story of her young life? Without dredging up the reality of a child's poverty in the midst of wealth. Yet, in spite of what they signified, she had loved the little miniatures and, when she began working, had continued the collection.

"That's a bag of money there," he commented, his eyes accusing her of she didn't know what. "And a damned big bag, too. I'd better turn in." He left her, taking with him the joy that had suffused her when she looked up and saw him leaning against her door.

Half a hundred Wesley Arne sculptures. Priceless miniatures. He shook his head. No, he wasn't going to stoop to investigating her, and he wasn't going to interrogate her about her affairs. He should have done that before he hired her. But from now on, he was going to use his God-given senses, and maybe he'd get over his raging hunger for her. He tossed his duffle bag in the closet and thought about how he'd practically risked his life speeding back home. To her. He ran his hand over his tight curls. She couldn't be as perfect as she seemed, and if she had one frayed edge, he'd see it sooner or later. He'd gone to Curtis Bay to think. A mistake. All he'd done there was need her. The place for him was home with her, where he could see her shortcomings, her faults, see the little things that would remind him to keep his distance.

What a time for him to walk in there. If she had needed a reminder of the fragility of her status with him, he'd just demonstrated it. When she'd looked up, his eyes had been fiery balls of desire, but when he saw her treasures, they became icy pools of disinterest. She wrapped the pieces, put them in the box, and stored them in the back of her closet. Duncan had jumped to a conclusion when he saw them, and she couldn't blame him. Nannies weren't expected to own art of that quality nor to have other tastes that she'd exhibited. She wondered when he'd finally confront her.

The ring of her telephone interrupted her thoughts. "Hello."

"How are things going, girl? I can't seem to get you off

my mind. You don't have to write that column, and if you give it up, that's one less thing you'd be hiding from him."

"Uncle Hugh. I'm so glad you called. Things aren't any better." She told him as much as she thought he should know. "The column is the least of my problems. I'd have told him about it if my contract didn't forbid it. You're the only person who knows other than the folks at the paper."

"Arnold doesn't know?"

"No. Daddy still doesn't return my calls."

"I see. I may have a talk with that fellow. He's not perfect, and I'm one person who knows it. You can ask your boss for permission to tell Duncan about the column."

He offered other suggestions, but none would solve her dilemma. After hanging up, she went over to Tonya's room and found the child singing and playing with her bears. She dressed her, took her down to the basement, and sat her in a high chair while she played Chopin waltzes. After a while, she moved from the piano, got a book, and began to read *The Song of Hiawatha.* She knew Tonya didn't understand the words, but she loved the hypnotic rhythm of the phrases and hummed as though singing to music. The child clapped her hands, enjoying the rhythm of Longfellow's epic poem.

"Want to read *Beowulf, The Brave Prince?*" she asked Tonya.

"Yes. Yes." Tonya slapped her hands. "Baywuf."

Justine read a passage of the Scandinavian tale, while Tonya tried to mouth the words, stopped, and asked her, "Why don't you like Dunbar's poems?"

"Baywuf," the child replied, and kissed Justine on the cheek as though to make sure she'd get what she asked for. Justine covered her face with her hands and lowered her head for a second, getting her bearings. She had so much. And nothing. But she wouldn't let it break her; five months earlier, she hadn't had this much. She'd cherish it while she had it.

* * *

Duncan stood at the door of the large basement room trying to deal with his emotions as he watched Justine and Tonya. Here was proof of the care she gave his child, for Tonya had heard those stories so many times that she knew and enjoyed them. He didn't think he'd ever be able to separate them, unless Justine gave him a criminal reason. But who was she? Polished. Well educated. Self-assured. A woman with class and style. And she hired herself out as a nanny. The idea returned that she might be a part of an experiment. He pushed back the anger that had begun to unfurl in him. Neither the relationship between her and Tonya nor his hunger for her was going to make him hold still while she hoodwinked him. If he had a wife, Tonya would transfer some of her affection for Justine to his wife, the woman who would be her mother.

A wife. What had happened to the numerous phone calls that had once driven him nearly to distraction? He walked into the room, ignored Tonya's gleeful welcome, and asked Justine, "Have you taken any calls from women who asked to speak with me?"

She shifted Tonya to the other side of her lap, "Are you suggesting that I wouldn't have given you your messages?"

He looked closely at her. "I should have gotten some calls, and it is strange that there haven't been any since . . . for the last few months."

She looked straight at him, and he saw no guilt in her expression. "I'm sorry if you've been disappointed."

He thought about that for a moment. Sorry? She didn't look it. "By the way, that's the first time I heard you play. You're gifted, and you're . . ." He spun around toward the stairs.

Tonya held out her arms to him. "Daddy. Daddy. Kiss Tonya. Ice cream. Baywuf."

He took her from Justine's lap without looking into the eyes of the woman who flitted through his dreams. "You're getting big," he said, as he kissed her cheek and received some wet ones in return. Justine held out her arms, and he gave the child back to her, but he knew it had been an involuntary gesture, a reaching out to him. Sorrow filled him as he headed upstairs.

"Mattie, have any women called here for me recently?"

She took her time turning around to look at him and, when she did, she had her hands stuck on her hips. "Why you axin me, Mr. B? You know I don't answer no phones when I can help it. Far as I'm concerned, whoever invented them coulda kept his smartness to hisself."

Annoyed at Mattie's flippancy, he whirled around and headed for the basement. He wanted some answers. But when he reached it, Justine sat where he'd left her and held Tonya close to her breast while her closed eyes guarded a stricken expression. Hopelessness if he'd ever seen it. Desperation like the subdued chirp of a bird no longer able to sing leaped out from her and settled round him. The hurt in her tore at his insides and, shaken with the need to protect and shelter her, he rushed to her and eased down beside her on his haunches.

"Justine, can't you tell me what's eating you? Half a dozen times since you came here, I've seen this raw pain in you. Sometimes, it passes so quickly that I think I imagined it. But I know something is wrong, Justine. Why can't you trust me? Haven't I shown you that I'm honorable? Don't you know that by now? You're holding in a lot. Talk to me."

When her bottom lip quivered, every instinct he had wanted her in his arms, to hold her and cherish her. But he knew where that would end, so he steeled himself against the empathy.

"Talk to me."

She held Tonya closer, possessively, and began to rock her, and her attempts to speak ended in noiseless declarations. Disgusted with himself that he might have added to her unhappiness, he spoke softly. "I couldn't be more pleased about the way you're caring for my daughter. I couldn't ask for more. You're a born mother."

Her eyelids flew up, and he'd swear he'd never witnessed such raw vulnerability. She did little more than mouth the words, "I don't want Tonya to experience what I went through." He had to lean forward to understand her. "After my mother's funeral, my father took me and my belongings to my older aunt. I stayed with her one week and with my other aunt the next week. And that was the pattern until I went to college. I didn't have any friends, because they didn't want children destroying their perfect homes, and when I wasn't eating or practicing the piano, I had to be in my room. Nobody ever hugged and kissed me. They didn't mistreat me, but if either of them loved me, they kept it a secret. When I complained they wouldn't let me be like other children, either an aunt or my father gave me one of those Wesley Arne figures as an appeasement. I loved the miniatures, because the old men had such dignity and were so beautiful, but I've never been sentimental about them. When you judged me because of them, well . . . I had looked forward to your coming back and . . . just now, you were mean."

"Yes. I was. But there's so much that isn't right with us, Justine; my words of apology would ring hollow to me. I can tell you truthfully, though, that I can't stand to see you hurt. I want to hold you, but I dare not; this time, I don't think I could stop."

The mockery of her smile stunned him. "Oh, yes, you could. Mattie's right upstairs."

He raised an eyebrow. "Mattie doesn't have the key to the basement; I do. I'm not usually reckless, honey, but a challenge may spur me to unusual behavior, and where you're concerned, I want to move with a sound mind and an unfettered ego. I've told you twice that we have to talk. One day we will." As he stood, he leaned over and kissed her lips. "I'm going back upstairs."

Midway up, his cell phone rang. "Yeah. Hello," he added, correcting himself.

"Hi. This is Banks. Mama will be sixty-five in a few weeks. Let's give her a party."

"Sixty-five? Oh. Okay. Good idea. How're things going with you and Wayne?"

"Fine. I figured I was moving too fast, so I took Justine's advice and we're getting along."

"Long as you're satisfied, but if it doesn't fit, don't force it. The world is full of men."

Her laughter came to him as bells in a warm spring

breeze. "Duncan, I expect to have Roundtree on my tombstone, so not to worry; it's all settled."

He held the phone away from him and stared at it. Was she crazy? "Who said it's all settled? Getting to that point takes two people."

"Adam and Melissa are home with their new son, and that's all Wayne can talk about He's nuts about that baby. I sure hope he's getting ideas."

"Leah, watch out. If a man hasn't said the words, he hasn't made a commitment, and sometime he isn't committed if he does say the words. So be careful."

The bells tinkled again. "I hear you. Where's Justine?"

He transferred the call to the hall phone and asked Justine to take it. He wasn't sure he cared for the growing affection he observed between Justine and his sister, because he didn't want Leah to suffer if he and Justine went their separate ways.

Banks had other thoughts. She intended to do whatever she could to make her brother see that Justine was the woman for him. She told Justine about her mother's coming birthday. "I want you to come and so does Mama, and I'm sure Duncan wants Mama to see how Tonya's growing."

"Banks, I'd love to come, but it's up to Duncan; it has to be."

"All right. All right. Mama will tell him to bring you and Tonya. Be sure and don't plan anything else for that weekend."

She hung up, called Wayne, and told him about her mother's coming birthday event.

"Speaking of mothers, mine wants to meet you," Wayne said.

He might as well have dashed cold water on her. "Wayne, Miss Mary knows who I am, and she's seen me plenty of times. Isn't that enough?"

"You wouldn't be afraid to meet my mother, would you? Every time I ask you over here, you give me an excuse. She's like anybody else."

"Are we talking about the same person?"

"Leah, we're talking about my mother."

"Wayne, she's a . . . a heavy duty lady."

His deep rolling laughter could make her giddy with happiness. And he let the laughter pour out. "Why don't I drive over and we go to *The Watering Hole*? Okay?"

"Half hour." She hung up, rushed to the shower, got a quick one, and was zipping up her blue velveteen jumpsuit when the doorbell rang.

He whistled when she opened the door. "Hi. You move fast. I thought I'd catch you without your 'tweeds' this once. Ready to go?"

She folded her arms and braced herself against the wall. "Absolutely not! I didn't get dressed up to walk out of here with you without at least a peck on the cheek, Mister."

Even white teeth sparkled against his dark skin, and lights danced in his hazel eyes. For two cents, she'd just fold herself in his arms and stay there. "You want a kiss?"

She glared at him. "Perish the thought." She got her coat from a closet in the foyer and would have put it on if he hadn't taken it from her.

"Come here, Leah."

Why didn't he just kiss her and quit stalling. "What for?"

He threw the coat across a chair and pulled her into his arms. "For this." His lips teased hers, brushing across them, and she refused to ask for more, but when he gave the impression of releasing her, she wondered if she'd overplayed the coolness. She put her hands on his shoulders, and felt his finger raise her chin. He wasn't smiling.

"I can't tease all the time, Leah. I need to feel you tight in my arms, but if you don't want that . . ."

She loosened her grip on his shoulders and relaxed against him. "Don't pay any attention to me, Wayne. When it comes to you, I don't know what I'm doing."

The sweetness. She slumped against him while he tortured her mouth, holding her head to increase their pleasure, and when he released her lips, she let her head loll on his shoulder for a minute. Then she reached for her coat.

"What's the matter? You didn't like the kiss?"

She put her arm in a sleeve while he held the coat. "It was . . . wonderful."

"Then what's the problem?"

Might as well be honest. She laid her head to one side and looked at him from beneath long lashes. "The problem is I don't like having my brain scrambled."

His laughter wrapped around her like warm sunshine. "Let's go."

After dinner that night, Duncan telephoned Justine, though she was across the hall from him, because he didn't care to be dragged into her orbit when he was on his way to Capital View. In that dangerous environment, his survival could depend on having his wits sharp and his feet ready to move.

"Hello."

He wondered why she'd hesitated so long before speaking. "This is Duncan. I've got to run a couple of errands. If you need me, call my cell number. See you in the morning."

"Take care."

The concern in her voice said she might fear for his safety. But why should she? She didn't know where he went nor what he did, though she'd tried to guess. "That I will," he replied, keeping it light. "Good night." He stopped in Tonya's room, saw that she was asleep, and headed for the garage where he put on the "street" clothes that he wore as an undercover journalist, pulled a navy blue woolen cap down to his eyebrows, and drove off.

He parked several blocks from his destination and walked to Bladensburg.

"Say, brother." A man sidled up to him at the edge of an alley. "You wouldn't have a light?"

Duncan turned off his cell phone, because a ring would trigger the man's suspicion. He pressed his recorder and pretended to look for a lighter. "Looks like some cat took it off me, man," he replied. If he'd said he didn't smoke, he'd have provoked the man's curiosity, because everyone on the street smoked *something*.

"What can I get you, man?" the stranger asked.

Alert to trouble, Duncan only gave the appearance of being relaxed. "Not even a drink of water, brother. The guy who went off with my lighter got every cent."

The man looked from side to side, lit a cigarette, and assured Duncan, "No problem. Your credit's good."

"Thanks, man, but I owe everybody on the street from here to East of the River, and you know what happens when you can't pay up. If it gets bad, I'll look you up." He extended his hand to the stranger. "My name's Dunc. Don't forget it."

"If you get stuck, Dunc, here's my pager. Six to nine every evening. Just ask for Joe." He walked on, and with that slip-slide gait, he'd be easily recognizable if they met again.

Duncan stood there long enough to be sure the man who called himself Joe wouldn't return, and struck out for East of the River. Kids taking orders for drugs with pagers and regular business hours. He flicked off his recorder and quickened his steps. He'd begun to tire of the seedy side of his job. And now that he had Tonya, he had to consider the dangers involved.

He passed a woman sitting on the street beside her belongings, and his mind went back twenty-seven years to that day when his family sat homeless on the sidewalks of Bolton Street in the freezing cold. His hatred for Hugh Pickford flared anew.

His cell phone rang. "Yeah."

"Say, Pops, this is Mitch. Haven't seen ya 'round, and me and Rags heard you been looking for us. Not to worry. We're going to school every day, and we been checking out the shelter like you said. It beats that roach trap of ours, and the food's pretty good. When you coming 'round? Some guy came by here said he wanted to teach us how to play chess. Is that legal?"

"Chess? Legal as taxpaying, so long as you don't gamble. Take him up on it. Supposed to be a great game. Where's Rags?"

"He's right here, man. You be 'round tonight?"

If the boys were all right, he could go home and write.

"I'm headed home. Call me if you two need anything, Mitch."

"Gotcha, Pops."

Duncan reversed his steps, got into his car and went home. He parked in the garage, walked to his front door, and stopped. Why had the women stopped calling about his marriage proposal? He read Dee Dee's column every day, and the notice appeared at the end of each one, but nobody called. Maybe marriage prospects for women twenty-eight to thirty-four were better than people thought. He told himself he wouldn't glance toward Justine's door. But when he got to the top of the stairs, his gaze went straight to the light beneath her door. He had to laugh at himself.

"Justine, woman," he said as he closed his bedroom door, "all you need is a big black hat that has a wide brim and a pointed top, and a broom. A normal woman couldn't do this to me."

The following afternoon, Duncan stopped by his office at *The Maryland Journal*, checked his mail, and would have headed for CafeAhNay if Dee Dee hadn't challenged him when he passed her open door.

"Still single, I see. You sure you're not just putting up a front?"

He stepped inside her office and leaned his right shoulder against the powder-blue wall. "The problem is your column. If I've stopped getting responses, maybe it's because nobody's reading your column."

"I'm crushed," she said, leaving her desk and strolling to where he stood. "Half a dozen women have called here and said that line I run for you is a hoax, that you're already married. I don't know why they'd think that, but if you're still looking, I could run your handsome picture."

He grimaced. "Definitely not. No way."

She eyed him from beneath her lashes. "Maybe you should look a little closer to home. I wouldn't be a bad companion for a man-about-town."

He was about to tell her how foolish an idea it was when

he realized that she was serious. He put an arm around her shoulder. "Dee, I couldn't marry my sister, and that's what you are to me."

Her rueful smile told him that her suggestion had been anything but casual. She shrugged. "Your sister, huh? Knowing you, that's an honor, though I have to say it's a dubious one."

He told her good-bye and left the building. Something wasn't right; why would any woman who called his house think he'd gotten married? As he drove, light, drifting snow flakes obscured his vision, and he decided he'd better go home and finish his series.

Duncan walked into an empty house. Knowing that Justine and Tonya were out in the snow, even a light one, annoyed him and, besides, he hated getting home and finding that she wasn't there. The hall phone rang.

"Hello."

A woman wanted to know if he was Duncan Banks and if he was still satisfied with his choice for a wife and didn't intend to interview anyone else.

Wait a minute, he thought, as his mind jumped into action. "What do you mean, am I still satisfied?"

She hesitated as though unsure of her facts. "Well . . . The lady said the position had been filled and, you know—"

His hand gripped the phone, bruising his palm. "When was that?"

"I called a lot of times, and every time, that's what she said. Is it open? I mean did you get married yet or did you change your mind or . . . or something?"

He jotted down her name and phone number and told her he'd call her back. Mattie had said she hadn't taken any calls, and he couldn't believe Justine would do such a thing. But who else? Tonya couldn't even pronounce her own name properly.

Half an hour later, Justine, Mattie, and Tonya burst into the front door. Tonya greeted him with open arms and Justine explained that someone had stolen the battery out of Moe's car and taxis weren't answering calls, so she'd gone to Mattie's house and gotten her.

"I would have left a note, but I thought we'd be back before you got home," Justine explained.

"No harm done, but I'm getting you a cell phone and, if necessary, I'll glue it to you. Woman, you're going to give me gray hairs. When you get Tonya settled, I want to ask you something." He kept his voice light. "I'll be in my office."

She nodded, and he watched her trudge slowly along so that Tonya could climb the stairs. When he could no longer see them from where he stood in the foyer, he went to the kitchen to speak to Mattie, though he knew he wasted his time.

"Mr. B, did you think I was lying to you?" she asked, when he mentioned the calls. "That woman don't have to be telling the truth. Why you care, anyhow? I got sick of them women callin' here and acting like they was the Queen of Sheba, but I never told them nothing. Just took they names. Them callin' all the time wasn't a good thing for Tonya."

He patted her slight shoulder. "I didn't think you'd tell me an untruth; I had to check. It's settled, now, so don't worry about it."

He had a theory, but he didn't think testing it would earn him any points with Justine. Curiously, she didn't display annoyance when he asked her about it.

"Either the woman was lying or you had what you considered a justifiable reason for doing it. Did you tell any woman that I'd settled on a wife?"

She showed no remorse, but looked him in the eye and said, "I don't remember saying that you'd settled on a wife. In fact, I know I didn't. In every case, I was careful to state that the position had been filled. They didn't ask which position, and I let them think what they liked."

He fingered his chin, wondering why he wasn't surprised. "How many women did you tell that?"

Her right shoulder bunched in a careless shrug. "I don't know exactly, Duncan. Maybe fifteen, or it could have been more."

"Why'd you do it?" The huskiness in his voice astonished him; what was he hoping she'd say?

Without hesitating, she told him, "Because I didn't want anyone else to take care of Tonya."

He mused over that and decided that it didn't ring true; it was an excuse, not the reason. "I wasn't looking for a nanny, but a wife, and I suspect you knew that. Why would you think you couldn't be my child's nanny if I got married? Was it because you didn't want to see me—"

She almost knocked over the chair as she got up and bolted out of the room. He didn't stop to think, but raced after her. She shoved at her bedroom door with all of her body's force, but he grabbed the door knob, and they plowed into her room together.

"Have you lost . . . Duncan, are you crazy?"

He pulled her to him, wrapped her in his arms, and with his free hand, tilted up her chin so he could see the grayish-brown eyes that followed him everywhere he went.

"You called them off because you want me for yourself. Don't deny it."

She had guts and plenty of it. "If you're not going to fire me, please leave me alone. I told you the truth."

Her mouth was so close and so sweet. God help him, he had to taste her, feel her spin out of control while he kissed her, had to shatter her will, to assure himself that if he chose, she was his. When, as though impatient for him, she reached up, clasped his head and brought his mouth to hers, he thought he would explode as he soaked up the passion that she poured over him, lost himself in her frenzied kiss and gloried in her wild abandon. Then, it was he who nearly lost command of his will, he who had to battle the influence of her woman's scent, to resist the sweet torture of her soft mounds pressing against him. He looked around for . . . Good Lord. He was in her bedroom, seconds from disrobing her. Minutes from pouring himself into her warm tunnel of love. Minutes from heaven and the devil take the morrow. He backed away. Damned if he'd let his libido lead him as though he were a puppy on a leash.

He took her hand, walked with her to his office, and offered her a straight back chair. This was the fourth time they'd been headed for the limit and the fourth time he'd put on the brakes. He told her as much.

"If you're counting on my self-control, Justine, don't. On the other occasions, I didn't want us to make love, but tonight for some reason, I wanted it. Badly. And I still do. If this ever happens again, I don't promise to stop; protecting you from myself is getting harder and harder."

She got up and walked to the door, then turned and faced him. "If you knew what you were doing, that would probably be sufficient to assure your self-control. But you don't, so—"

"And you aren't telling me," he cut in.

"So don't put your hands on me. That way, you won't start a fire, because I certainly am not going to walk up to you and begin testing my feminine powers."

"But you don't resist."

"What happens when you pour water on a thirsty plant, Duncan?"

"You're telling me you're missing something?"

"No, I'm not. You have to know a thing in order to miss it. Good night."

For the next hour, he sat as she'd left him. Not for anything would he take that sentence apart. Maybe he hadn't been fair; after all he was as much a participant as she. He let his thoughts roam. What kind of life was it for an intelligent woman cooped up in a house six or seven days a week with a baby for company? True, she took the position voluntarily, but she needed a respite from it. It occurred to him that he hadn't been to the Adirondacks since his divorce. Several days at the log cabin he rented in Indian Lake might be just what she needed. To his astonishment, she embraced his suggestion with enthusiasm.

"Just the three of us?" she asked, as if on second thought.

He tried to put her at ease. "The place has two bedrooms, and Tonya could share with you, if you don't mind. The owners serve great meals and their place is a short walk away, so we wouldn't have to cook, although the cabin has a full kitchen. Okay?"

The glow on her face nearly undid him. He started downstairs to tell Mattie that she would have some days off then stopped. When Justine had smiled, she'd reminded him of someone, but he couldn't place the person. He'd known her from somewhere, he'd swear it.

CHAPTER NINE

Justine reflected on her feelings while her child played around her feet. She had always reached toward her father, grasping for any straw of warmth that might accidentally escape him. She had looked for affection in her aunts, her husband. Always denied. Oh, Kenneth had gone through the motions of warmth, but she now knew that it hadn't poured from his heart, that she had married a man who'd had her father's temperament. And she knew it because she'd been in Duncan Banks's arms, known his unrestrained affection and warmth, and because she had the constant and unfettered love of her child. Because, at last, she knew what love was.

She had answered all the letters to Aunt Mariah that were in her possession and couldn't risk sending in another warmed-over column. She had to go to the post office.

"You're getting heavy," she told Tonya, as she lifted her and walked up the mottled gray stone steps of the old post office.

"Walk, Juju. Tonya walk?"

She shifted the child to a more comfortable spot on her hip. "Not this time, Love. I can't have you running away from me the way you like to do at home," Justine said and headed toward the mail drop where she posted several letters. When she turned toward the mail boxes that were located just around a corner, a short man walked directly to her and stopped in front of her.

"You Justine Taylor?"

Her first impulse was to clutch Tonya close to her breast. "Who?"

The short, mustached man repeated his question.

"Sorry. I can't help you, Mister."

He didn't move, effectively blocking her way, but she didn't take her gaze from his eyes as he pulled off the baseball cap that he wore with the bill turned backward, ran his hands over his hair, put it back on, and appeared to consider her reply.

"You sure?"

Taking advantage of his indecision and the opportunity to throw him off balance, she smiled as warmly as she could. "Of course I'm sure. Hope you find who you're looking for." As if there was no reason why he shouldn't move, she smiled again. "Excuse me, please."

He stepped out of her path, but instead of going to the mail boxes, she headed for the stamp window, bought some stamps, and got her nerves under control. After assuring herself that she had the cell phone Duncan had given her, she took her time walking down the steps, carefully observing her surroundings as she did so. She could almost hear the accelerated racing of her heart when, across the street, she saw the man get into a red Oldsmobile Cutlass Supreme and drive off.

That voice. The same voice that had warned her in one of those mysterious phone calls to mind her own business. She drove past Duncan's house, didn't see the red car, circled the block, drove into the garage, and closed the door from the inside.

"What you doing coming in that way?" Mattie asked when she let her in the side door. Mr. B don't like that door opened 'cause it's too easy to forget and leave it unlocked."

The little woman picked Tonya up and hugged her. "You shore is a cute little tike." Then she set the child on her feet, braced her left hip with her fist, and looked at Justine. "That scruffy little man was back here looking for you. This the second time he axed me if you was home. I told him you don't live here, but looks like he don't believe me."

Justine had learned that Mattie wasn't as simple a person as she seemed. She studied the woman. "Why did you tell him I don't live here?"

Mattie shrugged, rolled her eyes toward the ceiling, and let the slow rising of her upper lip expose her large front teeth. "My Moe tells me to always figure out what kind of person a man is. And I knew no woman the likes of you has anything to do with that man. His kind ain't never up to no good. Humph. Him with his beady little eyes that don't look straight at you. Shady character if my name is Mattie Swindell."

Justine patted Mattie's shoulder. "You're a treasure, Mattie. Thanks."

Mind her own business. She hadn't meddled in anyone's affairs . . . except, maybe . . . She dialed Al's number.

"Al, have you given anybody other than Warren information about me and where I live?"

" 'Course not, babe. Why? You having problems?"

She told him about the calls and the man who had confronted her in the post office. "He could only be someone incensed by something that I put in my column."

"I should have had you use the paper's address, and maybe we'd better change. Anybody can find out who a P.O. box belongs to if they know how to go about it."

And that would cause more problems. She'd have to tell him she lived at Duncan Banks's home, and he'd want to get buddy-buddy with Duncan. "Wait on that, Al, 'til I get to the bottom of this."

She hung up and faced a truth that she'd rather not have to deal with. She had to tell Duncan that she was Aunt Mariah.

She waited until after dinner when he'd gone to his office, crossed her fingers, looked up to heaven, and knocked on his door.

If he'd asked her to come in, she'd have had time to

put on an expressionless face and stroll in, but the door opened abruptly.

"You want to see me?"

What could she say but, "Yes. I . . . I need to speak with you."

He stared down at her, and his inquiring look was neither friendly nor unfriendly. Just curious. You've had all evening, at least two hours, his expression seemed to say. Why now and what?

He motioned for her to sit in the chair near his desk, but her discomfort increased when she realized that he intended to stand. She didn't know where to start.

"Any problems?" he asked, as though anticipating something unwanted.

She nodded. "Yes. I didn't tell you what I'm writing about."

He shrugged. "As long as you aren't doing an expose on me or using Tonya as a guinea pig for some kind of research, I wouldn't think it would be something we couldn't . . . well, handle." His gaze bore into her, a well drill seeking an underground spring, and she shifted in her chair.

"No. Nothing like that. It's . . . I'm the person who writes Aunt Mariah's column for *The Evening Post.*"

He straightened up from where he'd leaned against a cabinet of books. "You're kidding. Why didn't you say so when you came here?"

She made herself look at him with all the honest innocence she could muster. "Al, that's my editor, had it inserted in my contract that I couldn't divulge Aunt Mariah's identity."

He seemed to muse over that, and she knew what he'd say next. "Then why are you telling me now?"

"Because . . . Duncan, a man has been calling here and pestering me. He said he'd teach me to mind my business. And today I took Tonya with me to the post office to get Aunt Mariah's mail, and a man with that voice confronted me. I told him I didn't know who he was talking about. I hung around there for almost an hour hoping he'd gone, but as I came out of the building, I saw him getting into his car. Mattie said he came here before I got home, and that he'd been here before asking for me."

"What did she tell him?"

"That she'd never heard of me. She said he seemed unsavory."

"I see. Did you get any letters from women who complained about their husbands or boyfriends?

"Quite a few, but I only told three or four of them to take strong measures."

He moved closer, more relaxed now and his voice softer. "Like what?"

"Leave the abusive man; go to work and exert some independence, that sort of thing."

He knelt on his haunches and took both of her hands. "In the future, when you have a problem, don't be afraid to tell me about it. This is dangerous. I don't want you to go to that post office ever again. I'll get your mail every day. And for a time at least, if you have to go to that paper, or anywhere, take a taxi and give me the receipt. Don't take Tonya out unless I'm with you."

She thought it over for a few minutes. If he and Al ever met and her name was mentioned, the fat would be in the fire. "I don't go to the paper, Duncan. I mail my columns in once a week. Al and I speak by phone."

"All right. If you still have the letters those women wrote to you, I'd like to see them."

"I have them."

He stood and began pacing the floor, and she didn't doubt that his mind had begun working, misgivings sneaking into his thoughts. "Why couldn't you have asked for my confidence and told me about your work? Did you think I wouldn't wonder why you, a fledgling writer, never asked me, a journalist, to read anything you'd written?"

"I'm sorry, Duncan. Maybe I was unwise. Do you want me to leave?"

A look of incredulity flashed over his face. "About this? Of course not. Your contract demanded your secrecy and, like your word, it's your bond."

She didn't know whether to be pleased by that remark. It could be a forewarning of an intractable impasse somewhere down the road. And she already knew that when he took a position and decided not to budge, you'd need an earthquake to move him. He'd given her a reprieve, but she knew it was a temporary one.

She rose to leave. "I hadn't picked up my mail in over a week because of the man's threatening phone call and the calls I got when the caller didn't identify himself."

"I'll get your mail tomorrow morning."

"Thanks."

He said he was glad to do it, but it seemed to her that his whole demeanor mocked his words and belied his apparent calm, and she had an intuitive sense that a storm was brewing in him.

"I'd better go," she said, for want of a better way of announcing her desire to leave him.

He didn't attempt to detain her, and she suspected that she'd lost some points with him.

He walked to the door. "See you in the morning."

He let her pass close enough to brush his body and, from what she could tell, he didn't move a muscle. She didn't look him in the face. Who knew what he was thinking and feeling? He was magnanimous in overlooking her negligence, generous in his offer to collect her mail, and ice-cold in his behavior.

Aunt Mariah! And he'd bet that wasn't the half of it. He hadn't forgotten that she'd derailed his efforts to find a woman who would agree to marry him and care for Tonya in exchange for a comfortable, if celibate, life. Never mind that he had scuttled the idea for reasons of his own. She'd been out of line, and she hadn't seen fit to apologize. Irritation bubbled up in him like stale bile, and he knocked on her door.

"I'm trying to understand about your column," he said when she opened the door, "but it isn't so easy, and the worst of it is, you didn't trust me."

"I'm sorry, Duncan. I offered to leave."

"That wouldn't solve anything, and you know it. Furthermore, it isn't what I want. You're in danger and my home and my child are in jeopardy. I ought to call Al Jackson and give him a good dressing down. Your mail should have gone to the paper."

"You said you'd collect it for me. Have your changed your mind?"

He didn't want to upset her too much, but she had to know that she'd displeased him. "I keep my word, Justine." He leaned against the doorjamb and crossed his legs at the ankles. "What's done is done. That man has seen you, and I can't risk your going outside alone."

Her rueful smile tugged at his heart. "So I'm relegated to the back garden?"

He straightened up and put his hands in his trouser pockets. "Well, we're going up to the Adirondacks for a few days. After we get back, we'll work something out. It's comfortable up there, so you'll be able to work on your column, if you want to, and you can walk all you like. By the way, I forgot to tell you Warren called a few days ago."

She rolled her eyes toward the ceiling. "Thanks."

He'd been right. Warren wasn't on her list. "Suppose we fly to Albany Friday afternoon, pick up a rental car, and drive on to Indian Lake?"

She regarded him carefully. "Are you sure you want to do this?"

"I don't volunteer to do what I don't want to do."

"All right," she said. "Friday it is."

Justine walked out onto the log cabin's front porch, gazed at the sun's reflection in the lake, and took a deep breath of clean, crisp air.

"Glad you came?"

She turned toward the direction of Duncan's voice. "I could stay here forever."

He raised an eyebrow at that. "Without a TV, telephone, internet, air conditioning, a microwave oven, and central heating?"

She turned fully to face him. Did he think her so frivolous? "I'm not married to material things, Duncan. This place is comfortable, peaceful, and attractive. And the environment is spectacular. It's . . . It's wonderful."

His fingers warmed her forearm. "I'll make us some coffee. After Tonya wakes up, we can go up to the lodge and get our breakfast.

Later that day, she strolled alone along the lake glancing occasionally toward the forest of thick trees and shrubs that grew almost to the water's edge. She sat on a boulder, serene, almost happy, and regarded her surroundings. The six log cabins and central lodge sat at the edge of the lake nestled in the woods with a quarter of a mile or more between them. That Duncan's cabin stood farthest from the others, inside the woods, was not an accident, she decided, but in keeping with his penchant for privacy. She picked up a sturdy stick and trudged over the rough terrain, back to Duncan's cabin.

"Thought you'd gotten lost, or worse, that you met a bear," Duncan said. "Say, did you bring a radio?"

She hadn't thought of it. "No. Why?"

"Up here, you need to know what the weather's going to do, especially this late in the year." He put some logs on the fire and closed the screen. "We have to keep Tonya away from this fireplace."

In spite of the idyllic environment, Justine couldn't relax. She didn't believe in premonitions, but something made her uneasy, and she wondered whether Duncan had brought her to the Adirondacks to confront her with her deception.

Around three o'clock the next afternoon, Duncan decided to gather chestnuts from the cluster of trees that grew in the forest. "Nothing like fresh roasted chestnuts," he told Justine. "I can't imagine Christmas or Thanksgiving without them. If I'm lucky, the squirrels will have left me some. See you shortly."

She walked to the back door with him and watched as he headed into the woods. Before leaving home, they had agreed to avoid all semblances of intimacy, and he hadn't offered her a kiss, though his eyes had begged for her sweetness. For the next two hours, she answered Aunt Mariah's mail, struggling with her reply to "Restless," a teenager who wanted to leave home and who had good reasons. She looked up from her writing and stared, dumbfounded, at the grainy snow that fell so thickly as to obscure her view of the lake that lay a mere seventy-five feet from her window. She went to the back porch and could barely see the forest. Where was Duncan? And how would he find his way back to the cabin?

As night settled, her anxiety for him mounted. She looked in the shed on the back porch, found three lanterns, some fares, flashlights, light bulbs, and a cord, along with firewood. Another hour passed, and he hadn't come back. Without a phone to call the lodge and with the path to it blocked by snowdrifts, she had to look for him, and that meant going into those woods. But she couldn't leave Tonya alone in the house. She dressed herself and Tonya warmly, found a terry cloth bath sheet and tied it lengthwise around her hips. Then, she sat on the bed, put Tonya in the sheet facing her and tied its top lengthwise around her neck to make a pouch in which to carry the child. Unaware of the implications, Tonya bubbled with joy as though beginning a new game. Justine put on a cap and a pair of gloves, got the lanterns, flares, cord, and flashlights and eased her way down the back steps.

She tied one end of the cord to the back porch, hung a lantern on it and tied the other end to the branch of a tree. With the flashlights and flares in her pockets and lanterns in each hand, she trekked through the icy snow toward the forest. She hung one lantern on a limb that she could barely reach, and its red blaze penetrated the night. If only she had a cane to help sturdy her steps as walking became more hazardous. But she couldn't turn back; he was out there somewhere, and he needed her.

"Juju love Tonya?"

Justine wondered at the question and asked the child whether she was cold, but Tonya's response was to sing, "Tonya loves Juju. Tonya loves Daddy," oblivious to the danger they faced.

The wind gathered momentum, whistling ominously through the trees as though searching for her, and grains of snow like sharp icicles bruised her face. She closed her eyes for a minute, glad that she wore glasses, and trudged on. Increasingly desperate now, her fingers numb, she hung the third lantern and prayed that the snow wouldn't wipe out her tracks and she and Tonya would also be lost.

She got a flashlight from her pocket, flicked it on, and its yellow beam penetrated deep into the woods. She rotated it several times and thought she saw a moving object. Again and again, she moved it in circles until she saw something settled against a tree trunk. Slowly, she blinked the light, fearful of attracting a wild animal and of wandering from her path. She looked back and could barely see the red blaze of the third lantern.

The grainy snow stung her cheeks like tiny needles. She put one arm beneath Tonya's bottom and satisfied herself that her child was secure. Then, she blinked the light again, and the object moved. She had to risk it.

"Duncan," she called. "Duncan, where are you?"

She stood still and her nerves seemed to scatter as though reassembling themselves. When there was no answer, she called again. Louder.

"Duncan. Can you hear me? Duncan, where are you?"

In the silence, she brushed the snow from the pouch in which she carried Tonya, from the cap on her head, and from her face. Again she called him. The low sound was not a growl, but more like a moan. Then she remembered the flare and lit it. If that was Duncan, he'd be able to see her. She stood still and waited as the object moved toward her, seemingly groping its way.

"Duncan," she called, allowing herself a last chance to escape.

"Jus . . . Justine."

She thought her heart would burst, but she knew she couldn't celebrate when the task of getting him to the cabin lay before her. She held the flare until he reached her and slumped against the tree.

"Duncan. Honey, are you all right?"

"Soon . . . Soon as I g . . . get warm."

Six hours in that weather without hat, top coat, or boots. She shook her head. With one arm around him, she led them to the third lantern. He slumped again, and she had to slap his face in the hope of energizing him. For what seemed like hours, she struggled with Duncan and Tonya until, at last, they reached the lantern at the door of the log cabin, and she knew they'd made it safely.

She got them into the house, put Tonya in bed without awakening her, and turned to the task of taking care of Duncan.

She ran a tub of hot water, led him to the bathroom, and helped him undress. "You have to get in that tub, Duncan. For all we know, you could be suffering from hypothermia and frostbite."

"But I don't—"

"Get in there, Duncan. I didn't risk my life and Tonya's for no good reason, so don't be a baby."

Unused to taking orders, he sat on the edge of the tub, put his feet in the hot water, and grimaced. She pushed him into the tub. "You'll get used to it."

She had to get out of that bathroom. Not even the raw condition of her nerves from their near catastrophe was sufficient to keep her libido quiet when she looked at Duncan's body, nude but for a G-string.

Half an hour later, Duncan walked into the living room and sat down. "That was close. I've been coming up here for years, but that's the first time I've gotten lost. The snow came so suddenly and so heavily that I couldn't find my way. I couldn't see a single landmark."

"Let's not think about it."

His eyes stroked her with adoration. "I hadn't given up, but I didn't see how I would make it. You're a brave woman, and a smart one, too."

And right now, a happy one. "What I want right now is some food."

He leaned forward, took the poker, and pushed a log in place. "We were going to have a cook-out tomorrow. Let's eat the hot dogs. We can roast them and some potatoes here in the fireplace. How did Tonya react to that adventure?"

Her mind hadn't been on Tonya, but on the man whom her soul loved. She thought for a minute. "For once, she used a complete sentence."

"Like what?"

"Tonya loves Daddy."

A grin streaked across his face. "Well, I'll be."

They finished the modest meal and sat before the fire, lost in their individual thoughts. Justine listened with consternation as the storm whistled around the log cabin.

"I might still be out in that storm, if you'd been like Marie—scared of anything she couldn't eat, wear, or spend. I'm tired, and I need to lie down, but I don't want to leave you."

She didn't want them to get into a lovers clinch. Feeling about him as she did, glad he was alive, she wouldn't have let him stop.

"We'd better turn in," she said, as she looked into eyes that were turbulent pools of desire. "I know how you feel, Duncan, because I feel that way, too, but this time, I'm prepared to stop it. So let's stick to our agreement. Goodnight."

She felt his gaze on her, but controlled the urge to look at him, went into the room she shared with her daughter, and closed the door.

That had been close. Because of her ingenuity and guts, he was sitting there staring into the fire. He wanted her in his bed as he'd never wanted anything, but he couldn't break his covenant with her. He got some coal from the back porch, banked the fire, and went to bed.

"Sorry you didn't have as many opportunities to enjoy the outdoors at Indian Lake as I'd hoped. We'd better wait 'til spring before we try it again," Duncan said, as the taxi stopped in front of his home.

"It had its great moments," she answered, "and I enjoyed it."

He lifted Tonya and took Justine's hand. "Don't forget to stay in the back garden if you want to spend time outside, and I wouldn't venture into those woods alone. Okay?"

He could see from her face that it was not all right, but

until he figured out a different strategy, she'd have to stay out of sight. He told her so.

"Will we try to catch this guy?"

He opened the front door with his keys. "We'll get him."

He settled down at his desk to work on the last article of his series on juveniles. The sooner he finished it, the quicker he could get started on that exposé of Baltimore slumlords. Several hours later, he reread what he'd written. Bland. No guts. No hard facts. He shredded it, put on his "street" clothes and headed for "East of the River." Something always happened down there, and it almost always involved young boys.

He parked on Bladensburg Road in front of a fried chicken carry-out, got out, and started toward Fifteenth Street. The air didn't smell right, and the flesh on his back was too warm for a cold night. Suddenly, his hair crackled, and he dived behind an old Chevrolet minivan seconds before a bullet whizzed past. He didn't think it was intended for him, but what difference would that have made if it had torn into his head? He eased up from his crouched position, sped down the narrow side street, and didn't breathe deeply until he was a block away. Winded, he ducked into Hurley's combination poolroom and bar, took his usual booth near the door, and cocked his ears. "What's going on?" he asked Hurley.

But the usually loquacious man was tight lipped, and merely shrugged. Something untoward had the regulars in a state of disquiet. Not even Buck, one of his most reliable informants, had anything to say.

"Anybody dead?" he asked a bystander.

"Who knows?" the man replied. "Could be several. We all heard the shots and the ruckus, Pops, but we don't know who got brought down."

Duncan thought of the bullet that had mercifully missed his head and asked, "Where? Right around here?"

The man raised his shoulder nonchalantly. "The police set up another one of their sting operations, man, and it turned deadly."

His blood pounded in his head. "Any kids?"

The man nodded. "Bunch of 'em. Couple of blocks down."

He didn't wait to hear more, but raced toward Benning. As he hastened along, pictures of Tonya and Justine flashed through his mind along with the thought that he'd better be careful, because they needed him. He forced his mind away from Justine. If he started thinking about her, he'd be a sitting pigeon for any crook who wanted to take a shot at him.

Duncan turned a corner into Rock Alley and stopped at the sight of Mitch sitting alone on the steps of the Christ First storefront church.

"*Mitch!* Where's Rags?"

His flesh began to crawl when the boy dropped his head in his hands and sobbed.

"I said, where is he?"

Horror siphoned off his breath as Mitch sputtered and sobbed until Duncan understood that a junkie had attempted to rob Rags and, when he found that the boy had no money, had spitefully pulled the trigger of his semi-automatic.

"The ambulance took him to D.C. General."

"Was Rags involved in that ruckus around on Benning?"

Mitch shook his head and explained that the junkie had escaped the sting, but hadn't gotten his fix, and probably didn't have the money to buy anything from an unfamiliar source.

"Whatever. Maybe he was just mean."

"Do you know that junkie?"

Mitch nodded and described the man who had attempted to sell a substance to Duncan a week or two earlier. "Calls himself Joe, but his real name is Rudolph Hester."

Duncan nodded. "You and I are going to the hospital to see that Rags gets proper care. Then you're going home." He watched Mitch drag himself up, a seventeen-year-old who'd seen ninety years of hard living.

"Where you going after that, Pops?"

He didn't want Mitch to follow him. "I don't know. Let's go."

Duncan had Rags, who was recovering from a shoulder wound, moved to a semi-private room, sent Mitch home, and went looking for the junkie who'd shot his young friend. If he gave the information to the police, the case would end there. In a file. Forgotten. But if a journalist of his stature handed the man over to them and reported the crime, the junkie would be off the street for a long time.

His search of local bars and dives proved fruitless, but he went on looking. He couldn't stop, because that man knew Rags could identify him, and he'd kill Rags to prevent it. With seconds to spare, he slipped through a broken window on the ground floor of an abandoned building when he recognized the slip-slide gait of the man he hunted, the man who might have recognized him had it not been for the smog.

Crouching out of sight, he used his cell phone to call the police, saw the man get a ride to police headquarters and, as the sun broke through the clouds, he crawled out of the old building and limped four blocks to his car. Once inside of it, his clothes dirty and torn, he slumped in the driver's seat, exhausted. He had his story, but every word he wrote would come out of him as though he were trying to chisel stone with a blunt object.

Justine fed Tonya, but had no taste for food herself. Eight-thirty in the morning and Duncan hadn't come home.

"No point in driving ourself crazy," Mattie told her. "No news be good news." She took her usual place at the table. "It ain't like him though. I tell you in this life they's always problems. Me and my Moe been looking at houses and axed the agent to hold one for a few days while we thought it over. Now the agent says we got to buy it, 'cause some people wanted it but she kept it for us. Justine, we can't afford no eighty-thousand dollar house."

In spite of her own uneasiness, it saddened her to see Mattie so deeply worried, and she patted the woman's frail shoulder. "I know someone who'll straighten that out for you, Mattie. So stop worrying. He'll make certain that agent doesn't try that trick again." She made a mental note to call Kenneth's fraternity brother in the Mayor's office and ask him to deal with it.

Mattie thanked her. "You know, Justine, you be one beautiful, classy lady. Such a good person. I can't see why you want to be a nanny, but I'm sure glad you come here. You and Mr. B shore oughta get things together, though, 'cause you'd make Tonya a good mother. Shucks, she already look like you. I'm gonna have to pray for this, and especially since you getting me and my Moe outa hot water with that real estate agent."

Cold tentacles of fear began a wild rampage through her body like sharpened icicles stabbing whatever they touched. Tonya sat in the high chair beside her, and Mattie faced them. How much more time would she have with Tonya before Mattie guessed, or Duncan realized why she seemed familiar? She left the table as soon as she could without exciting Mattie's curiosity, put Tonya in her crib, went to her room, and looked around for something to distract her—something to take her mind off the inevitable.

Her right eye began to tear, and she went to the bathroom to cleanse her contact lenses. Looking at herself in the mirror, an idea sprang to mind. *Eyeglasses.* She didn't have to wear contacts, and the resemblance between Tonya and herself would be less noticeable if she wore glasses. She phoned her optometrist, told him that she wanted to stop wearing contacts for a while, and asked that he check her records and send her a pair of glasses.

Satisfied that she had at least postponed her day of reckoning, she decided to develop a teaching course for barely literate and illiterate adults. She'd give the materials that she developed to the Literacy Society without charge and with the understanding the gifts were to be recorded as anonymous. That would keep her busy. Unable to work, she decided to write a song for use in the literacy classes. She scored a few bars, gave up, and walked out on her little porch and let the bracing air chill her body. She couldn't let herself give in to her feelings—*if anything had happened to Duncan.* Anything. She dare not dial his cell phone number, because she didn't know whether a ringing phone would cause trouble for him. But suppose he . . . needed her.

Riddled with anxiety, she threw up her hands and went back inside. What would she do? How could she live without him? She couldn't. She stood at her bedroom window, staring down at the cold, wind-swept garden. What a fool she'd been to let herself fall in love with him, when she knew he'd one day shut her out. Away from Tonya. Out of his life.

Mattie's soft knock shattered her reverie. "I don't know if I ought to leave, Justine, when Mr. B ain't home yet, but today's Thursday, my regular afternoon off. I could stay if you think you need me."

She draped an arm around Mattie's slight shoulders, intent on comforting her, but the gesture showed her how much she herself needed caring, assurance that someone loved her. She hugged Mattie and sent her home with the promise that, if there was a problem, she'd call. The doorbell rang, and she nearly fell down the stairs getting to the door, but was relieved to discover that the caller was a messenger with her eyeglasses.

She was halfway back up the stairs when the doorbell rang continuously as if someone leaned on it. With marbles fighting for space in her belly, she went to the door and called out, "Who is it?"

"Duncan."

The voice, tired and sluggish, was unlike the dark, mellifluous sound that always flowed from his throat. She locked in the chain, cracked the door, and peeped out.

"Open up, sweetheart. I'm bushed."

She slid off the chain, flung open the door, opened her arms, and clasped the big man to her breast. "Are you all right? Tell me. Are you all right?" As best she could, she pulled him into the house and locked the door.

He let the door take his weight. "If I can eat, take a shower, and get some sleep, I'll be fine. You must have been terribly worried. I would have called a couple of hours ago, but I fell asleep in the car."

She released a long breath. He hadn't been with a woman, though from the looks of him, he'd been into something. "You don't have to apologize. I'm just so happy you're here and that you're all right. I sent Mattie home. If you want to take a shower, go ahead. I'll get you some breakfast."

"No, you don't have to—"

"I said I'll get it," she broke in.

A sheepish grin crawled over his face. "Thanks. I'll be back down in a few minutes."

She knew he'd opened Tonya's door when the child's joyous squeals reached her ears. He never came home without greeting Tonya and never left without kissing her good-bye. If only there was some way that they could both love and care for their daughter openly without deceptive charades. But she'd tested fate already, been given a chance to know and love her child, and she wouldn't count on anything more.

It was already afternoon, so she made a brunch of waffles, sausages, fresh fruit, and grilled chicken nuggets, set the table quickly, and looked in the refrigerator for the biscuits that he and Tonya loved. She glanced toward heaven and gave silent thanks at the sound of his footsteps loping down the stairs. Twice in one week, she'd wondered if she'd ever see him alive again. But he was alive, and he was there.

"What can she eat?" he asked, referring to Tonya, whom he held in his arms.

"Scrambled eggs, banana, and biscuits. Some orange juice, maybe."

He ignored the high chair and put the child on his knee. "You sit here and behave yourself so daddy can eat. Okay?"

Tonya bounced up and down, her face glowing in smiles. Justine wondered how he'd feed himself and the child, and watched in awe as he managed and Tonya cooperated.

"Thanks for that great meal. Don't let Mattie catch you cooking like that; she thinks she's the only one who can do it. If you'll straighten up the kitchen for me, I'll get Tonya ready for her nap. Then I'll stretch out for a while." Minutes later he was back in the kitchen, obviously intending to wash a cup that Tonya had no doubt dropped.

She gazed at him, a far cry from the beat and bedraggled man who'd struggled into the house an hour earlier. She had no idea what kind of expression her face showed to him; she only knew what she felt—love from the tip of her longest strand of hair to her toes. As swiftly as lightning strikes, his own visage changed, and what she saw there wasn't gratitude for a good meal, but explosive desire. His Adams' apple bobbed, and he swallowed with obvious difficulty.

Frightened at her vulnerability and for want of other words that might reduce the heightened tension, she asked him, "You still angry at me for—?"

He looked into her eyes, rested the cup on the counter, and stroked her left cheek. "I've never been angry with you in my life." His voice wooed her, made love to every inch of her. He stared down at his fists, his legs wide apart, the way he always stood when he was hot for her, and when he looked up, his eyes were fiery orbs of primitive want. His hands went toward her body, but when she thought she would feel them on her, he dropped them to his sides. His intense stare held her riveted, and she bit her lip to stop its quivering response. His heat swirled around her, and she could see every masculine inch of his body revolting against its prison of denial. His aura sucked her to him until she smelled him, tasted him, and wanted him. Near panic, she spun away from him, but her backward glance nearly undid her, for his full arousal greeted her eyes.

Stunned, she rushed to the kitchen sink, gripped its rim, and held on to it until, fully fifteen minutes later, she heard him walk slowly up the stairs. He'd wanted her many times, but never like that. Whatever he'd done and wherever he'd been the night before, the experience had intensified his need. She rubbed her sides with her palms, now damp because she wanted him as badly as he wanted her. Damp, because the lessons of her life told her that they flirted with disaster. Hers, if not his.

She cleaned up the kitchen, went to her room, and tried to outline some reading lessons for the Literacy Society, but she couldn't get her mind on the lessons and had to put them aside. She could clean out her closets, but she had done that last week. Frustrated and unsettled, she fell across her bed and rested her face on her arm. In her mind, he stood before her holding Tonya, his eyes declaring his desire and promising her the ecstasy of which she had dreamed, longed for, and never experienced.

Desire burned the seat of her passion, stunning her, and she gripped the bed covering, her nails scoring and streaking the silk satin material. For once in her life, couldn't she have what other women took for granted? In a few weeks she'd be a thirty-year-old woman who'd had a four-year marriage but still wore the flower of her birth. He would love her. She knew he would, because whatever she'd seen him do, he'd done it thoroughly. Maybe tomorrow or the next day or the next, he'd discover her secret and ask her to leave and she'd never have known him. She twisted and turned until the bed covering entrapped her, and she fell over on her stomach and her breasts, themselves erect, rubbing the bedding.

"I can't stand it," she confessed to the silence. "I may lose, but I will have known passion in the arms of the man I love."

He'd told her that if she came to him, he'd welcome her. She forced herself not to think, took a quick shower, slipped into her favorite lace underwear and red silk kimono, crossed her fingers, and tapped on his door.

"In a minute." Suddenly, she wondered what he was doing, whether she was disturbing him. How would he react? He didn't keep her guessing.

She'd picked the devil of a time to knock on his door. Temptation personified. If she'd learned anything about him, she had to know that when she'd walked away from him, he'd been a man trussed and immobilized. Tired as he was, he hadn't slept a second, and anybody looking at his bed would know that he'd spent the last hour in it, wrestling with himself and his demons. He didn't blame her for rejecting the idea of intimacy between them; he also knew it wasn't wise. But he'd never wanted a woman as badly as he desired her, never felt as if he had to have *any* woman—except Justine Taylor. Damn all his reservations if she lingered at that door; he was starved and hurting with the pain of it.

That soft tap again. She'd never been in his room and, as best as he could remember, had never knocked on his bedroom door. He slipped a robe over his nude body, walked in his bare feet across the room, and opened the door.

"You wanted me for something?"

He looked down at her—hair flowing around her shoulders, those silver hoops in her ears and red silk on her body—vulnerable. Tension gripped him and threatened to settle in his groin. Her face was open, sweet, questioning. He told himself not to let her blind-side him, but her tongue rimmed her lips, dampening them for his mouth, and shudders raced through him.

"*Justine! What do you want?*" He hadn't meant to frighten her, but something akin to terror flashed across her face, and she turned as if to go back to her room. His hand shot out and grasped her arm. "Why are you here?" he asked, this time as softly as he could make the words.

She didn't look at him. "I . . . I was just . . . just . . ."

It couldn't be. Not when he needed . . . He had to take the chance. "Have you come to me? Have you?"

She looked up into his face, and when she didn't answer, his heart pounded so furiously and loudly that it nearly frightened him.

He opened his arms to her, and she dashed into them. His hands rested on her body, but he couldn't let himself hold her to him the way that he needed to. "Sweetheart, if you're not staying, please go now." She held him tighter, and he nearly choked on his breath.

"I . . . I want to . . . to stay here with you," she finally managed.

Blood rushed wildly through his body as desire gripped him. He wanted to shout to the world that she would be his, but he set her away from him and looked her in the eye. "Are you sure? I don't want you to be sorry later, or ever."

Her voice came to him like a newly polished bell, tinkling in a warm breeze. "I need . . . to be with you."

Air hissed out of him, and he lifted her in his arms, stepped into the room, and kicked the door shut. He ran his hands beneath her kimono, found the naked flesh of her back, and crushed her to him. Her mouth, ripe and sweet, opened like rose petals beneath his searching lips and, this time when she asked for his tongue, he plunged into her, giving in to her greedy request.

Her fingers at his nape moved restlessly as though unable to find enough of him to touch. Then, with her hands at the back of his head, she increased the pressure of his kiss.

"Duncan. Duncan. I'm . . . I'm on fire. I'm . . ."

He swallowed the rest of her words, and she moved against him. Asking. Demanding. He held her closer, and the tips of her breasts teased him until it was all he could do not to throw off his robe. He let his hand roam her naked back until she twisted, letting him know she wanted his hands on her breasts. Nearly out of his mind with desire, he put his hand in her right bra, cupped her breast, and toyed with it until she undulated against him.

"Kiss me," she urged in a breathless tone that he knew signalled mounting desire. He needed to slow down, or he'd explode. She swung her hips into him, her only thought seeming to be the pleasure he gave her. When she tried to fit her body to him, he lifted her off her feet, carried her to his bed, and lay her there. Her rapid breathing nearly undid him, and when she spread her legs, he jumped to full readiness.

"May I take this off?" he asked, his voice deep, guttural, as his fingers gripped her robe. He thought he saw a flash of discomfort—or was it fear?—in her face. "You're so beautiful," he said, hoping to reassure her, as he looked down at the rich treasure awaiting him. "So lovely." He unhooked her bra and gazed in awe at the sexy lode. She raised her arms to him in an unmistakable invitation and he let his own robe drop to the floor.

He knelt on the bed, leaned over her, and fell into her open arms. At last. She could feel his body, his power, his maleness. His lips caressed her neck and moved slowly, too slowly, to her mouth, where he drove her nearly wild plunging his tongue in and out, teasing her with what was to come. His fingers tortured first one breast and then the other until she pleaded.

"Duncan, please. I can't stand it. I want to feel your mouth on me."

His tongue circled an aureole and tortured it until she lifted her body to him, and he took her into his mouth and dragged a keening cry from her. She'd never wanted, needed, anything like she needed him inside her, but he took his time, learning her body with his fingers, his five senses, and suckling her until she cried aloud. Seconds later, his hand began a slow journey down her body, skimming her flesh, brushing, caressing, and teasing. Burning her. Branding her. His mouth closed over a nipple, and his educated fingers began a dance of love at the nub of her femininity. Out of her mind with want, she reached for him.

"You're not ready yet, honey."

"I am. I am. I'm going crazy." But he continued the torture, his lips and hands possessing her until, wonder of wonders, a strange, tight fullness gathered inside her and heat seared the bottom of her feet as the liquid of love dampened his fingers.

"Duncan, what's happening to me?"

"Shhhh, darling. I'm loving you."

"Duncan, what's happening to me? I feel like I'm going to explode."

Frustrated, she found him and took him into her hands, and he moved above her.

What was he waiting for? "Duncan?"

"May I?"

"Yes. Oh, Lord, Yes!"

He stopped to protect her and then, staring into her eyes, he slowly began to enter.

"Relax, and let yourself go, honey. It'll work just fine. Just relax and trust me. I'll take us where we want to go."

Quit fighting it and let yourself go. Kenneth's words reverberated through her brain, and she froze, unable to move.

Duncan locked her in a fierce embrace. "Listen to me,

sweetheart, it's you and me here and nobody else. I'm yours. Give yourself to me. That's it. Relax and let me love you."

She pushed the past out of her mind, let herself relax, and he began to move. She found his rhythm, and that tight, full feeling was soon in her again, all over her. She thought she'd die if she didn't burst.

"Duncan, I want to . . . to burst open. Honey, do something."

With his hands beneath her hips, he thrust deeply, vigorously, until she couldn't hold back the screams, and erupted in a vortex of throbbing pulsations that sucked her into a whirlpool of ecstasy. She threw out her arms, exhausted, but he hadn't finished with her, and within minutes he drove her to another wild, volcanic eruption. She was one with him, uncertain where she began and he ended. The words came to her lips, and she had to bite her tongue, as he plunged again and again, wringing herself out of herself, drawing from her a thunderous explosion, and then collapsing, splintered into her arms.

She held him to her as tightly as she could, squeezing him until she thought her arms would break. If only she could tell him what she felt, how she loved him. She caressed his head lying on her shoulder and skimmed her hands over his back. As though to let her know he understood, he kissed her cheek, and then, resting on his elbows, gathered her to him and kissed her as though he couldn't get enough of her, wanted to devour her. Savored. Cherished. She thought her heart would burst with joy and with love. He'd given her all that she had dreamed of, sated her with loving, and now, he adored her.

He looked into her eyes, and a dazzling smile took possession of his face. "Are you all right?"

Didn't he know? "I've never been so happy in my life," she told him. "You gave me something that had eluded me. Thank you. I'll never forget this time with you. Never."

His smile broadened. "I finally guessed that. You shot my ego into the stratosphere. Why haven't you had . . . been fulfilled? You are the most sensuous, the most physically alive woman I've ever known."

Maybe what she'd had with Kenneth hadn't been love, for it didn't approximate or even come near to her feelings for Duncan. She locked him in her arms and told him, "At least I know it was never my fault."

He kissed her, fell over on his back, tucked her to his side, and said, "We couldn't miss, Justine; the chemistry between us is so strong that we didn't stand a chance of avoiding it, nor of staying away from each other. I've done everything I could to prevent this, but the night you came here for the interview, I knew I wanted you. I could handle that, but these other feelings crept in and . . . When you knocked on my door, I was going crazy for you."

She wanted to ask him where they went from there, but she knew it had to be a one-time thing, because he wouldn't forgive her deception, and the more she had of him, the more devastated she'd be when he ended their ties. And what should she expect anyway? She was still his employee, nanny to his child, the child to whom she'd given birth. Shudders plowed through her at the thought that this may be the only time she would fly to the sun in his arms.

She threw her left arm across his flat belly and stroked him. "Duncan, make love to me until I don't know who I am."

He sat up and looked down into her face. " What happened? Why are you frightened? Don't tell me you're sorry."

"How could I be sorry? I don't usually get what I want from life," she whispered, "so let me cheat Providence this once. I want to know one more time what I felt with you just now."

He gazed at her for a long time before he said, "Let's not cross our bridges before we get to them." Then he bent to her lips and began their next tumultuous ride to paradise . . .

Replete. Sated. She held him in her arms and in her body and knew beyond a doubt that the heaven she'd found with him would cost her, that the price would probably be more than any woman should have to pay. She hadn't meant to communicate her momentary trepidation to him, but she must have, because he put both arms beneath her shoulders and looked deeply into her eyes.

"I'm asking you again. Are you sorry?"

It was so strange being with him that way, her senses filed to a fine point, totally in tune with him. Her body still bloomed from his marksmanship. Echoes of his murmurs, his lover's entreaties, resonated through her head. She gazed up at him. Brazen. Assured. Her soul knew him. He shifted slightly, and she clutched at his hips. Surely he wouldn't separate from her, from the place in her where he belonged.

"Are you? Sorry?" He persisted, his eyes on her and his mouth barely a centimeter from hers.

"How could I be? I knew the score, Duncan, and I can't be sorry for knowing at last who I am, for coming alive in your arms—as if I'd been reborn. What about you?"

His lips brushed her mouth. "Only if you are. You gave me something so special, that I can't regret it, nor will I forget it. I don't know about the future, but I—"

The fingers of her left hand went to his lips, cutting off his words. She didn't want to hear about tomorrow. "Don't. Please. Not now. Don't interfere with what we have right now."

His kisses drugged her. "Sweetheart, we can't share what we've had in this bed and pretend it's business as usual. It won't be the same with us, so there's no use pretending that nothing happened. As far as I'm concerned, everything has changed."

She shoved back a rising panic and put a cool tone in her voice. "Does that mean you want me to leave?"

She failed to see the humor in that or anything right then and pinched his shoulder in reprimand when he laughed.

"You're kidding, I hope."

Then, to her amazement, he kissed her left breast, put his head on her shoulder and went to sleep. And he could sleep; he wasn't living a lie. But she had just quadrupled her chances of misery, just added one more certain cause for heartbreak.

CHAPTER TEN

She didn't want to arouse him and end the moments of incredible peace with him in her arms, but the call could be important. She stroked his head, caressing him with a tenderness that flowed from her whole being. "Duncan, your phone's ringing."

"Huh?"

He was upright immediately. "Did you say telephone?"

It rang again, and he reached for it. "Hello?" After listening for a minute or so, his muscles flexed with alertness, and she knew that for the present, at least, she'd lost him. "All right, I'll be over there in the morning."

He hung up, fell over on his back, and stared up at the ceiling. "Wayne wants me to start on something urgent tomorrow, which means I have to finish my series on juveniles tonight and take it in with me. I'd hoped for a couple of days, but I'll get it done. If you'll feed Tonya and yourself, I'll get a sandwich or something." He raised up, braced himself on his left elbow, and looked steadily at her. "Will you give me this time I need and not torture yourself about answers or solutions or feel as though I'm a rat for ignoring you? Will you?"

She took his hand. "Of course. After all, I understand pro . . . I know you have a job to do."

She'd almost told him she understood professional responsibility, which, as a clinical psychologist, she certainly did. But he'd apparently missed her slip, and she let herself breathe deeply. He leaned over her, kissed her so quickly that she barely felt it, got up, and headed for the bathroom. She couldn't help feeling bereft, as though he'd taken her most precious possession. And he could do that if he chose, for he had everything that mattered to her. He had Tonya and himself. Not that she intended to get morose. Not after what he'd just given her. *All right, so I'm messed up; what can I expect after a loving like that?*

She dressed and went to look after Tonya, who greeted her with laughter, bouncing up and down, exuding love. She picked up the happy child, kissed her, and received kisses in return. "I've got the world on a string," she sang out, happier than she'd known she could be.

" 'Atta girl."

She whirled around in time to see him wink and head downstairs. An hour later, he walked into Tonya's room and handed Justine a shopping bag full of mail. He had the nearly impossible task of finishing his series that night, but he'd kept his word and had spent a precious hour getting her mail.

Using the self-control of a righteous person, she thanked him. "Consider yourself kissed."

His wide grin told her that she had found the right vein.

At nine-thirty the next morning, Duncan stepped off the elevator in the Roundtree Building, energized with the prospect of beginning a new, exciting assignment, though he'd begun the drive to Baltimore after little more than two hours sleep. Finishing that story hadn't been easy, for his thoughts had gone repeatedly to Justine and his mind-blistering experience with her that afternoon. He'd reminded himself repeatedly that he wasn't going to fall for her, that he'd had his last emotional attachment to any woman. Then he would remember how she'd given herself to him. Totally. Completely, without false pride, and with none of the hysterical faking of his former wife. She had enjoyed everything he'd done to her and had made sure of his own satisfaction, though all he'd needed was his place within her.

He knew she would want to know where they stood with each other; any woman would, and especially if she had deep feelings as he now suspected Justine had for him. A woman couldn't give her body with such abandon, such complete trust unless she cared, deeply. And he wondered about himself—the way he'd felt with her—the way in which he'd loved her. He'd be a fool to tell himself that a man could make love to a woman as he'd done if he didn't care. He'd have to settle a few things with himself before he got back home. He knocked and entered Wayne's office.

Wayne skimmed Duncan's report, his smile broadening as he read. "Man, this thing reads like Mozart's chamber music, everything where it's supposed to be when it's supposed to be there. Congratulations."

Both of Duncan's eyebrows went up. He didn't want to be reminded of Justine right then. "Don't tell me you freak out on Mozart, too."

"You betcha. Who else does?"

There was no escaping it, he thought, rubbing his chin reflectively. "Justine. And now my daughter loves it too."

Wayne tapped his Mont Blanc pen on his desk a few times as though weighing his next words. "How is Justine?"

"Fine."

Wayne's laughter reverberated through the room and into the hallway. "Sorry, man, but if you had committed a murder, what you're wearing on your face right now would get you a life sentence."

Duncan shrugged. At age thirty-five, he didn't have to discuss his business if he didn't want to. Not even with Wayne. "As a detective, you'd probably flunk. What's the latest on this slumlord situation?"

"The City Council is beginning an investigation of slum housing, and I want your story out before one of those politicians gets a chance to whitewash it."

"Yeah. Every paper in town will be after this. I'll get right on it. By the way, when have you seen my kid sister?"

Wayne laughed, mainly in embarrassment, he thought. "Man, stop thinking of her as a kid; she's twenty-seven. And I see her or talk with her every day."

Walking toward the door, Duncan glanced at a woman's framed picture that always sat on a bookcase near Wayne's desk. "You never did tell me who that gal is. You seeing her, too?"

Wayne leaned back in his chair and locked his hands behind his head. "I keep that picture where I can see it. There's an identical one on my night table. Their job is to ensure that I don't make a fool of myself, to remind me to watch my step with women. You could say that's why, when it comes to women—Leah included—I move at a snail's pace."

He hadn't dreamed that he and Wayne had in common disappointment with someone they'd loved. "Put them face down, Wayne. We're letting people who let us down prevent us from living fully. I know it's hard, but we have to deal with it. See you, man." With a ton of luck, he'd be able to take his own advice.

Duncan set out for CafeAhNay, his first stop for information about anything relating to Baltimore's inner-city street life. Lottie walked over to his booth as soon as he sat down.

"Anything going on?" he asked her, as he gave her an order for scrambled eggs, toast, and coffee, pulled out his Frederick Douglas carving and began whittling.

She nodded. "Head over around Westchester and Fairfax and knock on some doors. You oughta get something."

He'd planned to do that, but he appreciated confirmation of his hunch. He stayed there for about an hour picking up loose bits of conversation and making mental notes of what he overheard. On his way to Grace's place, he flipped on his recorder and summed up the information he'd gotten at CafeAhNay.

Her smile greeted him as she opened the door. "I checked several tenements," he told her, "but I can't find out who owns them, and there's a reason for that."

"I wouldn't think anybody in Graystone Alley would be

afraid to tell you what they know; that area's hardly fit for swine."

"Thanks. I've heard about the place. I'll walk through there."

"Make sure it's morning," she warned.

So far nothing concrete, but he'd get the story if he had to cover every inch of West Baltimore by foot. After several fruitless hours, he met two teenaged boys who let him into the building in which they lived, and he jotted down the name and identification number of the elevator inspector. Sensing success, he collected that information in as many apartment buildings as he could enter. Around four o'clock, with night approaching and hunger pangs reminding him that he hadn't eaten lunch, he saw an old woman limp from one of the most deteriorated buildings he'd seen. He gave her a hand and asked to whom she paid her rent.

"Mister, on the first of every month, I write a check for six hundred dollars to Hugh Pickford to live in a one-room apartment in this rat-infested place. I mail it to a post office box."

Hugh Pickford. His pulse accelerated and his heart thundered in his chest, as he grasped the old woman's bony arm. "Are you sure, Ma'am? Really sure?"

"Of course, I'm sure," she said, obviously aggravated.

Hugh Pickford! By damn, he had him at last, right where he wanted him, and when he'd finished, Hugh Pickford would be living rent free—in jail. For twenty-eight long years, he'd dreamed of the day he'd face the man who had set his family out on the street in the dead of winter not caring if they froze or starved. Talk about the chickens coming home to roost! Excited at the chance for revenge, adrenalin rushed through him, a gushing torrent, energizing him. But he didn't believe that Hugh Pickford was Baltimore's only slumlord, and he'd find the others just as he'd found Pickford, but he had the propeller for his story. He itched to expose that man and all of the rest.

The Beltway traffic to Washington and home slowed him down and his mind took him back to the previous afternoon when, in Justine's arms, he'd known at last his potential as a man. If there was more to him, he wasn't sure he could survive experiencing it. Horns honked, a cacophonous symphony playing to the tune of human frustration. He barely heard it. What would he say to her? What could he say? That he'd gone to heaven in her arms, thank you but no more? Or thank you, please move across the hall? Neither. He wasn't a cad, but neither was he ready for marriage, legal nor common law. Maybe they could work it out together.

At home, Justine was having similar concerns. Her euphoria of the previous afternoon had begun to ebb, and guilt of a measure such as she'd never experienced had sunk into her. How could she justify having gone to him when she lived a charade that would bring him pain? She could tolerate his anger, but not his disgust when he came to the false conclusion that she'd made love with him as a safeguard against his firing her after learning that she was Tonya's birth mother. But how could she pull back? He'd taught her the lesson of love, whetted her appetite, and the thought of him sent her blood racing and her mouth watering for more of him. She walked to her bedroom window and looked out at the last of the gray November day. *I'm his daughter's nanny, not his lover.* It would be business as usual. She couldn't expect or justify more. The phone rang as the front door opened.

"Hello." She waited, but no sound came from the other end.

"Was that another call from our mystery man?"

She nearly dropped the phone. "Duncan, stop frightening me."

When he leaned forward and kissed her beside her mouth, she stared at him, trying to read him, and hoping that was his way of setting their course.

"Maybe we ought to keep the answering machine on, and you listen to the voice before picking up. First chance I get, I'll check those letters you gave me and see if I can get a clue."

She thanked him and attempted to pass him, but he stopped her. "I hope you got along all right today. I managed to get my work done, but I'm having trouble with what to do about us. I don't want to walk away from what we found, but I can't embrace it. At least not yet. Can you tell me how you feel about it?"

She should have known that he'd face it head on and that he'd behave with honor and considerateness. "My feelings are similar to yours. I didn't act impulsively. Emotionally, I'm . . . well, I'm ready for it, but intellectually, I am not. So we're in agreement? You're my employer, and nothing more."

He shook his head. "I'm not quite that good at fooling myself, but basically, let's be good friends and keep everything else at bay."

Her smile must have pleased him, for a crinkle beneath his wonderful, reddish-brown eyes soon blossomed into a full grin. He stuffed his hands in his pockets, and she knew he'd begun his trial of self-control.

By some miracle, they managed to maintain a platonic relationship for the next few days, though she couldn't get used to the strangeness of it. Yet, with a peculiar contentment, she concentrated on her column and her child. Tonya loved watching the flames that danced over the logs in the fireplace, so she had begun reading to her in the living room. Several evenings after she and Duncan had made their pact, she sat there with Tonya and read aloud Emerson's *Eldorado*. Tonya didn't like nursery rhymes, but loved long poems with a pronounced rhythm. She clapped her hands and tried to hum the "tune".

"How do you do that?" Duncan, who had observed them from the doorway, asked her. "She's a baby, but she loves these poems you read to her."

Careful, she cautioned herself, because she could so easily become the psychologist. "She enjoys the music, the lilt. When she begins to talk, she may remember the words, too."

He walked over, reached down, and took the child from her. "Whose baby are you?"

He'd asked Tonya that question often since she'd been

there, but this time his little game cut her to the quick, for it was the first time Tonya had answered him. "Daddy," she sang out. Justine had to lower her gaze so that he couldn't see her pain.

Still holding Tonya, Duncan stepped into the hall to answer the phone. "It's for you, Justine."

Who would call her at seven in the evening? Maybe Banks or her godfather. She took the phone from him. "Hello." After listening, she said, "Sorry, Warren, I'm busy tonight."

Duncan looked at her, his dark face devoid of expression. Then a mask settled over it, a veil of pain powerful and intense, electrifying like the sun going down. He started toward Tonya's room, reversed himself, walked over, and handed the child to her. She thought he looked from Tonya to her and back again and thanked God that she wore her glasses.

"Is there any reason why you wouldn't want to go to Frederick with Tonya and me Thursday? That's turkey day, and Saturday is my mother's birthday. She'll be sixty-five. She wants you to come, and I told her I'd bring you."

She longed to go, to be with him and her child on that special holiday, but, as an outsider . . . "Thanks, but it's a family holiday, and I—"

He held up his hand to stop her. "I want you to come with us. What kind of Thanksgiving do you think I'll have knowing you're here alone? Besides, Mama and Leah are expecting you." He tweaked her nose. "You'll enjoy it. Will you come?"

"All right."

"And you're off duty from Wednesday night until Sunday morning. Got it?"

Oh, how she loved this wonderful man. If only she could open her soul to him and pour out everything. Everything. "Thanks. I'll . . . Thanks."

"Mama, this is Justine."

Justine bowed slightly in deference to his mother and extended her hand but, to his amazement, his reserved mother opened her arms and enveloped Justine in a warm embrace.

"I'm so glad you'll be with us this holiday, Justine. I want you to feel at home here."

Justine seemed taken aback at his mother's reception, and she showed her pleasure in a warm smile, her beautiful grayish-brown eyes sparkling. "Thank you, Mrs. Banks. Is this generosity a family trait? I've noticed it in Duncan and Banks, and now you."

"I see my daughter's had you understand what her real name is. Next time I have to write her a letter, I think I'm going to address it to Miss Banks Banks."

Justine let them hear the sound of her laughter, a rarity, for he'd seldom heard her laugh aloud. Her big grayish-brown eyes sparkled with merriment, beautiful and wicked, and he had to force himself not to touch her. His mother's small talk with a stranger about Leah's attitude toward her name—a matter that had always displeased her—was proof that she accepted Justine without reservation. Leah hugged first Justine and then him. He made himself a bystander and watched the interplay among the women in his life.

His mother reached for Tonya, but the child wanted Justine. "Juju sing. Sing. Pay panno," Tonya insisted, holding her arms out to her nanny. When Justine took her, she bounced with joy, clapped her hands, and kissed Justine's cheek. "Baywu," she said, referring to the story of Beowulf.

His mother watched the two of them, obviously scrutinizing and, if he knew her at all, adding up some things. Her eyes narrowed, and Justine turned away. Something had passed between them or from one to the other, and he'd give a lot to know what it was, but he didn't expect either one of them to enlighten him.

Arlene Banks turned on the dishwasher and clicked off the kitchen lights. The past few hours had been an eyeful and a head full.

"Well, what do you think, Mama?" Banks asked as she entered the kitchen door, their first chance to speak of the evening's happenings.

"About Justine?" Arlene asked.

Banks nodded. "I think she's super. What about you?"

Arlene spoke truthfully, "I wish he had known her before he met Marie. She is the woman for him, a giving person. Did you see his face as he watched her cuddling Tonya? Did you?"

Banks leaned against the wall. "I saw that and then some. I just hope they know what they'd lose if they threw it away. I'm just learning, but I know that much. She isn't what you'd expect in a nanny, is she?"

Arlene lifted both eyebrows. "Nanny? I'm surprised at you." She clicked off the remaining light. "I want to tell Tonya good night. She has to get to know me."

She started down the narrow hallway to the stairs and surmised that the dialing she heard was her daughter calling Wayne Roundtree. She had never accepted the reasons that Duncan and Leah had given her as to why the woman they described Justine to be would work as a nanny. As much as they'd both seen Justine and Tonya together, it amazed her that they hadn't guessed. Didn't Duncan know why he thought he'd known Justine? The woman had a story to tell, and she suspected from the aura of veiled sadness she detected in her, even when she laughed, that hers was a tale of unhappiness. She treaded the carpeted, upstairs hallway on her way to the room that Justine would share with Tonya. She stopped, not wanting to shatter the unifying force that ricocheted between Duncan, Justine, and Tonya, binding them, glowing on their faces, echoing from the walls and lighting up the room like the rays of an early morning sun. Didn't Duncan know that he was in love with Justine? She went into the bathroom, closed the door, and prayed that God would smile on the three of them and keep them together. And they'd need a lot of prayer, because Duncan was in for a shock, and he hadn't yet learned how to forgive and forget.

Alone in her room, Banks held her breath, hoping that Wayne and not his mother would answer the phone, but it was Mary Roundtree whose voice she heard. "This is the Roundtree residence. With whom do you wish to speak?"

Reminding herself to be thankful that she'd been given a different mother, she said, "Miss Mary, this is Leah Banks. I want to speak with Wayne."

"Oh, yes, Leah. I've been asking Wayne to bring you to see me, since the two of you spend so much time together, but he always gives me a reason why he can't do it that day or that weekend. So how about Sunday afternoon?"

Thank goodness, she had a legitimate excuse. "Thanks, Miss Mary, but my brother and niece and my girlfriend are spending the weekend with us, so this isn't a good time. I'll let Wayne know when it's good. Could I please speak with him?"

"Yes, of course."

Ice water. How did a man like Wayne get such a snowflake for a mother? Her bones jellied when his deep baritone reached her through the wires.

"Hello, Leah. Still got the Roundtrees on a merry-go-round? What's up?"

"Wayne, what are you talking about?"

She imagined that his faced glowed with innocence. "Still scared to meet my mother. Shame on you."

She hoped she didn't have to go near the woman until she wore Wayne's ring on the third finger of her left hand. "Who's scared? I'm just real careful in case your mother is your confidant and advisor."

"Tell me you didn't say that," he growled.

"You told me you can't stand people who don't tell the truth."

"That's right, I did. You love me?"

"Will you hold me to my answer?"

His laughter warmed every molecule of her being. "I'll hold you, all right. Wait 'til I get my hands on you."

Just the opening she needed. "How about an hour from now? Justine and Duncan are here for Thanksgiving, so the four of us could check out *The Watering Hole.*"

"Meet me at your front door in half an hour; I need thirty minutes before your brother gets into the act."

Eager anticipation and warmth surged through her, but

she steadied her voice and needled him. "What could we possibly do for thirty whole minutes?"

She'd known he'd laugh at that, and she relished it. "Baby, I wouldn't take a million dollars for you."

"You'd take two million?"

"Go ahead. Press your luck. You've got twenty-eight minutes. See you."

"Bye." She hung up and dashed upstairs. "Put on something, girlfriend. Wayne's coming over, and the four of us are going to *The Watering Hole.*"

Duncan's questioning look accused her. "Who decided this?"

"Me. Come on Duncan. I want to see Wayne, and us going out together gave me an excuse to ask him. You going, Justine?"

"Of course, if it's all right with Duncan."

"It's all right with him. I'm going to put on a pink lace dress, sleeveless and miniskirted."

"Something similar," Justine said. "Come on, Duncan, be a good sport."

"Sure," he grumbled, "and spend the evening watching Roundtree ogle my kid sister."

"You think you're the only one entitled to ogle?" Banks shot back. "I'm getting dressed."

"Me, too," Justine said and ushered Duncan to the door. "Meet you downstairs in forty minutes."

Duncan held Justine's coat while she slid out if it. When she turned to him and smiled her thanks, he let out a soft whistle. "Isn't that thing cut a little low? I mean, it's kind of skimpy, isn't it?"

Justine glanced toward Banks, whose gaze went skyward as though Duncan was hopeless. "It doesn't approach the line of indecency," Justine said of her red, cleavage-revealing shift. "It's practically Victorian."

His tongue poked his right jaw. "You don't say."

"Why don't we go to the lodge Saturday morning and do some fishing?" Wayne asked Duncan.

"You want to go fishing?" Duncan asked Justine.

She looked down at his hand high on her thigh as though it belonged there. And didn't it? "Guarantee me I'll catch something."

"I wouldn't touch that with a fishing rod," Banks said.

"You will definitely catch something," Wayne assured her. "I'm aiming at a pretty good harvest myself."

"Wait a second," Duncan said to Wayne. "What are you talking about?"

"Fishing. What else?"

Banks slapped Duncan on his hand. "He has a right to hope."

Justine told herself not to think of what could be, but enjoy the present. She had never spent time matching wits and telling tall tales with friends. Happiness filled her and spilled out of her, a wild river suddenly undamned. She laughed. And laughed. Duncan kissed her mouth, and she sobered.

"What happened to you?" he whispered in her ear with Banks's gaze locked on them.

I'm going to be honest with him, she told herself. If he didn't like what he heard, she couldn't help it. "It was too much all of a sudden. I'm happy, and I know it can't last."

He eased himself around her, shielding her from the eyes of Wayne and his sister. "It sounded to me like sadness," he said, for her ears only. "Remember, we promised not to cross our bridges until we got to them. You're not alone in this whirlwind."

They didn't hear him, but they had to know that his words weren't for their ears. "Thanks," she whispered, "but maybe we'd better continue this another time. Your sister may think you're making a public statement about us."

"Let her think what she likes. And she will. Besides, it's been years since Leah and I surprised each other, if we ever did." He moved away from her and, as she had suspected, they had Wayne's and Banks's full attention.

"How many Thanksgiving dinners are you eating tomorrow, Wayne?" Duncan asked, obviously to divert the focus from himself and Justine. "Two?"

"Looks like it."

Justine could see in Banks an aura of contentment, a softness that came with knowing that Wayne cared for her. She didn't want to stare at them, so she turned to face Duncan and caught him off guard. If only she dared to trust what, in that fleeting moment, she'd seen flashing in his eyes. Was what he felt so strong that he would forgive her? Or was he a man who could toss her off like a pair of worn-out shoes even if he loved her? She dare not hope.

Thanksgiving dinner was served with all the trimmings. Arlene Banks sat at one end of the table and Duncan at the other, and when the older woman asked Justine to sit at Duncan's right, Justine accepted it as a gesture of good will, though guilt diminished her pleasure in it all.

Arlene looked at her son, then bowed her head. Duncan, Arlene, and Banks reached for the hands of those nearest them, and Justine lowered her head and closed her eyes as Duncan said grace. An inner peace, buttressed by the strength of his fingers joined with hers, flowed through her, powerful in its solace, its reassurance that he was there for her. She fought back the knowledge that she had sowed the seeds sure to destroy all that she meant to him, that what bound them now could prove as fragile as a feather in a wind storm.

CHAPTER ELEVEN

They laughed, joshed each other, told tales, and lied outrageously about little things, while the soft sounds of Duke Ellington's "Creole Love Song," "Mood Indigo," and "Prelude To A Kiss"—songs Arlene loved—filled the room. *As a child, I had people around me,* Justine thought *but this is a family.* Silently, she vowed that Tonya's life would be filled with love no matter what she had to pay.

"I'm surprised that your mother excused you from dinner," Arlene said to Wayne.

His pained expression told the tale before he spoke. "She didn't. She just scheduled dinner at five o'clock instead of two, so I could eat with Leah." He turned to Leah. "And if I can eat two big meals within three hours, so can you."

Arlene looked aghast. "I certainly hope you'll eat dinner with him," she said to Leah, "since he's eating with you."

Leah eyed her mother. "You taught me to chart my own course, and I'm doing my best to obey you."

Justine dragged herself out of bed at six o'clock the next morning, groggy from lack of sleep. There seemed little point in arousing Tonya; Duncan's mother would enjoy dressing and feeding her. She still hadn't figured out the message she'd gotten from Arlene Banks soon after she arrived at the Banks home. The woman had looked her over as she held Tonya and her eyes had seemed to say, *I know you*. But how could she, when they had not previously met? Yet, Arlene's perusal had not been hostile, and she had received her warmly. She dressed and went down to the dining room, where Banks and Wayne sat at the table, holding hands and gazing into each other's eyes while they sipped coffee.

"Hi. Don't tell me you two have been here all night," she said to them.

Wayne seemed to take his gaze from Banks with reluctance. "Hi. I went home to Beaver Ridge."

"And I slept upstairs, girlfriend. Can't you tell?"

Justine joined them at the table and poured herself a cup of coffee. "How would I know?"

Banks looked straight at her. "Same way I could tell. Some things scream out at you. Want me to go on?"

Wayne went to Justine's defense. "You don't have to say everything you think, Leah."

Banks shrugged. "What makes you think I do? I don't miss anything that goes on around me. Not one thing." She tweaked his nose. "If I said everything I thought, you'd probably run. Anything you want to know, just ask."

He put his left arm around her shoulder and tugged her closer. "With your bluntness, I'm not sure I'd want to. All right. Why won't you come home with me? My folks were disappointed that you didn't come to dinner yesterday."

She looked him in the eye. "I told you. Your mother's formidable, and you're the only person in Frederick who disagrees with me. She and I like each other from a distance, and I think we ought to keep it that way, at least for now."

"She's got a strong personality," he said, "but she also has two sons who are strong-willed, independent, and have made good lives for themselves. That ought to tell you she respects individualism."

The seriousness of Banks's tone matched her words. "I didn't think it was the time for me to visit Miss Mary, not with a crowd of family at a holiday meal, because I don't want to get off on the wrong foot with her. If she and I don't have an audience, we're more likely to get on well. So, try not to push it, Wayne. We'll get there."

The tenderness that glowed on his face as he gazed at Banks reminded Justine of Duncan's expression when he rocked Tonya and sang to her and when he'd held her own body in his arms.

She glanced toward the open door just as Duncan filled it. "Good morning. I didn't expect that you'd all be here, so I've been working in my room."

"Sure," Banks taunted, "any excuse will do. You sure we should go fishing? We could freeze on that river."

"Not to worry, babe," Wayne said. "We'll have a fire, and the forest is so thick that we won't get much wind. But dress warmly. I got enough donuts to last you a week, and we'll have plenty of coffee, so you ought to be happy." He looked up at Duncan. "This will be Leah's first visit to the lodge. I tried to get her to go when Adam and Melissa were here a couple of weeks ago, but she begged off. I still don't know why."

Banks raised an eyebrow. "You hadn't called me in four days, and I didn't feel like pleasing you."

Wayne's shoulders shook as he let himself laugh. "Sometime when I realize I spent thirty-four years of my life without having known Leah, I think about what I've missed and I get mad at the world."

As though to say, the heck with Duncan, he leaned over, pulled Leah into his arms, kissed her mouth, and prolonged it until she wrapped him in her arms. Observing them and their shared passion, Justine squirmed. Finally, she could no longer resist looking at Duncan, who had locked his gaze on her. Without thinking, she let her right hand go to her left breast, as she sucked in her breath. Within seconds, he was there, bringing her out of the chair and into the heaven of his body. Frissons of heat shot through her like hot, metal arrows seeking magnets. His lips adored her mouth until she opened to him, longing to take him in.

But he eased her away, winked, and whispered, "Looks like we can't be trusted in private or public. You mad 'cause I did that?"

He had made another public statement of their relationship; how could he ask if he'd angered her? "I'm so mad, I never want to see you again."

"What?"

"Right. It's a kind of madness that sends me spinning out of this world."

His even white teeth glistened and sparkles danced in the eyes that she adored. "That kind of talk will get you in trouble, sweetheart, and nail you there."

This time when she saw that Banks, though nestled in Wayne's arms, watched them with an inquiring look, she shrugged it off. Let Duncan handle it.

Wayne looked at his watch. "It's time to get going, folks. The lodge is a good hour from here."

They went in separate cars. "Too bad we couldn't take Tonya," Justine said to Duncan as he sped behind Wayne's maroon Town Car.

"Another time. She's better off there with my mother."

"I know," Justine said, and in her mind's eye, she saw her child bonding with the woman whom she would call grandmother and who, if Duncan cut his ties with her, could be the one who reared Tonya and taught her about life. She had a sensation of being crushed between towering forces. The morning slowly lost its darkness, and shades of gray crept into the skies. Like her life. From night to shrouded morning, from not having her child at all to having her and knowing that, at any minute, she could lose her forever.

"You've been silent for miles," Duncan said. "What's wrong?"

"Paying for last night's lost sleep."

He pulled up to the lodge behind Wayne. "This is a great place. You'll see," he told her, holding her hand and walking around the house. "That's the most wonderful woods back there, and the river is magical, but it floods and can be dangerous."

She scrutinized the lodge. "Duncan, this is a house. I was expecting a log cabin."

They went inside, put on their fishing clothing, got their fishing gear and cooking supplies, and trekked down to the edge of the Roundtree property—about half a city block from the lodge—where the Potomac River ambled lazily toward the Chesapeake Bay. Wayne made a fire, and they spread out to try their luck with the fish. Duncan quickly caught six croakers, and Banks landed a large trout, but Wayne and Justine had no luck.

"I'll get these cleaned and in the frying pan in no time," Duncan said to Wayne and Banks. "Justine, would you put some coals on the fire? I'll mix some corn bread, and we can have fried fish, cornbread, and coffee for breakfast. If Wayne and Leah do get together, they'll have to hire a full time cook, because neither one of them can cook anything fit to eat." He measured the meal and some flour.

"I'm not sure I want any cornbread; it'll make me gain weight," Justine told him.

"Yeah? So what if you gain a little weight. You could add another ten pounds and still be perfect."

Was he aiming at her Achilles heel? "What do you mean by that?"

"What I said. To me, you're perfect."

Without warning, his mouth settled on hers with a powerful, searing hunger, and shudders racked him. The hard tips of her breasts proclaimed to him their need as he held her body to him, caressing, rubbing her shoulders, her arms, her back.

"I need you," she whispered. "Oh, Duncan, you don't know how I need you."

He rested her head on his shoulder and held her tightly. He had to be the gentlest, sweetest man alive, she thought, when he pulled away from her. "When we get back home, I mean to Washington, we'll have to talk about us, Justine. I'm not used to being indecisive, but . . . well, it seems as though neither of us is directing this drama. I don't believe in letting life happen to me, and I don't think you do. I accept that I care for you, and that I'm strongly attracted to you. I haven't gotten further, and I may not. So I want us to have an understanding."

"I want that, too, Duncan, and I thought we had one, but our understandings don't seem to count for much because they're not based in reality, but in denial. There's no point in us talking unless we face what we feel. I don't know that I want to go through that."

He hugged her. "Are you suggesting we try to stay with what we worked out before we left home?"

She nodded.

"All right, but if it doesn't work, we try it my way." He looked around. "What happened to Leah and Wayne? They're not out there fishing."

"Your sister can take care of herself and especially with Wayne. He adores her."

"You don't know that guy. Women are crazy about him."

"Take a good look at him. Sure they are."

"Where'd they go?" Duncan asked.

Justine flexed her right shoulder. "Probably somewhere making out " she said reminding him that it wasn't really his business and enjoying the glare he gave her for her daring comment.

Banks and Wayne were at that moment walking through the woods hand in hand discussing Duncan and Justine.

"My brother's crazy in love with Justine and doesn't realize it."

Wayne disagreed. "That would surprise me. G. Duncan Banks is in tune with himself and the rest of the world. Besides a man knows how he feels about a woman."

Banks stopped walking and looked at Wayne. "Always? You're telling me that all men are that clever?" She sucked her teeth. "Well fly me to the moon in your Cesena—"

His hands grabbed her shoulders and he turned her to face him. "Leah stop hiding your feelings behind these clever remarks you like to make. You want to know how I feel about you? Do you care how I feel about you? Do You? Well, ask me!"

"Do I . . . Wayne. Wayne."

She wanted to take off her jacket so she could feel his hands on her body when his arms went around her.

"I feel something special for you, Leah. Special and strong. Do you think you could get rid of your sharp tongue when you're with me and . . . just be yourself. I thought you'd cry when you lost that first big fish this morning, and I was hoping you would. I need to know when you're vulnerable."

"I don't have such a sharp tongue. Honest, Wayne, I just tell the truth, and you don't hear it often. Besides, when people see your weaknesses, they take advantage of you."

He kissed her eyelids. "Not me. Never. I just want to know who you are, who it is that's worming herself into me."

She cocked her ear, and when he repeated it, she let her delight shine on her face. "You talking about me?"

"Who else, Leah?"

She didn't want to get weak and throw herself around him, so she said, "We'd better get back to the fire before my brother sends out a posse for you."

He shook both of her shoulders. "See what I mean?"

"Not a bad way to express your feelings," she said of Wayne's gentle shake. "I enjoyed it."

His hug wrapped her in heaven, and she sensed that she'd gotten closer to him.

Duncan and Justine sat on a stone bench beside the hot coals. His mind had drifted back to his work when Justine remarked, "You're awfully quiet."

He patted her hand. "I'm on a story, and every time I get a lead, it takes me nowhere." He paused, realizing that it was the first time he'd discussed his work with Justine. Marie hadn't shown an interest in what he did, and he hadn't considered discussing it with Justine.

"I don't remember ever before having gotten so many false tips or gone down so many dead ends," he went on.

"What's the problem?"

He was silent for some minutes, deciding whether and how much to tell her. He didn't discuss his assignments, but he wanted to share it with her. "I'm investigating housing conditions in West Baltimore for a series of articles Wayne asked me to write, and I can't find out who's managing those tenements and, in some cases, who owns them."

"My godfather deals in Baltimore real estate. Maybe he can give you some leads." She must have been taken aback at what he knew was a stunned look on his face at her offer of help but, nevertheless, she wrote something on a piece of paper and handed it to him. Still preoccupied with his thoughts of her and of his assignment, he thanked her, folded the paper, and put it in his pocket without looking at it.

"Any time. We aim to please."

"You do please me, and in ways that you may not have contemplated."

"Duncan, I wouldn't expect you to be a loose-tongued man, so don't tease my about my . . . my size."

"I'm not teasing. You do suit me."

A woman with an influential godfather. All at once, his mind plunged into its old habit of tormenting him with thoughts of who she might be, whether she was who she represented herself to be.

"By the way," he heard himself say, "would you mind telling me why you told those women who answered Dee Dee's ad that the position was closed and that I'm not looking for a wife?"

If he was looking for a way to put some distance between them, he'd found it. "I already told you. I just couldn't see turning Tonya over to a stranger."

"And I said you can remain her nanny as long as you like. But day before yesterday, you told another woman she was out of luck. Look me in the eye and tell me you did that."

She refused to lie about it or to apologize. As she looked into the distance beyond his shoulder, she knew that her culpability blazed across her face.

His next words stunned her. "If you want me for yourself, tell me. I like a woman who knows what she wants and goes for it. The way things are moving between us, I wouldn't dare guess where or how it will end. Who knows, I might take a call from another one of Dee Dee's readers on a day when my ego needs stroking."

"You unfaithful creature."

"Me? I'm the epitome of fidelity." he growled, stood, and held out both hands to her. "Come here, baby."

If they didn't stop it, she'd lose everything, and he'd break her heart. "Duncan, I work for you, and I live in your house."

"Okay. You're fired," he said, without the semblance of humor. "Now, come over here. I'm cold, honey."

She walked to where he stood with his back to the fire, took his hand, and stood beside him with her head against his shoulder where he'd put it.

Banks and Wayne found them holding each other, their demeanor quiet and somber.

"Where's the food?" Wayne asked.

Duncan looked at Wayne's arm around his sister's shoulder. "The stuff's been ready half an hour."

Justine let herself enjoy the interplay between Banks and Duncan. He played the role of big brother, and she teased him about it. "You could have eaten already, if you hadn't been otherwise busy," she told Duncan.

Wayne's fingers grasped both of Banks's shoulders. "Honey, the correct response is 'sorry, I hope it didn't get cold.' "

Banks half nodded. "Right."

Duncan eyed them curiously. His sister had actually agreed with Wayne without first giving him a smart comeback. "Well, hallelujah, there've been some changes made."

"Yeah?" Banks asked. "What happened while we were gone?"

Wayne's laughter echoed through the woods. "You're incorrigible, honey."

Duncan remembered the note Justine had given him, took it out of his pocket, and looked at it. His heart began to bounce around in his chest and perspiration beaded on his forehead. Her godfather. *Hugh Pickford was Justine's godfather.* He'd gotten into something and, whatever it was, he wasn't going to like it. For a long time, he contemplated his course of action. Quiet. Pensive. He knew that Justine sensed his cooled feelings, but she wouldn't question him about it. He admired her innate dignity. No matter how much a thing distressed or hurt her, she laid her shoulders back and raised her head. If he knew one thing about her, it was that she would never crawl.

As though she'd read his thoughts, she looked him in the eye and said, "Who am I looking at right now, Duncan? Same man? The thunder of your silence is almost deadly, ear-splitting like the sound of . . ." she looked skyward, "of the . . . the moon bleating at the clouds. What you're not saying is stronger and louder than anything I ever heard. I hope you know what it is." She didn't wait for his response, but walked away from him and joined Banks and Wayne, who talked a few feet away.

"It seems colder. Could we head back to Frederick?" she asked Banks.

Banks looked over at her brother. "Yeah. Let's." She put an arm around Justine as though, having sensed the rift between her and Duncan, she sought to comfort her. "It's great out here," she said, "but I need some real coffee." She opened a pack of cigarettes and put one in her mouth.

"Can't you do without those things for a couple of hours?" asked Duncan who had joined them.

"Not to worry friend," Wayne interjected coming to Banks's defense. "She's blowing her smoke my way."

Duncan had made Justine uncomfortable but he couldn't tell her why. Not yet. Not until he got his man. "If you want to leave," he told her, "I'll take you."

Sunday morning Justine stood at the door with Duncan as they prepared to return to Washington. His mother's birthday gala had been a gathering of the town's notables, as well as Arlene Banks's less well-placed friends. Justine had enjoyed meeting Adam and Melissa Roundtree,

Wayne's brother and sister-in-law, and had marveled at the similarity in stature, physique, and good looks that Melissa and Banks shared. It was the kind of party that she had attended so often during her life with Kenneth and she'd been glad when it ended.

Duncan went to pack their things in the car, and his mother walked over to Justine, placed Tonya in her arms, and kissed both of them. "Justine, I hope you've decided what to do about Duncan. He—"

"Mrs. Banks, you know I'm Tonya's nanny."

The woman didn't back down. "And you and I both know that you're more than that. Duncan suffered during his first marriage and after it ended, and you can hurt him more than Marie ever did. But if you do, remember that my son will always fly. No matter what you do to him, he has it in him to pull himself up and fly. So be careful. No matter how deeply he cares for you, he has the strength to turn away from you. I hope for all your sakes that it doesn't come to that. If you ever need me, just call."

The woman's ambiguous remarks unsettled her, but Justine hugged Arlene, for she truly liked Duncan's mother and knew that she reciprocated her feelings. One more source of pain, her conscience reminded her, and she turned away and walked to the car.

Duncan packed them in and headed for Washington. They rode mostly in silence, each unsettled by the morning's events. Duncan was certain that Justine would not forgive his exposure of her beloved uncle, and Justine's premonition that her brief idyll of joy was approaching its conclusion was almost more than she could bear.

CHAPTER TWELVE

The next morning, Duncan stood at the bottom of the stairs looking up at Justine, who stood at the top holding his daughter. He had to talk to himself to keep from running up those stairs and taking her in his arms. She'd gotten to him, deep down in his gut where he lived, sticking there like the sweet honey of a queen bee, and he didn't know who she was. If he'd had any doubt that he'd given her her first job as a nanny or any other kind of servile position, seeing her at his mother's party, in fact the entire weekend, had dispelled it. This regal, well-bred woman would be at home with kings.

His mind rambled on as he stood there gazing up at her. If she had a rich godfather, what about her own parents, who had to have been in his social and economic class and that of his close personal friends; at that level, African Americans rarely crossed class lines. She had kept two secrets from him, and he didn't want to imagine what others she might have. Yet, he'd lay his life on her sense of honor and decency. She loved Tonya and would protect the child with her life, and he knew beyond a doubt that her response to him was real, that her body and emotions overrode her genuine desire not to get involved with him.

Her low, sultry voice halted his musings. "You leaving now?"

"Yes. I'll be in Baltimore for a couple of days. If I'm too beat to get home in the evenings, I'll stay at Wayne's place. In any case, I'll call you." He turned toward the front door.

"Aren't you going to kiss Tonya good-bye?"

Her honeyed voice peeled away layers of his determination, and her words pierced his hastily donned armor. Substitute Justine for Tonya and he'd have their real meaning. "I did that already," he said, steeling himself against his seething emotions.

"I . . . Justine, for God's sake!" His feet propelled him up the stairs, increasing their speed the closer he got to her. *"Justine!"* He crushed her to him, found her eager mouth, and let himself come alive.

She broke the kiss and stroked his face with her free hand. "I know things aren't good between us right now, that for some reason you've pulled back, and that's probably a good thing. But let's not hurt each other more than we have to."

He stared down at her. "You're saying we have to hurt each other?"

She nodded, and he looked into eyes that glistened with unshed tears. "Looks like it. We don't want to, but we will. Kiss Tonya and . . . look after yourself."

She passed the child to him, and he marveled at childhood innocence as Tonya kissed him, rubbed his cheek, and wrapped her little arms around his neck. He handed her back to Justine, whom he kissed on the cheek, and raced down the stairs.

She had made his house a home. She belonged there. He wished he could understand why he doubted, why his mind had catalogued her as a temporary fixture in his life when he knew he cared for her; she had given him more than any woman he'd known.

He left his car on Calvert Street in the garage beneath the Roundtree Building, got a Taxi to CafeAhNay, and took a seat in his usual place, a booth near the door facing the bar. The weather had gotten mild for late November and brought out most of the lunch time regulars. He'd just begun whittling on the little Frederick Douglas statue that accompanied him wherever he went, when Lottie brought him two glasses of water but no flatware, a signal that she had news. He put the carving back in his pocket.

"What's up, Lottie?"

"You been asking questions about the slums 'round on Dolphin Street?"

"Yeah. Why?"

"Everybody's buzzing about it, so watch your back."

In his business, nothing surprised him. "Thanks. Any idea who I'm looking for?"

She glanced toward the rear of the room. "Like I said before, somebody's always fronting for somebody. There's a couple of our fellows that owns blocks of slums and some white guys, too. Take a look at some of the rundown buildings with mostly white tenants and see who manages them."

"I'm doing that. You saying it's the managers I want?"

"I'm saying they're what you'll get. At least at first. And that's a dirty bunch. Ever hear of a guy named Kilgore?"

Duncan sat forward. "I thought he was a supplier for local schools."

She shrugged. "He's into everything, including the horses. Did you want anything? A cup of coffee maybe?"

So she needed a cover. "Sure. Coffee and French toast. No syrup." When she returned, he asked her loudly enough to be overheard, "How's your mother these days? Still shut in?"

"She gets around a little, but she can't leave the house."

He paid for his order, folded a large bill, and handed it to her. "Buy your mother something nice."

Lottie looked first at the money, then at him, and with the sleeve of her black uniform, brushed away the moisture that dripped from her eyes. "She's been wanting a little radio, and when I get there tonight, I'll take one to her. God bless you."

He finished his toast and coffee as quickly as he could and headed for Wilma's Blue Moon Restaurant. Wilma greeted him at the door. He knew he could trust whatever she told him.

She led him to a corner table, snapped her fingers for a waiter, and sat down. "Bring us some coffee," she ordered, and turned to Duncan. "You wanna eat or talk?"

"Talk." He told her what he was looking for. "Know anything?"

"Of course I do." She confirmed what Lottie had told him, adding, "Those owners launder their tracks with all kinds of covers, so be careful you don't write anything libelous."

He thanked her and headed for the worst of the slums. If anybody was under the impression that slumlords were bigots who victimized the African-American poor alone, let him think again. They victimized all the poor, race and ethnicity notwithstanding, and with equal disdain for the quality of human life. Broken glass, graffiti, litter, and ugliness greeted his eyes wherever he went. Living Hell.

Near the end of a long day, he had two names: Hugh Pickford and Buddy Kilgore. He wasn't far from Grace's apartment, so he used his cell phone and called her. "Mind if I drop by for a few minutes?"

"You didn't have to ask. I'm here."

When he got to her place, he asked her whether she knew an agent/manager of the building that faced the one in which she'd previously lived. She told him of a man named Cap.

"He plays low down, Dunc, and he's got eyes and ears everywhere, so you watch out."

He thanked her and left before she had a chance to try pulling him back into her life. It was seven forty-five and he hadn't even had a good lunch. He got in his car and drove to drove to Wayne's pied à terre, a large, well-furnished one-room apartment that Wayne used when he had to spend a night in Baltimore. He let himself in, pulled off his jacket and sweater, sat on the edge of the long leather hide-a-bed sofa, and telephoned Justine.

"I've had a gruelling day, so I'm staying over at Wayne's place tonight. I'll try to get home late tomorrow. How . . . how are you?"

"We're okay. Tonya's gone crazy over that piano. Every time I tried to work, she sang piano, and if I ignored her, she screamed it. I think I may have created a piano monster."

He chuckled with pride. "Does she try to play it?"

"With all ten fingers, and she sings while she plays or, rather, bangs."

"I'll be darned. Will she let you play for her?"

"Strangely, yes. When I get tired of the noise, I move her hands and play a sonata or some eight-to-the-bar."

"What's that?"

"Boogie-woogie. Where've you been? Anyhow, she loves it and doesn't make a sound. Any progress today?"

"Yeah, but it's slow going. Did you get another crank call?"

"One. He didn't say anything, though."

Maybe he should have gone home. The man could know his movements. "Don't answer the door tonight and turn on the answering machine. If you don't know who's calling, don't pick up. Next week I'm going to install caller I.D. You okay otherwise?"

"I'm fine, Duncan."

What else could she say? He hung up and telephoned his sister.

"Banks."

"I was hoping Wayne would break you of that. You're a girl, for heaven's sake."

"I'm a woman, for heaven's sake, and don't think he doesn't try."

"At least you don't complain when he calls you Leah."

"Make sense, Duncan. It's Leah or nothing, so I answer to Leah."

"It's like that, is it?"

"He's wonderful, Duncan. I'm never going to let him go. Never. I'm so happy when I'm with him."

He could not believe what he heard. He had thought she'd enjoy a short fling with a man she could trust, but she'd maintained from the beginning that Wayne was the man for her. "How were you so certain that he's the one?"

"I was with Melissa a couple of years ago and overheard him telling another man his views on life, women, and family in that wonderful voice of his, and then I looked at him and something happened to me."

"What about him?"

"He didn't see me. Melissa told me who he was. When I met him at your house, I flipped."

The way he'd reacted to Justine? "How's it going?"

"We are getting closer, and I'm settling down kinda, because he said he cares for me, and wants me to . . . well . . . be like you said."

"And are you?"

"Duncan, you know a leopard doesn't change its spots. I told him I'm trying, and he accepts that. Why should I stop being me?" He heard her pull air through her teeth. "I like me just like I am."

He had never been able to resist needling her. "Sure, but you're willing to tone down for old Wayne. Way to go, man. How is Mama?"

"She's okay. Whatta you know? She flipped over Justine. Says there is something special about her."

He knew that, but at times he wondered what it was. "She's right about that. I'm signing off."

Peels of laughter came through the wire. "Sure you are. You can grill me about Wayne, but if I mention Justine, you don't want to hear it. Get used to it, bro, Justine is your destiny."

"So you're a psychic now. Don't forget you promised to go to the Kennedy Center honors gala with me."

"How could I? I'm getting a new evening gown, split up the sides to—"

He couldn't help laughing. "I know better than that."

He hung up, heated one of Wayne's frozen pizzas in the microwave, got a bottle of pilsner, propped his feet on the coffee table, and watched CNN's nightly news. He had put his finger on the switch to turn off the TV, when Arnold Taylor of the Virginia House of Delegates was heard to say, "Rent control is an abomination. Our maintenance costs escalate yearly, and we're stuck with these low rents."

The camera roamed over a block of tenements in the nation's capital.

"But, sir," the reporter countered, "these houses haven't been maintained in twenty years."

Duncan jumped to his feet. Mitch and Rags lived in that building. Who *was* Arnold Taylor? He ran his left hand over his tight curls, mentally reaching for an explanation that was on the edge of his consciousness and that had been there before, always eluding him. He wasn't after conditions in Washington, he reminded himself as he sat down to finish his pizza. Baltimore was his purview.

He wrote up the day's notes, cleared off his tape recorder, and got in bed, but whenever he closed his eyes, Justine danced before him, a vision in a red silk kimono with beautiful brown skin and large grayish-brown eyes. He fell over on his belly and permitted himself a groan to release the tension. But she wouldn't leave him. After two hours of it, he sat up and looked at his Jaeger le Coutre. Eleven o'clock.

He called her. "Justine, this is Duncan. Pick up the receiver."

"Hello, Duncan?"

"Yeah. You wouldn't let me sleep, so I won't apologize if I woke you," he said when she answered.

"I wasn't sleeping, and your call won't be of much help when I try to sleep after you hang up."

He could not say what he felt, not until he was sure of his ground, and he didn't want to chat. He went for the jugular.

"Something is keeping us apart, Justine. I didn't want to get emotionally involved ever again. That's why I considered a marriage of convenience. But there is no denying that I am involved with you. Something isn't what it should be. You want me, you care one hell of a lot for me, but you act as if it's all right with you if I leave you alone. There isn't a man alive who's dumb enough to accept that at face value. I want to know why you're so sure we're going to hurt each other."

He knew from her silence that he was on target, that this was what they needed to talk about, but he also knew that they ought to be together when they did.

"Are you all right, Justine?"

He listened for sniffles and relaxed when he didn't hear any.

"No, I'm not all right, and yes, there are things that will keep us apart. I promised you that I'd take care of Tonya to the best of my ability and that I'd behave respectfully in your home. Please, don't ask more of me. Duncan, I didn't plan for us to get involved, but for me, it was hopeless from that first evening. I am not sorry for what's happened between us; I wouldn't have missed it for anything. Because of you, I see the world through different eyes. But there can't be more." He heard the catch in her voice. "Not . . . not ever."

He sat up. Don't be a fool, he told himself, but suddenly he had to know. He'd regret it, but he regretted a lot of things.

"Justine, do you love me?" Cold shivers skittered through his body as he waited for her answer.

Her voice came to him strong and even. "Yes, I love you, and I knew it long before we made love. You don't reciprocate it, and you don't want to love me or any woman. I know that, and I try not to encourage you to love me, as much as I'd cherish it if you did, because there is no future for us."

"You are sure of that?"

"Yes, I'm sure."

"Do you have a husband or a man to whom you're committed?"

"No. Nothing like that."

"I didn't think so. Is there anything you want to tell me?"

"Yes, but nothing that I *can* tell you."

Just as he guessed, she had secrets. Well, he'd let it go for now, but after he turned in his story, he'd get busy. He propped himself up on his elbow. "Do you realize that if I were there with you right now, I would not sleep until I made love to you? Do you hear me, Justine?"

Her low, sultry voice caressed his ears and shot powerful signals to his libido. "On this night, Duncan, I'd meet you half way."

Eleven thirty-two. What the hell! He hung up. Twelve minutes later he was headed for Route 95 south.

Justine replaced the receiver and cupped her face with her hands. Duncan was her daylight, her sunshine, and she didn't want to imagine her life when he would no longer be a part of it. He was afraid of loving her, and he teetered on the edge of it. She wanted to tell him who she was, but she couldn't take the chance that he would scorn her and send her away. She got up, tiptoed across the hall, opened Tonya's door, and looked down at the sleeping little girl. She didn't know how long she stood there, rubbing her arms, praying for guidance, and calculating the risks if she told him. At last, she closed the door, went back to her room, and got in bed.

She bolted upright when she heard the tap on her door. "May I come in, Justine?"

Duncan! She sprang out of bed and sped to the door, her soul soaring and her feet on wings. "Duncan. Duncan."

She was in his arms. He picked her up, carried her back to bed, and lay her there. She gazed up at him and saw eyes that glowed with the pleasure he planned for them.

"Did you think I'd sleep in Wayne's apartment after what you said to me? I had to get to you, Justine."

He stood beside her bed and looked down at her. What was it about this one woman that could tie him into knots? "Woman, what have you done to me? I need you!"

She raised her arms to him. "And I need you. I want you to love me like it's the last time, as if tomorrow morning will bring Armageddon and end it all." Moisture streaked her cheek. "Love me like I'm the whole world to you."

She barely heard his hoarse words, "You are the world to me. Believe that." He pitched his jacket over to her chaise longue and pulled his black T-shirt over his head. She loosened his belt, unzipped him, and dropped his trousers to his feet. When her hands went to his shorts, he stopped her.

"If you touch me, honey, it'll be over before we start."

He knelt beside her, took her into his arms, and gazed into her face. "Are you crying?"

She brushed away a tear. "I don't know. I'm so full, so . . . What I feel is exploding inside of me."

"What you feel for me?" he whispered, and she thought that hope filled his voice.

"There is so much of it. I . . ."

"Then shout, scream, do whatever you like. Tonight at least, we're here for each other." His right hand stroked her cheek, and his gaze roamed over her face until she wanted to drown in those reddish-brown eyes that she loved.

"You're so beautiful, so sweet, and so much a woman. Justine, hold me."

She wrapped him in her arms, and kissed his eyes, throat, and chest. Her tongue traced his lips and he parted them for her. Did he want her to make love to him? Her fingers skimmed his back and thighs, and his breathing quickened. She let the palm of her hand stroke lightly over his pectorals, and his groan told her she'd excited him and that he liked it. But when she reached for him, he grabbed her wrist, stopped her, and flipped her onto her back.

His lips savored every part of her face, roamed around her neck and the inside of her arms, getting responses where she hadn't known it was possible, branding her, making her his own. He whispered tantalizing, suggestive words in her ears. "When I get inside you, I am going to show you who you are and who I am."

His words sent sparks flying through her body, stirring up the hot coals of desire, singeing her nerve ends.

"Yes, yes," she replied, eager for whatever he would give her. She tugged at his hand, but he wouldn't be led, and slowly his lips brushed lightly over her breasts until she thought she would die if he didn't take her nipple into his mouth. Her body began its demands, and she clasped his head in her hands and led him to her left breast.

"Tell me what you want, what you need."

"I'll go crazy if you don't kiss me."

While he suckled one, his right hand toyed with the other, and she thought she'd incinerate when his left hand began a slow, teasing journey to the seat of her passion. She couldn't restrain her cry when at last he touched her, and his magic fingers began their dance of love.

"Duncan, please. I can't stand it."

But he suckled with increased vigor while he worked his witchery at her pleasure seat. He took his lips from her breast and kissed her waist, her belly, moving his lips downward at a slow, tormenting pace, until he reached his goal and wrung from her the essence of her being. Screams of ecstasy tore from her throat, yet the squeezing and pumping would not end. He intensified it, commanding her to give all. And she gave until he stripped her of every emotion but her love for him. Exhausted, she fell back on the pillow.

"Do you still love me?"

She looked up to the man who loomed over her and could have truthfully answered, "until I die." Instead she breathed his name softly, "Yes. Yes, I love you. If I believed it was so ephemeral, thoughts of the future would be less painful."

"And are they . . .?"

She put two fingers on his mouth. "Shhhh . . . Something for you." Her lips found his pectorals, and she teased until she felt his tremors. She let her hands skim lightly over his flat belly and his thighs and then she touched him and found him ready. She glanced up at him and saw desire and, yes, adoration shining in his eyes. She took him in her hand, caressed his length, and would have stroked him, but he shook his head and she guided him to her portal of love. He would not enter but stayed there teasing, stroking, and heating her blood. When she could no longer tolerate it, she raised her body, clasped his hips, and urged his entry. He filled her slowly, firing up the delicate nerves of her lover's tunnel. When he began the dance, slowly, locked in her arms and legs, she caught his rhythm and swung her hips to his beat. Almost at once, heat flushed the bottom of her feet, skittered up her body, and concentrated at her feminine center. She couldn't breathe.

"Give yourself to me, love. Come on. Fly with me."

"Darling, it's . . . it's almost unbearable."

He thrust higher and harder. "You are mine. Mine, Justine. Do you hear me?"

"Yes, yes. Yes, I'm yours." The waves reeled faster, and the squeezing and clutching would be the death of her.

"Duncan."

"I'm with you, love."

He clasped her to him, wrung the last bit of passion from her, and let himself go as he erupted like a long-dormant and violent volcano into the only woman he would ever want. Shaken by the force of what he felt for her, and acknowledging at last all that she was to him, he gathered her to him, closed his eyes, and looked at his troubled future.

He awakened later that morning to find her sleeping on her belly with one leg thrown across him and her head on his shoulder. She had turned his life around. He wanted to love her again, but he had done that time after time until four o'clock, and he didn't want to make her sore nor, heaven forbid, to make her tired of him. What a woman! She fitted him the way his leather gloves fitted his fingers. He didn't know where they were going, but he hoped they had the same destination. He expelled a deep breath. A smart man wouldn't bet heavily on their getting together, not with her secrets and her insistence on keeping them to herself.

He kissed her until she opened her eyes. "It's getting near to eight o'clock, honey, and I have to get back to Baltimore. I'll be home tonight—unless something unexpected happens."

She sat up, clutching the sheet to her breast, and looked at him. Rays of recognition floated over her countenance and she covered her face with both hands and, in the process, dropped the sheet.

"Don't tell me you're shy." When she buried her face in his chest, he asked her, "What's the problem? Did you discover something about yourself that you didn't know?"

She moved away from him. "Did I ever! And a lot about you, too."

He poked his tongue in the right side of his jaw. "You and me, both. Try not to engage in any guilt-producing foolishness while I'm gone. Okay?"

She nodded. "And you take your own advice."

He had to taste her before he left there, so he leaned over and brushed her lips. Immediately, her nipples became erect, and awareness slammed into him. "You feel like that?"

She lowered her lashes and grinned, flirting with him. "You may say I'm a quick study. You've taught me that I get the goodies as soon as you know I'm ready for them. If you have to leave, go on. I'll be here when you get home."

A quick kiss and he put his feet on the floor. It was a night that he would remember for the rest of his life. After dressing, he checked on Tonya, whom he found playing with her rubber alphabets and musical notes, and sat down to a breakfast of coffee, biscuits, jam, and scrambled eggs.

"I thought you wasn't coming home last night, Mr. B, and I didn't leave you no supper."

"I ate in Baltimore, Mattie, and I got here late."

She stood at the table holding a spatula in one hand and tugging on her canary-yellow wig with the other one. "Mr. B, me and my Moe found a house over on Columbia Road that we can afford, and I'm axin if I can borrow a little on my salary."

"How much do you need?"

She hung her head. "A lot. We short of ten thousand for the down payment."

"Tell you what. I'll loan you half of that and you can have the other half as a house-warming present. How's that?"

Her eyes widened, and she treated him to her best Bugs Bunny grin. "Lord, Mr. B, the Lord is shore gonna bless you this very day. You hear? And I shore do thank you."

"Just let me know when you need it."

Her grin spread wider. "Any day this week, sir. And I shore do thank you."

He wrote her a check and, remembering that he had to handle Justine with care, started back up the stairs to tell her good-bye. She met him halfway with Tonya in her arms.

"When did you start wearing glasses?"

"Ages ago. Sometimes I wear contacts."

He kissed them both and headed for Baltimore.

He parked his car and went to find Cap. If Grace's information was accurate, he'd get the lead he'd been looking for. He entered the dingy little bar and grill shortly after eleven that morning. Cap sat at the bar with his back to the room, but that didn't fool Duncan; the man could see the entire room in the mirror facing him.

Cap proved to be surly and threatening. "Why do you think you're entitled to interfere with me when I'm having my beer? People have been put to sleep for less."

Duncan was on alert. Someone had tipped off the man. A slap on his breast pocket turned on his recorder. "Sorry, man. I was told you might have some information, and that if you said it, it was good as gold. No offense meant."

Cap put down his beer. "Good as gold, huh? Whatta you after?"

Duncan took an uneasy look at the tattered seat beside Cap, sat down, and began talking.

"All right," Cap said, after a few swallows of his beer. "These owners are covered. Well, most of them are. Go after the managers. They are crooks, and they'll squeal to save their hides."

How far could he trust a man who'd change his demeanor for a few words of praise? An ego that needed stroking. He'd take the chance. "Ever hear of a man named Pickford?"

"Yeah. Get him, and I hope you nail the bastard. My sister died in one of his fire traps. Not a sprinkler in the place. Buddy Kilgore fronts for him. You can catch him down at CafeAhNay every evening at seven-thirty."

Duncan stood. "Thanks, man. I'll do my best to get justice for your sister."

"All right. Keep a low profile."

Duncan thanked him and left. He went first to his office

in the Roundtree Building, called Justine, and told her he'd be late getting home, if at all. Seven-thirty found him at his regular booth in CafeAhNay.

"He'll be in any minute," Lottie told Duncan.

Kilgore arrived at his scheduled time, took a seat at a center table and, after turning on his recorder, Duncan joined him. An hour later, he had his story. He left the cafe and decided to make good use of the clear, crisp moonlit night by walking the streets in search of background material for his report. Long after midnight, he let himself into Wayne's apartment.

The next morning, Lottie called him at his *Maryland Journal* office. "I just wanted to make sure you knew Buddy Kilgore plays the horses. Cap was in here after you left. He said he made some inquiries today, and that Buddy gambles away a lot of the rents he gets from Pickford's buildings and tells Pickford he spends it on maintenance. He said Kilgore doctors his accounts."

"Can't Hugh Pickford see how those buildings are kept?"

"No, he lives in Florida. Be sure and check out your story before you put it in the paper."

He spent the remainder of the day in the city government offices checking the information he'd gotten from Wilma, Cap, and Lottie. While he weighed his evidence during the next few days, the Baltimore County Attorney General indicted Hugh Pickford for the condition of his rental property, and brought more than a dozen charges. Duncan put his article aside, and went to the trial.

"I'm not going to think about where this thing between Duncan and me is headed," Justine promised herself, while she tried to feed Tonya. Duncan had stayed in Baltimore the previous night, though he'd called twice. Each time, what he didn't say blasted itself to her through the wires, like a ship's horn in a heavy fog. Knowing that he loved her wasn't much comfort as long as he couldn't bring himself to say it. And she didn't want him to say it, because she'd have to tell all. She looked closely at Tonya.

"Mattie, come here, please."

Mattie stepped into the dining room with a purple bandanna tied around her head. "I couldn't find the key to my closet this morning, and the only wig on my dresser was a blue one," she explained, when she noticed Justine staring at her head. "I knew when I woke up that this wasn't no blue day. What you want me for?"

"Tonya isn't eating. She ate almost nothing for dinner. It isn't like her, and she's listless."

"She don't have no fever?"

Justine got a thermometer and took Tonya's temperature. "No. I can't imagine what's wrong with her."

Mattie offered Tonya orange juice, but she wouldn't drink it. "Better call Mr. B. This child loves orange juice."

"I can't. He's in court, so his cell phone wouldn't be turned on. I'm taking her to the pediatrician."

"But Mr. B said we wasn't to take her out 'less he was here."

"Then you come with me. I'm taking her to the doctor as soon as I get her dressed."

Mattie seemed uncertain. "Well . . . I don't know." Her face lit up as though she had seen a heavenly vision. "I know what. My Moe will go with us. He don't leave for work 'til twelve-thirty."

"Then call him," Justine threw over her shoulder as she carried Tonya upstairs.

Justine wasn't prepared for Moe. No one who knew Mattie would have been. She thought she might be hallucinating when the six foot, four inch robust man walked into the foyer. Her gaze shifted to Mattie, who didn't stand more than five feet tall in her low heel shoes.

"Glad to meet you, ma'am," he said, when she greeted him. "My Mattie has your name on her lips with just about every other word. She says you're a real classy lady."

Justine stared at him. He was tastefully dressed and spoke perfect English. She told herself to say something. "I'm so glad to meet you at last, Moe, and I appreciate your helping us out."

"Pleasure's mine."

Mattie beamed. "Ain't he just somethin'? People is so

surprised when I introduce them to my Moe. Well, let's be going."

The doctor examined Tonya and couldn't find anything wrong, but wrote a prescription. "This will perk her up. It could be a virus. She'll be her old self in no time."

Justine thanked her and asked Moe if he would get her mail from her post office box. He did that, got Tonya's prescription filled, and saw them safely home.

The phone rang as Justine entered the foyer. Duncan's voice came over the answering machine, and she raced to the phone.

"Hello."

"Justine. Where were you? I've been calling non stop for the last hour and a half. I was ready to go home."

She told him what had happened. "Tonya may have a virus."

"I hope that's all it is. I have to call Moe tonight and thank him. That was good thinking on Mattie's part. I'll phone you every hour, since you can't call me while I'm in court.

"Do you think that's necessary? I'll take good care of her, Duncan."

"I know that, but I also have to know how she is. Don't worry, though. She'll be fine."

Justine knew he was reassuring himself. Tonya was his heart. She gave the child a dose of medicine and put her to bed. Tonya's smiles and happy hand clapping filled her heart with joy when she went in the room later to feed her.

"Panno, Juju. Pay panno."

Justine hugged Tonya, dressed and fed her, and took her down to the basement.

"What do you want me to play? she asked her.

"Pay Towpan."

Justine couldn't restrain the laughter that poured out of her, releasing her fear. "Chopin. SHO PAN, darling."

"Tow pan, Juju."

She played a sonata and couldn't believe it when Tonya watched her hands intently and didn't move or say a word.

Duncan's call interrupted what she was certain would have been an afternoon at the piano.

"That's Daddy calling." She picked up the receiver and held Tonya in her left arm. " Hello."

"Is everything all right?"

"She is fine now. Tonya, say hello to daddy." She put the phone where the child could speak into it. "Daddy. Daddy. Daddy."

"Thanks Justine. I don't know what I'd do if anything happened to my child."

They talked for a few minutes, and as soon as she hung up, the phone rang again. She answered it automatically without waiting to hear the caller over the answering machine.

"Hello."

"Is Pops there?"

"You must have the wrong number."

"No, ma'am, I don't." He described Duncan. "I need to talk to him real quick. My brother, my half-brother that is, fell off the stairs, and he's hurt. Pops tells us that if anything happens to us or if we get into trouble, we have to call him. I need for my brother to go to a decent hospital."

"He can't be reached for the next hour. I—"

"That's too long, lady, he could die."

She sat down with Tonya in her lap. "What's your name?"

"Mitch, and my brother's named Rags."

"Tell me where you are and I'll get an ambulance over there."

"Capitol View, and I ain't got no money for no ambulance."

"All right, Mitch. Calm down. Give me your address. I'll call the ambulance and pay in advance with my credit card, and I'll send your brother to the George Washington Medical Center. What's his full name?" He told her his brother's name and address. "Wait for the ambulance. I'm putting him in semi-private. Okay?"

"Yes ma'am. What's your name, ma'am?"

"Justine."

"Thanks, Justine. I owe you, and I always pay."

"You are welcome. Call me as soon as Rags is checked into the hospital."

She called the hospital and the ambulance. *Capitol View.* Misery personified. The boy couldn't be more than sixteen or seventeen. So that's where Duncan went at night. A Good Samaritan. The more she learned about him, the dearer he became.

Duncan knew Justine could take care of his child and his home, as well as he could, but he didn't want her there alone. If she had to take Tonya to the hospital at night, she'd be a sitting duck for that stalker, and he had no idea what time that trial would recess. He called his sister.

"Banks."

Would she never learn? "Leah, this is Duncan." He told her about Tonya's illness and of his concern for Justine's well-being. "I can't get away from here, and I'd feel better if you'd stay with them tonight."

"Okay. Not to worry. I'll get there by six-thirty. How's it going?"

"It's been a long time since I sat in court, and I'd forgotten how boring all these tedious questions can be. Other than that, fine."

"Uh . . . Duncan, Wayne asked me to go fishing with him next weekend. Maybe you can take Justine to the Kennedy Center honors awards instead of me. Huh?"

"I can ask her. Are you certain you want to go fishing with Wayne?"

The voice that reached him was not one to which he was accustomed. Its softness stunned him. "We love each other, Duncan, and he's . . . he treats me like . . . Well, I'm his princess. He's . . . He's wonderful. I'd even quit smoking if he asked me to."

"Leah, don't do it for him; quit for yourself." Now, what had she found to giggle about?

"I just wanted you to know how serious it is. Who knows what I might agree to if he got on his knees in Town Square at high noon on the Fourth of July and—"

"All right. I get the message. You haven't changed, and

you never will. Be certain you're doing the right thing, sis. A few things can only happen once with one person. If he's the one, and you're sure of it, I say no more. But if he louses up, he'll hear from me."

"How do you know so much?" she asked, her voice low with a touch of testiness.

"I helped raise you, and we've always been close. Also, I'm a man, and I understand women. End of topic."

"Right. I'll be at your place tonight."

He hung up and went back into the courtroom, but both lawyers were speaking with the judge, so he stepped out again and telephoned Justine.

"Any news?"

She told him about Mitch's call and what she'd done. "Is that okay? I didn't know what else to do. He was frantic."

If he could have gotten to her right then, he'd have kissed her silly. "More than okay, sweetheart. Be sure you put those bills on my desk. When he calls back, tell him to ring me at exactly eight o'clock. Leah will be over there tonight. I hope you don't mind."

"Mind? I can't think of anyone I'd rather see."

He stared down at the phone in his hand. "Run that past me again. You had rather see—"

Her laughter interrupted what was about to be a foolish question, but what the heck, he was feeling fragile where the woman was concerned. "You are getting clever."

"How so?" he asked her.

That laughter, once so rare, thrilled him again. It was like bells tinkling in a warm breeze. "You didn't finish that sentence and lay an egg."

"Men don't lay eggs."

"I'm glad to know it. You coming back tonight?"

How he longed to do just that. "I'm not sure, but if I can, bet on it."

He hung up and went to find some lunch. He settled on a small Chinese restaurant off Charles Street, pulled out a copy of *The Maryland Journal,* and prepared to eat alone.

"Mind a little company?"

Duncan looked up at the man, judged him, and slapped

the breast pocket of his jacket. "And if I do, you are joining me anyway."

The coarse, craggy voice did not reassure him. "I'll get down to business. Whatever they are paying you to rat on these landlords, I got more."

Duncan figured he must have given himself away before he spoke, because the man's lips began a slow curve upward.

"I work for *The Maryland Journal.* Period."

The man leaned forward, a menacing scowl taking over his face. "You wanna be sure you're not making a mistake."

Duncan narrowed his eyes and tapped his fingers on the linen tablecloth. "I'm sure I'm not making one, but I don't know about you."

"You ain't smart, mister," the man replied, and left the restaurant.

"Take your order?"

Duncan's gaze fell on the first African American who'd waited on him in a Chinese restaurant. "This is a day for surprises," he said.

"My mother is Chinese. What can I get for you, brother?"

Duncan gave his order. "Any idea who that man is who stopped at my table?"

"No, sir."

Duncan finished his shrimp in garlic sauce, rice, and Chef Lu's vegetable delight more quickly than he had planned and got out of there.

Justine opened the door for Banks, and they enjoyed a warm exchange of embraces.

"How's Tonya?"

So that was why she'd come in midweek when she had to work the following day. "Much better. Come on in. I'm glad you're here."

Banks hung her coat in the foyer closet, dropped her overnight bag on the floor, and strolled into the living room. "How's it going with you and my brother?"

Justine had to laugh. "You believe in cutting to the chase, don't you?"

Banks's right shoulder flexed lazily. "You could say that. Well?"

"I don't know, Banks. I really don't."

"Then let me rephrase it. Has he found out that he's in love with you?"

"Not to my knowledge. He hasn't said so."

Banks looked toward the ceiling as though to ask why she had to suffer the stupidity of foolish people.

"I take it you, at least, have sense enough to let him know how you feel about him."

She would have laughed if she hadn't begun to hurt. And she'd gotten tired of pretending, of living a charade every day of her life. "I love him, Banks, and he knows it."

Banks kicked up her heels, slapped her hands, and did a jig. "Hallelujah, one of 'em's got sense." She sobered and put both arms around Justine. "Mama wishes he'd met you years ago, but she's glad he has you now. Me, too."

"He doesn't have me, Banks."

She shrugged. "Mama says he does, and I hope she's right. Straighten out whatever is between you, Justine, and do it soon. He's crazy about you, but he's tough enough to walk away from you."

"Your mother said that, too."

Her voice lost its buoyancy. "We know him, girlfriend."

"What's with you and Wayne?" Justine said, deliberately changing the subject.

She'd never seen eyes get so dreamy so fast. "We're in love."

"Hmm. You've told him you love him?"

Banks's expression was that of a child caught robbing the piggy bank. "No. But Wayne's a clever man. I'm sure he's figured it out."

Justine decided to lean on her. "And Duncan isn't that clever. Right?"

Banks pulled air through her teeth as though disgusted.

"Please! I'm wide open, but you, girlfriend, are tight as a clam."

Ignoring that jab, Justine asked her, "And you are certain Wayne loves you?"

Her expression darkened. "I hope so, Justine. I'm going away with him this weekend. It's a good thing for us. I know it is. And I told Duncan that it's right for Wayne and me."

Justine didn't try to control her gasp. "You told Duncan?"

"Yeah. Why not'? I told Wayne I intended to, and he didn't object. Duncan asked me a lot of questions, talked things he was not supposed to know, and left it to me."

Justine thought about their conversation for a long time and wished she'd had a brother. When she answered the phone around seven o'clock, Mitch's voice greeted her. He'd called to tell her that Rags was resting comfortably with a fractured left wrist and a concussion. She told him to call Duncan at eight o'clock that evening and to keep her posted.

It was Thursday, and Hugh Pickford's trial was to go to the jury Friday afternoon. Duncan had sat through every hour of it, heard all of the testimony, the truths and the lies. He paced the halls of the courthouse, wrestling with his conscience. Hugh Pickford had set his family and all their belongings out on the street in the coldest month of the year because of a meager four hundred dollars, and had indirectly caused his father's death. He'd waited twenty-eight years for this moment, for the chance to get even, to laugh in the man's face. But he knew that Buddy Kilgore and Lim Haskins had lied on the witness stand, because he'd been through the Housing Division's records, had seen the two managers' replies to their tenants' complaints, and had interviewed people who lived in the building.

The evidence before the jury would send Pickford to jail for a dozen years.

Could he live with himself if he didn't disclose what he knew? And what about Justine? She loved Hugh Pickford.

He headed home Thursday night after having been in Baltimore since Tuesday morning. His blood rushed through his veins, almost making him dizzy, when he thought of Justine there. Justine, who'd said she loved him.

When he neared Primrose Street, his heartbeat accelerated, and he slowed down, letting himself take control. He turned into Primrose and stopped. A stretched-out Lincoln stood across the street from his house. Remembering the threat he received, he backed up, went around the block, and entered Primrose from the opposite end. Another limousine stood between him and his house, blocking his way. He backed up, skirted the block, and headed for Georgia Avenue, where he called the police from his cell phone. Three squad cars met him and escorted him home. The police blocked both ends of his street and, minutes later, he had the pleasure of seeing the police handcuff the man who had followed him into the Chinese restaurant in Baltimore and who had threatened and attempted to bribe him.

Justine met him at the door. "Something weighing on you?" she asked, after his brief kiss.

He forced a smile. "Am I so transparent? I have a tough decision about my work to make tonight," he told her, "so I probably won't be good company. But I'll make it up to you."

Her smile warmed him the way the July sun always soothed his body when he lay supine on a sandy ocean beach.

"No apology is needed. Mattie has the kitchen reeking with wonderful odors. Let us know when you're ready to eat."

"Give me fifteen minutes." If only she knew how refreshing she was; she gave him all the space he wanted.

Throughout the night, he wrestled with his demon, hatred. Why should he go to Pickford's defense? After three hours of sleep, he got up, dressed, pushed a note under Justine's door, peeped in on Tonya, and headed for Baltimore.

At a quarter to nine, he knocked on the judge's chamber, and the bailiff let him in. He'd done it. Now if he could only forget how he'd felt that long-ago January day sufficiently to say what had to be said.

The judge announced that he would appear as a friend of the court, and he took the stand. He began by telling of his family's eviction from Hugh Pickford's apartment building, and of his hatred for the man and his desire for vengeance that had endured almost three decades. "I hated him so passionately that, although I witnessed an accident for which many people still believe he was responsible, I refused to exonerate him, knowing he had nothing to do with it. I was seventeen.

"But, Your Honor, I have in my hand proof that, at various times, Hugh Pickford instructed these two managers in writing to repair these buildings, and that they defrauded him of funds he supplied for the maintenance. My job for my paper was to get the goods on Baltimore's slumlords, and I went after Hugh Pickford to get even. But in my view, if he's guilty, Your Honor, it is of failing to inspect his property."

He related Buddy Kilgore's scheme to defraud the city schools, and the arrest of Lim Haskins' associate for attempting to bribe him, threatening, and intimidating him.

"Your Honor, this is the story that will appear in the weekend edition of *The Maryland Journal* under my byline."

He'd done it. He didn't know whether his mother would be angry or proud, and he didn't intend to worry about it. How Justine would take it was another question, but he wasn't planning to sweat over that, either. The judge excused him after the prosecuting attorney declined to cross-examine him. Everyone in court knew that Duncan had destroyed the city's case against Hugh Pickford.

CHAPTER THIRTEEN

Justine opened the front door to pick up the morning paper and saw the red Osmobile Cutlass Supreme parked across the street. She grabbed the paper, quickly stepped back inside, slammed the door shut, and leaned against it, her heart pounding. That discolored sedan belonged to the man who had confronted her in the post office several weeks earlier, and that same man sat in the driver's seat.

"Mattie, would you please come here and look at this car?"

Mattie turned off the vacuum cleaner and peeped out. "You mean that red one? It's been out there a lot the last few days. Why?"

Justine explained where she'd seen it. "I think I'd better phone Duncan. If he comes to this door, don't open it."

Mattie's hands went to her hips. "Do I look like I lost my mind? That's the same little old man come here axin for you. What he want with you anyway? He shore ain't your type."

Justine explained about her column and her belief that the man was somehow connected to one of the women she'd counseled.

Mattie's eyes rounded and her upper lip skimmed over her front teeth to reveal a grin.

"You go 'way from here. You mean I been spending my good money buying that *Post* just to read Aunt Mariah, when I coulda got it from you for nothin'? Well starch my apron."

Bells of alarm rang in Justine's head. She wasn't supposed to reveal that. "Mattie, you can't tell anyone, not even Moe. It's in my contract that I am not supposed to reveal it, and I wouldn't have told you, if I hadn't been upset about that fellow loitering out front. Please don't mention it."

Mattie's expression could only be described as a long, slow boil. "If you say don't mention it, I don't breathe it in my prayers. Telling me two times is exaggeratin' it. I know how to keep secrets; I'm keeping one every single day."

Justine stared at Mattie, and goose bumps popped up on her arms when Mattie stared back at her without an expression on her face. Did she know?

The butterflies in her belly settled down when Mattie suddenly smiled and said, "Well, I do declare. Aunt Mariah. I knowed you wasn't any ordinary nanny. You too refined and classy."

Justine went to the living room window and looked across the street. The Osmobile was no longer there, but she'd phone Duncan anyway. His cell phone didn't ring.

"How did you think Tonya seemed this morning?" she asked Mattie.

"A little bit pallid, but she ate good."

That comment didn't placate Justine. It was unlike Tonya to be still. The child usually bounced, sang, and exploded with energy. She went to her computer to look up childhood ailments associated with lethargy, but the phone rang before she began.

"Ms. Taylor, this is Assemblyman Taylor's office calling. The assemblyman intends to transfer some rental property to you, and we need your signature on some papers that I'm faxing to you in a few minutes."

She nearly swallowed her tongue when she attempted

to reply. Of all the shocks he could throw at her, she trusted this the least. Arnold Taylor was a tight-fisted man who gave nothing away unless he had to cover his tracks.

"Why does he want to give me his rental property? Is he seriously ill?"

"The Assemblyman is enjoying excellent health," came the crisp reply. "May I please have your fax number?"

She bristled at the woman's audacity. "If you'll give me the address and deed number of this property, I'll take a look at it. Then, if I decide I want it, I'll send you my fax number."

"Are you suggesting that you're in a position to refuse two forty-unit buildings? Your father is being very generous with you, and he wants to sign the buildings over to you now."

If only she could tell him personally the words that roared through her head! "As his secretary, you are aware that he refuses to so much as give me the time of day. I'm not sure I want this kind of fatherly love. I'll be in touch." She hung up. What was he up to? She phoned the mayor's office and asked for Leland, Kenneth's fraternity brother.

"What's up, Justine?"

She told him the story.

"I can fax you the information sometime late this afternoon, pictures and all."

She gave him her fax number, thanked him, and hung up. Why would her father give her those two buildings? Conscience? Taxes? Enemies? Political liabilities? She'd think about it when she got the material from Leland. With the sack of mail Moe had collected at the post office, she had more than enough to keep her busy. Now, if the phone would stop ringing. She heard Al's voice on her answering machine and lifted the receiver.

"Hello."

"Hey. Big Al, here. I just got two extra passes to the Kennedy Center honors thing tomorrow night. I know it's a little late, and I have to give one to Warren, so I wondered if you'd meet him and the two of you could maybe go together?"

Justine had to laugh at the thinly veiled ruse. "Al, Warren

should be able to handle his affairs without your help. Thank you, friend, but someone else has already invited me. Tell him I'll see him at the reception."

Al's whistle pained her ear. "You mean you're going to the reception, too?"

Her chest went out a few extra inches. "So I'm told."

"Way to go, babe. That's what I call big time. Real big time. Your column's doing great. Increasing the paper's circulation, too."

"Really? Then what about a raise?"

"Raise? All right. All right. See what I can do. Keep the faith."

"You, too." She hung up, went to look in on Tonya, and found the child playing with her musical notes. She didn't like it. Tonya was too quiet.

She heard Duncan's Buick turn into the garage. She'd seen little of him since Tuesday morning, and her heart raced as though he'd been gone for years.

"I'm not going to pretend I'm not anxious to see him," she told herself, and sped down the stairs to open the front door just as his finger hit the bell.

"Now this is what I call a welcome," he said, lifting her and twirling her around. "Where's Tonya?"

"Tonya's upstairs playing in her playpen. Are you here for a while?"

He took her hand and started toward the stairs. "I expect so. I have to get this story written by Thursday latest if it's going in the next weekend edition."

He'd stopped midway up the stairs, and his voice carried a plea for understanding. "Then I thought maybe we'd take Tonya over to Frederick, leave her with my mother and Leah, and the two of us could go away somewhere and figure out what to do with our lives. Maybe we won't do anything, but who knows? We may find the way. In the meantime, let's just be good friends and not louse up what we already have. We could continue as we are, but without an understanding, we won't get much further."

So it would end sooner than she had feared. Well, she'd given it all she had, and if she lost, she'd lose graciously.

"You've done some thinking, some self-searching, haven't you?"

He nodded. "Yes, I have, and from now 'til we get that time to ourselves, I want you to do the same. Just work out how much you're prepared to lose."

He must have seen in her eyes the despair she felt, for he lifted her chin with his finger and told her, "Understanding and trust can set a lot of things right. Don't forget that. Now, let's not worry about any of this. When the time comes, we'll deal with it. Okay?"

"You're right. Our relationship needs some resolution. What I feel for you and what I think of myself deserve more than a convenient affair that's headed no place." She reached up and kissed his cheek. "Whatever happens to me, you'll always be a special man."

He held her gaze so long that she had a sense of floating, drowning in his wonderful eyes. At last, he spoke. "Let me look in on Tonya."

The child squealed and bounced with joy when she saw her father. She raised her arms to him and sang out, "Daddy, Daddy," over and over. Justine wondered if Tonya had been quiet and listless because she missed her father and decided not to tell him that she had been worried about her.

She told Duncan, who held the laughing, bubbling child in his arms kissing her, "You can see who's king around here. She's so happy to see you."

"Yeah," he said, hugging the little girl, "and Daddy's happy to see his baby."

She looked at them until she had to turn away. No more "if only's" for her; reality was about to settle in. "What are you wearing tomorrow night?" she asked, rechannelling her thoughts.

"I'll be in a tux. Let me know what color your dress is, so we don't go looking like Mattie's wigs."

"She's got on a purple bandanna today; seems her available wig was blue, and this isn't a blue day."

A half-smile floated over his face, revealing his one dimple. "I'd better get back there and give her a big hug before she threatens to leave. Mattie demands recognition and plenty of attention." He winked, put Tonya in her play pen, and loped down the stairs.

Justine didn't tell him about the man in the red car, because she knew that, although he needed every minute to work on his story, he'd stop and deal with any problem that affected her. Her fax phone rang, and she waited for Leland's letter. Just as she'd surmised, Arnold Taylor wanted to give her buildings in a state of disrepair and in one of Washington's seedier neighborhoods. But why? The buildings had full occupancy and no unmanageable debts. She locked up the papers and called her father's office.

"Please tell my father that I don't want the buildings, because I'm not interested in refurbishing tenements. That's all."

"Now, wait a minute. Those buildings bring in a tidy sum every month, and he's giving them to you."

She blew out a long breath and tapped her fingers against the phone. "Tell him, I'd exchange all that for a chance to have a nice long talk with him. Bye." She hung up, but she knew she hadn't heard the end of it.

She could hardly contain her relief when Tonya sat on her father's lap, ate all of her dinner, and entertained them with her usual exuberance.

Mattie presided over their evening meal as though she'd been serving it at her own table. "Mr. B, ax Justine what she thought of my Moe." She glanced at Justine. "Honey, ain't he somethin'?" She stopped eating and confided to Duncan, "People always surprised he married me, but theys a lot they don't know. My folks was sharecroppers in the backwoods of South Carolina, and I never got to go to school if they was any work I could do. I done everything a person can do on a farm, right down to roaming the forests in the wintertime lookin' for fat wood that my papa would split and bundle up for us kids to go out and sell. I left home when I was seventeen, went to Charleston, and got a job in a cafeteria. That's where I met my Moe. He was studying in one of they colleges down there, and I used to slip him food, otherwise he'd a' starved. He got pneumonia from living in that place with no heat, and after I found out where he lived, I went and looked after him. We stuck to each other till he graduated and got a job. We both come from poor families, but theys good, Godfearing people. When he axed me to marry him, I fainted and scared him to death. I was so crazy 'bout that man, I couldn't sleep at night. I tell you, he is somethin'. Justine, you quit foolin' round, honey."

Knowing Mattie's penchant for bluntness, Justine hurried to congratulate her on her fine husband, making certain that she kept her mind on him and not on Justine Taylor.

"You've done well for yourself, Mattie," Duncan said. "Not many of us began with so little and managed as well as you have." He reached over and tapped Justine's fingers. "I'm going to get Tonya settled in bed, then I think I'd better check on Rags before I start work. Did you hear from Mitch today?"

"He hasn't called, and I didn't know how to reach him."

Duncan excused himself and left the table. "I'll find him."

He'd planned to work, but he hadn't heard from the boys, and he didn't like it. He got Tonya to bed, read her some pages of *Hiawatha* which was what she wanted, put on a pair of jeans, grabbed the rest of his street clothes, and went downstairs.

"Be back when I get back" he told Justine and Mattie, and left. He got in the car, changed into a jogging shirt, sweater, and his old leather jacket, checked his gas gauge, and headed for Capitol View. After about twenty minutes, he found Mitch where he had least expected him, in the shelter.

"Man, it was cold out there, and with all those stringers and their cameras hanging around the building, I split."

"Stringers?"

"Yeah, man. Rats. News guys."

Duncan allowed himself a hearty laugh. "I thought you knew that I'm a writer."

Mitch didn't seem impressed. "Sure, Pops, but you don't rat on people. You tell it like it is. Not like those *News* and

Times rats that can't find nothing good to write about nobody black."

Duncan didn't feel like arguing that, if indeed it needed arguing. "It's seven-nineteen," he said to Mitch. "We can still see Rags for a few minutes."

En route to the hospital, Mitch questioned him about Justine. "She's *forty karat,* Pops. Is she your girl?"

Now, what did he say to that? "I'm working on that, Mitch."

The boy's face clouded in a frown. "She must think a lot of you. All I had to do was tell her you looked after us and, man, she pulled out the stops. A bird like that one. Man, I'd do more than work on it."

Duncan pulled up to the hospital and cut the motor. "Trust me, Mitch, when I work on a thing, the job's well done."

Mitch beamed as he jumped from the car. "You the man, Pops."

After a short visit with Rags, Duncan drove Mitch back to the shelter. "Any idea why those newsmen and cameramen gathered around your building?"

"No, but if they only want to see slums, they sure don't have to come all the way out here."

Duncan had been thinking the same thing. He gave the boy some money for transportation to and from the hospital and headed home. Washington slums weren't his concern right then; he had to deal with Baltimore, and daylight found him hard at work on his story of the Baltimore slums.

Justine strolled with Duncan along the Kennedy Center's promenade, as the mammoth crystal chandeliers and the lighted lanterns that hung from the ceiling cast a romantic glow against the majestic windows that towered at least three stories high, the bronze bust of John F. Kennedy a regal figure in the midst of it. She allowed herself a proud glance at the tall, good-looking man who walked beside her, resplendent in a navy-blue tuxedo and accessories that matched her royal-blue velvet gown, and peace washed over her when he held her hand as they left the reception to take their seats at the performance.

Warren Stokes stopped in front of Justine, effectively blocking her passage. "Well. Well."

" 'Evening, Warren," Duncan said and propelled her in another direction.

If she'd needed a clue to Duncan Banks's personality, he'd just given her one.

"Good grief," she exclaimed, when the President and Mrs. Clinton entered the auditorium. "He seems as tall as you are. How tall are you, Duncan?"

"Six four-and-a-half. How tall are you, shorty?"

He stroked the back of her hand as though to sooth her, in case his remark might have opened a wound.

"I'm five-seven, almost. Well . . . five-six."

An amused look settled over his features as he regarded her. "Yeah. A regular little totem pole."

She held her hands close to her sides and made certain that they stayed there. "I haven't had any complaints so far."

A grin spread over his face. "No? You're not likely to get any from me, either. Whatever you are, sweetheart, is what boils my water."

"You're meddling with me."

"Sure thing. You make it easy. " He leaned forward. "What do you say we take Tonya to Frederick Wednesday after I turn in my story, leave her with Leah and my mother, go on to my lodge on Curtis Bay and have the next few days to ourselves. It'll be late when we get there, but we can shop on the way." When she didn't answer immediately, he said, "I won't pressure you to do or say anything."

"Then why are we going?"

He stared into her eyes, and his own were flames of enticing warmth that promised her the heavens. "I want us to learn each other, to know each other without the sham of status between us. I want us to be out of that house, where you conveniently use your job to avoid seeing us as we are. I want you to go with me because I'm the man you want and you're the woman I . . . I need."

Her disbelief that he'd said it must have been obvious,

because he reiterated it. "That's right, *need.* I didn't plan it, but it's part of me now, and I have to deal with it. From now on, I'm counting chicks and naming names. I have to know where I'm going. Are you with me?"

When had he shed his determination to avoid emotional involvement? She'd never considered herself a coward, so she looked him in the eye and told him, "You said we need to resolve this, and I agree. If this is the way you want to do it, I'll go with you to Curtis Bay."

He cocked his left eyebrow and rubbed his chin. "You don't seem optimistic."

How could she be? "No, I'm not, but anything can happen."

He tightened his hold on her hand and led her to her seat. Her head pounded, but at least they could no longer talk. She put her hands together in a mild applause as the curtain opened and Cronkite stepped onto the stage.

Duncan helped Justine into his car for the trip home, got in, and started the engine. He looked over his right shoulder to check the traffic before he backed out, glanced over at her, and seemed to freeze. He turned off the ignition and stared down at her. "You can look at me that way, Justine, and not feel as strongly as I do that we have to do something about our relationship?"

She said the only thing that she could say. "One of these days, Duncan, you'll wonder why you asked me that question. You promised not to push me, and that shouldn't be difficult, because you know what I feel."

"All right."

He backed out and drove off. When they got home, he checked on Tonya and kissed Justine's cheek. "Thanks for your company tonight, lovely lady. I'm taking the sitter home. See you in the morning."

He didn't rush back after the short trip, because sleeping across a six-foot hall from Justine wasn't something he relished doing. But he'd meant it when he said they should be friends only until they knew where their relationship was headed. When he got to the top of the stairs, his gaze found her door, and when he didn't see a light there, he breathed deeply in palpable relief. Deciding against work, he looked in on Tonya and went to bed. But as he was about to turn out the light, he bolted upright. Screams. He'd locked all the doors. Who could . . . He sprang out of bed and dashed into the hallway. Screams. Sobs. *Justine!*

He shoved open her door and rushed to her bed, where she thrashed wildly, sobbing and moaning. Should he shake her? "Justine," he called, softly and repeatedly. Exasperated, he crawled into the bed, gathered her to his body, and began to rock her. She curled into him, and her tears wet his chest. When at last she was quiet, he turned on the light and whispered to her.

"It's all right, Justine. I'm here with you, and nothing can happen to you. I'm here, sweetheart."

She cuddled closer, and he held her for half an hour while she slept. Who and what were her demons? Nothing and no one would convince him that those nightmares and flashbacks weren't tied to her secrets. What memory could have dragged her into the clutches of such abject misery as he'd just witnessed? He gazed at her face—peaceful, almost smiling—eased away from her, and went back to his room. Half an hour of the torment of holding her to his almost nude body was as much punishment as he cared to take.

If she knew he'd been in her room the previous night, held her, and rocked her, she didn't mention it at breakfast that Sunday morning.

If Duncan thought his relationship with Justine was at a crossroads, Wayne had arrived at approximately the same conclusion in regard to himself and Duncan's sister. He'd asked her to go away with him for the weekend; the suggestion of a fishing expedition had merely been a gracious way of phrasing it. Four days had passed and she hadn't given him an answer. He telephoned her at her office Friday morning.

"What about it, Leah? Should I pick you up after work?"

"Where're we going?"

He let out a long breath. If she decided to match wits with him, he'd disintegrate. He didn't have the patience for it right then.

"To the Roundtree Lodge. Did you pack a bag for the weekend?"

"Wayne, I'm not going to strut out of here with a suitcase and jump into your car in the presence of every gossip monger in Frederick, Maryland."

Don't lose it, Roundtree, he told himself. "All right. Leave it at *The Watering Hole* at lunch time, and I'll pick it up around four-thirty. Then, I'll drop around to your place and get you. That suit you?" He held his breath for what seemed an eternity.

"Okay. Pick me up at home at five o'clock."

He stared at the phone after she hung up. She was a handful but, between then and Sunday night, he intended to make putty out of her. He couldn't help laughing at himself. Leah as putty in his or anybody's hands was a joke. To his amazement, their plans materialized without a hitch. They reached the lodge around seven o'clock, but her first act was to establish her ground rules.

"Why do you want to carry me in here when I can walk?"

He let her walk through the door, but he wouldn't let her carry her bag. "Leah, are you planning a hard time for me? It would be a help if I knew what to expect."

Dreams seemed to take shape in her long-lashed, reddish-brown eyes and all of her fantasies settled in them and on him, shaking his very foundation. She promised much, but she was asking plenty. He started toward her, and she met him halfway, scooting into his arms and burying her face into his shoulder. He wasn't certain of the message, but he knew he'd better figure it out.

"Let's get unpacked and get some dinner together," he said, needing a breather. "I stocked the kitchen yesterday." A thought occurred to him. "Why did you put me through hell for ten days when you knew you were coming with me this evening? Why, Leah?"

"You asked me to go fishing with you, and what did I say?"

"You said you loved to fish."

She shrugged and poked her tongue into her right cheek as he'd so often seen Duncan do. "Wayne, even a mentally challenged person could figure out that was a yes."

He refused to match wits with her. "Did you want to be with me?"

She nodded. "Yes, but let's eat. Then we can go outside and watch the moon."

Laughter bubbled up in him. He had to touch her. He knew he'd better not rush her, but right that minute he wanted her in his arms. He hadn't come there to practice high-level restraint, but that was what she needed, so he checked himself and settled for a kiss on the side of her mouth. Her face softened into a half-smile and she lowered her eyes.

Damn! "All right. My mother mixed up the hamburgers and made the patties, since she knows I'm no cook."

Her mouth opened, and she sucked in a lot of air. "Your mother knows you're here with me?"

He pinched her nose and let the back of his hand drift over her face. "She knows I'm someplace where I need hamburgers, shucked corn, and biscuits. Period."

After eating, Wayne straightened up the kitchen and brought Banks her jacket. "You wanted to watch the moon. Let's go. Her hand found his as they started toward the river at the edge of the woods. He heard sticks cracking and cocked his ears.

"Any bears out here, Wayne?"

"Sure. Lots of 'em."

She pointed toward the woods. "Over there?" When he nodded, she whirled around. "I want to go back."

They stood on the deck of the lodge and gazed at the clear moon. "Except for those bears we heard," she said, "it's so quiet, I can touch the silence."

He opened the door and walked in with her. "Want to sit by the fire for a little?"

She shook her head. "Wayne, I haven't ever gone this far with a man. I'm not afraid, though. I'm scared to death, Wayne, but I'm . . . I'm so happy."

He pulled off her jacket and eased her sweater over her head. "Come with me. All I want is that you trust me. And, sweetheart, I know you've never obeyed anybody in your life, but—"

"I have so," she argued. "Ask Mama. I even obey Duncan."

"As I was saying, I want to make this night perfect, one that we will remember forever, and I can do that if you do as I ask. Trust me?"

He could have tanned in the sunshine of her smile. "Oh, I do. Give me a few minutes."

Twenty minutes later, she stuck her head out of her room and called, "Wayne. For Pete's sake, how long is a minute in Beaver Ridge?"

He stepped to her door, picked her up, and carried her to bed.

Her nerves rioted in her body. If he didn't hurry and do something, she'd go berserk. He leaned over her and brushed her lips with his, but she wanted to tell him that she'd been in a constant state of desire for him for almost as long as she'd known him. He took his time, showering her with kisses, and her restlessness increased. At last his fingers touched where no man's hand had gone and dragged a keening cry from her. She thought she'd die for whatever it was he'd give her. His fingers tortured her nub of passion and his lips feasted at her breasts until she pulled him over her body and begged for relief.

He stared into her eyes. "Look at me, Love. This can only happen to us once."

Passion flared up in her, and she raised her body to meet his as he slowly began his entrance. She bit her lips at the first stabbing pain.

"Try to relax, sweetheart, and it will be better in a second."

"I know it's supposed to hurt, and I don't care if it does. It's wonderful, even hurting."

She felt his arm around her shoulder and his right hand beneath her hip. Then he kissed her, and she took his sweet tongue into her mouth as he burst into her. He looked down in her face and kissed moisture from her lashes.

"I love you, Leah. I've never loved another woman. Never. I . . . I'm in love with you. Do you love me, Leah?"

"I do. I love you. I hardly remember when I didn't." She twisted beneath him. "Isn't something else supposed to happen?"

His face beamed and a grin spread over it. "You're priceless. I'm just giving you time to adjust to me."

"Okay, I'm adjusted."

He bent to her breasts, put a hand between them and brought her back to passion's peak. Minutes later, she shouted his name as he hurtled them both into ecstasy. Then, he wrapped her tightly in his arms and cherished her.

The expression on her face as she looked at him had to be one of awe. When he asked what the matter was, she answered, "If I had known this, I would have seduced you long ago."

"Seduced *me?* Is that what you think you did?"

"If I didn't," she purred, raising her arms and stretching like a sated young cat, "I need some pointers."

"Woman, you don't need anything. You wouldn't be more perfect for me if I'd made you myself."

If she were any happier, she'd probably start shouting. "Now what do we do?" she asked him. What was he so serious about, she wondered, as he gazed into her eyes.

He didn't keep her guessing. "Are you going to marry me?"

"Am I going to . . . *what did you say?*"

"I said, will you marry me?"

"Of course. Do you think I would have done this if I wasn't planning to marry you?"

She loved to hear him laugh, and happiness suffused her and it rolled out of him. "Say, do you realize it's ten o'clock and you haven't smoked a cigarette since before we left Frederick at five o'clock?"

"Yeah, I know. You don't like my smoking, but since you were smart enough not to ask me to quit, I'm trying to stop."

"But if I'd asked you to stop, you wouldn't have considered doing it. Right?"

She snuggled closer to him. "Something like that. I would've eventually, though, 'cause I don't want my children to smoke." She stroked his arm, loving the feel of the silky hairs that got thicker the closer she got to his wrist "I just wish Justine was as happy as I am right now."

"You like her?"

"I think she's a wonderful person, and she loves my brother."

"They'll work it out." He rolled her over on her back. "Who do you love?"

She let her fingers learn his silky eyebrows as she stroked them. "Hmmm. Can't think of his name."

"I'll see if I can't refresh your memory," he said, and set himself to the task.

Justine hugged and kissed Tonya for the third time. As much as she looked forward to being alone with Duncan, she didn't want to leave her child. Duncan leaned against his mother's refrigerator watching her.

"Juju kiss Tonya. Daddy kiss Tonya," the child said repeatedly, enjoying the fun of having been passed from one of them to the other as they kissed her good-bye.

"Girlfriend, I've got something to show you," Banks said to Justine, and ushered her into a nearby bedroom. "Don't miss the opportunity of a lifetime, honey," she advised Justine. "Let him love you. Considering the person you are, nothing could be so awful that he won't accept and forgive. You two love each other. Anybody can see it. Mama is always singing an old hymn, 'Work for the Night Is Coming.' Think about that."

"You're saying I'm keeping something from him?"

"Yes. I'm also saying that if you weren't, the two of you would be open to each other and to the world about what you feel. Like Wayne and me. Don't let it pass you by." She crossed her right index and middle fingers. "I'm rooting for you."

"We'd better be going," Duncan said, when Justine and Banks came back into the kitchen. "If you need me, call my cell phone number."

Arlene Banks hugged Justine and whispered, "God bless you, honey."

Duncan's mother and sister stood at the door waving to them. "I hope they work it out," Arlene said. "She loves this child so much."

"More than you'd expect of a nanny," Banks added.

Arlene looked her daughter in the eye. "She's more to Tonya than a nanny."

"I know," Banks replied. "I can't figure out why he doesn't see it."

"He doesn't want to see it, and he won't learn it from us, either."

"Good Lord, no. I want her to be my sister-in-law, and if we get in it, that'll be the end."

Arlene looked around for Tonya, who was pulling a glass vase on herself, and rushed to the child. "He needs her. I just hope he realizes how much."

Duncan took the Baltimore National Pike out of Frederick wondering whether his plan was defeated before it began. Justine was too quiet for his comfort. Judging that it wasn't a time for seriousness, he said, "I bet you can't name two famous black parks."

"Sure I can. Rosa and Gordon. Let's see if you can name two famous black highways."

"That's easy," he said, warming up to the challenge. "There's the Jackie Robinson Memorial in New York City, and the Martin Luther King Jr. highway in just about every big city in the country. Who was the most famous African-American man to pitch in both the Negro league and the major leagues?"

She laughed, and he began to relax. "Now you're about to learn that I love baseball. It was Satchel Page. Since you started this, and being a journalist, maybe you'd like to give me the names of five members of the Harlem Renaissance, including the last one who died recently. *Duncan, look out!*"

"Sorry." He switched over to the right lane and slower

traffic. Some nanny. She'd just about given up all pretense. The Harlem Renaissance, for goodness sake. "Let's see. Langston Hughes, Countee Cullen, Alain Locke, Zora Neal Hurston, James Van Der Zee, and Dorothy West, who died last year."

"Six of them. Not bad."

"As you said, I'm a journalist." And what a surprise she'd get when he brought her the weekend edition of *The Maryland Journal.* He didn't want to think about it. "I've been writing since I was a boy. From elementary school on, I managed to get on the school paper. When I was a junior in college, I got to interview First Lady Barbara Bush. She was reading to some kids, and I sent my credentials to her and asked for an interview. She granted it. That was my first big one. I sent her the copy before I filed the piece with my editor, and she called the principal and congratulated me on the story and on my fairness."

"I love writing, too," Justine said. "Aunt Mariah doesn't keep me as busy as I'd like to be or could be, because Tonya is at the age now where I shouldn't interfere with her too much, though she's so precious that it's difficult to give her the space she needs. She ought to have freedom to explore, and I try to give her that. I'm developing a series of instructions for use in adult literacy classes. I'll give them to the Literacy Society. I don't want to profit from helping people learn to read, because illiteracy is such a handicap, and I want to do all I can to help."

He eased up on the accelerator. The entire scenario was getting to be a barrel of laughs. His daughter's nanny was developing materials for use in adult literacy classes. He told himself to remember their agreement, conditions that he had set, and that learning about each other was what they were supposed to be doing.

He made himself sound casual. "I'd already realized that you're interested in education. That's a wonderful thing you're doing." It didn't surprise him that he meant the compliment.

They'd left the pike and had been driving on Route 695 for over half an hour. "We'll be there in a couple of minutes. I hope you'll like it as much as I do. It isn't as big as the Roundtree lodge, but it's just as comfortable."

"I should hope not," she said. "Why would you need a five-bedroom lodge?"

Darkness settled around them soon after they reached their destination, and Duncan made a fire in the great stone fireplace. "Did you bring some good walking shoes and some sweaters?" he asked her.

Assured that she had, he suggested that they walk over to the beach. "It's wonderful at night."

"In the darkness?"

"Bundle up and come with me. You'll enjoy it. When we get back, it'll be warm in here."

They walked along the beach, letting their shoes sink into the white sand. Justine marveled at the peace all around them, a vibrant harmony that linked them as surely as a vine connected the leaves it nourished. His ungloved hand tightened around hers, communicating his understanding of their oneness at that moment, and she turned and held him to her. But all that she was and everything she felt for him, for Tonya, and the eminent end to it all shredded her joy at being with him and tore into her soul.

"It's all right, sweetheart," he said as he held her and stroked her back. "This is why we're here, to come to terms with what we feel for each other."

She took herself in hand and calmed herself. Seeing Kenneth tied in that plastic bag hadn't thrown her, and neither would this. They walked to the other side of the pier, where the sloshing of water against the small boats interrupted the calm. The breeze strengthened, and she tightened her jacket. How could it be that they had walked so far, hardly speaking, and yet she felt as though they had communed as never before.

"Justine, look at this." He pointed to the moon that seemed to rise from the ocean.

A sliver of electricity jetted up her spine as the big bright disk emerged onto the horizon, and he whispered, "Life for us can be like this always, if we let go and embrace it."

"I can't let you talk this way, Duncan. I told you that, in the end, we'll separate, and nothing has happened to change that."

"Aren't you willing to try?"

She stepped away from him. "I can't try, Duncan. Knowing what I know, it would be no use."

He grabbed the lapels of her coat and pulled her to him. "Why can't you level with me?"

She shook her head. "When I met you, you'd sworn off emotional involvement, so even when I knew I loved you, I didn't worry for your sake, because I alone would suffer the consequences. Are you saying that you . . . you're—"

He interrupted her. "That was before I knew you. Before I held you in my arms and exploded to life inside you. Before I loved you."

"Duncan, don't . . . you can't."

"You must know it. How could you not know that I love you?"

His eyes were shimmering promises of forever, and she had to lower her gaze lest she foolishly commit to what could never be. "Can we . . . can we have this night together? This one last night together?"

He shook her shoulders as if to reawaken her to the truth. "Tell me you can walk away from me. And from Tonya. Tell me that you can wipe us out of your life and walk on. I don't question your love for me, and I know you love Tonya as much as if you had given birth to her."

Thank God he wasn't looking into her face when he said it. She couldn't pretend. Not now, when the truth seethed within her, and to look at him would be tantamount to agreeing with his words.

"Answer me," he challenged. "Can you do that? Can you relegate me and my child to the back corner of your life, old clothes that you've discarded, and take a hike? Can you?"

I won't let him beat me down, she told herself, but words wouldn't come, and when he held her face to his shoulder, she let him comfort her. After some minutes, while wrapped in the cold night, holding each other, he asked her, "Is this your answer?"

She looked up into the storm that raged in his eyes, at the passion and anger that wrestled with his love for her. "If I had the right, I'd tell you I never want to leave you, that the thought of being away from Tonya sickens me, but I don't have that right."

He released her, took her hand, and headed down the beach toward his lodge. "I promised not to pressure you, but I did, and it was a mistake. Let's go get something to eat."

She doubted she could swallow a morsel. They walked in silence until they reached the lodge and entered it as his cell phone began to ring. He raced to answer it.

"Hello."

He listened for a second, his face ashened and grim, and passed the receiver to her. "It's Leah. Something's wrong with Tonya."

She grabbed the phone. "Justine, she didn't eat any dinner; she wouldn't sit up when I tried to bathe her; she didn't have any interest in anything. I read from the books you brought, but she ignored me. What's the matter with her?"

That was the third time Tonya had behaved that way. "I took her to the doctor with those symptoms a couple of weeks back, but it must not be a virus as the doctor thought." She turned to Duncan. "We'd better go get her and take her to the doctor."

Duncan took the phone. "We'll be there by seven tomorrow morning. If she worsens, call me." He hung up. "Let's get some sleep. We may have a rough day ahead."

She told him good night and went to her room. Whatever Providence had in store for her, she wasn't going to like it.

CHAPTER FOURTEEN

The next morning, Duncan parked in front of his mother's house in Frederick, cut the motor, and jumped out. In his haste, he forgot to open the passenger's door for Justine, but she raced beside him up the wide, paved walkway. As they reached the porch steps, he stopped her and took her hand.

"We don't yet know whether there's anything to be concerned about. So don't worry. My mother is probably worrying enough for both of us."

She nodded. "I'm calm, Duncan. I think." However, her breath came with difficulty.

"Take a deep breath," he coaxed. "You shouldn't be panting this way. She'll be all right, baby. And if she's sick, she'll get the best care; you know that. Now, chin up." Worry clouded his own face, but he tilted up her chin, pressed a kiss to her lips, winked at her, and rang the doorbell.

She pushed her glasses to the bridge of her nose, smiled tremulously, and told him, "I hope she someday knows how lucky she is to have you for a father."

He punched the bell again. "How's she doing?" he asked his mother when she opened the door.

"About the same. Come on in and get a bite to eat. Soon as I put her jacket on her, she'll be ready." She looked at Justine. "Honey, I'm so sorry you had to break up your vacation this way. I hope nothing's wrong and you can go on back tonight."

Justine thanked her. "Where's Leah?"

Arlene smiled as she led them through the kitchen to the breakfast room. "At least there's some good news. Wayne was over last night after we called you and asked for permission to marry Leah. I hadn't expected that so soon, but she was certain she was going to marry him. How do you feel about that, son?"

From the grin on his face, Justine thought the question redundant. "Wayne's my best friend, my soul-brother, and he's a great guy. I couldn't ask for a better man for her." He ran his left hand over his tight black curls and blew out a long breath. "Boy, does that guy work fast! But that's the way he is. He takes forever to make up his mind, but when he does, look out."

Arlene led Justine to Tonya's room, and she put herself to the task of dressing the child. At that moment, anything would have been a task; if she had been anxious before, her feelings now bordered on alarm, for Tonya had barely greeted her. She took her into the breakfast room and let Duncan judge for himself.

He looked at the two of them, set his coffee cup down, and got up from the table. "Thanks for everything, Mama. Tell Leah I'll catch up with her later. We'd better leave."

When they reached Washington, he drove directly to the George Washington University Medical Center, identified himself, and asked for the chief of pediatrics. In less than an hour, Tonya was in a room gaily decorated with animals, balls, and mobiles that children love, but which she barely noticed.

Duncan prepared to leave, but Justine hung back, concerned that Tonya didn't cry or seem to care that she was in a strange place. He walked back to Justine, but not even his strong arms around her reassured her. He held her to his side until they reached his car.

"We're in this together, honey, so don't shut me out.

You couldn't hurt as badly as I do, so let's be here for each other. Whatever it is, we'll beat it."

She couldn't manage more than a nod. Once more, he'd implied that her concern for Tonya couldn't equal his, because he was her father. Listlessly, she settled into the car. He buckled her seat belt and caressed the side of her face until she looked at him. Then, without a word, he leaned to her, took her into his arms, and held her.

"She'll be all right, Justine. We don't know that it's serious, so let's try not to worry."

She tensed when Duncan turned into Primrose Street. "That car. That red car in front of the house. It's the man who confronted me in the post office that day, and this isn't the first time he's been parked out there."

Duncan stopped the car and unbuckled his seat belt.

"What are you doing?"

"If I drive up there, he'll see me. I want the number of his license plate. Stay here."

Minutes later, he got back in the car. "You've seen him parked in front of our house before, and you didn't mention it to me?"

"When I would have told you, you had to finish a story and turn it in the next morning. I didn't want to distract you. Mattie told me she'd seen him out there several times."

"Next time you notice something this important, tell me even if I'm on my way to interview the President of the United States."

He drove into the garage and closed the door behind them. "We'll go in through the back. I don't want him to see you, or me, for that matter."

"Y'all leave Tonya in Frederick?" Mattie asked as they entered the house through the breakfast room, where she was dusting furniture.

Justine didn't pause, but let Duncan do the explaining. She went into her room, closed the door, and headed for the bathroom. Alone at last, she braced herself against the wall with the palms of her hand, and she prayed for Tonya and for the strength to deal with whatever she had to face. She heard the explosion seconds before he knocked, ran from the bathroom, and jerked open the bedroom door.

"Duncan, what was that?"

"I . . . I don't know." He grabbed her hand. "Whatever it was, I want you right with me."

He ran down the stairs with her and into the breakfast room. "Are you all right?" he asked Mattie.

Her eyes were round saucers of fright. "Whatever in the name of the Lord was that?"

"You two stay right here while I check out the place."

Duncan stepped out of the front door and let his gaze sweep his property. He clenched and unclenched his fists as anger seethed in him at the sight of his prized crabapple tree split with what had to have been a Molotov cocktail. He walked over to the tree, examined the burns, and went back into the house. So the goons were still trying to intimidate him—or were they after Justine? He telephoned the police, went into the breakfast room, and told the two women what he'd found.

"It's probably a one-time thing, but I want the two of you to stay away from the front windows until I get to the bottom of this stupidity."

He phoned the hospital, learned that Tonya's condition hadn't changed, and called his source in the Municipal Building. "Can you check plate number LRP897 on a red 1988 Oldsmobile?"

Within minutes, he had the information he wanted, hung up, and checked it with the names Justine had given him of women she'd counseled against accepting abuse from their mates. *Bingo!* Elsa Modeen and Cage Modeen. With such an unusual last name, it couldn't be a coincidence. If Justine could pick Cage Modeen out in a police line-up, they'd be rid of the pest. He went downstairs and asked her.

"I sure can. I'd even recognize his voice."

"Me, too," Mattie said. "I probably seen him more times than Justine. He been to this door at least three times axin for her. 'Course I always told him she don't live here. Looks like he didn't believe me."

"He won't be back here again soon, because I'm going to press for his indictment as a stalker."

His nerves stood on end when the phone—the number of which he'd given hospital authorities—rang in his office, and he took the stairs three steps at a time. "Banks."

"Duncan, this is Banks. How's Tonya?"

He wiped the perspiration from his forehead. "The same when I called an hour ago. They're running some tests, so we ought to know something in a day or so. Try not to worry; it's all I can do to keep Justine from losing it. So you tied Wayne up?"

"For your information, the gentleman asked my hand in marriage."

He laughed, and it felt so good to let it out. "Sure he did. Poor guy was a goner from the minute I introduced you to him."

"Duncan, I think I'm going to capitulate and pay Miss Mary a visit. Why couldn't he have some other mother?"

"If I could answer that, I'd be the Solomon of our times. I'm happy for you, kiddo. Wayne is a good man."

"Thanks. Are you and Justine going to get it together? Too bad your vacation got torpedoed, but there'll be other times. Mama and I like her, Duncan."

"Yes, I know that, but don't lean on me. We're a long way from anything definite. I'll keep you posted on Tonya's condition. And don't worry, Wayne's mother has mellowed since Adam and Melissa gave her a grandchild. She thinks Melissa can do no wrong."

"You serious? She once knocked herself out cold when she ran into an iron post trying to avoid meeting Melissa."

"That's in the past, evidently. I promise you'll like her."

He hung up, and his cell phone rang. "Hello."

"Say, Pops, this is Mitch. We having landlord trouble. I told the guy's secretary that Rags still don't get around too good, but she said he can't have two kids living alone in his building. I told her our mother is just off right now, but she won't listen to reason."

She'd been "off" for sixteen months. "Don't leave the

building; he can't put two minors on the street. I'll get back to you."

Frustrated and angry, he slammed out of his office and almost knocked Justine to the floor. "What's the matter?" she asked, after he'd helped her regain her equilibrium.

He walked with her back into his office. "The poor get poorer," he began, and relayed Mitch's story. She asked him where the boys lived and, when he told her, her eyes widened and a scowl shadowed her face.

"You know something?" he asked.

Her shoulder lifted in a careless shrug. "You can find in that area the genesis of just about every problem in this city. Something has to be done."

He studied her for a long time, thinking that every day, a little more of the real Justine emerged. He'd be angry about it, if what came out was less attractive. He observed her wan expression and didn't like what he saw; indeed, he couldn't understand it. She wasn't a woman to cave in at the first sign of trouble, yet Tonya's illness seemed to have sucked the wind out of her.

"Yeah, something ought to be done," he said after a long while. "And I'm tired of putting Band Aids on a sore as big as this town. Stay put, you two. I'm going down to police headquarters."

He filed the charges against Cage Modeen, against whom two others—one of wife beating—were pending and, on an impulse, decided to go to the hospital. Tonya's slothful greeting didn't lighten the weight on his heart. He remained with her for an hour, but she paid little attention to him. He didn't know how he got out of her room. As he passed the newsstand leaving the hospital, he bought a copy of *The Maryland Journal* and was reminded that it carried his story of Baltimore slumlords and Hugh Pickford. He'd have no choice but to show it to Justine.

When he got home, he made sure that nothing untoward had happened in his absence, went to his office, and read his story. He could take pride in what he had accomplished with that piece, but he didn't expect Justine to smile at him after she read it. No point in postponing the inevitable. He knocked on her bedroom door.

"Duncan. May I see you for a second?"

He scrutinized her face for evidence that she was coping with their mutual problems, because he was about to hand her another one.

"My story on slumlords is in here, and before you indict me, ask yourself how you would have reacted and what you would have done if you'd been wearing my shoes."

She looked from him to the paper he gave her, and he didn't have to be told that, after what he'd said, she'd rather not read it. Her face expressed as much apprehension as he'd ever seen mirrored on anyone. He wanted to step into that room, take her in his arms, and love her, lose himself in her until she rocked him into oblivion.

"See you later," he managed, stuffed his hands in his pockets, and went back to his office.

How naive she'd been, telling Duncan that her godfather could help him, when he was the man whom Duncan hunted. Yes. Hunted. A man Duncan had hated for almost thirty years. She'd heard her aunts talk about "the trouble Hugh got into" by running a red light, supposedly hitting a pedestrian, and not stopping to help. And they would invariably add: "Child, it doesn't hurt to have influence, and Hugh has more than his share. "All those years and all the hurt her godfather must have suffered knowing he wasn't guilty and, for thirty years, Duncan had let him sweat it out. Her conscience reminded her that her godfather had put a family out in the cold for a debt the repayment of which would have amounted to an infinitesimal fraction of his vast wealth. She read again the last two sentences of that incredible piece of writing.

"Hugh Pickford may not have known that his buildings were in such a state of disrepair as to endanger the lives of his tenants, but he is guilty of disinterest, of not caring enough to oversee his criminal managers. A man who doesn't check his property or his employees for eight years doesn't care."

He was expecting some comment from her, but she didn't feel like talking to him. For most of her life, Hugh

Pickford had been the one person to whom she'd been able to turn for affection, comfort, and understanding, and the man she loved had stood between her beloved godfather and the respect he craved. He'd told her many times that, because of that incident, he needn't consider running for public office.

She put her hands to her face, closed her eyes, and tried to put herself in Duncan's place. He'd been a teenager, but he knew what was right and what was wrong. In his article and in his court testimony, he hadn't tried to exculpate himself and had said that he'd erred. She telephoned her godfather.

"I just read Duncan Banks's story in *The Maryland Journal,*" she told him. "I'm sorry. And to think that I gave him your phone number believing you could help him with his story."

"Tell you the truth, I didn't remember any of that stuff he told in court; it all happened such a long time ago. I believed him, though, because I'd had a Marshall dispossess tenants plenty of times if they didn't pay up. I'm pretty much ashamed of it, 'cause I didn't need the money. I don't hold it against him, though; this time, if he had kept his mouth shut, I'd have gone to jail for a good long spell. He didn't have to point the finger at Kilgore and my other crooked managers after they pocketed my money and falsified accounts instead of keeping up my buildings, and lied on me in court. I thought I was in for it. Half the people on that jury looked as though they lived in a tenement."

She couldn't believe that he expressed no anger, and she couldn't help wondering when he'd changed from the swaggering, romantic figure she'd adored from childhood.

She hung up, went to her dresser, picked up her comb and put it down. The image of Justine Taylor Montgomery stared at her from the mirror—the haggard way she'd often looked when nightmares of Kenneth and his horrid end had plagued her nightly and wouldn't let her sleep. How long had it been since she'd last known interminable despair? Not since she'd first held her child or made love with Duncan or realized how much he cared. How can you judge him? her conscience needled. Is he worse than you? You deliberately deceived him. You held him in your body, told him you loved him, while you skillfully misled him. His sin was the act of a troubled adolescent. You are thirty years old. She wiped her tears with the back of her arm, walked over to the window, and stared out at the dreariness. In three weeks, it would be Christmas. She wouldn't think of it. She couldn't.

She was still in her room when Mattie rang her private phone. "Dinner's in the oven, Justine. Mr. B says I can have the rest of the day off 'cause my Moe is gonna run me by to see Tonya. You want to come down so I can show you where everything is?" No, she did not, but she pulled off her robe, slipped into a jumpsuit, and went to the kitchen.

"She ain't no better and no worse," Mattie said. "I'm gonna just peep in on her." She looked at Justine. "Honey, you're a wreck. Ax Mr. B to get you a sedative or somethin'."

"Ask me what?"

Justine whirled around and faced him. What could she say to him? "I read your article. It was fair, and you have a wonderful talent for writing."

He gazed into her eyes, searching, seeming to judge her, though she couldn't imagine for what. "You aren't irritated or angry?" he asked.

She looked over his shoulder at a distant object. "I'm not happy. You could have told me when you discovered that he was my godfather, but . . . well, you packaged it neatly, and in the end you were his salvation. I don't think I have a right to judge you."

Her left hand was the one nearest him, and he grasped it in both of his. "I'm relieved. I would never intentionally do anything to hurt you or distress you in any way." He seemed to weigh a decision. "I went to see Tonya while I was out this afternoon." Her heart leaped inside her chest. "No change. I'll drive you over if you want to go, but I don't advise it. She paid almost no attention to me. Maybe when she sees Mattie, she'll perk up a bit."

Mattie preened. "I think I'll put on my red and purple

wig when I go home; Tonya loves that one. She just laugh every time she see it."

But would she laugh this time? "Duncan, do you think that man's in custody? If he is, I'd like a few hours off tomorrow morning. I have to run an errand."

He released her hand and put both of his in his pockets. She'd never seen him pace, but he walked to the door, walked back, and repeated the action several times.

"They ought to have him by now, since he wasn't expecting to be taken in. I'll check."

Minutes later, he told her, "Yes, he's in custody, and they want you and Mattie down there Monday morning. Your time's your own."

Sunday morning at seven o'clock, she got in her car and headed for Richmond, Virginia. Arnold Taylor wouldn't answer her calls to his office, but she'd catch him before he went to church. Church. He shouldn't defile the door by walking through it. Two hours later, she parked in front of his white Georgian home and stared at the place where, during her youth, she'd dreamed of living with him. But instead of letting her share his home, he'd made her live with her aunts. She rang the bell, and after what seemed like forever, he opened it. His loud gasp and harsh swallow told her she'd robbed him of his customary aplomb, his iron-clad composure.

"Hello, Father." He'd always insisted that she call him that and had scolded her whenever she said "Daddy." "May I come in?"

He stepped aside. She'd surprised him, and he had no comeback. "To what do I attribute this unexpected pleasure?"

She walked into the place and looked at the trappings of wealth—wealth that she had never questioned until now. The wall covering of silk tapestry in the foyer and living room, marble fireplace with its shinning brass accessories; Persian carpets, porcelain vases, sterling silver everywhere, a painting of Thomas Jefferson, and works of James Porter, Elizabeth Catlett, Doris Price, and, strangely, one of a mother and child, entitled "Family" by Josie Miller. Why would he have something like that? But the opulence had a chilling effect on her, and she pitied him.

"Why have you come? Have you left Banks? Aren't you ashamed to live with a man who isn't your husband? Didn't you do enough when you married my bitterest enemy, a man who trashed my name like a pile of rotted refuse? Why are you here?"

He was so much older than when she'd last seen him, six years earlier. Gray and drawn. She spoke with more gentleness than she felt. "I tried so many times to speak with you, Father, but your secretary never put you on the line. I'm here about this."

She showed him the papers setting forth the transfer of property from himself to her. "Father, I want you to tell me that you aren't trying to dump these buildings on me to avoid a civil suit and damage your chances for reelection. Have you forgotten that I have a doctor's degree, which means I'm capable of reasoning. When that boy fell off that staircase, from which the railing had been ripped months earlier, I am the person who got him into the hospital. Me. I paid his bills. And I would never have made the connection if his brother hadn't given Duncan the address. You see, Duncan is big brother to those two boys. Now, you want to put them out on the street. Over my dead body. How could you do it?"

He slumped into a chair, a beaten man. "I knew you were living with Banks, and I know his reputation. He would never let you take the heat for it, because he has contacts all over the country. He could have bought you out of it, but it will ruin me. I don't want you to think I expected you'd have to suffer for it. I thought he'd get you off." He shook his head. "I might as well not run for reelection."

She stared at him. "Does being an assemblyman mean so much to you that you'd risk my well-being? Duncan buy me out of that mess?" She laughed aloud. "Get a copy of *The Maryland Journal* weekend edition and see what he thinks of slumlords. Father, I advise you to get a lawyer. A good one." His face, so heavily lined since she'd last seen him, seemed to sag before her eyes. She stepped toward him, paused, and stepped back. "Maybe . . . maybe if you'd offer some kind of restitution, you could avoid a suit."

She turned toward the door, and his hand on her arm stopped her. "Would you care for some coffee?"

She gaped at him. "Well . . . well, yes. Thanks."

She followed him back to the kitchen, a large airy masterpiece in design and equipment that would no doubt have Martha Stewart's approval.

"I'm by myself on Sundays," he confided. "Cook's off."

She sat at the kitchen bar with him and sipped coffee. Six weeks earlier, she would have been overjoyed to be with him, but on that morning, she felt only sympathy for him in his loneliness. "Those boys have lived alone since their mother flew the coop a year and a half ago, Father. Duncan says they're seventeen and fifteen years old, they go to school regularly, and the older one looks after himself and his younger half-brother."

He leaned forward. "How do they live?"

"Mitch, the older one, found a way to cash their mother's monthly welfare check, but Duncan supplies most of their needs."

"I see. This Mitch must be quite resourceful."

"I suppose so." It occurred to her that this was the longest conversation of substance that she'd ever had with him. "I don't live with Duncan Banks, Father," she said, offering an olive branch. "I take care of his child. After Kenneth's death, I had a hard time, and I decided to change my life. Why didn't you take my calls once in the last six years?"

"I didn't know you'd been calling me. I'll have to speak to Lerlaine if she hasn't been putting my calls through."

"Would you have talked to me if you'd known?"

"I don't know. Probably I would have, because I always wondered why you went against me and married him."

She sighed. Why beat a dead horse? "Because you told me that you forbade it, and I didn't think you had that right."

"I see. Well, maybe we can do this again sometime."

He looked around him, waving his hand in a sweeping gesture. "This is a big house."

"Yes. I know. It always was."

Duncan slowly replaced the receiver and stood at his desk staring into space. He refused to believe it. Tonya with Myelogenous Leukemia? He wanted to believe that the radiologist had made an error, but the doctor had assured him that they'd done the test three times to make sure. Her chance for complete recovery rested on finding a match for a bone marrow transplant. If he told Justine, she'd be frantic. He called the hospital and was informed that Maryland law forbade the unsealing of adoption papers, so how would he find the parents? He called his mother and sister. There was time enough till he had to face Justine with it.

"No need to despair," his mother told him. "We'll pray. It'll work out."

He reeled in his rising impatience. She didn't understand. "Mama, this thing is serious. Tonya could die if I don't find a donor."

"I know, son, but have faith. That's what I'm going to do. We'll all get tested. Maybe by some miracle . . ." She let it drift.

He telephoned Wayne, and they rounded up mutual friends. Mitch and Rags were among the first to volunteer, though they weren't allowed to test because of their ages. Workers in the hospital took the test, but none matched, and the doctor warned him that the chances of finding one were nearly nonexistent. He hated keeping the seriousness of it from Justine, because he knew how deeply she loved Tonya, but finally, he had to tell her.

"I didn't want to alarm you, because I know how you love her, but it doesn't look good for her. She hasn't improved since she's been there. You could see that." He threw up his hands. "I'd give everything that I have, but I can't help her."

Justine opened her arms to him, and he went into them, a ship sailing into safe harbor in the midst of a violent, life-threatening storm. "Hold on to me," he said, when the tremors shook her and tears cascaded from her eyes. "Sweetheart, if we ever needed each other, it's now."

His arms hadn't been around her since they'd begun to suffer in their individual hells over Tonya's illness, not since they'd taken her to the hospital. It seemed as though, in that one week, she had doubled her age. Her thoughts as he held her were not of her love for him, but of thanksgiving that she had at last reached a rapport—however tentative—with her father, for they could be the only ones alive who had a chance of giving her child the bone marrow that she needed. No thoughts of the future, of the consequences of what she must do, occurred to her.

She moved away from Duncan and looked straight at him. If he guessed, so be it; what happened to her was no longer of any import. "Do you mind if I take the test?"

He smiled, indulgently she thought. "It's an unpleasant business, and we know it's not going to work. I don't want you to put yourself through it when we know it will be useless."

When she didn't answer, he tugged her close to him. "Half of the people we know in Frederick have taken the test, but none of them match. It's driving me up the wall."

She hugged him, instinctively offering him solace, but her heart and thoughts were elsewhere. Just be calm, she cautioned herself. She had a lot to think about; if she or her father weren't a match, she'd trace every one of her relatives and Kenneth's, no matter what it cost her.

"I have to call Big Al and tell him to use some of my early columns for the next few days. I don't feel like dealing with the frivolous concerns some of those women think are so important."

He squeezed her to him and released her. "I'd better go downstairs and talk to Mattie. I hadn't told her earlier, because she'd have spilled all of it to you no matter what I said. Chin up, now."

She closed her bedroom door, called the hospital, and made an appointment for Justine Montgomery to take the test. Not a camouflage, for none made sense any longer; her charade was at an end. But what if she wasn't a match? She dialed her father's office and, to her amazement, a different voice answered.

"I'm Justine Taylor, and I'd like to speak with my father, Assemblyman Taylor."

When he answered, his voice reflected astonishment. "Well, this is a pleasant surprise. Did you notice I have a new secretary?"

She had indeed. Where to start? "I hope you're sitting down, Father," she said, and over the next twenty minutes told him what her life had been for the past six years.

His long silence thundered his shock at what he'd learned. Finally, he told her, "I think I can just make that age limit for a bone marrow donor. I just turned fifty-nine. Let me know if you need me."

An avenue of her life, once strewn with rubble and long closed, was opening at last, and though she knew debris would remain until she could bring herself to forgive, she rejoiced that they had at last made a beginning.

"Your previous secretary once asked if I had a message for you. I told her to tell you that I loved you."

"She didn't mention it; I wish she had. I hope things will work out so I can see my grandchild."

He hadn't told her he loved her, she mused, but that would take time. At least he was willing to help.

One week later, Duncan slammed down his office phone and shrieked for joy. In his state of near delirium, he shoved open Justine's bedroom door, but the room was empty. He had forgotten what it was to slide down a bannister, but he did exactly that as he went looking for Justine or any human he could find with whom he could rejoice.

"Mattie, where's Justine? We've got a donor." He picked her up and swung her around, set her on her feet, and hugged her. "Did you hear me? *Tonya has a donor!*"

A grin bloomed on her face. "Didn't I tell you to quit worrying. I knowed you'd find one. Well, I tell you, Mr. B, this is a happy day."

"Where'd she go? Where's Justine?"

"She left in her car this morning while you was out. Said she be back in a few hours."

He telephoned his sister at her office. "Can you believe it, Leah? We've found a donor."

"Thank goodness. I know how relieved you must be. Mama's been on a continuous prayer vigil, and . . . Duncan, I'm . . . I'm so happy."

Why were they all taking the news so casually? First Mattie and now Leah. He hung up and called his mother.

"Thank God, my prayers have been answered," she said. Another calm one. He called Wayne and got the drum-rolling kind of excited response he'd expected from the others. But Justine. He couldn't wait to tell her. When he heard the front door open, he raced down the stairs and dashed into the foyer. As he rushed to her, she gazed up at him as though in anticipation.

"Duncan, what is it? What's happened?"

He pulled her into his arms and rocked her. "She's going to make it, Justine. She has a donor. Imagine. She's going to be all right. She's . . . *Justine!*"

She slumped in his arms. He carried her to the living room sofa, lay her there, and went for some water. "Justine fainted when I told her. What can I get for her?" he asked Mattie.

She poured some spirits of ammonia in a cup. "Let her breathe that in. Poor thing, she been under a load. They tell you who this donor is?"

"Why, no. I forgot to ask."

Justine lay across her bed, a myriad of emotions swirling within her. Her child would live. The procedure hadn't caused much discomfort, and she had only a little soreness as a reminder, but through it all, she'd had a feeling of incomparable joy—an exhilaration that defied description. Once more, she'd given her child life. She'd been told to be quiet and relaxed, but she could have danced all night with relief. She telephoned her father and godfather and rejoiced with them. Barely able to endure the happiness that suffused her, she stretched out her arms and shouted with laughter. Minutes elapsed and her laughter became hysterics and her hysterics turned into sobs.

When she tried to calm herself, she only cried louder. Her world lay in shambles, for he was certain to send her away. Behind closed eyelids she looked at pieces of her soul, scrambled like the disintegrated scraps of her naiveté, and scattered around her feet. She cried out as pain seared her, and she didn't hear Duncan burst into her room, but when his arms eased around her body, it knew him, and relaxed against him, drinking in the solace that he offered. She turned over on her back and looked into his eyes. He didn't know, and she didn't know how to tell him.

For the first time since she'd known him, he seemed unable to communicate his thoughts and feelings. "Would you . . . like to go with me to the hospital to see her?"

She doubted she'd be able to stand. Her earlier ebullience had deserted her, and when he'd touched her, she could think of nothing but the dark mourning that was sure to follow her triumph. Fate had exacted a price, for she had been forced to purchase her child's life at the cost of nurturing her and of loving Duncan.

Better begin now to separate herself from them. "I'm not sure I can keep back the tears when I'm with her, and I don't want to alarm her. You go, and tell her I love her."

He stood there, obviously reluctant to leave her. "Go on, now," she prodded. "She needs to see at least one of us."

His kiss reminded her of what she was about to lose, and she gave herself to it, parting her lips in quest of his tongue and feasting upon his generous offering. His gaze became strangely questioning when he licked from his top lip what she knew was the brine of her tears.

"We're over the worst of it, so let's be thankful." His voice softened. "Please don't cry any more, sweetheart. There's no need."

Duncan couldn't banish his anxiety about Justine—her unusual behavior—sadness when she should have been rejoicing, and her refusal to share with him her feelings. And she'd kissed him as though it were the last time, something he couldn't understand. With everything else going on in his life, his testosterone had taken a nap and he hadn't wanted a desire-ladened kiss.

He answered his phone on the first ring. "Duncan, this is Leah, How's—?"

He gulped. "This is who? Leah? Who *is* this?"

"It's your sister. My future husband wrote down Banks Banks when we went to order the wedding invitations, and the clerk at Weller's Engravers—you know, Miss Avery—laughed until somebody had to give her some water. He did it for a point, and Mama says her name can't go on the invitation unless I'm Leah Banks, so I'm giving in until after I get married."

"You mean you're going to sign your married name Banks Roundtree? Leah, you're crazy."

"I'm changing the subject. Has Tonya had the transplant yet?"

"Yeah. Today."

"How's Justine?"

"She's fine." He reconsidered. "Actually, she's behaving strangely. You'd think she'd be deliriously happy, and in a way she does seem happy, but she's also sad."

"She loves Tonya, you know."

"Yes. She couldn't love her more if she'd given birth to her. Look, I've got to get over to the hospital. Give Mama our love."

The head nurse greeted Duncan as he stepped off the elevator on his way to Tonya's room. "She's looking brighter, and in a few days she'll be able to go home. We'd just about given up hope that you'd find a donor."

They walked along the corridor toward Tonya's room. "How do I get the donor's name? I have to write and thank her. By the way, was it a man or a woman?"

"A woman. I didn't meet her, but give her my thanks, too."

He bade the woman good-bye and opened Tonya's room

door. Her color had improved but, apart from that, he saw no change. She seemed more alert when he played the Mozart tape, and he stayed with her for about an hour, playing it repeatedly. On his way out of the hospital, he noticed the administrative office, knocked, and went in.

"I'm G. Duncan Banks. My daughter received a bone marrow transplant this morning, and I'd like the name of the donor so I can thank her."

The clerk flipped through record folders until she found Tonya's, studied it, and wrote something on a slip of paper. He looked at it and read: *Justine Montgomery,* age 30, (202) 811-1188.

Through a fog of unreality, he heard the clerk say, "We had all despaired of helping Tonya, but this woman was a perfect match."

He didn't know whether he thanked the woman. He stumbled out of the office and propped himself against the wall. Perspiration soaked his under clothing and his breath hung in his throat, nearly choking him. Somewhere in the dark labyrinth that was his mind, he'd known from the start. Why she seemed so familiar, why he'd felt as though he knew her. How could he have missed the resemblance? Those eyes were absolute replicas. He pulled himself away from the wall and made his way to the car. At last, he understood Justine's sadness.

He drove into his garage and sat there. She'd had no choice but to do the noble thing; she loved her child. But she had lived a lie, more than one, in fact, and he wanted some answers. If his mother hadn't called him away from his lodge at Curtis Bay, he would probably have asked her to marry him. What was he to think? She knew what he felt for her, because he'd told her and he'd demonstrated it repeatedly. She had discouraged him, had warned him that there was no future for them, and then, she'd blown his mind with the gut-level loving he'd always longed for and never had. He got out of the car, locked it, and entered the house through the breakfast room.

"How's Tonya doing, Mr. B?"

He couldn't infuse his voice with any enthusiasm. "She'll

be all right now." He'd thought Mattie a keen observer, so he asked her, "Any idea who the donor was?"

She directed her gaze away from him, and that meant she knew. "I don't look no gift horse in the mouth, Mr. B. I prayed, and I got answered. That's enough for me."

He stood there, in effect daring her to dismiss him. "So you do know. You've known all along."

"It don't make no difference now," she said, letting her impatience show. "I don't meddle in what ain't none of my business." She turned her back, bent to the oven door, and started humming.

He had no right to pressure her and, he supposed, no right to be angry. If Justine hadn't taken the job, he could have lost his child. But on the other hand, if Tonya hadn't needed that transplant, Justine's charade would have continued indefinitely. And he would have been in an indefinite dilemma about her. No wonder she'd maintained that nothing could come of their relationship.

When he reached the top of the stairs, he didn't look toward her door, but went into his room, threw himself across his bed, and tried to come to terms with his feelings for Justine. Who was she? He reached over and dialed his mother's number.

"I just left Tonya," he told her after they'd greeted each other. "She'll be fine now."

"You seem down. What's the matter?"

He sat up. "I've just been clobbered with a two-by-four. Do you have any idea who donated that transplant?"

Her long silence was pregnant with significance. "Do you?" he repeated.

"Well, I can imagine."

His eyes widened, and he jumped out of bed and walked as far as the length of the phone cord would allow. "What do you mean, 'you can imagine'? Mama, talk to me in plain English."

"Duncan, I cannot tell you what you must discover for yourself."

"So you knew. How long have you known that Justine is Tonya's birth mother?"

"Since the first time I saw them together. From what

Leah had told me, I had suspected it, but once I saw her, I was positive. She loves Tonya, and she loves you."

He looked toward the ceiling. "I'm not dealing with that right now. Does Leah know?"

"Son, she knew before I did. But we both love Justine, and we hope you move with care. You understand?"

"Uh . . . I'm not a foolish man, Mama."

CHAPTER FIFTEEN

She'd heard him come home from the hospital and go into his room without stopping to tell her about Tonya's progress. So he'd found out already. She looked at her watch. At any minute, Mattie would call to announce dinner, so she freshened up, put on a Dior blue silk jumpsuit, gold hoops, let her hair fly around her shoulders, and made her way downstairs.

Mattie greeted her with a wide grin that exposed her top front teeth. "Justine, honey, it shore is wonderful 'bout Tonya. I tell you, I am glad it's over. I didn't worry none, though, 'cause I prayed, but you never can tell. My Moe said, sometime brothers and sisters can't even match." She looked down at the sauce she stirred. "Mothers ain't a shore bet neither. We have to thank God."

So she knew and had had the grace not to mention it. She put her arms around the little woman and hugged her. "Thank you, Mattie, for being a real friend."

"Oh, shucks, child. It ain't nothing you wouldna done for me."

He entered the dining room and walked back to the kitchen where she and Mattie stood arm in arm, but she didn't turn around. From now on, it would be he who orchestrated whatever happened between them.

To her amazement, he said, "Justine, there's a string quartet concert down at the National Gallery tomorrow night. Would you like to go?"

She faced him. "I'd love it. Thanks for asking me."

He wasn't himself. Duncan Banks didn't flounder, but the man before her had the appearance of one at a precipice, forced to jump, but uncertain as to the right direction.

Mattie must have sensed their uneasiness with each other, for she tried to smooth over their awkwardness. "Mr. B, I stretched myself like you said I oughta and made you a scallop mousse with shrimp sauce. My Moe bought me the book." She dipped the spoon in the fragrant sauce. "Here, taste that. If it don't make you hop, skip, and jump, my name ain't Mattie Swindell. All y'all don't eat, I'm taking home to my Moe."

Justine watched Duncan dutifully taste the sauce, run his tongue over his top lip, and smile in a way that she hadn't seen him do in two weeks. "Mattie, I doubt there's anything else you could have done that would have made me feel this good." He looked at Justine. "This is right up there with Justine's quenelles."

Mattie's eyes held a mischievous twinkle. "So, you made him quenelles. Looks like you know a few things, too."

At dinner, the three of them talked about French food, Cajun food, Soul food, anything but what bore on their minds. Several times, Justine glanced at Duncan and found him staring quizzically at her, as though she were a riddle that he couldn't decide whether or how to solve. They finished Mattie's excellent meal, and Duncan said he'd do the dishes. Justine knew he'd given her a chance to avoid the inevitable, and she went to her room.

Banks's call was the last that she would have expected, for Banks had told her bluntly that she had secrets, but that she should trust Duncan. Was her friend calling to scold?

"Justine, you did what you had to do, and Mama and I are proud of you," Banks said, without preliminaries. "I discovered your big secret the week after we met, and

Mama figured it out when you came for her birthday, but we didn't know your reasons, so we kept it all to ourselves. Just wanted you to know we're on your side."

"Thanks, Banks. What I have to tell goes to Duncan's ears first, provided he gives me the chance, but I can tell you that I'm a good person, and I never planned on getting involved with him. I tried to prevent it, but nature had other ideas."

"Enough said. I love my brother, and I want you for my sister-in-law, girlfriend, so get busy and fix it up with him. Bye for now."

Justine looked at the phone as the dial tone hummed. Well, that was something with which to begin.

The next afternoon, Sunday, she went alone to see Tonya and couldn't believe the change in her. "Juju. Juju kiss Tonya. Juju read Hiwattie."

She grabbed the child into her arms and smothered her face with kisses. Duncan walked in and found them hugging each other.

"How's Daddy's girl?"

"Daddy kiss Tonya," she said, leaning away from Justine and opening her arms to him. He took her into his arms and closed his eyes, and she watched in awe as tears streaked his face. Things weren't right with them, but she put her arms around the two of them, and when she opened her eyes, she looked into fiery masculine orbs that brimmed with passion, and her heart began to gallop in her chest. Maybe she could hope.

"Would you rather go to dinner than a concert?" he asked as they left the hospital. "I . . . we need to talk, Justine."

"I know. I'd rather get a bag of hamburgers or some Chinese food and go home. If we're going to talk, really talk, we'd better be alone."

"All right. Hamburgers and fries."

He built a log fire in the living room fireplace, got a bottle of wine and some glasses, and settled with her before the fire—the room's only light. After their silent meal before flames that undulated among each other and cast their shadows across the bodies of the troubled lovers, Duncan cleared away the evidence of their dinner. He sat on the floor at her feet with his arms wrapped around his knees and looked up at her.

"What the devil!" he said, when the phone rang.

"Banks."

After about five minutes, he came back. "That was Warren. He wanted to tell me who you are. I let him know that I didn't care to discuss you with him. What was it about?"

Thank God, she could tell the truth. "He knows my background, and he tried to blackmail me into sleeping with him. In exchange, he wouldn't tell you about me. As you may see, I refused."

"Well, you can forget about him. I put the fellow in his place."

He sat at her feet, as he had before the phone rang, but sitting above him on the sofa, unable to look directly into his face when she spoke, magnified her discomfort. "Would you . . . sit up here with me, please. I need to see your face."

He got up, sat beside her, and took her hand. "If you can't tell me everything right now, everything I ought to know, this is where I get off."

Fair enough, she thought, and oddly, she had no fear; she'd take whatever came. "My name is Justine Taylor Montgomery. I'm thirty years old. I have a Ph.D in psychology, and I am a widow. I was married to Kenneth Montgomery until he died in a motel fire with his white mistress of more years than I'd been married to him. Seven hours after I left the scene of that fire, Tonya was born one month prematurely."

He said not one word, as she continued to speak, leaving out nothing that had happened to her from that fatal day until she answered his ad for a nanny.

"I did not intend to become involved with you or any man. Never. My father and Kenneth had been lessons enough. The first person to love me after my mother's death was Tonya. I thought Kenneth loved me—until I met you; until I watched you with Tonya, I knew I'd had no idea what love was. And until you held me in your arms and made love to me, I knew I had never before loved any man. I fought getting involved with you, because the burden of my guilt was so awesome—at times, almost unbearable. The day before we learned that Tonya needed a bone marrow transplant, I paid an unexpected call on my father."

He spoke for the first time. "Is he the Virginia Assemblyman?"

"Yes." She told him the remainder of the story, including her father's offer to test for the transplant."

"That's my story, Duncan. Unvarnished. I can't excuse myself for the deception, but considering how things turned out, I don't know if I should apologize."

He slid down on the sofa until his head rested on its back. "It's a lot to digest. If you'd told me you were her mother, I certainly wouldn't have hired you. Yet, I can't say I'm sorry I did. I always knew that nothing about you fit the role. With your nurturing, she developed so rapidly, a mushroom swelling to maturity in the summer rain. Don't jump to any conclusions. You've given me a lot to think about, and I'd better get started on it." He got up, extended his hand, and helped her to her feet. "I'll say good-night. Wednesday morning, we have to bring Tonya home." He left her standing there and, as though with feet of lead, climbed the stairs. She stared after him as he walked off, leaving an empty hole in her soul.

Wednesday arrived too quickly for Justine. She didn't see how she could live with Duncan in a platonic relationship when she loved him so deeply, yet she didn't know how she could live separately from her child. They brought their daughter home, put her in her playpen, and sat on the floor beside it while the child reacquainted herself with her toys. He'd given no hint as to what he felt about her or thought of her deception.

Unable to tolerate it any longer, she left him in Tonya's room laughing and playing with the child. Half an hour later, when he knocked on her door, she opened it and spoke first. "I have to leave here, Duncan."

His eyebrows lifted and a frown darkened his features. "You *what?*"

She walked to the window and stood with her back to him. "I can't stay here. I know I'll never have a peaceful moment without my child, and I have no legal claim to her, but I can't live in this house with you as your mistress any more than I can sleep across the hall from you night after night and not go insane wanting you. At least, you'll let me see her once in a while . . . won't you?"

"You can't leave, Justine. Tonya needs you."

Icy fingers circled her heart, but she straightened her back and turned to face him. "I know she needs me, but . . ." She bit her tongue and said it. "What about you?"

When he didn't answer, she turned her back to him and stared unseeing at the endless darkness. The heat of his fingers on her shoulders renewed her hope and sent jolts of passion hurtling through her, awakening in her desire that for weeks had been unappeased.

"Please don't touch me, Duncan. If you're not going to hold me, don't play with me."

His fingers dug into her shoulders until she turned and faced him. "I have no right to judge you harshly. Few people could have had your experience and weathered the turbulence as you have done. You're a brave woman. You expected that when I learned who you were, I'd walk away from you. Yet you didn't hesitate to give your child life a second time, knowing that doing so would expose you. Justine, it hasn't occurred to me to ask you to leave here. Don't you have any idea what you mean to me? You've held me in your arms, in your body, and you still don't know?"

She shook her head. "With my experience, I no longer take anything for granted."

He lifted her chin with his index finger and looked into her eyes. "What do you see?"

She thought her heart would fly out of her body. "I . . . I see half a dimple." She traced it with her fingers. "The most beautiful eyes in this world, an—"

"You don't see that I love you?"

"Duncan. *Duncan!*"

* * *

Her words, the quivering of her lips, and the hard tips of her breasts against her shirt sent wild fire roaring through him, exacerbating his pent-up hunger for her, intensifying his pain of wanting her non-stop since he'd held her sobbing in his arms on Saturday. He struggled to check the desire that threatened to tie him in knots, to render him as ineffectual as a sinking ship.

"Justine, I'm yours to take."

He could sense her hesitance, her uncertainty. But he knew that he had only to touch her in familiar places. He let his left hand drift down her shirt and over her right breast, the more sensitive of the two, and watched her lips part and her tongue dart out to lathe them.

"It's been like this from the moment we first looked at each other, Justine, and you know it. Tell me you can walk away. Tell me you don't belong here with me. In my arms. In my bed. Tell me I don't belong inside you. You told me you loved me, and I believed you, because I already knew it. Tell me it's no longer true."

"Duncan, it's . . . I—"

"I'm trusting you, sweetheart, and you have to trust me. Put your arms around me."

The sweetness of it. The hell of it. She locked him in her arms, parted her lips, and sucked his tongue into her mouth.

He thought he'd burst if he couldn't get inside her. "Baby, slow down."

But she paid no attention to his pleading. Her hips rolled against him, and when she shifted from side to side, rubbing her breasts against his chest, he found her right breast inside her shirt, released it, fastened his mouth on it, and nourished himself on her sweet flesh.

"Duncan, I need you. I *need you!*"

He looked around him, stunned. Daylight. "Sweetheart, Mattie's in the house."

"Tell her to leave. Lock the door. I don't care what."

He picked her up, carried her to her bed, and stood looking down at her, her breath already coming in pants, eager for him. He closed the door, braced her desk chair beneath the door knob, and rushed back to her. Standing beside the bed looking down at her, he wondered if he could get the control she needed. Her smile almost took his breath, and he quickly disrobed her, unbuttoned his own shirt, and reached for his belt buckle, but she was there before him. His trousers dropped to the floor, and he stepped out of them, but when he would have joined her in bed, she reached for him and caressed him. He threw back his head and gritted his teeth, but she didn't stop.

The full power of his virility loomed before her and, unable to resist, she sat up, stroked him, and kissed him. "Justine, sweetheart, you're playing with fire. I'm just a man, baby."

She held out her arms to him and he fell into them. His lips brushed her ears and neck and travelled to her breast. He toyed there, knowing what she wanted and making her wait.

"Honey, kiss me. I need you to kiss me."

His answer was a kiss on the inside of her arm, and a skimming of his fingers over her belly. When she could stand it no longer, she grasped his head and led him to her breast.

Heart-thumping, spine-tingling rockets shot through her, and she swung her leg across his hips, while he tortured her breasts with his honeyed mouth. Unable to contain her rising passion, she raised her body until she could feel his hard arousal and undulated against him. He gripped her hips to still her, and continued his assault on her nervous system. His tongue traced a line from her breast to her belly, reminding her of what he had done to her the last time, and the seat of her passion pulsated in anticipation of his lips. He made good on his promise, loving her, possessing her, branding her as his for all time until he brought a keening cry. He raised himself up and smiled into her face.

"May I, Justine?"

She opened to him and her pent-up passion exploded as he found his home within her. She had no secrets from him now and no reason to hold back. Free at last, she opened herself to him and let him know her, as she undulated and danced beneath him, gripping his hips and rocking to his beat.

"Slow down, sweetheart, and let it catch up with us."

She hardly heard him, as frissons of heat shot through her. "Duncan, *please!*"

His lips stilled her murmurings. "Yes, sweetheart. I'm going to love you until you won't think of leaving me. Do you hear? Give yourself to me. I want all of you."

His deep thrust set her nerve endings afire. She didn't want it to end. Didn't want it to be the last time. But he turned her inside out, obliterated her inhibitions, and exposed her soul. The musky smell of him intoxicated her, his hands held her in his lover's prison, and he was over her, beside her, and all around her as he drove within her.

"I said give yourself to me."

"I am. I am."

"No, you're not. But you will."

He bent to her breasts, put his fingers between them and teased her while he accelerated his powerful thrusts. She bucked beneath him and gave herself up to the powerful vortex into which he pitched her.

"Come with me, honey. Love me, Justine. You hear me? I want you to love me."

Tremors shook her as wave after wave of ecstasy sucked her into his orbit and her body clutched him. "I do."

"That's it, love. I want all of you."

"I love you. I love you," she screamed as he stripped her of herself and made her one with him. He drove once more, folded her tightly to him, and unravelled in her arms.

He didn't move away from her, but continued to hold her after he separated himself from her body. Minutes passed before he said, "Justine, are you willing to give us a chance? You've already given me so much that I didn't have before I knew you. What do you say? Will you marry me, Justine?"

"Will I—"

"Will you? You don't want an affair, and I don't either. I love you, and I can't envisage life without you."

"I . . . Yes. Yes. *Oh, yes!*"

He slipped on his trousers and stepped out of the room. There was one more thing that he had to settle. He kicked open the door and walked in with Tonya in his arms.

"Juju pay panno wi Tonya."

Duncan put Tonya in her arms, sat on the side of the bed, and shook his finger at the child. "It's time you learned how to say Mother. No more Juju. Say mother. Mother."

"Muwa."

He leaned over and kissed them both. "Muwa. That'll do for now."

Dear Reader:

I hope you have enjoyed meeting Justine and Duncan and following their joys, pain, conflicts, passions and triumphs as much as I enjoyed giving them life. I saw in Duncan the black *everyman*, who rose from the harshness of his early youth to honor, dignity and notable accomplishment, and whose love for his child and his woman defies description. For me, Justine may well be the prototype black woman of the next millennium—intelligent and accomplished, challenged but undaunted, gentle yet strong and independent, passionate and loving.

A great number of you asked me for the story of Wayne Roundtree and Banks, whom you met in my book, ***AGAINST ALL ODDS***, and I hope you liked the way in which their relationship comes to fruition.

I want to take this opportunity to thank the many, many readers among you who have made writing romance novels so rewarding for me. Some of you have written me after publication of each of my previous eight titles and have come to my book signings. I cherish each of you and always look forward to hearing from you and, of course, to meeting you in person.

If you haven't read any of my previous books, check the note, *About the Author*, near the back of this book and chose one or two. If you enjoyed this one, you'll find those a pleasure as well. I love hearing from my readers and try to answer letters within three weeks, and e-mails immediately. So please be in touch and let me know what you think of ***FOOLS RUSH IN***. Write me at P.O. Box 45, New York, N.Y. 10044; E-mail—GwynneF@aol.com And don't forget to visit my web page to see what I'm doing. My web address is http://www.infokart.com/gwynneforster

Fond Regards,
Gwynne Forster

ABOUT THE AUTHOR

Gwynne Forster is a best-selling and award-winning author of six romance novels and two novellas. Her January 1999 book, ***BEYOND DESIRE,*** is a Doubleday Book Club selection. Gwynne holds bachelors and masters degrees in sociology and a masters degree in economics/demography. As a demographer, she is widely published. She is formerly chief of (non-medical) research in fertility and family planning in the Population Division of the United Nations in New York and served for four years as chairperson of the International Programme Committee of the International Planned Parenthood Federation (London, England), positions that took her to sixty-three developed and developing countries. Gwynne sings on her church choir, loves to entertain, is a gourmet cook and avid gardener. She lives with her husband in New York City.

Gwynne's previous books include ***SEALED WITH A KISS*** (October 1995), ***AGAINST ALL ODDS*** (September 1996), ***ECSTASY*** (July 1997), ***OBSESSION*** (April 1998) and ***NAKED SOUL*** (July 1998, paperback—August 1999). Her first novella, *Christopher's Gifts,* is included in the anthology, ***SILVER BELLS*** (December 1996), her Valentines Day 1997 novella, *A Perfect Match,* is in the anthology, ***I DO***, and *Love for a Lifetime,* her story of two passionate, battling attorneys is in the BET/Arabesque anthology, ***WEDDING BELLS*** (June 1999). She is represented by the James B. Finn Literary Agency, Inc. P.O. Box 28227A, St. Louis Missouri 63132. Readers may write to her at P.O. Box 45, New York, N.Y. 10044-0045.

Web page—http://www.infokart.com/gwynneforster
E-mail GwynneF@aol.com